U0073689

39大情境 × 239段職場萬用對話
只要一本在手,升官發財絕不是夢!

學習有捷徑
夢想最接近

User's Guide 使用說明

職場如戰場，本書貼心列出5大生存法則，讓你的辦公室英語無師就能自通、活用，縱橫沙場無往不利！

生存法則 No.1

39大情境、近2000句對話，想看什麼都能看到！

職場就是生活的一部分，百百種狀況哪是幾段制式死板的對話就能隨便打發的？所以我們給你39種情境、近2000句對話，光是處理糾紛的說法就針對各個對象、各種主題，讓你吵架也不怕吵輸人家，抓住自己的權益絕不被人占便宜！

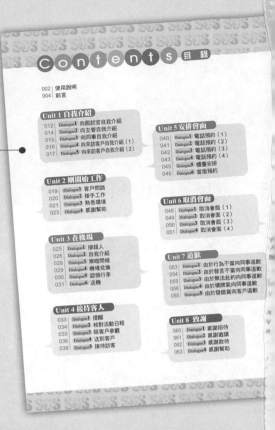

SOS Unit 4 接待客人

Dialogue ❶ 提醒 ◀ Track 016

打電話到客戶的旅館房間打擾人家，感覺總有點不好意思，所以至少也要和對話中一樣，客氣地問對方一句睡得好不好。

Mr. Smith: Hello, Smith speaking.
Kathy: Hello, Mr. Smith . This is Kathy from Flora International Cosmetics Company . How did you sleep last night?
Mr. Smith: Okay, thank you.
Kathy: You're welcome. I just want to remind you we have an appointment at 7 tonight.
Mr. Smith: Yes, I remember. Thank you.
Kathy: I am going to pick you up at 6:30 .
Mr. Smith: I'll be waiting in the lobby. See you later.
Kathy: Talk to you later.

★全文中畫色塊的地方，可以依自己的狀況套入不同的名字、公司名、職稱、學校名等等。

中文翻譯1
史密斯先生：你好，我是史密斯。
凱　西：你好，史密斯先生。我是芙羅拉國際化妝品公司的凱西。昨晚休息得怎麼樣？
史密斯先生：滿好的，謝謝。
凱　西：別客氣。我是打來提醒您，我們晚上7點有約。

生存法則 No.2

活潑會話搭配活用句型，想說什麼都能說出！

「Hello, Smith speaking.」簡短有力的句子，給人感覺專業又幹練，在職場上最好用了。什麼？你說「這句子我不能用，因為我是女生、我不叫Smith」？那就把Smith換成你的名字就好啦！書中把所有可以依狀況代換成其他人名、地名、公司名、時間的地方，全都用紅色色塊標出來，如此一來，就成了到處適用的百變說法！

生存法則 No.3　專業外籍人士親錄MP3，想聽什麼都能聽到！

雖然很無奈，但不管書中內容多有趣，還是一翻開就想睡？雖然很勤奮，但總是加班到半夜，根本沒空讀書？那也沒關係，本書搭配外師親錄、口音道地的會話MP3，讓學習者只要放在手機、電腦裡反覆聆聽，不管是讀書會犯睏還是忙得天昏地暗，一樣可以把握時間學英文！

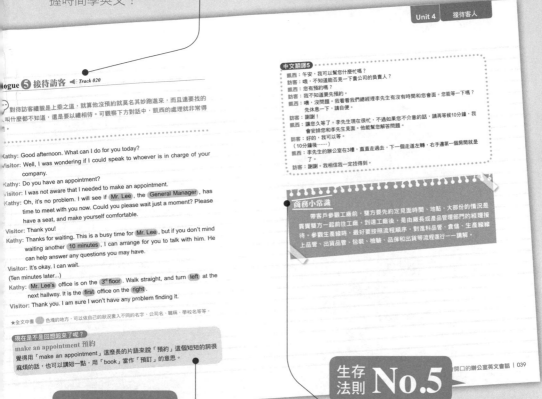

Dialogue ❺ 接待訪客 ◀ Track 020

對待訪客禮貌是上策之道，就算他沒預約就莫名其妙跑進來，而且連要找的人叫什麼都不知道，還是要以禮相待。可觀察下方對話中，凱西的處理就非常得

Kathy: Good afternoon. What can I do for you today?
Visitor: Well, I was wondering if I could speak to whoever is in charge of your company.
Kathy: Do you have an appointment?
Visitor: I was not aware that I needed to make an appointment.
Kathy: Oh, it's no problem. I will see if Mr. Lee, the General Manager, has time to meet with you now. Could you please wait just a moment? Please have a seat, and make yourself comfortable.
Visitor: Thank you!
Kathy: Thanks for waiting. This is a busy time for Mr. Lee, but if you don't mind waiting another 10 minutes, I can arrange for you to talk with him. He can help answer any questions you may have.
Visitor: It's okay. I can wait.
(Ten minutes later...)
Kathy: Mr. Lee's office is on the 3rd floor. Walk straight, and turn left at the next hallway. It is the first office on the right.
Visitor: Thank you. I am sure I won't have any problem finding it.

★全文中畫 色塊的地方，可以依自己的狀況套入不同的名字、公司名、職稱、學校名等等。

現在是不是回想起來了呢？
make an appointment 預約
覺得用「make an appointment」這麼長的片語來說「預約」這個短短的詞很麻煩的話，也可以講短一點，用「book」當作「預訂」的意思。

中文翻譯5

凱西：午安，我可以幫您什麼忙嗎？
訪客：哦，不知道能否見一下貴公司的負責人？
凱西：您有預約嗎？
訪客：我不知道要先預約。
凱西：哦，沒問題。我看看我們總經理李先生有沒有時間和您會面。您能等一下嗎？先休息一下，請自便。
訪客：謝謝！
凱西：讓您久等了。李先生現在很忙，不過如果您不介意的話，請再等候10分鐘，我會安排您和李先生見面。他能幫您解答問題。
訪客：好的，我可以等。
（10分鐘後……）
凱西：李先生的辦公室在3樓，直直走過去，下一個走道左轉，右手邊第一個房間就是了。
訪客：謝謝。我相信我一定找得到。

商務小常識

帶客戶參觀工廠前，雙方要先約定見面時間、地點，大部份的情況是買賣雙方一起前往工廠。到達工廠後，是由廠長或產品管理部門的經理接待。參觀生產線時，最好要按照流程順序，對進料品管、倉儲、生產線上品管、出貨品管、包裝、檢驗、品保和出貨等流程進行一一解說。

生存法則 No.4　重要單字片語小提示，想記什麼都能記得！

千萬別覺得職場英文有多難，其實它們根本都是由你學過的字組成的！「現在是不是回想起來了呢？」的欄位，就是要挑出好用又好記的單字跟片語，告訴你使用時機和其它同義字，用你想得起的單字，學新的說法、用在不同的情境！

生存法則 No.5　專欄提點商務常識，想知道什麼都能知道！

和外籍人士談生意、談合作，怕的就是因為文化差異而造成誤會，所以來點基本的「商務小常識」是絕對必要的！到底英文名字怎麼取才不會被取笑、道歉怎麼說才不會讓人覺得有負擔、說哪些話才比較委婉而不會得罪人，就在這裡補充你的職場知識吧！

Preface 作者序

　　身邊不少在職場打拼、奮鬥多年的朋友們都告訴我，他們很後悔當年沒有好好學英文，或是很後悔脫離大考、上大學後就再也沒碰英文了。因為，直到開始工作，他們才發現英文好在職場上有多麼吃香，做起事來又是多麼地輕鬆愉快。

　　根據人力銀行的統計，高達將近七成的企業，在招募新人時會將英文能力列入考量，在這些企業中，更有九成五的公司會給予英文能力好的員工更優渥的工作待遇。原因在於，如今的企業營運模式已經不再只是著重在國內，幾乎各個公司都會接外籍客戶的訂單，或者跟國外的公司有合作夥伴關係。因為這樣的轉變，讓現代上班族不管是出國洽公、接待貴賓，或是日常的電郵、電話往返，都非常需要用到國際通用語言──英文。

　　但是，一般隨著學校教育一路唸書上來的人們，大多都只會課本裡教的那些單字、課文，而那些為考試而設計的內容，並不是人人都知道如何使用在職場上。因為，職場就是日常生活的一部分，它只是說法比較正式、精鍊，時不時會需要用到各個行業的專門用語。但生活中有各式各樣的情境，層出不窮的狀況，僅僅靠著背單字、背課文才學會的英文，哪裡知道如何應用？

　　於是就有了本書的誕生。我們自己也曾在職場中打滾過，碰過各種光怪陸離的情況，像是一個商品的產出，有可能會在產線上品質出問題，也有可能是商品的包裝出問題，或者是送貨途中有什麼差池⋯⋯我們將這些情況一一整理起來，

匯集成39類情境，將近2000句對話，相信各位上班族，遇到棘手情形的時候，只要對照著本書的目錄，一定都能找到相對應的應急會話。

　　另外，為了所有辛苦加班、熬夜奮鬥、沒空讀書的可憐工薪族們，我們也特別聘請了專業的外籍教師，將本書內容以美式口音呈現，所以，如果沒機會翻開這本書，那就一邊工作時就一邊帶著耳機聽對話吧！多聽就能熟悉這些道地的職場說法，甚至可以趁著面對電腦辦公、沒人注意你的時候，跟著MP3無聲地練習開口說，當有朝一日必須派上用場的時候，就絕對不用擔心想說的話全都哽在喉嚨、說不出口了。

　　最後要鼓勵在工作之餘仍願意勤奮學習的你：不要被「職場」、「商業」這些字眼給嚇到了，我們自己在辦公室不也是用很白話、很容易了解的中文來開會、談公事，或是和同事東扯西聊嗎？根本就不會賣弄文采，講些很艱澀難懂的文言文。同樣地，職場英文也是很平易近人的，靜下心來，就會發現其實你絕對可以掌握它！那麼，接下來就讓我們開始吧！

　　另外，感謝參與本書編寫工作的張印、孫美秀、董海楠三位老師，因為有他們的付出，這本書才能更臻完美。

朱傳枝、夏洋

Contents 目錄

SOS Unit 1 自我介紹

Dialogue ❶ 向面試官自我介紹 🔊 *Track 001*

💬 面試的時間長度不一定，有可能一聊就是兩小時，也有可能一分鐘給你結束。在這種短短的面試中，就要抓準所有可能的機會彰顯自己的好處，如對話中凱西雖沒有被問到打工經驗的事，卻在回答其他問題時若無其事地帶出自己的打工經驗，就是個很好的作法。

• •

Mr. Lee: Come in, Kathy. Take a seat, please.

Kathy: Thank you.

Mr. Lee: Let me introduce myself. I am the General Manager of Flora International Cosmetics Company and this is our Personnel Manager, Mr. Song. We are looking for a secretary. I'd just like to make sure that all of the details on your resume are correct.

Kathy: Of course! How can I help you?

Mr. Lee: You're a graduate of Peking University, is that right?

Kathy: That's right.

Mr. Lee: Now, tell us, Kathy, why do you want to work for Flora Cosmetics?

Kathy: I heard that this company has a professional training programme for new employees, which is exactly what I need now.

Mr. Lee: The secretarial position needs to be filled by a responsible individual. How do you handle responsibility?

Kathy: I have always handled responsibility well, and I often worked part-time when I was at university.

Mr. Lee: I see, so you don't have any difficulties working without supervision?

Kathy: Not at all. I had to work independently when I did my part-time jobs in the past.

★全文中畫 ⬤ 色塊的地方，可以依自己的狀況套入不同的名字、公司名、職稱、學校名等等。

現在是不是回想起來了呢？

Take a seat 請坐

在正式場合要請人坐下時，可以說「Take a seat」，比較禮貌。不要直接說「Sit down」（坐下），就算加個「請」說「Sit down, please」，還是會有點強迫、命令的感覺，像是學校老師叫學生坐下一般。

中文翻譯1 ▶

李先生：請進，凱西。請坐。

凱　西：謝謝。

李先生：讓我先自我介紹一下，我是芙羅拉國際化妝品公司的總經理，這位是我們人事部的宋經理。我們想招聘一名秘書。我想核對一下妳履歷中的一些細節問題。

凱　西：沒問題！請問。

李先生：妳畢業於北京大學，對嗎？

凱　西：沒錯。

李先生：那請跟我們談一下，凱西，妳為什麼想來芙羅拉化妝品公司工作呢？

凱　西：我聽說貴公司有為新員工設立專門的培訓課程，我想我現在需要的就是這個。

李先生：秘書這個職位需要非常有責任心的人。妳看待職責的態度是什麼？

凱　西：我總是能盡職盡責，在大學期間也經常做兼職工作。

李先生：我明白了。所以如果讓妳獨立作業，不會有問題吧？

凱　西：沒問題。以前我在做兼職的時候，就都是獨立作業的。

💬 在和主管初次見面時，一般不會太熱情、親切地打招呼，至少也要先察言觀色看看主管的個性是否非常嚴肅，再決定如何開口。如下面對話中，我們可以看到是主管先說早安的，凱西再配合主管的口氣，用同樣熱情的方式打招呼。

• •

Mr. Song: Good morning! I don't think we've met.

Kathy: Good morning. I am a newcomer.

Mr. Song: I'm Song Gang , the Sales Manager here. It's great to meet you.

Kathy: Mr. Song , I'm glad to meet you, too.

Mr. Song: Which position do you hold?

Kathy: I am employed here as the secretary of Mr. Lee .

Mr. Song: Are you familiar with our working environment?

Kathy: I've just arrived, but I'm ready to work.

Mr. Song: Great! If you are ready, I would like to introduce you to your new colleagues.

Kathy: Wonderful! Thank you!

★全文中畫 ⬤ 色塊的地方，可以依自己的狀況套入不同的名字、公司名、職稱、學校名等等。

現在是不是回想起來了呢？

I don't think we've met. 我們好像沒見過。

這句在電視劇、電影中也能經常看到，用於兩人初次見面時，帶有「雖然我現在不認識你，但我有興趣更認識你」的含意在。就算你根本不想認識對方，還是可以假仙地用這一句表示親切。

中文翻譯2

宋先生：早安！我好像沒有見過妳。

凱　西：早安！我是新進人員。

宋先生：我是宋剛，銷售部經理。很高興認識妳。

凱　西：宋先生，我也很高興認識您。

宋先生：妳負責什麼工作？

凱　西：我是李先生的秘書。

宋先生：妳熟悉我們的工作環境嗎？
凱　西：我才剛來，不過已經做好了工作的準備。
宋先生：很好！如果妳準備好了，我想向妳介紹一下妳的新同事。
凱　西：太好了，謝謝！

Dialogue ❸ 向同事自我介紹 ◀ *Track 003*

身為一名初來乍到的新同事，不能太囂張，所以我們可以看到文中的凱西謙虛地說自己什麼都不會，讓同事覺得她有禮貌又好相處，願意教她更多。

Kathy: I'm Kathy , the new secretary . Pleased to meet you.

Amy: I'm Amy , the Financial Supervisor . Pleased to meet you, too.

Kathy: I hear that you are doing a great job. The division's finances are in top shape.

Amy: Thank you. Which university did you graduate from?

Kathy: I just graduated from Peking University .

Amy: What did you major in?

Kathy: My major was English . I'm a newcomer, and there are lots of rules that I don't know. Would you mind showing me the ropes?

Amy: No problem.

Kathy: Thank you.

Amy: I may need a lot of help from you. I hope we can help each other.

★全文中畫 ⬤ 色塊的地方，可以依自己的狀況套入不同的名字、公司名、職稱、學校名等等。

現在是不是回想起來了呢？

show sb. the ropes 教某人一些基本功

「rope」是繩子的意思。這和「基本功」有什麼關係？原來，剛開始航海的水手還不太懂怎麼操縱繩索，可是要航海就一定要會使用繩索，所以老手就會教他們怎麼拉、怎麼綁。同樣地，剛到一個新公司的員工也需要老手教他們在公司生存的基本功，這時就可以用「show sb. the ropes」來形容這件事。

中文翻譯3

凱西：我是凱西，新來的秘書。非常高興見到妳。
艾咪：我是艾咪，財務主管。我也很高興見到妳。
凱西：聽說您工作很出色。部門的財務狀況很不錯。
艾咪：謝謝。妳是哪所學校畢業的？
凱西：我剛剛從北京大學畢業。
艾咪：妳主修哪一科？
凱西：我的主修是英文。我剛剛進入公司，所以對這裡的許多制度都還不瞭解，還請
　　　您多多指教。
艾咪：沒問題。
凱西：謝謝您。
艾咪：在很多方面我可能都需要妳的幫忙。希望我們可以互相幫助。

Dialogue ❹ 向來訪客戶自我介紹（1） 🔊 *Track 004*

客戶對公司的事務不見得瞭解，公司裡的長官或許也不希望他們太瞭解。因此，當客戶好奇地打探一些事（如本文中客戶打聽前一個秘書的去向）時，如果沒有和長官確認過是否可以把真相說出來，就不要隨便說。

Kathy: Hi, Mr. Wang . I'm Kathy . Glad to meet you.

Mr. Wang: Hi, I don't think we've met yet.

Kathy: No, we haven't. I'm the new secretary .

Mr. Wang: Betty used to work here, what happened to her?

Kathy: She resigned because of her health .

Mr. Wang: Resigned? I haven't even been here for two months and there is already a personnel change.

Kathy: I'll be handling the contacts with clients.

Mr. Wang: What else are you responsible for?

Kathy: Anything related to the company's meetings and reception.

Mr. Wang: That will keep you very busy. No wonder Betty got sick. Will you be able to manage?

Kathy: I'll be fine, but please be patient with me.

Mr. Wang: Do your best; we'll really need your help.

★全文中畫 ⬤ 色塊的地方，可以依自己的狀況套入不同的名字、公司名、職稱、學校名等等。

現在是不是回想起來了呢？

contacts 聯絡人

contacts還有「隱形眼鏡」的意思，因此有這樣一個冷笑話：有個男子開車在路上蛇行，被警察攔下，問他為何不戴眼鏡在路上亂開。男子表示：「我有contacts（隱形眼鏡）啊！」警察則說：「我才不管你的聯絡人是誰，罰單還是要開。」真的很冷。

中文翻譯4

凱　西：您好，王先生，我是凱西。很高興見到您。
王先生：妳好，我們以前沒見過面吧？
凱　西：我們沒見過。我是新來的秘書。
王先生：貝蒂以前在這裡工作，她怎麼啦？
凱　西：她因健康問題辭職了。
王先生：辭職了？我才來這裡兩個月，就有人事變動了。
凱　西：我會負責與客戶聯絡的事。
王先生：妳還負責什麼事？
凱　西：還有所有與公司會議及接待有關的事情。
王先生：那會讓妳忙到不行的。難怪貝蒂會生病。妳能忙得過來嗎？
凱　西：沒問題的，但希望您能多多包涵。
王先生：盡力做吧，我們很需要妳的幫忙！

Dialogue ❺ 向來訪客戶自我介紹（2）　◀Track 005

　　身為公司的新人，來訪的客戶很可能還不認識你。這時，別讓對方瞎猜「這人在這裡幹嘛」，如同文中的凱西一樣，主動自我介紹吧！

Kathy: Nice to meet you, Mr. Green . I'm Kathy , the new secretary .
Mr. Green: Nice to meet you too, Kathy .
Kathy: Did you have any trouble finding us?
Mr. Green: No, no trouble at all.
Kathy: Would you like to meet Mr. Lee ?

Mr. Green: Oh, yes, that would be great.

Kathy: Well, I'll just see if he's free now. I hope you don't mind waiting a moment.

Mr. Green: No, that's fine.

Kathy: Mr. Lee is expecting you in his office. Would you follow me please?

Mr. Green: Thank you.

★全文中畫 ⬭ 色塊的地方，可以依自己的狀況套入不同的名字、公司名、職稱、學校名等等。

現在是不是回想起來了呢？

expecting you 等著你來

和客戶說你的主管正「等著他」，可以說「expecting you」。注意「you」不可省，要是說你的主管「is expecting」，就表示你的主管快生了，這意思差很多的。

中文翻譯5

凱　　西：很高興見到你，格林先生。我是凱西，新來的秘書。
格林先生：我也很高興見到妳，凱西。
凱　　西：我們這兒難找嗎？
格林先生：不，一點兒也不難找。
凱　　西：你想見見李先生嗎？
格林先生：哦，好的，非常好。
凱　　西：好的，我看看他現在有沒有時間，請你稍等一下。
格林先生：好的。
凱　　西：李先生正在辦公室等你。請這邊走。
格林先生：謝謝。

商務小常識

　　新進職員遇到客戶來訪時，可以主動向客戶作自我介紹。彼此先握手問候，然後交換名片。遞交名片要用雙手或右手，讓文字正面朝向對方，對方是國外客戶的話，記得英文面朝上。交換名片時，要清楚複誦一次自己的名字，以免對方誤唸，而且千萬要對對方的名片內容表示興趣，不能看也不看就收起來，這樣很不禮貌。

Unit 2
剛開始工作

Dialogue ① 客戶問路 🔊 *Track 006*

在路上隨便被人問路，結果好巧不巧，對方正好就要去你公司！除了像對話中的凱西一樣詳細和對方說明路線以外，直接和對方說「我也要去那裡，跟著我走就對了」（**I happen to be heading there too. You can come with me.**）也行。

. . . .

Stranger: Excuse me, Miss. Would you please tell me how to get to Flora International Cosmetics Company ?

Kathy: Yes, take Bus No. 202 , get off at the Peace Plaza , then transfer to Bus No. 406 , and get off at Flora International Cosmetics Company .

Stranger: How long does it take?

Kathy: About half an hour . Here comes the bus.

Stranger: Are you taking the bus, too?

Kathy: Yes, I'm going the same way.

Stranger: Nice to have you as my company.

Kathy: I work at Flora International Cosmetics Company .

Stranger: Glad to meet you. I'm David , a new client. May I have your name?

Kathy: Call me Kathy . Glad to meet you, too.

★全文中畫 色塊的地方，可以依自己的狀況套入不同的名字、公司名、職稱、學校名等等。

have you as my company 有你作伴

這句中的「company」和「Flora International Cosmetics Company」的「company」是不同的。前者是「夥伴」，而後者則是「公司」。

中文翻譯1

陌生人：打擾一下，小姐，能告訴我怎麼去芙羅拉國際化妝品公司嗎？
凱　西：好的，搭202路公車到和平廣場下車，換搭406路公車，然後到芙羅拉國際化妝品公司下車。
陌生人：需要多久時間呢？
凱　西：大約半個小時。車來了。
陌生人：妳也坐這班公車嗎？
凱　西：是的，我和你同一路。
陌生人：很高興有妳做伴。
凱　西：我就在芙羅拉國際化妝品公司工作。
陌生人：很高興認識妳。我叫大衛，是你們的新客戶。怎麼稱呼妳啊？
凱　西：叫我凱西就可以了，我也非常高興認識您。

Dialogue ❷ 接手工作 ◀ *Track 007*

前輩在交接的時候，身為新人的你要很有禮貌地聽對方說，不要自我主張很強地插入一堆意見。如文中凱西都回應得非常簡短，讓對方知道自己有聽懂即可。

Betty: Kathy, you are going to take over my job as secretary here starting next Monday. Now let me tell you the office rules first.

Kathy: Thank you.

Betty: The working hours are from eight to twelve in the morning and from one to five in the afternoon. Be sure not to be late or absent.

Kathy: I'll do my best.

Betty: To be a good secretary, you'll have to be quite familiar with office routines and try to learn to do a bit of everything.

Kathy: I understand.

Betty: Come here, please, Kathy . I'd like to explain the filing system to you.

Kathy: All right.

Betty: This is your filing cabinet and all the documents must be filed alphabetically.

Kathy: I see.

★全文中畫 色塊的地方，可以依自己的狀況套入不同的名字、公司名、職稱、學校名等等。

現在是不是回想起來了呢？

office routine 辦公室的日常事務

辦公室一般幾點開門？幾點鎖門？大家都什麼時候去吃午餐？會訂團購嗎？有固定的下午茶活動、教育訓練嗎？這些都算是「office routine」。

中文翻譯2

貝蒂：凱西，從下週一開始妳就要接手我的秘書工作了。現在我先跟妳說明一下辦公室的規定吧。

凱西：謝謝。

貝蒂：上班時間是上午8點到12點，下午1點到5點。注意不要遲到或曠職。

凱西：我會盡力。

貝蒂：要想成為一名好秘書，妳就得對辦公室的日常事務非常熟悉，每種工作也都要學著做一點。

凱西：我明白。

貝蒂：過來這邊，凱西。我解釋一下建檔系統給妳聽。

凱西：好。

貝蒂：這是妳的檔案櫃，所有的檔案都必須按照字母順序存檔。

凱西：我明白了。

Dialogue ❸ 熟悉環境 ◀ *Track 008*

和新同事見面，如果同事請你叫他綽號，那叫綽號就沒關係，但如果同事沒有請你叫他綽號，則不要自己主動幫他取一個，就算他名字很長也一樣。至少等熟了再來取比較好。

Victoria: You must be Kathy ! I'm Victoria , but you can call me Vicky .

Kathy: Hi, Vicky , nice to meet you.

Victoria: Nice to meet you, too. Are you familiar with the routines here?

Kathy: No, I've just started working here.

Victoria: Then I'm going to be running you through your orientation today. If you have any questions, just let me know.

Kathy: Okay, thank you.

Victoria: First, I'll just let you know how the company works and tell you specifically what your job is as a secretary . Your main responsibility is to arrange all the meetings and contacts .

Kathy: I see.

Victoria: So you must take down all the information clearly.

Kathy: I'll remember that communication is my number one priority.

★全文中畫 ⬤ 色塊的地方，可以依自己的狀況套入不同的名字、公司名、職稱、學校名等等。

> **現在是不是回想起來了呢？**
>
> **take down information 記錄資訊**
> 雖然整個片語中從頭到尾沒提到「寫」，但它的意思其實就是指把聽到的資訊老老實實地寫下來。

中文翻譯3

維多利亞： 妳一定是凱西！我是維多利亞，你可以叫我薇琪。

凱　西： 妳好，薇琪，很高興見到妳。

維多利亞： 我也很高興見到妳。妳熟悉這裡的日常工作了嗎？

凱　西： 還沒有呢，我剛來工作。

維多利亞： 那麼我今天會帶妳跑一次就任流程。如果有什麼問題，儘管問我。

凱　西： 好的，謝謝。

維多利亞： 首先，我會讓妳知道公司是怎樣運作的，然後具體說一下作為秘書妳要做哪些工作。妳的主要工作就是安排所有的會議和聯繫事宜。

凱　西： 我明白。

維多利亞： 所以妳必須清楚記錄下所有事情。

凱　西： 我會記住溝通是我最重要的工作。

Dialogue ❹ 感謝幫助 ◀€*Track 009*

請新同事幫忙一點，難免要比較客氣。在公司分秒必爭，時間就是金錢，對方願意花時間教你，就要感謝人家為你耗費了他的時間成本，因此我們可以看到文中凱西為自己「佔用對方很長的時間」感到抱歉。

Michael: Now, is there anything else I should tell you?

Kathy: No, I don't think so. I've already taken up a lot of your time.

Michael: Oh, don't worry about that.

Kathy: No, I really appreciate what you've done for me these past few days, Michael . Thank you very much for your help.

Michael: That's all right. If there is anything else I can do for you, do let me know.

Kathy: I certainly will. Well, thanks again.

Michael: My pleasure. Well, it's time to go home.

Kathy: Go ahead. I have letters to type.

Michael: Okay. See you tomorrow.

Kathy: See you.

★全文中畫 ⬤ 色塊的地方，可以依自己的狀況套入不同的名字、公司名、職稱、學校名等等。

現在是不是回想起來了呢？

appreciate 感激
appreciate除了用來當作「感激」以外，「欣賞」美麗的藝術品、漂亮的景色等等，也可以用這個字表示。

中文翻譯4
麥克：現在，還有什麼需要我介紹的嗎？
凱西：我想沒有了。我已經佔用你很長時間了。
麥克：哦，這沒什麼。
凱西：不，我真的很感謝你這些天來為我做的一切，麥克。真的非常感謝你的幫助。

麥克：沒關係，如果還有什麼需要，儘管告訴我。
凱西：我會的，再次感謝你。
麥克：不客氣。喔，該下班了。
凱西：你先走吧，我還有幾封信要打。
麥克：好的，明天見。
凱西：再見。

商務小常識

　　一般來說，有與國外客戶往來的公司，員工（尤其是祕書）一定都會有自己的英文名字。有些人會認為取些可愛、搞笑的英文名字會讓人印象深刻，疏不知英文名字如果亂取的話，給客戶的印象就會不佳，會被認為沒有常識或是不夠莊重。像Candy、Lucky這種像寵物的名字，或是Cherry、Dick等含有特殊意義的名字，就最好別用了。

在機場

Dialogue ❶ 接錯人 🔈 *Track 010*

別以為在機場接機接錯人這種事不可能發生，外國人的姓氏重複率不算很高，但如果你現在要接的客戶是華裔，搞不好會一不小心就接到別的「陳先生」、「王先生」，因為姓這些的人多到不行。參考文中凱西如何化解吧！

Kathy: Excuse me. Are you Mr. Smith from America ?

Mr. Smith: Yes, I'm Tom Smith . How do you do?

Kathy: How do you do? I'm Kathy , and my boss has asked me to come and pick you up.

Mr. Smith: That's very kind of him.

(In the cab)

Kathy: Please drive to Flora International Cosmetics Company .

Mr. Smith: I'm afraid I don't know the company.

Kathy: Really? Aren't you Thomas Smith from Los Angeles ?

Mr. Smith: No, I'm Tom Smith from New York .

Kathy: Oh, I'm sorry. I've got the wrong person.

Mr. Smith: That's fine. Could you drop me off at the airport arrival level?

★全文中畫 ⬤ 色塊的地方，可以依自己的狀況套入不同的名字、公司名、職稱、學校名等等。

drop me off 把我放下來

「drop」是「使掉落」的意思，但「drop me off」並不是叫人家把你拋到地上，而是用於「你人在車上，要人家把車停下來，把你放下車」這樣的情境。

中文翻譯1

凱　　西：打擾了，請問您是從美國來的史密斯先生嗎？
史密斯先生：是的，我是湯姆・史密斯。你好。
凱　　西：你好。我是凱西，我的老闆要我來接您。
史密斯先生：他人真好。
（在計程車上）
凱　　西：請到芙羅拉國際化妝品公司。
史密斯先生：我好像不知道這家公司。
凱　　西：是嗎？您不是從洛杉磯來的湯瑪斯・史密斯嗎？
史密斯先生：不是，我是湯姆・史密斯，來自紐約。
凱　　西：噢，對不起，我接錯人了。
史密斯先生：沒關係。您可以在接機樓層讓我下車嗎？

Dialogue ❷ 自我介紹 🔊Track 011

面對客戶，可以若無其事地稱讚對方一下，如本文中凱西提到老闆說客戶非常努力促進雙方合作，不但讓對方被稱讚很開心，也同時讓對方對自己與老闆的印象加分。

Kathy: Welcome to Shanghai , Mr. Brown . May I introduce myself? I'm Kathy , Mr. Lee's secretary .

Mr. Brown: Thank you. It's very kind of you to pick me up at the airport.

Kathy: Mr. Lee has asked me to come and meet you.

Mr. Brown: It's kind of your manager. I have been looking forward to this trip. It was so good of you to invite me to China .

Kathy: Mr. Lee said that you have done substantial work in promoting our mutual trade.

Mr. Brown: It is very kind of you to say so, but nothing can really be done without our close cooperation.

Kathy: Right. I am sure our cooperation will continue and become stronger in the future.

Mr. Brown: Yes, I believe so.

Kathy: The waiting room is over there. Let's rest a bit, then we'll claim your baggage.

Mr. Brown: Okay, after you.

★全文中畫 ⬤ 色塊的地方，可以依自己的狀況套入不同的名字、公司名、職稱、學校名等等。

現在是不是回想起來了呢？

claim baggage 拿行李

「claim baggage」是表示「拿行李」的動詞片語，而如果你現在在國外的機場要找「拿行李的地方」，它叫做「baggage claim」。

中文翻譯2

凱　西：歡迎來到上海，布朗先生。讓我先來作一下自我介紹，我是凱西，李先生的秘書。

布朗先生：謝謝。很感謝您來機場接我。

凱　西：是李先生要我來接您的。

布朗先生：您的主管真是太好了。我一直對此行很期待，謝謝你們邀請我來中國。

凱　西：李先生說，您在促進雙方貿易方面做了許多努力。

布朗先生：你們能這樣說我真是太高興了。但是如果沒有雙方的密切合作，什麼事也做不到。

凱　西：沒錯。我相信以後我們的合作還會持續下去，以後還會更加穩固。

布朗先生：是的，我也這麼相信。

凱　西：休息室在那邊。我們先去那邊稍微休息一下，再去拿行李。

布朗先生：好的，請。

Dialogue ❸ 寒暄問候 🔊 *Track 012*

💬 與客戶應對一定要格外地親切小心、噓寒問暖，所以本文中凱西一聽到客戶暈機，就立刻領他去休息室坐下。不過，雖然這樣的做法很體貼，但也要注意不要坐太久哦，不然客戶的行李可能會被收走了。

‧‧‧

Kathy: Excuse me, are you Mr. Smith ?

Mr. Smith: Yes, I am.

Kathy: How do you do, Mr. Smith ? My name is Kathy , a secretary at Flora International Cosmetics Company .

Mr. Smith: How do you do, Kathy ? Nice to meet you.

Kathy: Nice to meet you, too. I've come here to take you to your hotel. How was your trip?

Mr. Smith: Not very good. I'm afraid I was airsick, but I feel better now.

Kathy: Let's have a rest in the reception room over there, and then we'll pick up your luggage.

Mr. Smith: All right.

Kathy: This way, please.

Mr. Smith: OK.

★全文中畫 ⬤ 色塊的地方，可以依自己的狀況套入不同的名字、公司名、職稱、學校名等等。

現在是不是回想起來了呢？

airsick 暈機

和airsick類似的字還有seasick（暈船）、carsick（暈車）。一般非交通工具引起的「想吐」可直接說「feel sick」。

中文翻譯3 ‧‧

凱　西：打擾一下，您是史密斯先生嗎？

史密斯先生：是的，我是。

凱　西：您好，史密斯先生。我是凱西，芙羅拉國際化妝品公司的秘書。

史密斯先生：您好，凱西，很高興認識您。
凱　　西：我也是。我來接您去酒店。旅途愉快嗎？
史密斯先生：不太好，可能是暈機了，不過現在好多了。
凱　　西：我們到那邊的接待室休息一下吧。等一下再去拿行李。
史密斯先生：好。
凱　　西：這邊請。
史密斯先生：好的。

Dialogue ❹ 機場兌換 🔊 *Track 013*

如果要替客戶換錢、或替公司換錢，一定要先問好匯率，甚至需要更小心地與上級確認這樣的匯率應該換多少再下手，因為畢竟是職場，就算是一塊錢都要斤斤計較一些。

Bank clerk: May I help you?

Kathy: Yes, I would like to exchange some money.

Bank clerk: What currency would you like to trade in?

Kathy: I would like to exchange (pounds) for (RMB).

Bank clerk: No problem. How much would you like to exchange today?

Kathy: Well, that depends on the rate. What's the exchange rate please?

Bank clerk: The (pound) is now worth (RMB) (9.5). Will that be all right?

Kathy: Well, give me (5,000 pounds) worth of (RMB). I might as well exchange a little extra. Who knows what the exchange rate will be tomorrow!

★全文中畫 ⬤ 色塊的地方，可以依自己的狀況套入不同的名字、公司名、職稱、學校名等等。

中文翻譯4

銀行職員：有什麼需要幫忙的嗎？
凱　　西：我想換錢。
銀行職員：您想換什麼幣種？
凱　　西：我想把英鎊換成人民幣。
銀行職員：沒問題。您今天想換多少？
凱　　西：嗯，要看看匯率。請問匯率是多少？

Dialogue ⑤ 認領行李 ◀ *Track 014*

很多人行李沒到時會氣急敗壞地破口大罵，但偶爾也要為地勤人員想想，因為很可能根本不是他們的錯，對他們嚷嚷也沒意義。像文中這樣理性而平和的詢問方式，才能幫助工作人員快速確認你的行李外表，盡快找到你的行李。

Kathy: My luggage never arrived. What should I do?

Airport staff member: Can you show us your luggage claim tag?

Kathy: Yes, it's Flight 602 from London.

Airport staff member: All the luggage from that flight has been cleared.

Kathy: What should I do now?

Airport staff member: Look at these samples and tell me the color, type and unique characteristics of your luggage.

Kathy: It's this type in black.

Airport staff member: Okay, as soon as we find the luggage we'll deliver it to your hotel.

Kathy: Thank you.

Airport staff member: You're welcome. It's the least we can do. Sorry for the inconvenience.

★全文中畫 ⬤ 色塊的地方，可以依自己的狀況套入不同的名字、公司名、職稱、學校名等等。

現在是不是回想起來了呢？

luggage claim tag 行李認領牌
所謂的「tag」是一種「標示」，像服飾店商品上的價格標示吊牌就是「price tag」。

中文翻譯5

凱　　　西：我的行李一直都沒出來。我該怎麼辦？

機場工作人員：可以出示一下您的行李認領牌嗎？

凱　　　西：好的，是從倫敦來的602航班。

機場工作人員：飛機上的所有行李都已經清空了。

凱　　　西：那我現在應該怎麼辦？

機場工作人員：看一下這些樣品，告訴我您行李的顏色、類別和特徵。

凱　　　西：是這款的，黑色。

機場工作人員：好的，我們一找到您的行李就會送往您的酒店。

凱　　　西：謝謝。

機場工作人員：不客氣。這是我們起碼應該做的。對於給您帶來的不便，我們深表歉意。

Dialogue ❻ 送機 ◀ *Track 015*

在職場上，就算以後再也不會見到，和客戶維持良好的關係依然是再好不過的事。本文中的客戶不但和凱西約好下次見面的時間，還邀她到他的國家玩（雖然很可能不會真的去），就是維持人際關係的良好作法。

Mr. Smith: Thanks for seeing me off at the airport. I really appreciate it.

Kathy: No problem, it's my pleasure. I am glad you had a chance to visit our company, and I hope you can come back soon.

Mr. Smith: We should be back in about three months . We'll have another meeting next quarter . Will you be in the area at that time?

Kathy: I should be. Remember to send me an email and let me know when your flight arrives. I'll come and pick you up at the airport.

Mr. Smith: You're too kind!

Kathy: Here's your terminal. What airline are you flying with?

Mr. Smith: Um… Let me look at the ticket. Oh, that's right, Air China .

Kathy: The boarding gate for your flight is not far from here. All you have to do is walk straight through those doors and turn left , and then you should be able to see the check-in counter.

Mr. Smith: Thanks again for all of your help. If you're ever in my area, please be sure to look me up.

Kathy: Sure. Let's keep in touch.

★全文中畫 ⬤ 色塊的地方，可以依自己的狀況套入不同的名字、公司名、職稱、學校名等等。

現在是不是回想起來了呢？

boarding gate 登機門
在機場一定要認得這個單字。它也會出現在你的機票上！

中文翻譯6

史密斯先生：謝謝妳到機場為我送行。我真的非常感謝。
凱　　西：別客氣，我很樂意。非常高興您能來我們公司參觀，期盼您能早日再來。
史密斯先生：我們大概三個月後就會回來。我們下一季還要開一次會議，那時候妳會在那一帶嗎？
凱　　西：應該會。來的時候請記得寄電子郵件給我，告訴我你的航班時間，我會來機場接你的。
史密斯先生：妳人真是太好了。
凱　　西：航廈到了。您是哪家公司的飛機？
史密斯先生：呃，我看一下機票。哦，對，是中國國際航空公司。
凱　　西：您的航班的登機口離這裡不遠。只要穿過這些門直走左轉，您就能看見辦理登機手續的櫃檯了。
史密斯先生：再次謝謝妳的幫助。如果妳有機會到我們那裡，請務必來找我。
凱　　西：當然。那就再聯絡了。

商務小常識

　　在接機之前，一定要先熟悉自己的公司及產品的情況，並準備好相關文件和產品。接機的時候，可以跟外國客戶多聊本地的旅遊景點、美食（並打聽客人喜好的口味）、天氣狀況等，最重要的是要再跟客戶確認一次他（她）在本地的行程。初次聊天時則不要主動談到個人隱私、宗教信仰、政治等問題，這也是最基本的禮貌。

SOS Unit 4 接待客人

Dialogue ➊ 提醒 🔊 *Track 016*

💬 打電話到客戶的旅館房間打擾人家，感覺總有點不好意思，所以至少也要如對話中一樣，客氣地問對方一句睡得好不好。

Mr. Smith: Hello, Smith speaking.

Kathy: Hello, Mr. Smith . This is Kathy from Flora International Cosmetics Company . How did you sleep last night?

Mr. Smith: Okay, thank you.

Kathy: You're welcome. I just want to remind you we have an appointment at 7 tonight.

Mr. Smith: Yes, I remember. Thank you.

Kathy: I am going to pick you up at 6:30 .

Mr. Smith: I'll be waiting in the lobby. See you later.

Kathy: Talk to you later.

★全文中畫 ⬤ 色塊的地方，可以依自己的狀況套入不同的名字、公司名、職稱、學校名等等。

中文翻譯1

史密斯先生：你好，我是史密斯。

凱　西：你好，史密斯先生。我是芙羅拉國際化妝品公司的凱西。昨晚休息得怎麼樣？

史密斯先生：滿好的，謝謝。

凱　西：別客氣，我是打來提醒您，我們晚上7點有約。

史密斯先生：是的，我記得。謝謝。

凱　西：我6點半去接您。
史密斯先生：我會在大廳等您。待會兒見。
凱　西：待會兒見。

Dialogue ❷ 核對活動日程 ◀ *Track 017*

在閱讀接下來的對話中，你會注意到凱西在和客戶講每一段話的同時，總會加上一句句確認的話，例如「您覺得這樣可以嗎？」、「這樣的安排可以嗎？」等，這是禮貌的表現。

Kathy: Mr. Smith , I want to discuss the final itinerary with you if you don't mind.

Mr. Smith: Of course not.

Kathy: On the first morning, we'll have a meeting to discuss the progress of our cooperation project. Is that all right for you?

Mr. Smith: That's fine. What about the second day?

Kathy: On the second day, you'll visit the production line at the factory. On the third and fourth days, we'll take you on a tour.

Mr. Smith: Sounds good.

Kathy: On the last day, we'll host a dinner. Is the itinerary okay?

Mr. Smith: Yes, it sounds charming.

Kathy: If you would like to make any changes, please let me know.

Mr. Smith: There shouldn't be any problem.

Kathy: Great!

★全文中畫 ⬤ 色塊的地方，可以依自己的狀況套入不同的名字、公司名、職稱、學校名等等。

現在是不是回想起來了呢？

production line 生產線

「production」就是「生產」，而「line」就是「線」，不用懷疑，真的可以這麼直接翻譯。

中文翻譯2

凱　西：史密斯先生，如果您不介意的話，我想和您討論一下最終的行程安排。

史密斯先生：我當然不介意。

凱　西：第一天早上，我們開會討論我們合作項目的進展，您覺得可以嗎？

史密斯先生：好的，那第二天呢？

凱　西：第二天，您會參觀工廠生產線。第三天和第四天，我們會帶您逛逛附近的景點。

史密斯先生：聽起來不錯。

凱　西：最後一天，我們邀請您共進晚餐。這樣的安排可以嗎？

史密斯先生：當然，聽起來很吸引人。

凱　西：如果您有什麼需要更改的，請通知我。

史密斯先生：應該沒什麼問題。

凱　西：太好了！

Dialogue ❸ 陪客戶參觀 ◀ *Track 018*

客戶在參觀時，總會問很多問題，因此在陪同參觀前一定要先預想好會有哪些問題，尤其如文中數字相關的地方，更要記清楚。

Kathy: Welcome to our factory. I think it's the best way for you to get to know our factory and our product quality.

Mr. Smith: Do you process everything in your factory?

Kathy: Yes, we have employed several experts in the cosmetic field from both home and abroad.

Mr. Smith: No wonder your products are world-famous.

Kathy: Right, and we have a very strict quality control system.

Mr. Smith: Such as what?

Kathy: There are four inspection stops in our production process, and before shipment, our Quality Control Manager also personally does a random check.

Mr. Smith: How long has your plant been in production?

Kathy: About 10 years .

Mr. Smith: How many employees do you have?

Kathy: We have (7) stockholders and (over 100) employees.

★全文中畫 ⬤ 色塊的地方，可以依自己的狀況套入不同的名字、公司名、職稱、學校名等等。

現在是不是回想起來了呢？

plant 工廠
史密斯先生在這段對話中問到的「plant」並非大家熟知的「植物」，而是指大型工廠，尤其發電廠等特別常使用這個字來說明（例如：核電廠 nuclear plant）。

中文翻譯3

凱　西：歡迎參觀我們的工廠，我想這是讓您瞭解我們工廠及我們產品品質的最好方式。

史密斯先生：所有的生產流程都在你們廠內進行嗎？

凱　西：是的，我們聘用了幾位國內外化妝品生產領域的專家。

史密斯先生：難怪你們的產品世界聞名。

凱　西：是的，同時我們還有著極其嚴格的品質管制系統。

史密斯先生：像是怎樣的品質管制系統？

凱　西：生產流程上有4處檢查站，出貨前我們的品管經理也會親自抽檢。

史密斯先生：你們的工廠投入生產多久了？

凱　西：大約10年了。

史密斯先生：你們有多少員工？

凱　西：我們有7位股東，100多名員工。

Dialogue ④ 送別客戶 🔊 *Track 019*

這次客戶來參觀，時程很緊沒辦法帶他去玩，就可以如以下這段對話中一樣，主動說下次要帶客戶去玩，藉機也更鞏固兩者之間的合作關係，表示「還有下次機會」。

Kathy: I'm sorry that your visit was so short.

Mr. Smith: I wish I could stay a little longer, but I've lots to do back home. You know how it is.

Kathy: That's true. For a (businessman), (business) always comes first.

Mr. Smith: But I look forward to coming back.

Kathy: Hope to see you again soon!

Mr. Smith: So do I. It's very kind of you to see me off. I really had a lovely visit.

Kathy: It's a pity that you couldn't visit many places.

Mr. Smith: Business trips never leave much time for sightseeing.

Kathy: Perhaps we can make up for it next time.

Mr. Smith: I hope so.

★全文中畫 ⬤ 色塊的地方，可以依自己的狀況套入不同的名字、公司名、職稱、學校名等等。

現在是不是回想起來了呢？

see sb. off 替某人送行

雖然這個片語中有「off」，但和「下」沒有關係，而是「送某人離開」的意思。

中文翻譯4

凱　西：真遺憾您在此停留時間這麼短。

史密斯先生：真希望可以多待幾天，不過妳也知道，我回去還有很多事情需要處理。

凱　西：是啊。對於生意人來說，生意總是高於一切。

史密斯先生：但是我期待再次造訪。

凱　西：希望很快能再見到你！

史密斯先生：我也是。非常感謝妳來為我送行。我這次拜訪真的很愉快。

凱　西：真的很遺憾您沒能遊覽更多的地方。

史密斯先生：出差本來就沒有太多時間可以觀光的。

凱　西：或許我們下次可以去。

史密斯先生：但願如此。

Dialogue ⑤ 接待訪客 🔊 *Track 020*

對待訪客禮貌是上乘之道，就算他沒預約就莫名其妙跑進來，而且連要找的人叫什麼都不知道，還是要以禮相待。可觀察下方對話中，凱西的處理就非常得體。

• •

Kathy: Good afternoon. What can I do for you today?

Visitor: Well, I was wondering if I could speak to whoever is in charge of your company.

Kathy: Do you have an appointment?

Visitor: I was not aware that I needed to make an appointment.

Kathy: Oh, it's no problem. I will see if Mr. Lee , the General Manager , has time to meet with you now. Could you please wait just a moment? Please have a seat, and make yourself comfortable.

Visitor: Thank you!

Kathy: Thanks for waiting. This is a busy time for Mr. Lee , but if you don't mind waiting another 10 minutes , I can arrange for you to talk with him. He can help answer any questions you may have.

Visitor: It's okay. I can wait.

(Ten minutes later...)

Kathy: Mr. Lee's office is on the 3rd floor . Walk straight, and turn left at the next hallway. It is the first office on the right .

Visitor: Thank you. I am sure I won't have any problem finding it.

★全文中畫 ⬤ 色塊的地方，可以依自己的狀況套入不同的名字、公司名、職稱、學校名等等。

現在是不是回想起來了呢？

make an appointment 預約
覺得用「make an appointment」這麼長的片語來說「預約」這個短短的詞很麻煩的話，也可以講短一點，用「book」當作「預訂」的意思。

中文翻譯5

凱西：午安，我可以幫您什麼忙嗎？

訪客：哦，不知道能否見一下貴公司的負責人？

凱西：您有預約嗎？

訪客：我不知道要先預約。

凱西：噢，沒問題。我看看我們總經理李先生有沒有時間和您會面。您能等一下嗎？先休息一下，請自便。

訪客：謝謝！

凱西：讓您久等了。李先生現在很忙，不過如果您不介意的話，請再等候10分鐘，我會安排您和李先生見面。他能幫您解答問題。

訪客：好的，我可以等。

（10分鐘後……）

凱西：李先生的辦公室在3樓，直直走過去，下一個走道左轉，右手邊第一個房間就是了。

訪客：謝謝。我相信我一定找得到。

商務小常識

　　帶客戶參觀工廠前，雙方要先約定見面時間、地點，大部份的情況是買賣雙方一起前往工廠。到達工廠後，是由廠長或產品管理部門的經理接待。參觀生產線時，最好要按照流程順序，對進料品管、倉儲、生產線線上品管、出貨品管、包裝、檢驗、品保和出貨等流程進行一一講解。

SOS Unit 5
安排會面

Dialogue ❶ 電話預約 (1) \blacktriangleleft *Track 021*

電話預約時，如果是和自己熟悉的對象，就不用在那邊長篇大論地介紹自己。仔細看看這篇對話，應該就能發現凱西和貝蒂是熟人。

● ●

Kathy: Flora International Cosmetics Company , how may I help you?

Betty: Yes, this is Betty speaking.

Kathy: This is Kathy speaking. How are you, Betty ?

Betty: Fine, and you?

Kathy: Just fine, thank you.

Betty: I'm calling to see if we can arrange a meeting. There are several matters I'd like to discuss with you.

Kathy: Okay. When would be convenient?

Betty: Could we meet tomorrow?

Kathy: Yes. What time would be convenient?

Betty: How about 2 p.m. ?

Kathy: Great, I'm looking forward to seeing you.

★全文中畫 ⬤ 色塊的地方，可以依自己的狀況套入不同的名字、公司名、職稱、學校名等等。

中文翻譯1

凱西：芙羅拉國際化妝品公司，您有什麼需要？
貝蒂：妳好，我是貝蒂。
凱西：我是凱西。貝蒂，妳好嗎？
貝蒂：很好，妳呢？

凱西：還不錯。謝謝。
貝蒂：我打電話是想問能否安排一個時間見面。有幾件事情我想和妳討論一下。
凱西：好的，什麼時候方便？
貝蒂：明天可以嗎？
凱西：可以。什麼時間方便？
貝蒂：下午兩點怎麼樣？
凱西：好的，很期待跟妳碰面。

Dialogue ❷ 電話預約 (2) ◀ Track 022

如果是和已經聯絡多次，彼此都已明白不需客套的對象聯絡，可以避開繁文縟節，直接切入正題，如以下對話中直接和對方討論時間地點。

Kathy: Good afternoon.

Bob: Hello, this is Bob . May I speak to Mr. Lee ?

Kathy: Mr. Lee is in a meeting. This is his secretary speaking. May I take a message?

Bob: I'd like to discuss the new order with him. Would you ask him whether I can have lunch together with him at Garden Hotel next Wednesday ?

Kathy: Let me check his schedule. Er… I'm afraid he can't make it. He has to go to Beijing for a conference. He'll come back on Thursday .

Bob: That's a pity. Does Friday suit him?

Kathy: Yes, that would be fine. What time?

Bob: Is 12 o'clock convenient for him?

Kathy: Yes, that's fine. Next Friday at 12 at Garden Hotel .

★全文中畫 ⬤ 色塊的地方，可以依自己的狀況套入不同的名字、公司名、職稱、學校名等等。

現在是不是回想起來了呢？

take a message 記錄留言
某A要找某B，但某B不在，這時某A可能會請你幫他記錄下他要跟某B講的話然後代為轉達。你「記錄下留言」的這個動作就叫做take a message。

凱西：下午好。

鮑勃：你好，我是鮑勃，我想和李先生通電話。

凱西：李先生正在開會。我是他的秘書。你要留言嗎？

鮑勃：我想跟他談一談新訂單的事。麻煩妳問他下星期三可以和我在花園酒店共進午餐嗎？

凱西：讓我查一下他的行程。嗯……恐怕星期三不行，他得去北京參加一個會議，星期四回來。

鮑勃：太遺憾了。那星期五他有時間嗎？

凱西：可以，他有時間。要約幾點？

鮑勃：12點他方便嗎？

凱西：好的。下週五中午12點在花園酒店。

Dialogue ❸ 電話預約 (3) 🔊 *Track 023*

如果你像此對話中的秘書一樣，也是「代替某個人」打電話，就可以用「I'm calling on behalf on...」這個說法。參考看看凱西是怎麼用的？

Jane: Hello, this is Mr. Wang's office. May I help you?

Kathy: Hello, this is Kathy from Flora International Cosmetics Company. I'm calling on behalf of Mr. Lee.

Jane: I see. What can I do for you?

Kathy: Well, Mr. Lee would like to make an appointment to see Mr. Wang sometime this week. Could you arrange a time for Mr. Lee?

Jane: What is it concerning?

Kathy: Mr. Lee wishes to discuss the terms of the new contract.

Jane: I see, do you have any particular time in mind?

Kathy: Would 10 o'clock tomorrow be all right?

Jane: I'm afraid Mr. Wang will be completely tied up the whole morning. What about 2 p.m. tomorrow afternoon?

Kathy: A moment, please. I'll check Mr. Lee's appointment book. Yes, 2 p.m. tomorrow afternoon will be convenient for Mr. Lee.

Jane: Where does Mr. Lee wish to see Mr. Wang, please?

Kathy: What about Mr. Lee's office ?

Jane: All right.

★全文中畫 色塊的地方，可以依自己的狀況套入不同的名字、公司名、職稱、學校名等等。

現在是不是回想起來了呢？

tied up 忙碌

「tied up」可以指「被綁起來」，像是被綁架的人通常都會被「tied up」。在這段對話中，則是指「忙得抽不開身」，彷彿被一大堆事務「綁住了」一樣。

中文翻譯3

珍：妳好，這裡是王先生的辦公室。您有什麼事？

凱西：妳好，我是芙羅拉國際化妝品公司的凱西。我是代表李先生打這通電話的。

珍：我知道了。有什麼我可以幫忙的嗎？

凱西：李先生想在這個星期跟王先生約個時間見面，請妳幫李先生安排一下，好嗎？

珍：是為了什麼事呢？

凱西：李先生想與王先生討論一下新合約的條款。

珍：我明白了，妳想約在什麼時間？

凱西：明天上午10點可以嗎？

珍：恐怕明天整個上午王先生都會很忙。明天下午兩點怎麼樣？

凱西：請等一等，讓我看一下李先生的行程表。嗯，李先生明天下午兩點有時間。

珍：李先生打算在哪裡與王先生見面呢？

凱西：在李先生的辦公室，可以嗎？

珍：好的。

Dialogue ❹ 電話預約 (4) 🔊Track 024

如果接起電話搞不清楚對方是誰，對方又沒明說，可以像凱西一樣問：「Who is calling, please?」（請問您是？），不要直接問「Who are you?」（你是誰？），很不禮貌喔！

Kathy: Hello!

Sam: Hello, is Kathy available?

Kathy: This is Kathy. Who is calling, please?

Sam: Hi, Kathy, this is Sam calling from Import Company. I'm calling to confirm your appointment for tomorrow morning at 9 a.m. with Mr. Wang.

Kathy: Oh, thank you for your friendly reminder. Actually, I have a scheduling conflict, and I can't make it that early.

Sam: What time would be better for you?

Kathy: It would have to be after lunch. Will Mr. Wang be available at around 2 p.m.?

Sam: Sorry, he has another appointment at that time. But he might be able to meet you at 4 p.m. Would that be better?

Kathy: That's all right. Where should we meet?

Sam: How about at Mr. Wang's office?

Kathy: No problem.

Sam: Great! Tomorrow afternoon at 4 p.m. at Mr. Wang's office.

Kathy: Wonderful.

★全文中畫 ⬤ 色塊的地方，可以依自己的狀況套入不同的名字、公司名、職稱、學校名等等。

現在是不是回想起來了呢？

scheduling conflict 行程的衝突

如果同時兩個約會強碰，總有其中一個得取消，這時就得不好意思地和對方說：「I have a scheduling conflict.」（我的行程有衝突）。

中文翻譯4 ● ● ● ● ● ● ● ● ● ● ● ● ● ● ●

凱西：你好！

薩姆：妳好，凱西在嗎？

凱西：我是凱西，請問您是……？

薩姆：妳好，凱西。我是進口公司的山姆。我打電話是想確認一下妳明天上午9點和王先生的會議。

凱西：噢，謝謝你提醒。實際上，因為安排上有衝突，我不能那麼早去了。

薩姆：什麼時間妳比較方便呢？

凱西：得等午餐過後了。王先生2點左右有時間嗎？

薩姆：對不起，2點他另有一個會議。可能4點比較合適，可以嗎？

凱西：沒問題。那在哪裡見面呢？

薩姆：在王先生辦公室可以嗎？
凱西：沒問題。
薩姆：好！那就明天下午4點在王先生的辦公室見！
凱西：好的。

Dialogue ❺ 櫃臺安排　◀ *Track 025*

對付客戶一定要彬彬有禮，但如果是連你老闆都不耐煩、很不想理的客戶呢？這時就得用一些「委婉」的方式讓對方感覺到自己不太受到歡迎。看看凱西又說老闆最近很忙、又說「I suppose」（我想）這種不確定的話，是隱晦地表達了「老闆其實也沒那麼想見你」的意思，就看對方能不能聽出弦外之音了。

Kathy: Good morning, Sir.

Thomas: Good morning. I am Thomas , the Sales Manager from Import Company . I've come to see Mr. Lee .

Kathy: Have you got an appointment, Mr. Thomas ?

Thomas: No, I haven't.

Kathy: Mr. Lee is pretty busy these days.

Thomas: I see. Could you be so kind as to arrange it for me? I have something urgent to talk about with him. It will not take much time.

Kathy: I'll see what I can do. Just one moment, please. I'll look at his schedule.

Thomas: Thank you.

Kathy: Tomorrow morning he's all booked up. Will tomorrow afternoon be okay?

Thomas: All right. What time exactly?

Kathy: I suppose you could come here at 3 p.m .

Thomas: Good. That's settled then.

★全文中畫 ● 色塊的地方，可以依自己的狀況套入不同的名字、公司名、職稱、學校名等等。

> **現在是不是回想起來了呢？**
>
> **urgent 緊急的**
>
> 在寄送非常緊急的e-mail給同事等人時，可以在標題的前面加上一個
> 「urgent」，讓大家一看就明白這封信現在就得趕快打開來看。

中文翻譯5 ● ● ● ● ● ●

- 凱　　西：早安，先生。
- 湯瑪斯：早安，我是湯瑪斯，進口公司的銷售經理。我來見李先生。
- 凱　　西：湯瑪斯先生，您預約了嗎？
- 湯瑪斯：沒有。
- 凱　　西：李先生這幾天非常忙。
- 湯瑪斯：我明白。您能幫我安排一下嗎？我有非常緊要的事情要與他談一談。不會佔
  用他太多時間。
- 凱　　西：讓我看看我能做些什麼。請稍等。我看看他的行程。
- 湯瑪斯：謝謝。
- 凱　　西：明天上午全部排滿了。明天下午怎麼樣？
- 湯瑪斯：可以啊。具體什麼時間？
- 凱　　西：我想您可以下午3點來。
- 湯瑪斯：好，就這麼決定了。

Dialogue ❻ 當面預約 🔊 *Track 026*

💬 此段對話中，麥克所說的「**What's up?**」不但代表了大家熟知的打招呼意
味，也同時表示「有什麼事嗎？」的意思。

● ●

Kathy: Hey there! I was hoping to run into you. Are you busy tomorrow morning ?

Michael: Let me see. Wednesday morning ...Yes, I am booked solid all morning. What's up?

Kathy: Mr. Lee was hoping to talk to you about the sales plan for next year.

Michael: I do have a few ideas to discuss with him. It will just take about half an hour . How about Friday afternoon ?

Kathy: Oh, that's not good for Mr. Lee . He is tied up all day Friday . He'll be available next Tuesday afternoon .

Michael: Okay. Is 2 p.m. convenient for him?

Kathy: Sure, that'll be fine.

★全文中畫　色塊的地方，可以依自己的狀況套入不同的名字、公司名、職稱、學校名等等。

現在是不是回想起來了呢？

booked solid 約滿了

「solid」是「堅硬的、固體的」的意思。如果整段時間都約得滿滿，那就表示那段時間的計畫很「固定」、不會動搖了，所以才用solid來形容。

中文翻譯6

凱西：嘿，我一直希望可以碰到你。你明天上午忙嗎？

麥克：我想想，星期三上午喔……嗯，我整個上午都排滿了。有什麼事情嗎？

凱西：李先生想和你談談明年的銷售計畫。

麥克：我確實有些想法想要和他討論一下。大約半個小時就可以了，星期五下午怎麼樣？

凱西：噢，那個時間李先生不太方便。星期五整天他都很忙。下星期二下午他有空。

麥克：好的，星期二下午兩點李先生方便嗎？

凱西：可以，沒有問題。

商務小常識

　　在歐美，有一邊吃午餐，一邊洽談商務的習慣，這種午餐形式被稱為商務午餐（business lunch）。商談是商務午餐的主要目的，不過時間最好集中在飯前酒或餐後甜點的時間，這樣比較得體。良好的餐桌禮儀，可以表現修養、風範，給你的客戶留下良好的印象哦！

SOS Unit 6 取消會面

和人家約好了卻臨時取消，是一件不好意思的事，所以可以參考文中凱西所用的「**embarrassing**」（丟臉的）、「**sorry**」（抱歉）等等單字，以表達歉意。

....

Kathy: Hello, may I speak to Charles, please?

Charles: This is he. May I know who is calling, please?

Kathy: Hi, Charles, this is Kathy.

Charles: Hi, Kathy, nice to hear from you again. How is everything?

Kathy: Fine, thanks. Now Charles, I find myself in a very embarrassing situation. It's about the appointment. I have something urgent to attend to, and I'm sorry but I won't be able to meet with you tomorrow afternoon. We will have to rebook the appointment.

Charles: Not a problem. We can arrange another meeting. When will it be convenient for you?

Kathy: Thanks for your understanding. How about next Tuesday afternoon?

Charles: Okay, that's fine.

★全文中畫 ⬤ 色塊的地方，可以依自己的狀況套入不同的名字、公司名、職稱、學校名等等。

現在是不是回想起來了呢？

hear from sb. 得到某人的消息

這個片語常用的情況是「很久沒有聽到某人的消息、很久沒跟某人聯絡」的時候。可以說：「I haven't heard from you in a long time.」（我很久沒你的消息了）。

中文翻譯1

凱　西：你好，我找查理斯。
查理斯：我就是。請問是哪位？
凱　西：你好，查理斯，我是凱西。
查理斯：你好，凱西。很高興又接到你的消息了。一切都好嗎？
凱　西：很好，謝謝。查理斯，我現在有個情況滿尷尬的。是關於見面的事情。因為我有一些緊急的事情要處理，非常抱歉，明天下午不能和你見面了。我們得重新約個見面時間了。
查理斯：沒關係，我們可以再安排見面時間。你有什麼時間合適？
凱　西：謝謝你的理解。下個星期二下午可以嗎？
查理斯：好的，可以。

Dialogue ❷ 取消會面 (2) ◀ *Track 028*

取消會面時，雖然對方嘴上不說，但總是會有一點不太開心，因為都為你特別排出了時間，可能會造成對方的不便。這時可如文中一樣，為了造成別人的不便（inconvenience）而致歉。

Kathy: Hello, Jim . This is Kathy calling.

Jim: Oh, hi, Kathy , what's up?

Kathy: I'm just calling about Mr. Lee's meeting with your boss today. Is it possible to reschedule their appointment in the afternoon? Mr. Lee has a bit of an emergency that he needs to take care of.

Jim: Let me see, it shouldn't be too much of a problem.

Kathy: I'm really sorry, I hope it doesn't cause too much inconvenience.

Jim: No problem. Kathy , when will Mr. Lee be free?

Kathy: How about (tomorrow afternoon at three)?

Jim: Let me check. OK, so the meeting is rescheduled for (tomorrow afternoon at three).

★全文中畫 ⬤ 色塊的地方，可以依自己的狀況套入不同的名字、公司名、職稱、學校名等等。

現在是不是回想起來了呢？

reschedule 重新安排時間

「re-」這個字首有「重新」的意思，例如redo就是「重做」，rewrite就是「重寫」。這裡在「約定時間」（schedule）前加上re-，就是「重新約一個時間」的意思。

中文翻譯2

凱西：你好，吉姆，我是凱西。

吉姆：哦，妳好，凱西，有什麼事？

凱西：是關於李先生和你們老闆今天開會的事。能不能把今天下午的會改個時間？李先生有一點急事得處理一下。

吉姆：我想想，應該沒什麼問題。

凱西：真抱歉，希望沒有造成太大麻煩。

吉姆：沒關係。凱西，李先生什麼時候有空？

凱西：明天下午3點怎麼樣？

吉姆：我看一下。好的，那麼會議就改到明天下午3點。

Dialogue ❸ 取消會面 (3) ◀ *Track 029*

電話聯絡時，有時電話會有點問題，聽得不是很清楚。看看文中兩人是如何化解的吧！

Kathy: Hello, this is (Kathy). May I speak to (Mr. Green)?

Mr. Green: Hi, (Kathy), this is (Mr. Green) speaking. I didn't recognize your voice.

Kathy: Oh, yes, the line isn't very good. I'll speak a bit louder. Is that any better?

Mr. Green: Yes, it's much better now.

Kathy: (Mr. Green), it looks as if I won't be able to keep the appointment we've made.

Mr. Green: Did something urgent come up?

Kathy: Yes, I'm so sorry. I have to meet an important client from (America).

Mr. Green: I see.

Kathy: He's come from (America) specifically to see us. I hope you understand.

Mr. Green: Well, that's OK.

★全文中畫 ⬤ 色塊的地方，可以依自己的狀況套入不同的名字、公司名、職稱、學校名等等。

中文翻譯3
* 凱　　西：你好，我是凱西，麻煩請找一下格林先生。
* 格林先生：妳好，凱西，我就是格林先生。我都沒有聽出妳的聲音。
* 凱　　西：哦，是的，電話線路不是很好。我講大聲一點，有好一點嗎？
* 格林先生：嗯，好多了。
* 凱　　西：格林先生，看來我不能赴約了。
* 格林先生：妳有什麼緊急的事情嗎？
* 凱　　西：沒錯，非常抱歉。我得見一位從美國來的重要客戶。
* 格林先生：我知道了。
* 凱　　西：他從美國專程來與我們見面，懇請您理解。
* 格林先生：哦，沒關係。

Dialogue ❹ 取消會面 (4)　◀ *Track 030*

以下對話中，我們可以發現凱西很不好約，一直沒時間，但對方沒有表現出不耐煩。既然對方人這麼好，難怪凱西要說：「**You are very considerate.**」（你真體貼）。

Kathy: Hello, (Kathy) speaking. What can I do for you?

Charles: Hello, this is (Charles). My secretary said you called concerning our meeting (next Tuesday)?

Kathy: Yes, (Charles), thank you for returning my call.

Charles: You're welcome.

Kathy: I want to let you know I will not be able to make our meeting next Tuesday. I will leave for a business trip that day.

Charles: All right, can we reschedule for Monday?

Kathy: I'm sorry. I'm afraid I am completely booked on Monday.

Charles: Would it be possible to postpone until you have some free time?

Kathy: You are very considerate. What about Thursday afternoon? Would that work for you?

Charles: That should be fine. Shall we say about 2 p.m.?

Kathy: Perfect! I look forward to seeing you at two o'clock next Thursday afternoon.

Charles: If you need to change the time, please feel free to call me.

Kathy: Thanks. I'll see you on Thursday.

★全文中畫 ⬭ 色塊的地方，可以依自己的狀況套入不同的名字、公司名、職稱、學校名等等。

現在是不是回想起來了呢？

return sb's call 回覆某人電話

人家打來找你，你沒接到，後來再打電話回去給他，這個動作就叫「return sb's call」。簡單地說就是「回電」。

中文翻譯**4**

凱　西：你好，我是凱西，有什麼需要幫忙的嗎？
查理斯：妳好，我是查理斯。秘書告訴我妳打電話過來想和我說有關下週二見面的事情？
凱　西：是的，查理斯。謝謝你回電話給我。
查理斯：不客氣。
凱　西：我是想告訴你下週二的見面我不能如期赴約了。那天我要出差。
查理斯：好吧，我們星期一碰面怎麼樣？
凱　西：很抱歉，整個星期一都已經安排滿了。
查理斯：那等妳有空，我們再找個時間見面吧？
凱　西：你真是太體貼了。星期四下午怎麼樣？你方便嗎？
查理斯：沒問題。定在下午兩點左右怎麼樣？
凱　西：好！很期待下週四下午兩點與你會面。
查理斯：如果妳需要更改時間的話，請別客氣直接打給我。
凱　西：謝謝。星期四見。

道歉

Dialogue ① 由於行為不當向同事道歉 🔊 *Track 031*

💬 同事來跟你道歉，該怎麼回應？像文中凱西所說「不用想太多，我知道妳是無意的」就是個讓對方很安心的模範回答。

....

Mary: Hello, Kathy !

Kathy: Hi, Mary , what a nice surprise! Come in.

Mary: Thank you.

Kathy: Excuse me for my appearance, I've just taken a shower.

Mary: That's all right. I shouldn't have barged in like this.

Kathy: That's okay. Have a seat and make yourself comfortable.

Mary: Thank you. Kathy ?

Kathy: Yes?

Mary: I want to apologize to you for my behavior in the office this afternoon .

Kathy: Think nothing of it. I know you meant no harm.

Mary: Thanks for your understanding. You're really forgiving.

★全文中畫 ⬭ 色塊的地方，可以依自己的狀況套入不同的名字、公司名、職稱、學校名等等。

> **現在是不是回想起來了呢？**
>
> **barge in 闖進**
> 無預警地跑進人家的房間，不顧對方在做什麼就急吼吼地打擾人家，這個狀況可以用「barge in」這個片語來說明。

中文翻譯1

瑪麗：妳好，凱西。

凱西：妳好，瑪麗。真是稀客啊！請進。

瑪麗：謝謝。

凱西：真是不好意思，我剛剛在洗澡，所以外表有點邋遢。

瑪麗：沒關係。我不應該這樣就貿然拜訪。

凱西：沒關係。請坐，請隨便。

瑪麗：謝謝。凱西？

凱西：怎麼了？

瑪麗：我是因為今天下午在辦公室的行為，來向妳道歉的。

凱西：別想太多了。我知道妳是無意的。

瑪麗：謝謝妳理解。妳真是寬容。

Dialogue ❷ 由於發言不當向同事道歉 🔊 *Track 032*

道歉時想展現誠意，可以參考文中湯姆的說法。他說想道歉的事想了一個晚上，這樣對方一定感受到他滿滿的誠意啦！

Kathy: Hello, Tom .

Tom: Hello, Kathy .

Kathy: You look upset. Is there something wrong?

Tom: Yes. I owe you an apology.

Kathy: What for?

Tom: I've come to apologize for what I said yesterday.

Kathy: Why?

Tom: I shouldn't have said what I did.

Kathy: It's really not necessary.

Tom: But it kept me up all night.

★全文中畫 ⬤ 色塊的地方，可以依自己的狀況套入不同的名字、公司名、職稱、學校名等等。

現在是不是回想起來了呢？

keep sb. up 讓某人睡不著

說「某事讓某人睡不著」時可以用這個片語，如：The firecrackers kept me up all night.（鞭炮讓我徹夜未眠）。

中文翻譯2

凱西：你好，湯姆。
湯姆：妳好，凱西。
凱西：你看起來很心煩，怎麼啦？
湯姆：嗯，我該向妳道歉。
凱西：為什麼？
湯姆：我是來為昨天所說的話向妳道歉。
凱西：為什麼呀？
湯姆：我不該說那樣的話。
凱西：真的沒有必要道歉。
湯姆：但是這困擾了我整整一個晚上了。

Dialogue ❸ 由於無法赴約向同事道歉　◀ *Track 033*

像對話中的琳達這樣，因為事情多到不行，必須一直推掉人家的邀約，是有點過意不去的事，所以我們可以看到琳達用了大量「I'm afraid」（恐怕）、「I'm awfully sorry」（我非常抱歉）等字詞表達歉意。

Kathy: What a wonderful time we've had! How about going to see a movie tomorrow evening , Linda ?

Linda: I'm sorry, I can't. I have to work on Saturday evenings .

Kathy: What a pity! What about Sunday ?

Linda: Sunday is bad for me too. I am going to a party.

Kathy: Monday then?

Linda: No, Monday is out for me I'm afraid. I've got to stay home and write a report. I really must.

Kathy: Oh, what a shame. Well, I can't make it Tuesday . How about Wednesday ?

Linda: I'm awfully sorry but I've got a dinner appointment that day.

Kathy: Do you have to go? Can't you get out of it?

Linda: I'm afraid not. It's my good friend's birthday.

Kathy: Well, it seems we'll have to wait till next Friday then.

Linda: We'll see. Look, Kathy , I have to go now. I have to be home before ten .

Kathy: Fine. Try and keep Friday evening open for me. We'll talk later.

★全文中畫 色塊的地方，可以依自己的狀況套入不同的名字、公司名、職稱、學校名等等。

現在是不是回想起來了呢？

what a shame 真可惜

「shame」是「羞恥」的意思，但說「what a shame」並不是要罵人很羞恥，純粹是說這件事很可惜。

中文翻譯3

凱西：剛才我們玩得真是太開心了！明天晚上去看電影怎麼樣啊，琳達？

琳達：對不起，禮拜六晚上我得工作。

凱西：真是可惜！禮拜天怎麼樣？

琳達：禮拜天也不行。我要參加派對。

凱西：那禮拜一呢？

琳達：不，禮拜一恐怕不行。我得待在家裡寫報告。真的是非寫不可。

凱西：哦，真可惜。嗯，禮拜二我不行，禮拜三的話呢？

琳達：真的是非常抱歉，那天我有飯局。

凱西：一定要去嗎？不能不去嗎？

琳達：恐怕不行。那天是我好朋友的生日。

凱西：那，看來我們只有等到下個禮拜五了。

琳達：再說吧。凱西，我必須走了，我必須在10點前回家。

凱西：好吧。儘量空出禮拜五晚上出來見面哦。下次再聊。

Dialogue 4 由於壞脾氣向同事道歉 ◀ *Track 034*

這段對話中兩個人都非常客氣，不斷在向對方道歉。可以從中學到很多不同道歉的方式喔！

Kathy: Jack , I'm terribly sorry for what I said yesterday. I really didn't mean it. I don't know why I lost my temper and said so many stupid things.

Jack: Kathy , you don't have to apologize. It was my mistake in the first place. In fact, I hope you'll forgive me for starting the whole thing.

Kathy: Well, even if it was your mistake, I shouldn't have behaved like that. I do apologize.

Jack: Please don't. I know you were upset about the mistake I made, but I'll be more focused from now on. I promise.

Kathy: No, I'm not upset. I'm just concerned and don't want you to lag behind.

Jack: I understand.

Kathy: So you won't take offense at what I said yesterday?

Jack: I told you I wouldn't. Actually, I never did.

Kathy: Thanks very much for saying so.

Jack: Not at all.

★全文中畫 ⬤ 色塊的地方，可以依自己的狀況套入不同的名字、公司名、職稱、學校名等等。

現在是不是回想起來了呢？

take offense at 對某事生氣

這段對話中的「take offense at what I said」，意思就是「因我所說的話而生氣」。

中文翻譯4

凱西：傑克，我為昨天說的話道歉。我真的不是那個意思。我不知道為什麼發脾氣，還說了那麼多傻話。

傑克：凱西，妳不必道歉，是我有錯在先。事實上，這件事是我引起的，希望妳能原諒我。

凱西：即使是你的錯，我也不該那樣做。我真的很抱歉。

傑克：請不要這樣。我知道因為我犯的錯讓妳很煩。但是從現在開始我會更用心，我發誓。

凱西：不，我沒有不高興，我只是關心你，不希望你進度落後。

傑克：我明白。

凱西：所以你不會為我昨天說的話生氣了？

傑克：我說過不會了。事實上，我本來就沒有生氣。

凱西：真感謝你能這麼說。

傑克：妳太客氣了。

💬 因為無心的小錯誤把客戶趕跑，是職場上最可怕的事之一。因此，我們可以看到凱西在對話的最後，再三向對方保證不會再發生這種事情了，是很好的作法。

Kathy: Hello. Flora Cosmetics.

Bob: Hello, Kathy, this is Bob. I'm sorry to have to say this, but we have got a problem.

Kathy: What's the matter? Hasn't the consignment arrived yet?

Bob: The consignment arrived yesterday. Right on schedule. The problem is that the products are not what we ordered. You sent the wrong ones.

Kathy: Bob, I'm terribly sorry for this. I will get this sorted out immediately.

Bob: Kathy, it is essential that we receive the replacement by the end of this month. Otherwise, I am afraid we have to find a new supplier.

Kathy: Bob, we are very sorry for this incident. We will send you the correct products as soon as possible. I must assure you that it won't happen again.

★全文中畫 ⬤ 色塊的地方，可以依自己的狀況套入不同的名字、公司名、職稱、學校名等等。

現在是不是回想起來了呢？

sort out 處理好
這個片語是針對「處理好一團亂的事」用的，如果只是隨便一點小事要處理，連思考都不太需要，就比較不會用「sort out」來說。

中文翻譯5

凱西：你好，芙羅拉化妝品公司。

鮑勃：妳好，凱西，我是鮑勃。很遺憾告訴妳，我們遇到了個問題。

凱西：怎麼了？貨沒有到嗎？

鮑勃：貨昨天按時到了。問題是這些產品不是我們想要的，妳們送錯了。

凱西：鮑勃，真的很抱歉，我會馬上處理這件事情。

鮑勃：凱西，我們必須在月底前收到換貨。不然，我們恐怕得換家供應商了。

凱西：鮑勃，對於這件事情，我們真的很抱歉。我們會儘快把你們訂的貨送給你們的。我向你保證不會再發生這種事情了。

商務小常識

　　東西方文化在許多方面上都有差異，包括道歉這件事也是。在發生問題或爭議時，西方人會認為只有真正做錯事情了，才需要道歉；但東方人會常常因為注重禮儀而道歉（即使錯根本不在自己），而這有時都會造成錯誤會歸屬到道歉的東方人這邊。這樣的文化差異，在與西方國家做生意時，是非常需要注意的。

致謝

Dialogue ① 感謝招待 🔊 *Track 036*

💬 招待客戶，客戶即將離開時，可以禮貌地表示挽留，如下面對話中，史密斯先生就說：「我可以說服妳多待幾天嗎？」

• •

Kathy: Hello, Mr. Smith , how are you?

Mr. Smith: Very well, thank you. And how are you?

Kathy: Fine, thanks. I've come to say goodbye as I'm returning home tomorrow .

Mr. Smith: No, not so soon! It seems as if you just got here.

Kathy: I feel that way, too. But all good things must come to an end, as they say.

Mr. Smith: Couldn't I persuade you to stay a couple of days longer?

Kathy: Much as I'd like to, I can't. You know what I mean when I say duty calls.

Mr. Smith: In that case, I don't want to keep you. It certainly has been a pleasure to see you again.

Kathy: I had a great visit and I really appreciate you spending so much time showing me around.

Mr. Smith: Oh, it was fun for me, too. It gave me a chance to get away from my routine and do something a little different.

Kathy: You're too kind. Thank you again for everything.

★全文中畫 ⬭ 色塊的地方，可以依自己的狀況套入不同的名字、公司名、職稱、學校名等等。

現在是不是回想起來了呢？

duty calls 有公務在身

這兩個字直接翻譯，就是「我的職責在叫我囉」的意思。既然職責在叫你，那就當然得趕快趕回去處理它啦！有個有名的射擊遊戲叫「Call of Duty」，就是因為在這個遊戲中，射敵人就是角色的職責嘛。

中文翻譯1

凱　　西：您好，史密斯先生，您好嗎？

史密斯先生：很好，謝謝。妳呢？

凱　　西：我也很好，謝謝。我是來告別的，因為明天我就要回國了。

史密斯先生：不會吧！不要這麼早吧！感覺妳好像才剛來沒多久耶！

凱　　西：我也有同感，不過，如人們所說，天下沒有不散的宴席。

史密斯先生：我能留妳再多住幾天嗎？

凱　　西：我也希望如此，可是不行，您知道我有公務在身。

史密斯先生：那樣的話，我就不挽留妳了。能再次見到妳真是讓人高興。

凱　　西：我過得非常愉快，謝謝您花了這麼多時間陪我遊覽。

史密斯先生：哦，這對我來說也很有趣，我可以有機會擺脫日常工作，做些不同的事情。

凱　　西：您真是太好了。再次感謝您做的一切。

Dialogue ❷ 感謝邀請　◀℣*Track 037*

和客戶共餐完畢時，總想營造出一種「快樂的時光總是過得特別快」的氣氛，所以我們可以看到文中的查理斯假裝自己開心到搞不清楚時間（**Oh, dear, is that the time?**），就是個好用的說法。

Kathy: Well, that was a marvelous meal. Thank you very much.

Charles: I'm glad you liked it. Will you have some coffee ?

Kathy: Well, no, thanks. In fact, I have to be thinking of going.

Charles: Oh, not yet, surely?

Kathy: I'm afraid I'll have to. It's 10: 00 p.m .

Charles: Oh, dear, is that the time?

Kathy: Thanks again. It was really very kind of you to invite me.

Charles: It was my pleasure. You must come again.

Kathy: I'd love to.

Charles: Bye.

★全文中畫 ⬤ 色塊的地方，可以依自己的狀況套入不同的名字、公司名、職稱、學校名等等。

中文翻譯2

凱　　西：嗯，這頓飯很棒呢。非常謝謝你。
查理斯：很高興妳喜歡。要不要來一點咖啡？
凱　　西：哦，不了，謝謝。事實上，我差不多該走了。
查理斯：哦，一定要這麼早嗎？
凱　　西：我恐怕真的該走了。已經10點了。
查理斯：哦，天啊，都這麼晚啦？
凱　　西：再次謝謝你。你能邀請我真是太好了。
查理斯：別客氣。妳一定要再來。
凱　　西：我很樂意。
查理斯：再見。

Dialogue ❸ 感謝款待 ◀ *Track 038*

受到款待，對方不但是為你付出金錢，也付出了寶貴的時間。所以文中的鮑勃就特別感謝對方「為他付出那麼多時間」，是個很好用的說法。

Bob: Hello, may I speak to Kathy ?

Kathy: Yes, speaking.

Bob: How are you, Kathy ? This is Bob . I'm calling to thank you for the wonderful dinner we had yesterday. I enjoyed it very much.

Kathy: You're welcome. I'd like you to join me for dinner again sometime.

Bob: Thank you, Kathy . But I'm returning to America today.

Kathy: Today?

Bob: Yes, I appreciate all your help and in particular all the time you have spent on my account during my stay here.

Kathy: Don't mention it. I was only too pleased to help you.

Bob: If there is anything that I can do for you in the future, please let me know.

Kathy: I'll do that. Thank you. Have a good trip home.

★全文中畫 ⬤ 色塊的地方，可以依自己的狀況套入不同的名字、公司名、職稱、學校名等等。

現在是不是回想起來了呢？

Don't mention it 不要那樣說

受到別人感謝時，可以用這一句表示「不客氣、不用提這個沒關係」。

中文翻譯3

鮑勃：你好，請找一下凱西。

凱西：我就是，請講。

鮑勃：妳好嗎，凱西？我是鮑勃。我打電話是想謝謝妳昨天招待的晚餐。我非常喜歡。

凱西：別客氣。我想要改天再跟你一起用晚餐呢。

鮑勃：謝謝，凱西。但是我今天就要回美國了。

凱西：今天？

鮑勃：是的，謝謝妳的幫忙，特別感謝妳在我逗留的這段期間，為我付出那麼多時間。

凱西：不要那樣說。我非常樂意幫助你。

鮑勃：今後如果有什麼需要我幫忙的，請讓我知道。

凱西：我會的，謝謝。一路平安。

Dialogue ❹ 感謝幫助 ◀ *Track 039*

💬 感謝人家的幫助最好的方法，就是乾脆請他吃一頓吧！看看本文中凱西如何若無其事地拋出邀約！

Kathy: (John), I wish to express my gratitude and appreciation for helping me with this job.

John: Please don't mention it. I'm very delighted to be of help.

Kathy: Without you, I could not have finished it on time.

John: It's very kind of you to say so.

Kathy: Well, you really did help me a lot.

John: I'm glad to hear that. If you need any more help, please do let me know.

Kathy: I will. Thank you very much. By the way, do you have time tonight ?

John: I'm sorry, I have a dinner appointment tonight . Why? Did you have something planned?

Kathy: Oh, I just wanted to invite you to dinner.

John: Tomorrow night would be OK.

★全文中畫 ⬤⬤⬤ 色塊的地方，可以依自己的狀況套入不同的名字、公司名、職稱、學校名等等。

中文翻譯4

凱西：約翰，感謝你在這個工作上幫了我很大的忙。

約翰：別那樣說。我很樂意幫忙。

凱西：如果不是你，我不可能準時完成這個工作。

約翰：妳能這樣說真是太好了。

凱西：但事實上，你真的幫了我很多忙啊。

約翰：很高興聽到妳這樣說。如果妳還需要幫忙，請一定告訴我。

凱西：我會的。非常謝謝你。對了，今晚有空嗎？

約翰：不好意思，我今晚有飯局。問這個幹嘛？妳有什麼計劃嗎？

凱西：噢，我只是想邀請你一起吃晚餐。

約翰：明天晚上可以。

商務小常識

　　對於合作頻繁的公司或客戶，很容易就忘記感謝對方，尤其上司對於下屬更是如此，我問過的許多外國朋友就都說「老闆從來沒對他們說過謝謝，如果說了他們會嚇一跳」。但無論是以謝卡的形式，e-mail的形式或甚至是小便條的形式，都要盡量提醒自己要跟工作上的夥伴們道謝，雖然只是一個小地方，在對方的心裡會有非常大的加分作用。

建議

Dialogue ❶ 工作進度建議 🔊 *Track 040*

看到同事樣子不太妙，可以如以下對話中適時問一句：「**What's the matter?**」（怎麼了？）就算無法提供他實際的援助，至少也能表達一下關心。

Kathy: Hey, Mary , what's the matter? You look so upset.

Mary: Kathy , I should have finished the plan this morning , but it's 4 o'clock in the afternoon and I'm still working on it.

Kathy: Oh, that's not good news. When will the manager need it?

Mary: The manager needs it tomorrow .

Kathy: You'd better hurry up, forget your other projects and focus on it.

Mary: You're right.

Kathy: Do you need any help?

Mary: Sure. It's very kind of you to ask. Thanks very much.

Kathy: You're welcome. You've helped me a lot in the past.

Mary: Let's get started.

Kathy: OK.

★全文中畫 色塊的地方，可以依自己的狀況套入不同的名字、公司名、職稱、學校名等等。

中文翻譯1

凱西：嗨，瑪麗，怎麼了？妳看起來很不高興。

瑪麗：凱西，今天上午我就應該做完這份計畫的，可是現在已經下午4點了，我還沒做完。

凱西：哦，那可不是什麼好消息。經理什麼時候要？

瑪麗：經理明天要用。

凱西：妳最好一快點，先把別的事情放在一邊，專心做這個。

瑪麗：妳說得對。

凱西：需要什麼幫忙嗎？

瑪麗：當然。妳能這樣說真是太好了。非常感謝妳。

凱西：不用客氣。妳以前也幫過我很多忙。

瑪麗：那我們開始吧。

凱西：好啊。

Dialogue ❷ 休假建議 🔊 *Track 041*

同事頭痛得要命，你該對他說什麼？除了「多保重」外，像凱西在此對話中的「**That's no fun**」（這可不好玩）也是個不錯的說法，既帶點輕鬆，又表示同情與理解。

Kathy: Hi, Mary, how is it going?

Mary: Oh, hi, Kathy, not too well, I'm afraid.

Kathy: Why? What's the matter?

Mary: Nothing is really the matter except that I've got a splitting headache.

Kathy: That's no fun. Why don't you take a break?

Mary: I wish I could, but I have to finish this report today.

Kathy: Well, try some aspirins.

Mary: I did already, but they didn't help. I think all of the pressure from this job caused it.

Kathy: Well, you really should take a few days off and take your mind off your work.

Mary: Yes, I do need a vacation. Thanks so much. I'll talk to the manager about it later.

★全文中畫 色塊的地方，可以依自己的狀況套入不同的名字、公司名、職稱、學校名等等。

中文翻譯2

凱西：哈囉，瑪麗，最近如何？

瑪麗：哦，嗨，凱西，我恐怕不是很好。

凱西：怎麼了？有什麼事嗎？

瑪麗：沒什麼，只是我頭痛得很厲害。

凱西：這可不好玩。為什麼不休息一下呢？

瑪麗：我想啊，但是我今天必須完成這份報告。

凱西：那試試看阿司匹靈吧。

瑪麗：已經吃過了，但是沒幫助。我想是因為工作上的壓力太大了吧。

凱西：嗯，妳真的得把工作先放在一旁，休息幾天。

瑪麗：是啊，我確實需要休假。謝謝妳。我等一下會和經理談談看。

Dialogue ❸ 穿著建議　◀ *Track 042*

和比較熟（而且還很愛煩你）的朋友聊天，有時不需要太顧到禮貌。你反而可以參考下面對話中的班，用簡單隨便的短句，清楚表達「你很煩欸，不要來問我啦」的心情。

Kathy: (Ben), what do you think I should wear for tomorrow's trip to the carnival?

Ben: I think you can wear anything these days.

Kathy: For the top, shall I wear a silk blouse or a polo shirt?

Ben: I don't know.

Kathy: And shall I wear a skirt or jeans?

Ben: Anything comfortable. Really, it doesn't matter.

Kathy: Don't you think I will look too casual in a polo shirt and jeans?

Ben: Listen, you are going to a carnival, not a banquet. A polo shirt and jeans will be perfect. Save your silk blouse and skirt for more formal occasions.

Kathy: I guess you are right, but let me call (Mary) just in case and see what she is going to wear.

Ben: Whatever.

★全文中畫 色塊的地方，可以依自己的狀況套入不同的名字、公司名、職稱、學校名等等。

top 上半身

「top」這個單字是「上面」的意思，用在衣著方面，就代表「上半身穿的東西」，如襯衫、T恤等。像連身洋裝這種不只上半身，下半身也涵蓋了的服裝，就不能稱做top。

中文翻譯3

凱西：班，明天的嘉年華會，你覺得我該穿什麼？
班：我覺得這個年代穿什麼都可以。
凱西：我上半身是該穿絲質襯衫還是Polo衫呢？
班：我不知道。
凱西：那我該穿裙子還是牛仔褲呢？
班：哪件舒服就穿哪件吧。真的，穿什麼不重要。
凱西：如果穿Polo衫和牛仔褲，看起來會不會太隨便？
班：聽著，妳是去參加嘉年華會，不是宴會。Polo衫和牛仔褲就很夠了。把絲質襯衫和裙子留到更正式的場合穿吧。
凱西：我想你是對的，不過為防萬一我還是問問瑪麗，看她要穿什麼。
班：隨便妳啦。

Dialogue ❹ 出差建議 ◀ Track 043

和人家討論事情，對方講了一句有點扯的話時，你可以怎麼反應？建議可以像對話中最後一句的瑪麗一樣，重複一次對方說的話：「Three days?」三天遊完北京，哪可能啊！

Kathy: Have you ever been to Beijing before?

Mary: Of course, a couple of times.

Kathy: Great. Tell me something about the city. I don't know anything about it. I'm going to have a business trip there next week.

Mary: Well, you're lucky. The weather is perfect this time of year.

Kathy: What are some of the scenic places I should visit?

Mary: There are so many places to go, but here are a few locations you just can't miss: Tian'anmen Square, the Forbidden City, the Summer Palace, and the Heavenly Temple.

Kathy: Anything interesting on the outskirts of town?

Mary: Of course, there is the world-famous Great Wall and the Ming Tombs.

Kathy: Are three days enough to see most of the city?

Mary: Three days? You get a brief glimpse of Beijing. But to really appreciate the city you should stay for at least a week.

★全文中畫 色塊的地方，可以依自己的狀況套入不同的名字、公司名、職稱、學校名等等。

現在是不是回想起來了呢？

glimpse 一瞥

匆匆經過一個地方，迅速看一眼，這個動作叫做glimpse。如果看久一點、看得認真一點，就要叫look at 了，不能用glimpse。

中文翻譯4

凱西：妳去過北京嗎？

瑪麗：當然囉，去過好幾次了。

凱西：太好了。能跟我介紹一下這座城市嗎？我對北京一點都不瞭解。下個星期我要去那裡出差。

瑪麗：那妳滿幸運的。這個季節的天氣很好。

凱西：我該去哪些景點呢？

瑪麗：有許多可以去的地方。但有幾個地方是必去的：天安門、故宮、頤和園和天壇。

凱西：那郊區有什麼好玩的嗎？

瑪麗：當然有了，有世界聞名的萬里長城和明十三陵。

凱西：三天可以玩遍大部分的北京嗎？

瑪麗：三天？那妳只能走馬看花了。但要真正遊覽這座城市，妳至少需要一個禮拜的時間。

要給新來的同事一點忠告時，因為你比較資深，可以稍微用一點命令的口氣，如以下對話中的凱倫，就對新同事凱西說：「**Listen**」（聽好），這是不適合對上級使用的。

● ●

Kathy: Karen , I am new here. Could you give me some advice? It seems that Mr. Lee is very serious.

Karen: Why do you think so?

Kathy: He doesn't smile or talk much.

Karen: Listen, Kathy . You shouldn't worry about Mr. Lee . He is a very good man to work for, and he is willing to take suggestions from both men and women.

Kathy: I am very happy to hear that, Karen . It's good to know I'm working in such a fair and open environment.

Karen: I agree with you on that, Kathy . I've worked for Mr. Lee for nine years now, and I would never think of changing jobs.

Kathy: Good. Thank you for telling me this.

Karen: Any time. if you have a good idea, don't be afraid to speak up. This is a company that appreciates personal initiative.

★全文中畫 ⬤ 色塊的地方，可以依自己的狀況套入不同的名字、公司名、職稱、學校名等等。

現在是不是回想起來了呢？

Any time 隨時都行

在這段對話中，Karen說「Any time」，其實就是「你隨時來問我、找我幫忙都行，這是應該的」。當有人感謝你幫助的時候，你就可以說這短短兩個字來表示不用客氣，你隨時都願意幫忙。

中文翻譯5

凱西：凱倫，我是新人，可以給我一些建議嗎？李先生看起來非常嚴肅。

凱倫：妳為什麼會這麼樣覺得？

凱西：他不常笑，又很沉默寡言。

凱倫：聽好，凱西。妳不必擔心李先生。他是很好的老闆，而且他都會很樂意接受員工的建議，不論男女。

凱西：我很高興聽到這些，凱倫。很高興知道我是在這樣公平開放的環境中工作。

凱倫：關於這一點，我同意妳的想法，凱西。我已經為李先生工作9年了，而我絕不會考慮換工作。

凱西：很好，謝謝妳告訴我這個。

凱倫：隨時要我幫忙都行。如果妳有什麼好的意見，不要害怕說出來。我們公司很重視個人的積極主動性。

Dialogue ❻ 工作指導 (2) 　🔊 *Track 045*

如果只憑自己的判斷給人意見，可以不用說得很死：「You should...」（你應該……），而可以像這段對話中的瑪麗一樣，以「I think you should...」（我覺得你應該……）開始。

Kathy: Mr. Lee will fly to Beijing tomorrow for an emergency meeting with a client, but he hasn't purchased an airplane ticket yet. Should I call a travel agency?

Mary: I think you should call the airline directly.

Kathy: That's a good idea, but what if all the tickets are sold out?

Mary: He can always go to the airport on standby. Most airlines keep a small number of tickets until the last minute.

Kathy: By the way, do you have the airport's phone number?

Mary: Sorry, you can ask Jack, he is responsible for contacting the airport.

Kathy: But where is Jack now? I haven't seen him all day.

Mary: Oh, I remember. He is on a business trip to Beijing.

Kathy: Oh, do you have his mobile phone number?

Mary: Yes, it's 13800000000.

Kathy: Thank you very much.

★全文中畫 ⬤ 色塊的地方，可以依自己的狀況套入不同的名字、公司名、職稱、學校名等等。

on standby 候補

「on standby」的應用範圍很廣，除了「候補」外，也可以當作「備用」、「備取」、「隨時準備幫忙」等等的意思。

中文翻譯6

凱西：李先生明天因為有急事，要飛去北京跟一個客戶開會，可是機票還沒訂，我要不要打電話給旅行社？

瑪麗：我覺得妳應該直接打給航空公司。

凱西：好主意。但是萬一機票都賣完了呢？

瑪麗：他還是可以到機場等候補機票。大多數的航班在起飛前，還會保留幾張機票。

凱西：對了，妳有機場的電話號碼嗎？

瑪麗：抱歉，妳可以問問看傑克，他負責與機場聯絡。

凱西：但傑克現在在哪？我一整天都沒看到他。

瑪麗：噢，我想起來了。他出差去北京了。

凱西：噢，那妳有他的手機號碼嗎？

瑪麗：有，是13800000000。

凱西：非常感謝妳。

Dialogue ❼ 戒菸建議 🔊 *Track 046*

我們可以看到對話中的凱西很直接地建議老闆李先生戒菸，不過需要注意的是，李先生人很好，所以凱西才敢這樣。要是你老闆很嚴肅又兇，那就別像凱西這樣了。

Kathy: What's the matter with you, Mr. Lee ? You look a bit pale.

Mr. Lee: As a matter of fact, I feel terrible. I couldn't sleep a wink last night.

Kathy: You had insomnia, did you? I bet you have high blood pressure.

Mr. Lee: Yes, I do.

Kathy: Well, it might do you good to quit smoking or at least cut back. Watch your diet and…

Mr. Lee: A lot of people have told me the same thing, but somehow I just can't force myself to do it.

Kathy: Well, you'll only make things worse if you continue to smoke.

Mr. Lee: I know, I know. But quitting smoking is not as easy as you think.

Kathy: I think all these are excuses. Where there is a will, there is a way.

Mr. Lee: Maybe you're right. OK, I'll try.

★全文中畫 ⬤ 色塊的地方，可以依自己的狀況套入不同的名字、公司名、職稱、學校名等等。

現在是不是回想起來了呢？

as a matter of fact 事實上

當人家跟你講一些不太符合事實的話時，你就可以用這句開頭，來糾正他。

例如：

A: You never clean your room. 你從來都不清理房間的。

B: As a matter of fact, I cleaned it yesterday. 事實上，我昨天清過呢。

中文翻譯7

凱　西：您怎麼了，李先生？您的臉色有一點蒼白。

李先生：實際上，我現在很難受。昨晚一點也沒睡。

凱　西：您失眠了，是不是？我想您一定有高血壓吧。

李先生：是的。

凱　西：嗯，戒菸會對您幫助很大，至少少抽一點都好，還要注意飲食和……

李先生：很多人都跟我這麼說，可我就是做不到。

凱　西：嗯，一直這樣抽菸下去，只會讓身體越來越差。

李先生：我知道，我知道。可是戒菸不像妳想得那麼簡單。

凱　西：我覺得這些都是藉口。有志者事竟成嘛。

李先生：也許妳是對的。好吧，我試試看。

商務小常識

　　TPO是英文time, place, object三個詞首字母的縮寫。著裝的TPO原則是世界通行的著裝打扮的最基本原則。它要求人們的服飾應以和諧為美。著裝要符合時令、符合場合、符合著裝人的身份，並且應該根據交往目的、交往物件來選擇合適的服飾。

SOS Unit 10 達成共識

Dialogue ❶ 達成協議 (1) 🔊 *Track 047*

💬 和比較熟的對象協商時，可以像下面對話中凱西那樣，帶點耍賴的口氣，說：「Can't you give me a discount?」（不能打個折嗎？）尤其是這個「can't」，特別有親切請求的意味。

• •

Kathy: Can't you give me a discount?

Mr. Smith: Since we've cooperated for a long time, I can give you a break on the price. How about a total discount of 6% ?

Kathy: What did your boss say?

Mr. Smith: I told my boss, and he confirmed that if you take care of the shipping costs, we'll pay the insurance.

Kathy: What! I would have thought I'd get a better discount than 6% !

Mr. Smith: Could you make payment within a 30-day grace period? That shouldn't be a problem, right?

Kathy: No. As far as I know, we talked about the possibility of a 90-day grace period.

Mr. Smith: So, if all this is agreeable to you, I'll put it all down on paper.

Kathy: Okay.

Mr. Smith: If you can get a signed version of the contract we've agreed upon back to me by tomorrow morning, we can go ahead and make arrangements for the shipping of the product on Tuesday .

Kathy: Great!

★全文中畫 ⬤ 色塊的地方，可以依自己的狀況套入不同的名字、公司名、職稱、學校名等等。

現在是不是回想起來了呢？

grace period 寬限期

一旦兩方說定了一個日期，如果超過了那個日期才達成約定，理論上就應該要付違約金。而「寬限期」就是「超過了約定的日期，但還不用付違約金」的這一段時間。

中文翻譯1

凱　　　西：不能打個折嗎？

史密斯先生：因為我們已經合作很長一段時間了，我可以在價錢方面破例給妳，一共打9.4折如何？

凱　　　西：你們老闆的意見呢？

史密斯先生：我跟他說過了，他說如果你們負責運輸費用，我們就承擔保險費用。

凱　　　西：什麼！我原本以為折扣可以比9.4折再低一點！

史密斯先生：在30天的寬期限內付款，應該沒有問題吧？

凱　　　西：不對，就我所知，我們討論出的是90天的寬限期。

史密斯先生：那麼，如果這些條件你們同意，我就寫在合約上了。

凱　　　西：好。

史密斯先生：如果明天上午之前你能把我們談好的合約簽好字拿過來，我們就能在星期二安排裝貨事項。

凱　　　西：好的！

Dialogue ❷ 達成協議 (2) ◀ *Track 048*

仔細看看這段對話結尾處，史密斯先生在達成協議後，還提到合作關係的進步，這是一種禮貌的話術，表示「我在意的不只是錢，更在意我們之間的合作關係」。

Mr. Smith: We discussed your offer. We think your price is too high. We sent you a counter-offer two days ago.

Kathy: Yes, your counter-offer at 2,500 RMB per set was discussed, but we think this price really leaves us with no profit margin.

Mr. Smith: Then how much do you think will be acceptable for you?

Kathy: Do you think 2,800 is acceptable? At this price, we still give up most of our profit.

Mr. Smith: How about we meet each other half way at 2,700 ? We think this price is quite reasonable and is nearly the same as that of the world market.

Kathy: OK. We can do 2,700 .

Mr. Smith: Great. Could you manage to send the goods by September 15th ?

Kathy: Yes, we can.

Mr. Smith: All right. I'm glad we've reached an agreement. I believe the success of this transaction is an important step forward in our relationship.

Kathy: So do I.

★全文中畫 ⬤ 色塊的地方，可以依自己的狀況套入不同的名字、公司名、職稱、學校名等等。

現在是不是回想起來了呢？

meet each other halfway 各讓一步

這段直翻其實就是「在中間見面」的意思，也就是兩邊找到一個中間點，各妥協一點，不要只有一方犧牲。

中文翻譯2

史密斯先生： 我們討論過你們的報價，我們覺得價格過高，兩天前寄回去給貴方了。

凱　西： 是的，我們收到了，你們所報的每套2,500元的還價我們討論過了，我們認為這個價錢我們沒有利潤可賺。

史密斯先生： 那麼你們能接受的價錢是多少呢？

凱　西： 你覺得2,800元可以接受嗎？給你們這個價錢，我們還是放棄了一大半的利潤。

史密斯先生： 那我們各讓一步，2,700元成交怎麼樣？我們覺得這個價錢很合理，而且接近國際市場價格。

凱　西： 好吧，2,700可以成交。

史密斯先生： 太好了。你們9月15號之前能出貨嗎？

凱　西： 可以。

史密斯先生： 好的。非常高興我們達成了共識。我相信這筆交易的成功會使我們的關係向前邁進一大步。

凱　西： 我也是這麼想的。

Dialogue ❸ 在職業培訓方面達成共識　🔊 *Track 049*

對話中這兩名同事在討論主管的缺點，且非常實際地提出能夠改善的方法，這是相當不錯的，但若你打算也如法炮製，請確認你可以信任這個同事，知道他不會跑去在老闆面前捅你一刀。

• •

Kathy: I'm concerned about the ability of our supervisors to deal with the staff.

Mary: Yes, I agree that some of the supervisors need to improve their interpersonal skills.

Kathy: And they don't communicate very effectively at staff meetings.

Mary: That's true. Where do you think these problems come from?

Kathy: I think some of the problems come from the fact that they have risen through the ranks without ever having had any formal management training.

Mary: Yes, I think that's definitely true. They're good at their jobs but not so good at handling people.

Kathy: The other thing I've noticed is that at the staff meetings they are unwilling to share their ideas.

Mary: Do you think that has anything to do with a fear of speaking in public?

Kathy: To some extent, it probably does. A lot of people just clam up when they have to talk in front of others.

Mary: I think we need to find a good supervisor's training course.

Kathy: That would be of great help, I think.

現在是不是回想起來了呢？

clam up 一言不發

「clam」是蛤蜊的意思，像蛤蜊一樣閉得緊緊的，也就是「什麼都不說」的意思。

凱西：我們這裡的主管和下屬交流的能力讓我有點擔心耶。

瑪麗：嗯，我同意，有些主管需要提高人際交往能力。

凱西：而且他們在員工會議上還不能有效地溝通。

瑪麗：是這樣沒錯。在妳看來，問題出在哪？

凱西：我覺得這與他們是從基層逐漸升職，從未接受過正式管理培訓有關係。

瑪麗：嗯，說得對。他們擅長工作，但在與人交往方面比較遜色。

凱西：我還發現，在員工會議上，他們不太願表達自己的觀點。

瑪麗：妳覺得是因為他們害怕在大家面前說話嗎？

凱西：從某種程度上說可能吧。很多人需要在大家面前說話時卻一言不發。

瑪麗：我覺得我們需要找到一套好的主管培訓課程。

凱西：我覺得那一定大有幫助。

Dialogue ❹ 在招聘員工方面達成共識 🔊 *Track 050*

💬 身為像凱西這樣的新進員工，提出意見時，可以謙虛一點，說：「**Do you think it might be worth...**」（你覺得……值得嗎？）來詢問別人自己的意見是否聽起來值得採納。

Kathy: Good morning, Betty. How are you doing today?

Betty: A little tired. I am focusing on the report since it will be used tomorrow.

Kathy: Yeah, I have been up at the office until 9 p.m. these days.

Betty: I think we're all a little overworked these days.

Kathy: I definitely agree.

Betty: I think it's necessary for the company to hire someone. Four of us in the office just aren't enough.

Kathy: Yeah, I agree. What we really need is another full-time employee. I'm swamped these days. I am sure it's enough work for two people.

Betty: Same goes for me. I'm completely exhausted.

Kathy: Do you think it might be worth scheduling a meeting for everyone in the office to discuss it?

Betty: Good idea! I'll contact the others.

★全文中畫 色塊的地方，可以依自己的狀況套入不同的名字、公司名、職稱、學校名等等。

現在是不是回想起來了呢？

swamped 忙得不可開交的

swamp是沼澤、泥沼的意思。swamped表達的是「事情多得好像被泥沼淹沒一樣」的意思，非常有畫面感。

中文翻譯4

凱西：早安，貝蒂。妳今天還好嗎？

貝蒂：有點累。我正在努力寫明天要用的報告。

凱西：嗯，我這幾天也都是在辦公室待到晚上9點。

貝蒂：我覺得我們這幾天都有點過度操勞了。

凱西：非常同意。

貝蒂：我覺得公司應該再招聘一名員工。辦公室裡只有我們4個人根本不夠。

凱西：嗯，我同意。我們真正需要的是一名全職員工。這幾天我忙得昏天暗地的，這簡直就是兩個人的工作。

貝蒂：我也是。我已經筋疲力盡了。

凱西：妳認為有必要召集辦公室的人討論一下嗎？

貝蒂：好主意！我現在就去聯絡其他人。

Dialogue ❺ 在開拓市場方面達成共識　◀ *Track 051*

要問別人覺得自己的意見如何時，可以像對話中的王先生一樣，問：「Is that all right?」（這樣可以嗎？）快看看王先生怎麼用的吧！

Mr. Wang: (Kathy), things are running fairly smoothly at the moment. I thought it might be a good time for me to start expanding sales channels.

Kathy: Sounds like a good idea.

Mr. Wang: If you agree, I'll start in (Dalian) and move on to (Beijing).

Kathy: (Dalian) and (Beijing)? Great!

Mr. Wang: I'll go to these places soon. I know several sales chains which could be interested in our new product. Is that all right?

Kathy: Yes, why not? I hope you'll have a fruitful trip.

Mr. Wang: I've got quite a lot of phoning to do before I leave. I want to make sure that the people I need to see will be there.

Kathy: How long are you thinking of staying?

Mr. Wang: About one week .

Kathy: Well, good luck.

★全文中畫 色塊的地方，可以依自己的狀況套入不同的名字、公司名、職稱、學校名等等。

中文翻譯5

王先生：凱西，現在事情都正常運作。我想這正是開拓銷售管道的大好時機。
凱　西：聽起來想法不錯。
王先生：如果妳同意的話，我想從大連開始，然後轉入北京。
凱　西：大連和北京？太好了！
王先生：我之後就會去這兩個地方。我知道幾家連鎖店，他們可能對我們的新產品有興趣，怎麼樣？
凱　西：嗯，為什麼不呢？希望你收穫良多。
王先生：我走之前有很多電話要打，我必須先確保我要見的人都在。
凱　西：你打算在那裡待幾天？
王先生：大概一個禮拜吧。
凱　西：好的，祝你好運。

Dialogue 6 全票通過 🔊 *Track 052*

當人家主動提出要幫你忙，但你真的不需要時，也可以像對話中的海倫一樣，說：「你願意幫我忙真是太好了」。看看她是怎麼說的？

Kathy: How's the plan coming along, Helen ?

Helen: It was discussed at the meeting yesterday.

Kathy: No objection to it?

Helen: No, everyone thought it was a practical one.

Kathy: And when will you start putting it into practice?

Helen: Not until next week.

Kathy: Do you need to prepare anything?

Helen: Yes, so many things.

Kathy: Do you need any help?

Helen: No, it's very kind of you to offer. Thanks all the same.

★全文中畫 ⬤ 色塊的地方，可以依自己的狀況套入不同的名字、公司名、職稱、學校名等等。

中文翻譯6

凱西：計畫進行得怎麼樣了，海倫？
海倫：昨天在會議上討論過了。
凱西：沒有反對意見？
海倫：沒有，每個人都認為是可以執行的。
凱西：那妳什麼時候要開始做呢？
海倫：下個星期吧。
凱西：有什麼需要準備的嗎？
海倫：有啊，很多事情。
凱西：需要幫忙嗎？
海倫：不用了，不過妳能這樣說真是太好了，還是很謝謝妳。

商務小常識

　　在職場上，由於每個人對事情的看法多少有些不同，所以常常會出現需要溝通理解以達成共識的時候，下面是一些在溝通時常用的句子，可以讓談話過程更圓滑。

· Let's see if we can figure out how to deal with this situation calmly.（我們不妨想想看，怎麼樣可以心平氣和的處理這件事。）

· Perhaps we could try another way.（或許我們可以試試別的方法。）

· You have a deal.（我們接受你們的條件了。）

· That sounds like a good idea.（這個主意聽起來不錯。）

Dialogue ① 宴會中的注意事項 🔊 *Track 053*

要叮嚀別人注意某些事項時，除了直接說「欸，你要記得某事」以外，也可以參考對話中凱西的作法，以「問問題」的方式，確認對方都搞定每個細節了，比較沒有命令的感覺，更禮貌一些。

● ●

Kathy: Is everything ready for tonight's dinner party?

Susan: Yes. I have already checked everything twice.

Kathy: When will the party begin and where are we meeting?

Susan: It will start at 7 p.m. , on the 17th floor of the Hilton Hotel .

Kathy: How will our foreign guests get to the hotel?

Susan: We will arrange a car to pick them up, and the other guests can come by car or taxi.

Kathy: Will the dishes we ordered be okay?

Susan: I am sure our guests will enjoy the dinner very much.

Kathy: Make sure that no dishes contain unusual items like offal or liver.

Susan: I've already told the main chef.

Kathy: Actually I'm looking forward to this dinner very much.

Susan: Me too.

★全文中畫 ⬤ 色塊的地方，可以依自己的狀況套入不同的名字、公司名、職稱、學校名等等。

現在是不是回想起來了呢？

main chef 主廚

又叫做「head chef」或「executive chef」，反正就是掌管所有餐點烹調事務的那個人。

中文翻譯1

凱西：今天晚上的餐會都準備好了嗎？
蘇珊：準備好了。我已經核對過兩遍餐會流程了。
凱西：宴會什麼時候開始？在哪裡舉行呢？
蘇珊：晚上7點，在希爾頓酒店17樓。
凱西：國外國戶要怎麼到會場？
蘇珊：我們會安排轎車接他們。其他的客人可以自己開車或搭計程車到酒店。
凱西：宴會中點的菜沒問題吧？
蘇珊：我確定客人們會非常喜歡這頓晚餐的。
凱西：菜肴中一定不要含有動物內臟、肝臟之類的東西。
蘇珊：我已經和主廚交代這件事了。
凱西：事實上，我很期待這頓晚餐。
蘇珊：我也是。

Dialogue ❷ 提醒出貨 (1) ◀ Track 054

當老闆提醒你做某件事時，可以參考對話最後凱西的說法：「**I will handle this matter immediately**」（我馬上去處理）。

Mr. Wang: Have you checked on our order of air-conditioners for this month? We need them as soon as possible.

Kathy: I've already checked. Our distributor says that he will expedite shipment as soon as possible.

Mr. Wang: You know that air-conditioners are seasonal goods, and summer is the best time to sell them.

Kathy: So if the goods arrive later than June , we will miss our window of opportunity.

Mr. Wang: If that happens, it will be a disaster!

Kathy: What should I do now?

Mr. Wang: You'd better contact the distributor once more and tell him that an early shipment is of the utmost importance.

Kathy: Anything else?

Mr. Wang: We should remind him of the weather factor. It's been raining a lot recently.

Kathy: Okay, I will tell him via email.

Mr. Wang: Besides we should also emphasize that if he fails to deliver the goods according to the agreed-upon time, he should indemnify us for all losses and corresponding expenses.

Kathy: Okay, I will handle this matter immediately.

★全文中畫 ⬤ 色塊的地方，可以依自己的狀況套入不同的名字、公司名、職稱、學校名等等。

現在是不是回想起來了呢？

window of opportunity 機會之窗

所謂的「window of opportunity」指的就是「在某一個時間範圍內做這件事情會很有賺頭，但過了這段時間就來不及了」的意思。

中文翻譯2

王先生：妳檢查過我們這個月冷氣的訂單了嗎？我們急需這批貨。

凱　西：我已經檢查過了。我們的經銷商說他會儘早出貨的。

王先生：妳也知道，冷氣是季節性商品，而夏天又是冷氣最好的銷售季節。

凱　西：所以說，如果這批貨在6月以後到達的話，我們就錯過了銷售機會。

王先生：如果這樣的話，我們的損失就會很慘重！

凱　西：我現在應該做什麼呢？

王先生：妳最好再和經銷商聯繫一下，告訴他提早出貨對我們來說非常重要。

凱　西：還有其他需要我對經銷商說的事情嗎？

王先生：我們應該提醒他注意天氣的因素。最近很常下雨。

凱　西：好的，我會寫e-mail告訴他。

王先生：除此以外，我們也應該強調，如果他不能根據協定時間出貨，那麼他應該賠償我們的損失及相關的費用。

凱　西：好的，我馬上去處理這件事情。

Dialogue ❸ 提醒出貨 (2)　🔊 Track 055

邊聽這段對話，可以邊仔細觀察兩人的態度：凱西認為合約上說的就一定得達成，張先生則認為因為天氣的關係延期也是沒辦法的事，所以兩邊都認為自己對，互不讓步。你或許也會在職場上遇到一些死不讓步的人，可以參考兩人的說法，繼續堅定地堅持自己的立場！

Kathy: Hello, is this Mr. Zhang? Kathy calling.

Mr. Zhang: Oh, hello, Kathy. Is there anything I can do for you?

Kathy: Mr. Zhang, have you received the email I sent to you last week?

Mr. Zhang: Yes, I have, and the goods have already been delivered.

Kathy: The contract says that they should arrive at the latest this Monday, but we haven't received the goods yet.

Mr. Zhang: Actually the delivery was a little later than the agreed-upon time because of the bad weather, so I think the goods will arrive one or two days later.

Kathy: You know, June is the proper selling time for air-conditioners, and we don't want to miss the prime season.

Mr. Zhang: Yes, we know. We have delivered your goods as soon as we could after we received your email.

Kathy: You're aware that according to the contract we have the right to reject the goods if we fail to receive them this week.

Mr. Zhang: We have tried our best to reduce the delay and I hope the goods will arrive early enough.

Kathy: We hope so, too, because we are much in need of the goods and our competitor has begun promotion already.

Mr. Zhang: I do hope the goods arrive immediately so you can reduce your losses.

Kathy: Thank you. When we receive the goods I will call you. Goodbye.

Mr. Zhang: Okay, bye.

★全文中畫 ⬤ 色塊的地方，可以依自己的狀況套入不同的名字、公司名、職稱、學校名等等。

凱　西：你好，是張先生嗎？我是凱西。

張先生：妳好，凱西，妳有什麼事情嗎？

凱　西：張先生，我上個禮拜寄給你的郵件，你收到了嗎？

張先生：收到了，我們也已經出貨了。

凱　西：合約上說，這批貨最晚應該在這個禮拜一到。可是我們到現在還沒有收到這批貨。

張先生：事實上，因為壞天氣的關係，我們的出貨時間比預期的還要晚一點。所以我想，你們的貨會晚一兩天到。

凱　西：你知道吧，6月是冷氣的銷售旺季。我們不想錯過這個銷售旺季。

張先生：是的，我們知道。接到妳的郵件後，我們已經盡了最大的努力，儘早出貨給你們了。

凱　西：你是知道的，如果這個禮拜內我們還收不到這批貨，那麼根據合約，我們有權利拒收這批貨。

張先生：我們已經盡力縮短延誤時間了，我希望這批貨能儘早到。

凱　西：我們也希望貨能早一點到。因為我們急著需要這批貨，我們的競爭對手已經開始進行促銷了。

張先生：我真心希望這批貨馬上就到，這樣你們才可以減少損失。

凱　西：謝謝。如果我們收到貨，我會打電話通知你。再見。

張先生：好的，再見。

Dialogue ❹ 告知會議安排 🔈 *Track 056*

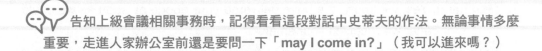
告知上級會議相關事務時，記得看看這段對話中史蒂夫的作法。無論事情多麼重要，走進人家辦公室前還是要問一下「**may I come in?**」（我可以進來嗎？）

Steve: Mr. Wang , may I come in?

Mr. Wang: Yes, of course. What can I do for you?

Steve: Here is today's agenda.

Mr. Wang: Is there anything special?

Steve: There is a board meeting this afternoon .

Mr. Wang: I thought the meeting was on Friday , not today.

Steve: I received an email from headquarters this morning, which says the meeting is at 2 p.m. this afternoon .

Mr. Wang: Same place?

Steve: Yes, the meeting is to be held at the (Shangri-La Hotel) just as it was arranged before.

Mr. Wang: OK, good. I should review the materials for the meeting and the relative data.

Steve: The reports and data you need are both on your desk. You can call me if there are any problems.

Mr. Wang: Thank you so much.

Steve: Not at all. (Mr. Wang), when shall we leave for the meeting?

Mr. Wang: How about (1: 30 p.m.)?

Steve: I think we should go a little earlier, because the hotel is quite far away, and we have to consider the traffic.

Mr. Wang: OK, we will leave at (1: 15 p.m).

★全文中畫 ⬤ 色塊的地方，可以依自己的狀況套入不同的名字、公司名、職稱、學校名等等。

現在是不是回想起來了呢？

headquarters 總部

雖然總部不見得會有很多個，但記得headquarters一定要有那個s，不會說
headquarter。這是一個固定用法。

中文翻譯4 •

史蒂夫：王先生，我能進來嗎？
王先生：請進，有什麼事情嗎？
史蒂夫：這是今天的行程。
王先生：有什麼特別的事情嗎？
史蒂夫：今天下午有董事會。
王先生：我以為董事會是在禮拜五，不是在今天。
史蒂夫：今天早上我收到來自總部的電子郵件，上面說董事會是在今天下午兩點舉行。
王先生：相同的地點嗎？
史蒂夫：是，像之前安排的一樣，會議在香格里拉酒店舉行。
王先生：好。我現在要看一下會議需要的材料和相關的資料。
史蒂夫：您需要的報告和相關資料已經放在桌子上了。如果有問題您可以打電話給我。

王先生：謝謝你。
史蒂夫：不客氣。王先生，我們幾點出發去開會呢？
王先生：下午一點半行嗎？
史蒂夫：我想想我們應該再早一點，因為從我們這裡到酒店滿遠的，而且我們還要考慮到交通的問題。
王先生：好吧，我們一點十五就出發。

Dialogue ❺ 告知貨物損壞 🔊 *Track 057*

貨物損壞了，也難怪凱西要這麼緊張。如果你也遇到了緊張兮兮的同事，可以像對話中的蘇珊一樣，說「Calm down」，要他別著急，才能把事情做好。

Kathy: Hello, is that Susan ? This is Kathy .

Susan: Hello, Kathy . Susan speaking. What's the matter?

Kathy: The shipment from our distributor is damaged.

Susan: Really? Was the damage extensive?

Kathy: I'm afraid about half of the goods are unusable. I think we'd better not accept the goods. What do you think?

Susan: I strongly agree with you. I will call our distributor later.

Kathy: Can I return to the company now?

Susan: Yes. By the way, did you note the damage on the bill of lading?

Kathy: Sorry, I forgot about that. I will do it at once.

Susan: Calm down. Be sure to go over the details.

Kathy: Okay, I will. See you later.

Susan: See you.

★全文中畫 ⬤ 色塊的地方，可以依自己的狀況套入不同的名字、公司名、職稱、學校名等等。

中文翻譯5
凱西：妳好，是蘇珊嗎？我是凱西。
蘇珊：妳好，凱西。我是蘇珊，怎麼了？
凱西：經銷商送來的貨有損壞。
蘇珊：是嗎？受損的貨多嗎？

凱西：恐怕有一半的貨不能用。我認為我們最好別接收這批貨。妳覺得呢？
蘇珊：我非常同意。等一下我會打電話給經銷商。
凱西：那我現在可以回公司了嗎？
蘇珊：可以。還有，妳把損壞情況寫在提貨單上了嗎？
凱西：對不起，我忘了。我馬上就註明。
蘇珊：別急。小心注意細節。
凱西：我會小心的。待會見。
蘇珊：待會見。

Dialogue ❻ 提醒名片設計細節　🔊 *Track 058*

此段對話中的艾咪搞錯了一個重要的細節，但王先生沒有責怪她，而是很詳細地跟她說明為什麼這樣不可以。遇到很笨的客戶的時候，你也可以試著用這樣的語氣來說，而非一開口就不耐煩。

Amy: Excuse me, may I come in?

Mr. Wang: Yes, please.

Amy: Mr. Wang , here is the sample of your new business card.

Mr. Wang: Oh, thank you.

Amy: Are you satisfied with the design? We can still change the layout before the final printing.

Mr. Wang: I'm afraid there is a problem.

Amy: What is it?

Mr. Wang: You printed my private phone number on it.

Amy: Isn't that a convenient way for our clients to contact you?

Mr. Wang: No. People only provide the office number on business cards, not the personal number.

Amy: Sorry, I don't quite understand.

Mr. Wang: People do this because they want to protect their privacy.

Amy: Oh, I get it. I will make the corrections right away.

Mr. Wang: Thank you.

★全文中畫 ⬤ 色塊的地方，可以依自己的狀況套入不同的名字、公司名、職稱、學校名等等。

sample 範例、樣品

無論是在大量購買物品前先用來參考的「樣品模型」，在香水店可以拿來試噴、試聞的香水，或是在超級市場試吃的東西，都可以叫做sample。

中文翻譯6

艾　咪：請問，我可以進來嗎？
王先生：可以，請進。
艾　咪：王先生，這是您新名片的樣本。
王先生：噢，謝謝。
艾　咪：您對這個設計滿意嗎？在最後印刷前，我們還可以修改排版。
王先生：這個名片恐怕有個問題。
艾　咪：什麼問題？
王先生：你們把我的私人電話號碼也印上去了。
艾　咪：這樣不是會方便客戶與您聯繫嗎？
王先生：不是的。名片上只會提供辦公室的電話，不能提供個人電話號碼。
艾　咪：不好意思，我不是很明白您的意思。
王先生：這樣做是為了保護隱私。
艾　咪：噢，我明白了。我馬上去修改。
王先生：謝謝。

Dialogue 7 提醒宴會服裝 🔊 *Track 059*

想表達自己因為公司的事務非常興奮，讓同事留下好印象嗎？就算對於宴會興趣缺缺，也可以像對話中的瑪麗一樣，來一句：「I can hardly wait」（我快等不及了）。

Mary: I hear our company has invited lots of important clients to today's dinner party.

Susan: Yes, the board really values these parties.

Mary: Do you know why?

Susan: Maybe the company wants to give our clients a fantastic impression during this financial crisis.

Mary: That makes sense.

Susan: There will be lots of foreign guests at our party as well.

Mary: I can hardly wait.

Susan: Me, too.

Mary: This is the first time I've taken part in such an exciting party.

Susan: Oh, I'm sure the party will be even better than you imagine. You must dress up and make yourself up properly.

Mary: What kind of dress do you propose?

Susan: A black dress suits you, I think.

Mary: Okay. Can we go together?

Susan: Sure, I will pick you up at 7: 00 p.m.

Mary: Okay, great.

★全文中畫 ⬤ 色塊的地方，可以依自己的狀況套入不同的名字、公司名、職稱、學校名等等。

現在是不是回想起來了呢？

dress up 打扮正式

打扮正式叫做「dress up」，而「穿上衣服」（不見得一定要穿得很正式，有穿就好）叫做「get dressed」，兩者還是有差異的。

中文翻譯7

瑪麗：我聽說今天的宴會上，公司邀請了很多重要客戶。

蘇珊：是啊，董事會很重視這些宴會。

瑪麗：妳知道原因嗎？

蘇珊：可能是在現在的金融危機下，公司想給客戶留下一個好印象吧。

瑪麗：很有道理。

蘇珊：到時還會有很多外國客戶到場哦。

瑪麗：我都等不及了呢。

蘇珊：我也是。

瑪麗：這是我第一次參加這麼刺激的宴會。

蘇珊：嗯，我很肯定宴會會比妳想得還要好。妳得穿正式衣服，再化一下適當的妝。

瑪麗：妳覺得我穿什麼洋裝好？

蘇珊：我想黑色的洋裝很適合妳。

瑪麗：好。我們可以一起去嗎？

蘇珊：當然，我七點去接妳。

瑪麗：好的，謝謝。

Dialogue ⑧ 提醒注意工地安全 🔊 *Track 060*

💬 參觀人家的工地（或其他場地）時，可以像這段對話的張先生一樣，先說一句：「我很期待參觀你們的工地」。

Kathy: Welcome to our factory.

Mr. Zhang: I've wanted to see your factory for a long time.

Kathy: Let me show you around.

Mr. Zhang: Sure, thanks.

Kathy: The tour lasts about one and a half hours . Before we begin the tour, you must wear this hard hat.

Mr. Zhang: Is that necessary?

Kathy: Yes, the factory safety regulations require that we wear them.

Mr. Zhang: Okay, I see, but I'm afraid this one is a little too small for me.

Kathy: What about this one?

Mr. Zhang: Much better.

Kathy: Please, this way. If you have any questions, you can ask me.

Mr. Zhang: Thanks, I will.

Kathy: This is our latest product.

Mr. Zhang: Wow. When is it being introduced to the market?

Kathy: It will be out next month .

Mr. Zhang: Could I have a sample free of charge?

Kathy: Sure. We hope you will be satisfied with our product and choose to place an order next month .

Mr. Zhang: Sure.

★全文中畫 ⬤ 色塊的地方，可以依自己的狀況套入不同的名字、公司名、職稱、學校名等等。

現在是不是回想起來了呢？

free of charge 免費

「charge」有「收錢」的意思，而「free of...」則是「沒有……」的意思。合起來就是「沒有收錢」，也就是免費啦。

中文翻譯8

凱　西：歡迎參觀我們的工廠。
張先生：我早就想來參觀你們的工廠了。
凱　西：讓我帶您參觀一下吧。
張先生：當然，謝謝。
凱　西：這次參觀大約需要一個半小時。參觀開始前您必須先戴上安全帽。
張先生：這是必須的嗎？
凱　西：是的。工廠的安全條例要求我們要戴安全帽。
張先生：好，我知道了。但是這頂帽子對我來說有點太小了。
凱　西：這頂怎麼樣？
張先生：好多了。
凱　西：請走這邊。如果您有任何問題，可以問我。
張先生：謝謝，我會的。
凱　西：這是我們的最新產品。
張先生：真棒。什麼時候上市呢？
凱　西：下個月。
張先生：我可以拿一個免費的樣品嗎？
凱　西：當然，希望您會滿意我們的產品，並且能在下個月訂購。
張先生：我會的。

商務小常識

　　在宴請外國客戶時，必須要優先考慮菜肴的安排。要問對方不吃什麼，有什麼禁忌，不同國家、不同民族的人有不同的飲食習慣，我們必須給予尊重。西方人一般有「六不吃」：(1) 不吃動物內臟；(2) 不吃動物的頭和腳；(3) 不吃寵物，尤其是貓和狗；(4) 不吃稀有動物；(5) 不吃淡水魚（淡水魚有土腥味）；(6) 不吃蛇、鱔等無鱗無鰭的動物。此外，還要注意宗教禁忌，比如伊斯蘭教禁忌豬肉和動物的鮮血，佛教禁忌葷腥、辛辣等。一定要事前瞭解清楚，給予合適的安排。

SOS Unit 12 祝賀

Dialogue ❶ 祝賀升職 ◀€ *Track 061*

祝賀別人時，可以像這段對話中的凱西一樣，以「I heard that...」（聽說……）開頭，讓對方知道自己為何會曉得他有好消息。

Kathy: Good morning, Rachel.

Rachel: Morning. Long time no see. How are you?

Kathy: Fine, thank you. I hear that you've been promoted to the Vice President of your company. Congratulations!

Rachel: Thank you. Actually, the board declared the promotion yesterday, and I will move to Beijing next week.

Kathy: You mean you have to move?

Rachel: I'm afraid so.

Kathy: Oh, that is a pity. We can't work together any more. You were a really good partner.

Rachel: Don't worry. I will call you regularly.

Kathy: OK, are you free tonight? I'd like to invite you to my house for dinner.

Rachel: Thank you so much. I'd love to.

★全文中畫 ⬤ 色塊的地方，可以依自己的狀況套入不同的名字、公司名、職稱、學校名等等。

中文翻譯1

凱西：早安，瑞秋。

瑞秋：早安。好久不見，妳最近還好嗎？

凱西：很好，謝謝。我聽說妳當上公司的副總裁了，恭喜啊！

瑞秋：謝謝。事實上，董事會昨天才宣佈這個消息。下個禮拜我就要搬到北京了。

凱西：妳是說妳必須去那邊工作？

瑞秋：恐怕是這樣。

凱西：太遺憾了。我們今後不能一起工作了。妳是一位很棒的工作夥伴。

瑞秋：沒關係。我會常打電話給妳的。

凱西：好的，今晚妳有時間嗎？我想請妳到我家吃飯。

瑞秋：謝謝，我很樂意。

Dialogue ❷ 祝賀研發成功 ◀ Track 062

像對話中的湯姆一樣，可以在參觀別人的工廠時，先說一句「我早就想來了」，讓對方有被重視的感覺。

Kathy: Is this the first time you have visited our factory?

Tom: Yes, it is. In fact I planned to come a long time ago.

Kathy: Let me show you around.

Tom: Thanks a lot.

Kathy: This is our R&D Department . Here is the latest product. Our engineers spent a lot of time designing and perfecting it.

Tom: When will they be on the market?

Kathy: They will be available for purchase in a month . We have already received many more orders than we expected.

Tom: Congratulations! Do you have a free sample?

Kathy: Yes, here is the sample and instructions.

Tom: It really does look great. I think I will place an order.

Kathy: Thank you. We look forward to cooperating with you in the future.

★全文中畫 ● 色塊的地方，可以依自己的狀況套入不同的名字、公司名、職稱、學校名等等。

R & D Department 研發部門

R & D就是Research & Development的縮寫，也就是「研究與發展」的意思，所以R & D Department就是研發部門。

中文翻譯2

凱西：這是您第一次參觀我們工廠嗎？

湯姆：是啊。實際上，我很早以前就計畫來看看了。

凱西：我帶您四處看看吧。

湯姆：謝謝。

凱西：這是我們的研發部。這是我們的最新產品。我們的工程師在設計和讓這件產品變得完美上花了很多時間。

湯姆：新產品什麼時候上市？

凱西：一個月後就會上市，我們已經收到很多訂單了，遠遠超過我們的想像。

湯姆：恭喜你們！你們有免費的樣品嗎？

凱西：有的，這是樣品和說明書。

湯姆：看起來真的很不錯。我想我會訂一些。

凱西：謝謝。我們期盼今後與你們合作。

Dialogue ❸ 祝賀加薪 ◀ Track 063

這位老闆麥克講話很有技巧，替凱西加薪時，還跟她說這個時節不可能幫所有人都加薪，以顯示她有多特別，是個很讓人開心的作法，可以參考看看。

Mike: Kathy, come to my office now, please.

Kathy: Okay, I will be there immediately.

Mike: Kathy, here you go. You've earned it. Congratulations!

Kathy: Oh, thank you. I didn't expect this. I actually thought I was being blamed for something I had done wrong.

Mike: You deserve it. You are the most industrious worker in my company.

Kathy: I just do what I've been told to do. Thank you so much.

Mike: The company has struggled this year because of the financial crisis. We can't raise the salary of every employee.

Kathy: I see. I am sure we can survive this crisis.

Mike: I hope so, too.

Kathy: Believe me, everything will improve.

★全文中畫 ⬤ 色塊的地方，可以依自己的狀況套入不同的名字、公司名、職稱、學校名等等。

現在是不是回想起來了呢？

raise the salary 加薪

除了這麼說以外，也可以說「give sb. a raise」表示「為某人加薪」。

中文翻譯3

麥克：凱西，現在到我辦公室來一下。

凱西：好的，我馬上來。

麥克：凱西，給妳，妳應得的。恭喜妳！

凱西：噢，謝謝。這太出乎我的意料了。剛才我以為是工作上有問題，要被罵了呢。

麥克：這是妳應得的。妳是公司裡最勤奮的員工。

凱西：我只是做了吩咐下來的事。真的很謝謝您。

麥克：由於這一次的金融危機，公司今年很辛苦，所以我們沒有辦法給每個人都加薪。

凱西：我明白，我確信我們會度過危機的。

麥克：希望是這樣。

凱西：相信我，一切都會好起來的。

Dialogue ❹ 祝賀訂單成功 🔊 *Track 064*

💬 訂單成功後，可以像對話中的王先生一樣，說一句「很高興與你們做生意」，來加強、鞏固雙方的合作關係。

Mr. Wang: Does this product meet your requirements?

Kathy: Actually, it is more than we need.

Mr. Wang: What do you mean? I don't quite understand you.

Kathy: The price you gave us is much higher than expected.

Mr. Wang: We have some cheaper ones.

Kathy: What is the price difference?

Mr. Wang: They will cost (10%) less.

Kathy: Does this model still use the same material?

Mr. Wang: Yes, the only difference is that the former has more functions.

Kathy: Oh, I'd like to order the latter then.

Mr. Wang: Okay. We are happy to have your business.

Kathy: Thank you.

★全文中畫 ⬤ 色塊的地方，可以依自己的狀況套入不同的名字、公司名、職稱、學校名等等。

中文翻譯4

王先生：這件產品符合你們的要求嗎？
凱　西：事實上，它超出我們的需求了。
王先生：什麼意思？我不太明白你的意思。
凱　西：我是說你們的要價比我們預期的要高。
王先生：我們也有便宜的。
凱　西：價錢差多少？
王先生：低10%。
凱　西：那這種型號採用的仍然是同樣的材料嗎？
王先生：是的，兩種產品唯一不同的地方，是前一種的功能比較多。
凱　西：這樣啊。那我還是訂後一種吧。
王先生：好的，我們很高興和你們做生意。
凱　西：謝謝。

Dialogue ⑤ 祝賀合作成功 🔊 *Track 065*

雙方討論完合作內容時，可以像這段對話最後面的地方一樣，學凱西說一句「希望合作成功」，表達友善的態度，也是為下一次的合作鋪路。

Kathy: We need our order packaged into (three) boxes.

Mr. Wang: How do you want it separated?

Kathy: I'll send you an email about it later.

Mr. Wang: Okay, I will package them when I receive the email.

Kathy: Thank you. We also hope you can send it via the earliest available shipment because the order is urgent.

Mr. Wang: No problem. We will do our best to meet your needs.

Kathy: Thank you. But I'd like to add that if we can't receive the goods by the deadline, we have the right to cancel the contract.

Mr. Wang: Don't worry. Our company can deliver your goods in time.

Kathy: This is our first cooperation and I hope it can be successful.

Mr. Wang: I hope so, too.

★全文中畫 ⬤ 色塊的地方，可以依自己的狀況套入不同的名字、公司名、職稱、學校名等等。

現在是不是回想起來了呢？

in time 及時

in time和on time的差別在哪裡呢？原來，in time是「在時間到之前」，而on time是「準時」。例如如果你準時來上班，就叫做「on time」，如果你趕在上班時間前幾秒及時打卡，則叫「in time」。

中文翻譯5

凱　西：我們訂的貨需要分裝3箱。

王先生：妳想怎麼分裝？

凱　西：稍後我會寫e-mail通知你。

王先生：好的。一收到e-mail我就開始裝箱。

凱　西：謝謝。我們同時還希望你們可以儘早出貨，因為訂單很急。

王先生：沒問題。我們會盡最大的努力滿足你們的要求。

凱　西：謝謝。但是我想補充一句，如果我們在截止日期前收不到貨物的話，我們有權利取消合約。

王先生：別擔心。我們會及時送到的。

凱　西：這是我們第一次合作，希望合作成功。

王先生：我也希望如此。

Dialogue ❻ 祝賀產品暢銷 🔊 *Track 066*

面對客戶，可以盡量表現出謙虛與禮貌，如這段對話中，可以看看凱西被祝賀產品銷售良好時，把功勞都歸給工程師，這是很好的說法。

Mr. Sun: How is the product selling?

Kathy: It's selling much better than we expected.

Mr. Sun: What are the advantages of this product?

Kathy: Compared with other products on the market, it is smaller and lighter .

Mr. Sun: What is the market share right now?

Kathy: It is at about 30% , and the number is increasing every month.

Mr. Sun: Well, that's good news. Congratulations to you!

Kathy: Thank you. In fact we should credit the product's success to our engineers. They worked hard on it.

Mr. Sun: Yes, you are right. Could I see your sample?

Kathy: Of course. We have prepared free samples for every agent.

★全文中畫 色塊的地方，可以依自己的狀況套入不同的名字、公司名、職稱、學校名等等。

中文翻譯6

孫先生：產品的銷售情況如何？

凱　西：比我們預期的還要好得多。

孫先生：這個產品的優點是什麼？

凱　西：和市場上的其他產品相比，它比較小而輕。

孫先生：現在的市佔率是多少？

凱　西：大約佔30%，並且市佔率還在逐月上升。

孫先生：這是好消息。恭喜你們！

凱　西：謝謝。事實上，我們應該把這麼好的銷量歸功於我們的工程師。他們花了很多心血在這款商品上。

孫先生：是啊，妳說得很對。我能看看你們的樣品嗎？

凱　西：當然可以。我們已經給每家代理商都準備了免費的樣品。

Dialogue ❼ 祝賀收到貨物 ◀ *Track 067*

注意看看這段對話，兩人用了不少假設語氣，討論「如果貨物沒到要怎麼辦」。不過貨物終究是到了，所以後來兩人發現他們根本沒必要煩惱，轉回使用現在式。

Bob: (Kathy), this is (Bob). I am at the dock to check our goods.

Kathy: Oh, the goods arrive finally.

Bob: Yes, I received the call this morning from the shipping company.

Kathy: If they couldn't arrive in time, there would be a huge loss for us.

Bob: If that would have happened, we would have had the right to reject the goods according to the contract.

Kathy: Yes, that is the only way that we could reduce the losses.

Bob: Whatever, they have already arrived. We are quite lucky.

Kathy: Yes, the weather is so bad recently.

Bob: I think I will return to the company in (two) hours.

Kathy: How about going for a dinner together?

Bob: That would be great!

★全文中畫 ⬤ 色塊的地方，可以依自己的狀況套入不同的名字、公司名、職稱、學校名等等。

現在是不是回想起來了呢？

have the right to... 有權利可以……

「right」當形容詞是「正確的」的意思，而當作名詞就是「權利」。「have the right to做某事」就是「有權利做某事」。

中文翻譯7

鮑勃：凱西，我是鮑勃。我正在碼頭驗貨。

凱西：哦，貨終於到了。

鮑勃：對，今天早上我接到了貨運公司的電話。

凱西：如果貨物不能及時抵達的話，我們的損失會很慘重。

鮑勃：如果那樣的話，根據合約，我們有權利拒收這批貨。

凱西：是啊，這是我們減少損失的唯一辦法了。

鮑勃：不管怎樣，貨已經到了。我們實在是很幸運。

凱西：是啊，最近的天氣太糟糕了。

鮑勃：我想兩個小時後我會回公司。

凱西：要不要一起吃晚餐？

鮑勃：太好了！

商務小常識

在祝賀國外客戶時，常常會使用e-mail或電話表示祝福。但在寫e-mail時有一些很基本但很容易就犯錯的小地方，不可不慎。例如對還不熟、甚至初次接觸的客戶，就不能在結尾用「Good luck,」、「Best wishes,」、「Love,」等，要用「Yours faithfully,」或「Faithfully yours,」才顯得得體哦！

Dialogue ❶ 面試服裝建議 (1) ◀ *Track 068*

給人建議時，可以使用「**You'd better...**」（你最好……）的句型。看看這個對話中是怎麼用的吧！

● ●

Kathy: Hi, Susan , I hear you have an interview tomorrow. How are you feeling?

Susan: I am very nervous.

Kathy: Stay calm. You'll be fine.

Susan: Thank you, but I don't have any experience with interviews. Would you please give me some advice?

Kathy: No problem. Happy to help.

Susan: You are so kind. What kind of clothes should I wear tomorrow?

Kathy: What kind of position are you applying for tomorrow?

Susan: An accountant in a bank .

Kathy: You'd better wear a suit and heels. This gives the interviewers the impression of seriousness.

Susan: Yes, you are right. First impressions are very important.

★全文中畫 ● 色塊的地方，可以依自己的狀況套入不同的名字、公司名、職稱、學校名等等。

Happy to help 很高興能幫忙

這句其實是「I'm happy to help」（我很樂意幫忙）的簡單說法。當別人感謝你幫忙時，就可以用這一句來回應。

中文翻譯1

凱西：嗨，蘇珊，我聽說妳明天有面試。妳現在覺得怎麼樣？

蘇珊：我現在很緊張。

凱西：保持冷靜，妳會沒事的。

蘇珊：謝謝。但是我以前沒有任何面試經驗。妳可以給我一些建議嗎？

凱西：沒問題。我很高興能幫妳。

蘇珊：妳真是太好了。我明天該穿什麼衣服去呢？

凱西：明天妳要應徵的職位是什麼？

蘇珊：是一家銀行的會計。

凱西：那妳最好穿西裝和高跟鞋，這樣可以給面試官一個很莊重的印象。

蘇珊：妳說得很對。第一印象很重要。

Dialogue ❷ 面試服裝建議 (2) ◀ *Track 069*

聽說人家要去面試，無論對方有沒有問你意見，都和這段對話中的凱西一樣，說一句「Good luck」（祝你好運）吧！

Susan: I have an interview this afternoon .

Kathy: Good luck!

Susan: Thank you. Could you give me some advice? Should I wear this suit this afternoon ?

Kathy: I think the suit fits you very well, but there is one problem.

Susan: What?

Kathy: I think you should put on make-up.

Susan: I'm not used to wearing make-up. It feels a little bit strange.

Kathy: But it is very important in a daily business routine. My company requires us to wear make-up during work.

Susan: You mean wearing make-up is a kind of necessary etiquette?

Kathy: That's right.

★全文中畫 ⬤ 色塊的地方，可以依自己的狀況套入不同的名字、公司名、職稱、學校名等等。

現在是不是回想起來了呢？

etiquette 禮儀

etiquette是「禮儀」的意思，它的念法比較特別，音標是 /ˈɛtɪkɛt/。

中文翻譯2

蘇珊：我今天下午有個面試。

凱西：祝妳好運！

蘇珊：謝謝。妳能給我一些建議嗎？我下午穿這套西裝好嗎？

凱西：我覺得這套西裝很適合妳，但是有一個問題。

蘇珊：什麼問題？

凱西：我覺得妳應該化妝。

蘇珊：我不太習慣化妝，那樣有點怪。

凱西：但在日常的商務生活中，這很重要。我們公司都會要求我們上班時要化妝。

蘇珊：妳是說上班時化妝是一種必備的禮儀？

凱西：是的。

Dialogue ❸　面試服裝建議 (3) 🔊 *Track 070*

想問其他人的意見時，可以用「**What about...?**」（……怎麼樣？）的句型。看看這段對話中是怎麼用的呢？

Kathy: How did your first round of interviews go?

Nancy: It was okay. The first round was a phone interview and I passed it.

Kathy: Congratulations! What about your next round of interviews? Have you prepared well?

Nancy: I am thinking about what kind of clothes I should wear.

Kathy: You'd better wear something fashionable.

Nancy: I think so. Because it is a (fashion journal) and I want to give the interviewers an idea of my sense of style.

Kathy: Yes, the proper attire will make the interview a success.

Nancy: You are right. What about this (red dress)? I think it fits me very well.

Kathy: Yes, you look beautiful and fashionable. Good luck during the interview.

Nancy: Thank you.

★全文中畫 ⬤ 色塊的地方，可以依自己的狀況套入不同的名字、公司名、職稱、學校名等等。

現在是不是回想起來了呢？

journal 期刊；雜誌
journal可以是「日記」的意思，此外，也可以當作「學術性的期刊」的意思。

中文翻譯3
凱西：妳的第一輪面試進展得怎麼樣？
南西：還好。第一輪是電話面試，我通過了。
凱西：恭喜妳！那妳下一輪面試怎麼樣？準備好了嗎？
南西：我正在想面試時我該穿什麼呢。
凱西：妳最好穿得時尚一點。
南西：我也這麼想。因為這是一家時尚雜誌，我想給面試官展示一下我的時尚品味。
凱西：是啊，適當的穿著可以讓妳成功通過面試。
南西：對。這件紅色洋裝怎麼樣？我覺得它很適合我。
凱西：妳看起來很漂亮也很時尚。祝妳面試成功。
南西：謝謝。

Dialogue ❹ 面試官的看法 (1) 🔊*Track 071*

同意對方的說法時，可以像這段對話中一樣，說「**Yes, definitely.**」（是的，當然了）。**definitely**是個語氣很強烈的字，表示你強烈地同意。

Mr. Wang: The interviews are finally finished. I'm very tired. What about you?

Kathy: Tired too, but we have to continue our work now.

Mr. Wang: Yeah! So what do you think of our candidates? Did anyone stand out?

Kathy: I think the girl named Ann is quite good, and she also did well on her professional test.

Mr. Wang: You mean the only one who wore a suit today?

Kathy: Yes. She looks older than her real age, but this can be advantageous in the business world.

Mr. Wang: You are right. It seems the older an accountant is, the more experience she has.

Kathy: And an experienced accountant always has lots of clients.

Mr. Wang: So Ann is our final choice, right?

Kathy: Yes, definitely.

★全文中畫 色塊的地方，可以依自己的狀況套入不同的名字、公司名、職稱、學校名等等。

現在是不是回想起來了呢？

stand out 表現突出

stand out是一個動詞片語，表示「表現突出」，而它的形容詞是outstanding，是「表現突出的」的意思。

中文翻譯4

王先生：面試終於結束了。我好累。妳呢？

凱　西：我也很累。但是現在我們還得繼續工作。

王先生：是啊。妳對這些面試者有什麼看法？有誰表現特別出色嗎？

凱　西：我覺得那個叫安的女孩子不錯，而且在專業考試中也表現得很好。

王先生：妳是說今天唯一一個穿套裝的那個人嗎？

凱　西：是的。她起來比實際年齡還大一點，但在我們的商務工作中，這恰恰是個優勢。

王先生：妳說得對。似乎是會計越老，經驗越豐富嘛。

凱　西：而一個有經驗的會計，總是會有很多客戶的。

王先生：所以安是我們的最終選擇了，對嗎？

凱　西：是呀，當然是她了。

Dialogue ❺ 面試官的看法 (2) 🔊*Track 072*

💬 想確認自己和對方的意見達成一致時，可以和這段對話中的凱西一樣，在最後再次重複結論，以確保自己沒有搞錯，結論真的就是要選擇這一個。

• •

Mr. Wang: What do you think of these candidates?

Kathy: It is hard to decide. Let's look at their resumes again.

Mr. Wang: Okay. Do any of them seem especially qualified?

Kathy: Linda and Ann . But we only have one vacancy.

Mr. Wang: What about Linda ?

Kathy: I think she is very elegant but her results on the professional test weren't so good.

Mr. Wang: And Ann ?

Kathy: Her professional test is good but she doesn't wear make-up at all.

Mr. Wang: I think professional records are more important. As for make-up, she can get tips from other employees.

Kathy: Yes, you are right, so Ann is our final decision.

★全文中畫 ⬤ 色塊的地方，可以依自己的狀況套入不同的名字、公司名、職稱、學校名等等。

中文翻譯5

王先生：那些面試者，妳覺得如何呢？
凱　西：很難決定。我們再看一下她們的履歷吧。
王先生：好。有誰看起來特別適任嗎？
凱　西：琳達和安。但我們只有一個職位空缺。
王先生：琳達怎麼樣？
凱　西：我覺得她很優雅，但是她的專業考試成績沒有很好。
王先生：安呢？
凱　西：她的專業成績很好，但是她一點妝都沒化。
王先生：我覺得專業成績比較重要。至於化妝，她可以從其他員工那裡得到建議。
凱　西：是的，你說得對。所以，安是我們的最終選擇囉。

Dialogue ❶ 職員間談論服裝 🔊 *Track 073*

💬 同事稱讚你的服裝時，要怎麼辦？那就也反過來稱讚對方的服裝吧！看看這兩個人的對話怎麼說。

Kathy: You look very smart today, Vincent .

Vincent: Thanks for the compliment, Kathy . I must wear a suit and tie today because I will meet some important clients.

Kathy: The tie really matches your shirt well.

Vincent: My girlfriend chose it for me. I'll tell her you liked it.

Kathy: Maybe your girlfriend can give me some fashion tips.

Vincent: You are too modest. I have heard lots of clients compliment on your attire.

Kathy: That's because they always see me in a suit but never in casual clothes.

Vincent: I think that's a good thing. We represent our company and should dress formally when we are at work.

Kathy: Yes, you are right. If everyone was dressed the same way as you, we would have very happy clients.

Vincent: Thanks again, Kathy . See you later.

Kathy: See you.

★全文中畫 ⬤ 色塊的地方，可以依自己的狀況套入不同的名字、公司名、職稱、學校名等等。

smart 時髦的、俐落好看的

大家可能都知道「smart」是聰明的意思，但用來說「服裝」、「外貌」的話，則是表示瀟灑時尚又好看的意思。

中文翻譯1

凱西：你今天看起來很時尚哦，文森。
文森：謝謝誇獎，凱西。今天我必須得穿西裝、打領帶，因為我要見一些重要的客戶。
凱西：這條領帶很配你的襯衫。
文森：是我女朋友挑給我的。我會告訴她妳喜歡這條領帶。
凱西：也許妳女朋友可以給我一些時尚建議。
文森：妳太謙虛了。我聽說很多客戶都稱讚妳的穿衣風格。
凱西：那是因為他們看到我的時候都是穿正式服裝，從來沒看過我穿休閒服。
文森：我覺得這是好事。我們代表著公司，在上班時應該穿得正式一點。
凱西：你說得對。如果每個人都穿得像你一樣，我們的客戶會很開心的。
文森：再次謝謝妳，凱西。待會見。
凱西：待會見。

Dialogue ② 會議服裝 🔊 Track 074

在工作上遇到了問題，想徵求同事意見時，可以像對話中使用「I don't know what to do」（我都不知道怎麼辦了），大家會覺得你很可憐，馬上幫你想辦法。

Kathy: What's wrong? You look unhappy.

Susan: The manager changed the agenda and now I have to present a report at the meeting later.

Kathy: Yes, I just heard of the meeting. Is anything wrong?

Susan: The trouble is that I'm wearing causal clothes, not a suit today.

Kathy: It isn't polite to present at a meeting in casual clothes.

Susan: I don't know what to do. There is little time left.

Kathy: Don't worry. I can lend you mine.

Susan: You mean you have a spare suit ?

Kathy: I always keep an extra one at the office in case of emergencies.

Susan: Thank you so much.

★全文中畫 色塊的地方，可以依自己的狀況套入不同的名字、公司名、職稱、學校名等等。

中文翻譯2

凱西：怎麼了？妳看起來不是很開心。

蘇珊：經理更改了行程。等一下我得在會議上報告。

凱西：我剛剛也聽說了這個會議。有什麼問題嗎？

蘇珊：問題是我今天穿的是休閒服，不是正式服裝。

凱西：穿休閒服在會議上報告確實不禮貌。

蘇珊：我不知道該怎麼辦。沒有多少時間了。

凱西：別急。我的套裝可以借給妳。

蘇珊：妳是說妳還有多的套裝？

凱西：為了防止意外，我都會在公司多準備一套正式服裝。

蘇珊：真是太謝謝妳了。

Dialogue ❸ 談判服裝 ◀ *Track 075*

很少有人會覺得自己的工作不辛苦的，可以和以下對話一樣，適時和別的部門的人說一句「好羨慕你啊」，說不定能讓達到讓對方覺得「哇，我的工作其實也會令人羨慕嘛」的鼓勵效果。

Mr. Sun: Your tie matches your shirt.

Mr. Wang: Thank you. I have a negotiation later, so I have to be formally dressed.

Mr. Sun: Yes, your sales department represents the image of the company.

Mr. Wang: And any possible mistakes we make could result in the loss of an important client.

Mr. Sun: You're right.

Mr. Wang: However, personally I favor casual clothes. They're more comfortable than suits.

Mr. Sun: That's right. Our R&D department allows us to dress casually in the office.

Mr. Wang: Sometimes I really envy you.

Mr. Sun: It's only because we work in a laboratory and don't need to negotiate with clients.

Mr. Wang: I suppose it's fair.

★全文中畫 ⬤ 色塊的地方，可以依自己的狀況套入不同的名字、公司名、職稱、學校名等等。

現在是不是回想起來了呢？

I suppose it's fair 這樣說也對啦

「fair」是「公平的」的意思，在這個對話中，王先生認為既然研發部門不用見客戶，所以可以穿得隨便點，「好像也蠻公平的」、「好像也蠻有道理的」，所以才說「I suppose it's fair」。

中文翻譯3 ● ● ● ● ● ● ● ● ● ●

孫先生：你的領帶和襯衫很搭。
王先生：謝謝。我等一下有個談判，所以我不得不穿得正式一點。
孫先生：是啊，你們銷售部代表了公司的形象。
王先生：而且任何失誤都可能會害我們失去重要客戶。
孫先生：是的。
王先生：但是就個人而言，我喜歡休閒服。休閒服比西裝舒服得多。
孫先生：是啊。我們研發部允許我們在辦公室裡穿休閒服就好。
王先生：有時我真的很羨慕你們。
孫先生：這只是因為我們在實驗室裡工作，不需要與客戶談判。
王先生：這樣說也是啦。

Dialogue ❹ 商務休閒裝 🔊 *Track 076*

💬 在公司聽到小道消息，就趕快找個應該知情的人，問問看到底是不是真的吧！像凱西一樣，問一句：「**Is that true?**」（是真的嗎？）

● ●

Kathy: I hear that our company will allow us to wear casual clothes if we don't have to meet any clients. Is that true?

Susan: Yes, the board will announce the decision (this Friday).

Kathy: That's really good news.

Susan: I agree with you. It is so boring to wear a suit every day.

Kathy: How do you define casual clothes in the business setting? Are jeans okay?

Susan: I don't think so. Things like jeans are too casual.

Kathy: What about pants and a polo shirt?

Susan: They are both okay. By the way, we'd better keep a spare suit at the workplace.

Kathy: Why?

Susan: Just in case.

★全文中畫 ⬤ 色塊的地方，可以依自己的狀況套入不同的名字、公司名、職稱、學校名等等。

中文翻譯4

凱西：我聽說，如果不需要會見客戶，公司將會允許我們穿休閒服上班。這是真的嗎？

蘇珊：是啊。這個禮拜五董事會將宣佈這個決定。

凱西：這真是個好消息。

蘇珊：我也這麼覺得。天天穿正式服裝上班真無聊。

凱西：妳覺得什麼是工作場合穿的休閒服？牛仔褲可以嗎？

蘇珊：我覺得不行，牛仔褲這種衣服太隨意了。

凱西：那長褲和Polo衫呢？

蘇珊：這些可以。順帶一提，我們最好在公司準備一套正式服裝。

凱西：為什麼？

蘇珊：以防萬一囉。

Dialogue ❺ 辦公室服裝 ◀ *Track 077*

就算是好久不見的好朋友，如果要忽然問到人家工作上的事情，還是會需要拘謹一點點。所以琳達在問問題時，還先禮貌地問了一句：「我能問妳一些問題嗎？」

Linda: Long time no see. How have you been?

Kathy: Fine. What about you? I hear you got a job.

Linda: Yes! It is my first job after graduation. May I ask you some questions?

Kathy: Okay, hope I can help.

Linda: Actually, I don't know what to wear besides a suit at work.

Kathy: Does your company have any specific requirements?

Linda: I don't think we do.

Kathy: Corporate casual clothes are okay.

Linda: What are those?

Kathy: Clothes like (pants and polo shirts) are okay, but (jeans and T-shirts) are forbidden.

Linda: Okay, I see. Thank you.

Kathy: I'm glad I could help.

★全文中畫 ⬭ 色塊的地方，可以依自己的狀況套入不同的名字、公司名、職稱、學校名等等。

現在是不是回想起來了呢？

forbidden 被禁止的

forbid是個動詞，是「禁止」的意思，forbidden就是它的相關形容詞，形容「被禁止的」。例如《哈利波特》系列小說中，提到霍格華茲魔法學院旁有座「禁忌森林」，就叫做Forbidden Forest。

中文翻譯5

琳達：好久不見。妳最近怎麼樣？
凱西：還好。妳呢？我聽說妳找到工作了。
琳達：是的。這是我畢業後的第一份工作。我能問妳一些問題嗎？
凱西：可以啊，希望我能幫得上忙。
琳達：事實上，我不知道在公司除了穿正式服裝外，還能穿什麼。
凱西：那妳們公司有具體的著裝要求嗎？
琳達：我覺得沒有。
凱西：商務休閒裝也可以。
琳達：商務休閒裝指什麼？
凱西：像長褲和Polo衫之類的可以穿，牛仔褲和T恤就不行。
琳達：好，我知道了。謝謝。
凱西：不客氣。

Dialogue ❻ 工作時的打扮 ◀ *Track 078*

💬 當要「罵」或「提醒」下屬一些事情時，可以參考對話中的作法，把他叫到
自己的辦公室來私下說，而不是當著大家的面罵他，這樣不是很好的作法。

Rachel: Linda, come to my office please.

Linda: Okay, I'm coming.

Rachel: Linda, how are the preparations for our commercial party going?

Linda: Great. Everything is going well.

Rachel: Okay. Linda, you've only worked here for one month and I appreciate
your attitude. But there is one problem I'd like to talk to you about.

Linda: What is it?

Rachel: I think it is inappropriate to wear shiny earrings at the office.

Linda: Sorry, I bought them the other day and I didn't think too much of it.

Rachel: It doesn't matter. I just want you to know your earrings may distract
others' attention while working. But to tell you the truth, they are very
beautiful.

Linda: Thank you. I will keep that in mind.

★全文中畫 ● 色塊的地方，可以依自己的狀況套入不同的名字、公司名、職稱、學校名等等。

中文翻譯6

瑞秋：琳達，請到我辦公室來一下。

琳達：好的，我現在就來。

瑞秋：琳達，我們的商務酒會準備得怎麼樣了？

琳達：很好，一切順利。

瑞秋：好的。琳達，妳才來一個月，我很欣賞妳的態度，但是有個問題我想和妳談
談。

琳達：什麼問題？

瑞秋：我覺得在辦公室戴閃亮的耳環很不合適。

琳達：對不起，我前幾天才買的，我沒考慮那麼多。

瑞秋：沒關係。我只是想讓妳知道，工作的時候妳的耳環可能會分散別人的注意力。
不過老實說，妳的耳環很漂亮。

琳達：謝謝。我會注意的。

Dialogue ❶ 請求擔任獨家代理 ◀ *Track 079*

💬 在見對自己公司還不熟悉的客戶時，恰當的作法就是把和公司相關的介紹、數據等重要資訊全部整理好，對方一要求要看，馬上能拿出來，絕對會讓他的印象加分。

• •

Kathy: Nice to meet you. I'm Kathy from ABB Company.

Susan: Nice to meet you, too. I'm Susan, the Marketing Manager of CBN Company.

Kathy: Our company wants to act on a sole agency of your garment products.

Susan: Could you give me some general information on your company first?

Kathy: Okay. We act on a sole agency basis for a number of companies, and we specialize in textiles and garments.

Susan: So you must have lots of sales experience in the field of garments?

Kathy: Yes, our company has been in this industry for about 10 years. We are confident you will be satisfied with our service.

Susan: I need some data on the potential market for our products.

Kathy: Actually our company has already prepared a market study. Here you are.

Susan: Wow, I'm really impressed.

★全文中畫 ⬤ 色塊的地方，可以依自己的狀況套入不同的名字、公司名、職稱、學校名等等。

中文翻譯1

凱西：很高興見到妳。我是ABB公司的凱西。
蘇珊：我也很高興見到妳。我是蘇珊，CBN公司的行銷經理。
凱西：本公司想獨家代理貴公司的成衣製品。
蘇珊：可以先簡單介紹一下貴公司嗎？
凱西：好的。本公司擔任多家公司的獨家代理，專營紡織品和成衣。
蘇珊：所以說你們有很多銷售成衣的經驗了？
凱西：是的，本公司在這行有約十年的經驗。我們相信貴公司會滿意我們的服務的。
蘇珊：我想要一些有關我們產品潛在市場的資料。
凱西：事實上，本公司已經做了市場調查。請看。
蘇珊：哇，很不錯呢。

Dialogue ❷ 獲得獨家代理權 (1) 🔊 *Track 080*

如果公司有尾牙、餐會等等，可以邀請可能要長期合作的客戶來參加，鞏固彼此之間的合作關係，如以下對話中所示。

Kathy: Nice to see you again. After we analyzed the market research data, we think you've clearly identified the potential market for our products.

Linda: As you know, silk goods are more and more popular in America , but not many stores offer them. We hope to meet this growing demand with your high quality goods.

Kathy: Your data identified it very clearly. I think we should discuss the contract next week . What do you think?

Linda: No problem. I will draft it up and deliver it to you next week .

Kathy: Okay. By the way, our company is hosting a dinner party this evening . Would you like to come?

Linda: I'd love to.

★全文中畫 色塊的地方，可以依自己的狀況套入不同的名字、公司名、職稱、學校名等等。

draft up 擬草稿

在開始寫正式報告、文章、講稿等等前，先起的那個草稿叫做「draft」，而擬
出一個draft的動作就稱為draft up。

中文翻譯2

凱西：很高興再次見到妳。分析了市場調查資料後，我們認為你們顯然已經為我們的
　　　產品找到了潛在市場。

琳達：如妳所知，絲綢製品在美國越來越受歡迎，但出售絲綢製品的商店並不多。我
　　　們希望用你們高品質的產品來滿足市場不斷增長的需求。

凱西：你們的資料已經把這點說得很清楚了。我想我們下個禮拜應該探討合約的內
　　　容。妳意下如何？

琳達：沒問題。我先起草稿，下星期送給妳看。

凱西：好的。對了，我們公司今晚有要辦一場晚餐會。妳願意來嗎？

琳達：我很願意去。

Dialogue ③ 獲得獨家代理權 (2) ◀€*Track 081*

注意凱西在此段對話中所說的「**That sounds reasonable**」（這聽起來很
合理）。兩方議價達到共識時，這是非常好用的句子。

Mr. Wang: Could you tell me a little bit about your company?

Kathy: Sure. We act on a sole agency basis for a number of manufacturers. We
specialize in textiles and garments .

Mr. Wang: So you must have a lot of experience in this field.

Kathy: Yes, our company has accumulated much experience over the years.

Mr. Wang: We'd like to cooperate with your company, but we think your
agency's fees are too high. Can you lower them?

Kathy: Due to the financial crisis, if we lower the agency's fees, there would be
little profit.

Mr. Wang: But if we could set the price comparatively low, there will be more
consumers.

Kathy: That sounds reasonable. I think we can give you another 2% off, so 10% is the bottom line.

Mr. Wang: Okay, we look forward to cooperating with you.

Kathy: So do we. Thank you.

★全文中畫 ⬤ 色塊的地方，可以依自己的狀況套入不同的名字、公司名、職稱、學校名等等。

現在是不是回想起來了呢？

comparatively 相對地

這個副詞指「和其他人比起來比較……」，例如要說「今天的溫度和其他天比起來比較低」，就可以說：The temperature today is comparatively low.

中文翻譯3

王先生：妳能簡單介紹一下貴公司嗎？
凱　西：好的。本公司擔任多個廠家的獨家代理，專營紡織品和成衣。
王先生：所以妳們在這一行有很多經驗了。
凱　西：是的。本公司這幾年積累了很多經驗。
王先生：我們想和貴公司合作，可是我們認為妳們的代理費用很高，能降低一些嗎？
凱　西：由於這次的金融危機，如果我們降低代理費的話，就沒有什麼利潤了。
王先生：但如果我們定價相對較低的話，就會贏得更多的消費者。
凱　西：有道理。我想我們可以給妳再打折2%，所以九折是底線了。
王先生：好的。我們很期待和貴公司合作。
凱　西：我們也很期待。謝謝。

Dialogue ❹ 申請擔任代理 ◀ *Track 082*

💬 在和客戶談合作前，不但要先做功課，瞭解自己公司相關的資訊，也要先瞭解對方公司相關的資訊，說出來會讓對方很驚喜，對你們印象加分。

Kathy: Our company is very interested in your products.

Susan: How long have you been in the clothing field?

Kathy: Around 3 years.

Susan: Can you introduce your company briefly?

Kathy: Sure! In fact our company acts as agent for around (6) brands, including (ONLY) and (ETAM).

Susan: You really are experienced! What do you think of our products? Have you conducted market research?

Kathy: I think your design is very modern and casual. Our study shows your brand attracts consumers between the ages of (20 and 30).

Susan: You've really done some in-depth research.

Kathy: Yes, I recommend your brand be marketed in (affluent but small) cities.

Susan: Give me some time to discuss it with our sales representatives. I will inform you after we make a decision.

★全文中畫 ⬭ 色塊的地方，可以依自己的狀況套入不同的名字、公司名、職稱、學校名等等。

現在是不是回想起來了呢？

in-depth 深度的

深入的談話叫做in-depth conversation，深入的知識叫做in-depth knowledge，深入的面試叫做in-depth interview。

中文翻譯4

凱西： 本公司對你們的產品很感興趣。

蘇珊： 你們從事服裝業多久了？

凱西： 大約3年。

蘇珊： 妳能簡單介紹一下貴公司嗎？

凱西： 當然可以。實際上本公司代理了包括ONLY、ETAM等在內的大約6個品牌。

蘇珊： 你們很有經驗呢！那你們是怎麼看我們產品的？有做過市場調查嗎？

凱西： 我認為你們的設計很時尚，也很休閒。我們的研究指出，貴公司的品牌適合年齡20歲到30歲之間的顧客。

蘇珊： 妳們確實做了一些深入的調查。

凱西： 是的。我建議貴公司的品牌應該要引進一些富裕的小城市。

蘇珊： 給我一點時間，我要跟我們的銷售代表們商量一下。等我們有結論後我會通知妳。

Dialogue ❺ 拒絕對方擔任代理 ◀₹ *Track 083*

　　對方拒絕和你合作嗎？也別氣餒，尤其絕不能表現出不開心的樣子。像對話中的琳達一樣，問對方是否可以過段時間再找他談談，就是個為未來合作鋪路的好方法。

● ●

Kathy: How long have you worked in this field?

Linda: Actually our company was established this year and we don't have much experience.

Kathy: Okay, did you conduct a market research?

Linda: We haven't yet, but we will later.

Kathy: What do you think of our products?

Linda: I think you have good quality linens, and your past publicity efforts were successful. I think your goods will have many consumers.

Kathy: Thank you, but I'm afraid we need another agency.

Linda: Can you tell me the reason?

Kathy: I think your company lacks experience and you are poorly prepared. I don't think we can do any business this time.

Linda: I'm so sorry you feel this way. May I approach you at a later date?

Kathy: Of course. Give us a call next year.

★全文中畫 ⬤ 色塊的地方，可以依自己的狀況套入不同的名字、公司名、職稱、學校名等等。

中文翻譯5 ●

凱西：你們在這個行業工作多久了？

琳達：實際上本公司今年才成立，所以沒有太多經驗。

凱西：好吧，那你們做市場調查了嗎？

琳達：還沒有，但過一陣子我們會做的。

凱西：妳覺得我們的產品怎麼樣？

琳達：我認為你們的亞麻織品品質很好，之前的宣傳也很成功。我想你們的產品會有很多顧客的。

凱西：謝謝。但恐怕我們需要別家代理商。

琳達：能告訴我原因嗎？

凱西：我覺得你們公司缺少經驗，而且準備得也不夠充分。我認為我們這次還不能合作。

琳達：讓妳這麼想，我很遺憾。過陣子可以再找妳洽談看看嗎？

凱西：當然可以。明年再打電話給我們吧。

Dialogue ❻ 試行合作 ◀Track 084

雖然被對方拒絕了，但可能還有轉機！像王先生明明都被對方說「下次吧」，還不死心地說「試行合作怎樣？」真是生意人的榜樣。

Mr. Zhou: Hello, Mr. Wang . I'm Zhou from ABB Company .

Mr. Wang: Oh, hello. I was waiting for your call.

Mr. Zhou: Thank you for your email suggesting that we grant you an exclusive contract for our goods, but I regret to say that our company doesn't think it is the proper time.

Mr. Wang: Why do you say so?

Mr. Zhou: There isn't any advertisement of our goods in your region, so not many consumers know our product.

Mr. Wang: What about a trial run?

Mr. Zhou: That could work.

Mr. Wang: If the turnover is high, then we could re-negotiate the contract.

Mr. Zhou: Okay, I'll be looking forward to hearing back from you.

Mr. Wang: Thank you.

★全文中畫 ⬤ 色塊的地方，可以依自己的狀況套入不同的名字、公司名、職稱、學校名等等。

中文翻譯6

周先生：你好，王先生。我是ABB公司的小周。

王先生：你好，我一直在等你的電話。

周先生：謝謝你寄郵件，建議我們授權貴公司做我們產品的獨家代理。但很抱歉，本公司認為現在時機不合適。

王先生：為什麼這麼說呢？

周先生：我們沒有在貴地區做廣告，所以並沒有太多的顧客瞭解我們的產品。

王先生：那試行合作怎麼樣？

周先生：這樣可以。

王先生：如果營業額很高的話，我們就可以重新談一下合約的內容。

周先生：好，期待你的回覆。

王先生：謝謝。

Dialogue ❼ 同意對方擔任代理 🔊 *Track 085*

💬 對話中，凱西雖然還是答應了對方可能可以打折，但她卻裝出一副很為難的樣子，說：「這很難耶」，以讓對方覺得自己為他犧牲很大，這是個技巧性的作法。

Kathy: After we analyze the relative marketing data, we'd like to hire you as our agent.

Mr. Wang: That's great. Thank you.

Kathy: Let's discuss the details now.

Mr. Wang: Okay. Actually our company thinks your price is a little high. Could you lower it?

Kathy: This is a difficult issue, because all of the raw material prices have increased. We'd have to raise the price, too.

Mr. Wang: If we order a large number of your goods, can you lower it then?

Kathy: That depends. Maybe we could give you 10% off instead of 8%.

Mr. Wang: Okay. We were wondering if you could allow our engineer to attend your training courses regularly.

Kathy: No problem. Here is the draft version of our contract. You can read it to see if we need to make any amendments.

Mr. Wang: Okay. Let me have a look.

★全文中畫 ⬤ 色塊的地方，可以依自己的狀況套入不同的名字、公司名、職稱、學校名等等。

凱　　西：我們分析了相關的市場資料後，想請你們做我們的代理商。

王先生：太好了，謝謝。

凱　　西：我們現在討論一下細節問題吧。

王先生：好的。事實上，本公司認為你們的定價有點高。你們能降價嗎？

凱　　西：這是個很困難的事情，因為所有原料都漲價了，我們也不得不跟著漲價。

王先生：如果我們大批訂購的話，你們能降價嗎？

凱　　西：視情況而定。也許我們可以把原定的九二折改成九折。

王先生：好吧。我們希望你們可以讓我們的工程師定期參加你們的培訓課。

凱　　西：沒問題。這是我們的合約草稿。你看一下是否需要其他補充。

王先生：好的，我看一下。

商務小常識

　　一個產品要打入新興市場，如果不是去當地設分公司，那一開始最重要的就是找當地的代理商協助代理產品銷售，所以又稱為通路商，這裡所謂的客戶就是代理商或是通路商。在聯絡過程中，要先清楚了解當地的國情及民性，例如印度人比較被動，但如果自己與對方有持續性的聯絡，那便是有合作的機會。在與國外客戶接洽時，僅記一件事，那就是「會吵的客戶才是好客戶」。

SOS Unit 16 專利許可談判

Dialogue ❶ 決定進行專利許可談判 🔈 *Track 086*

💬 注意文中蘇珊說的「**Do you have any ideas?**」，指的是「你有什麼好點子嗎？有什麼主意嗎？」，**idea**一定要加**s**，否則整句的意思會變成「你知道這是怎麼回事嗎？」

Kathy: This is our turnover for the year.

Susan: The statistics are favorable.

Kathy: But we have to pay 20% patent fees.

Susan: That's a large percentage.

Kathy: Right. After we pay patent fees, the profits will not be as high as we expected.

Susan: Do you have any ideas?

Kathy: I suggest we prepare a patent negotiation.

Susan: You mean we can buy the patent and then we don't need to pay the fees every year?

Kathy: That's right.

Susan: Okay, but first you'd better prepare a detailed proposal.

★全文中畫 ⬤ 色塊的地方，可以依自己的狀況套入不同的名字、公司名、職稱、學校名等等。

凱西：這是我們今年的營業額。
蘇珊：數據很不錯嘛。
凱西：但是我們還得支付20％的專利費。
蘇珊：佔的比例真不小。
凱西：是啊。在我們支付專利費以後，利潤沒有我們期待的那麼高。
蘇珊：妳有什麼建議嗎？
凱西：我覺得我們應該準備專利權談判。
蘇珊：妳是說我們可以把專利權買下來，然後就不必每年都支付專利費了嗎？
凱西：是的。
蘇珊：可以，但妳最好先準備一份詳細的計畫書。

Dialogue ② 準備專利許可談判 ◀ Track 087

在進行談判之前，對於不瞭解的地方一定要先搞清楚才不會吃虧，所以我們可以看到這段對話中琳達說她在「先做些準備」。

Kathy: Is the paper prepared?

Linda: I haven't finished it yet. I'm still reading the law, rules and regulations we need.

Kathy: It's difficult work.

Linda: Right. As you know, the patent negotiation covers many aspects of the law.

Kathy: Why don't you consult our legal counsel?

Linda: I will see him (tomorrow), but you know... I am not familiar with patent laws, so I want to prepare first.

Kathy: Oh, what's your opinion about this negotiation?

Linda: I think we should do our best in the negotiation, although the patent expenditure might be high.

Kathy: I agree with you. Here are the statistics you need.

Linda: Thank you.

★全文中畫 ⬤ 色塊的地方，可以依自己的狀況套入不同的名字、公司名、職稱、學校名等等。

現在是不是回想起來了呢？

paper 文件

大家一開始學到「paper」這個字的時候，應該都會知道它是「紙」的意思，但其實學術論文、報告、工作用的重要文件也都可以叫做paper。

中文翻譯2

凱西：文件準備好了嗎？
琳達：還沒做完。我還在看一些我們需要的法律、法規和條例。
凱西：這是很艱難的工作呢。
琳達：是啊。妳知道，專利談判會涉及很多法律方面的問題。
凱西：妳為什麼不諮詢我們的法律顧問？
琳達：我明天會找他。但妳知道……我不太懂專利權法，所以我想先做些準備。
凱西：那對於這次談判，妳有什麼看法呢？
琳達：我覺得儘管專利花費很高，但我們應該在談判時盡最大努力。
凱西：我也是這麼想。這是妳需要的資料。
琳達：謝謝。

Dialogue ③ 是否需要專利談判 ◀ *Track 088*

做專利談判之前，不但要回頭看過去的營利收支，也要看「未來」的營利收支可能會是什麼樣子，再下判斷，如對話中所示。

Kathy: What do you think about our patent negotiations?

Mr. Wang: Actually I don't agree with you. The expenditure on the patent will cost us too much.

Kathy: I know, but if we don't buy the patent, we have to pay 20% of our turnover annually as patent fees.

Mr. Wang: Here are our profits in the past 5 years. It has been positive.

Kathy: That's right, but I did further research. Here are the forecast profits for the coming 10 years.

Mr. Wang: Let me have a look.

Kathy: The data indicates the profits will reduce year by year due to the high patent fees. This will be very detrimental to our development.

Mr. Wang: That's true.

Kathy: So what do you think now?

Mr. Wang: Maybe we should plan the negotiation together.

★全文中畫 色塊的地方，可以依自己的狀況套入不同的名字、公司名、職稱、學校名等等。

中文翻譯3

凱　西：對於我們的專利談判，你的想法如何？

王先生：事實上我不贊同妳的看法。購買專利的費用太高了。

凱　西：我知道。但是如果我們不買專利的話，我們每年都得拿出營業額的20%來支付專利費。

王先生：這是我們過去5年的利潤。利潤一直是正的。

凱　西：是的。但是我做了進一步的調查。這是我們未來10年的預計收入。

王先生：我看一下。

凱　西：資料表明，由於高昂的專利費，我們的利潤會逐年降低。這很不利於我們的發展。

王先生：確實是。

凱　西：那麼現在你的看法是？

王先生：也許我們應該一起準備談判的事。

Dialogue ❹ 談判前準備 ◀ *Track 089*

在工作上不懂如何開始，卻又不好意思說自己不會時，不妨試試問一句「Where should we begin?」（我們從哪裡開始好呢？），把決定權推給對方。

Kathy: What do you think of the patent negotiation? Have you made a decision?

Susan: I think the negotiation is necessary. The patent fee is much too expensive!

Kathy: Where should we begin?

Susan: The first thing is to contact our attorney . He can give us some professional advice.

Kathy: Yes, patent trade requires many legal details.

Susan: The next step is to analyze the statistics and decide what price we want to pay.

Kathy: I hear their financial standing is not very good, so they may need the capital.

Susan: If that is true, it will be beneficial for us.

Kathy: You mean we'll have an advantage when negotiating the price of the patent?

Susan: That's right, so now I want you to prepare a plan for the negotiation.

★全文中畫 ⬤ 色塊的地方，可以依自己的狀況套入不同的名字、公司名、職稱、學校名等等。

現在是不是回想起來了呢？

attorney 律師

大家或許學過「lawyer」這個字，也是律師的意思。那lawyer和attorney有什麼區別？在美國大家幾乎都混著用，而在英國與一些其他英語系國家則會分得比較清楚。他們認為，lawyer是學過、懂得法律且領有律師執照，但不見得就以當律師為生的人，而attorney是以律師為職的人。

中文翻譯4

凱西：妳怎麼看這次的專利談判？下決定了嗎？

蘇珊：我覺得有必要談判。專利費太高了！

凱西：那我們該從哪裡開始呢？

蘇珊：第一件事是聯繫我們的律師。他能給我們一些專業建議。

凱西：好的，專利買賣會涉及很多法律細節。

蘇珊：下一步是分析資料，然後決定我們願意支付多少費用。

凱西：我聽說他們公司的財務狀況不是很好，所以他們或許需要這筆資金。

蘇珊：如果這是真的，就對我們有利了。

凱西：妳是說我們談判專利價格的時候會有優勢吧？

蘇珊：是的，所以現在我想讓妳準備一份談判的企劃案。

💬 想告訴對方無法降價，可以參考對話中張先生使用的「**we're not in a position to...**」（我們目前的狀態無法……），是個表示「我們也很想要幫你們降價，但因大環境等等諸多理由不得已，所以沒辦法」的推卸責任好用句。

Kathy: Nice to meet you, Mr. Zhang .

Mr. Zhang: Nice to meet you, too. What do you think of the patent price we offer?

Kathy: After we analyzed the relative statistics, we think your price is too high.

Mr. Zhang: I don't think so. The price is based on the market research and our investment in the patent application.

Kathy: We have cooperated with you for about 5 years . Perhaps you could offer us a more preferential price.

Mr. Zhang: I'm afraid we're not in a position to lower the price. What about a fixed patent fee rate?

Kathy: That sounds good, but I need time to think it over.

Mr. Zhang: Okay, I will wait for your reply.

★全文中畫 ⬤ 色塊的地方，可以依自己的狀況套入不同的名字、公司名、職稱、學校名等等。

中文翻譯5 ●●●●●●●●

凱　西：很高興見到你，張先生。

張先生：我也很高興見到妳。我們報的專利價格你們覺得如何？

凱　西：在分析了相關的資料後，我們認為你們的出價太高了。

張先生：我不這麼認為。這個價格是根據市場調查和我們在專利應用上的投資，才決定出來的。

凱　西：我們已經合作快5年了。或許，你們可以給我們一個更優惠的價格。

張先生：我們恐怕不能降價了。採用固定的專利費率怎麼樣？

凱　西：聽起來不錯，但是我得考慮一下。

張先生：好的，那就等妳的回覆。

Dialogue ❻ 專利許可談判 (2) ◀€*Track 091*

💬 如同對話中的宋先生，沒有馬上要求對方回應，而是說「你可以考慮一下」，是個在協商時不錯的作法，可以參考看看。

• •

Susan: Good to see you again, Mr. Song.

Mr. Song: It's great to see you, too.

Susan: We received the price list of the patent you offered last week. After we discussed it, we decided we can't accept your asking price.

Mr. Song: The price we offer is quite reasonable.

Susan: Your price is higher than we expected.

Mr. Song: If you think this price is unacceptable, we can offer you a fixed rate on the patent fees.

Susan: That seems reasonable.

Mr. Song: Here is the rate. You can think it over.

Susan: Okay, I will call you after we make a decision.

★全文中畫　　色塊的地方，可以依自己的狀況套入不同的名字、公司名、職稱、學校名等等。

現在是不是回想起來了呢？

think it over 好好想想

反覆認真思考一件事可說「think it over」。相關的說法還有think ahead（未雨綢繆）、think through（想清楚）、think back（回想）等。

中文翻譯6 •

蘇　珊：宋先生，很高興又見到你。

宋先生：我也很高興見到妳。

蘇　珊：上個禮拜我們收到了你們提供的專利報價單。討論後，我們認為不能接受你們的報價。

宋先生：我們的報價是很合理的。

蘇　珊：你們的價格還是高於我們的預期。

宋先生：如果你們覺得這個不能接受，那我們可以提供一個固定的專利費率。

蘇　珊：這似乎很合理。

宋先生：這是費率，你們可以考慮一下。

蘇　珊：好的，有結果後我會打電話通知你。

商務小常識

專利權談判應該分為申明價值、創造價值和克服障礙三個步驟。

(1)申明價值：此階段為談判的初級階段，談判雙方彼此應充分溝通各自的利益需求，申明能夠滿足對方需求的方法與優勢所在。

(2)創造價值：此階段為談判的中級階段，雙方彼此溝通，往往申明了各自的利益所在，瞭解了對方的實際需要。

(3)克服障礙：談判的障礙一般來自於兩個方面，一個是談判雙方彼此利益存在衝突；另一個是談判者自身在決策程式上存在障礙。此階段就要談判解決這兩個障礙。

Dialogue ❶ 決定談判 🔊 *Track 092*

談判失敗的話，還要有備案，所以這個對話中琳達提到她又找了三家公司可以合作，難怪凱西要稱讚她做得好。

● ●

Kathy: This is our net profit for this year and these are the other sales figures.

Linda: The figures are not so positive.

Kathy: No, due to the rise of the raw material prices and the financial crisis, our profit didn't reach the level we expected before.

Linda: Do you have any ideas?

Kathy: Yes, I think we should arrange a negotiation with our raw material supplier . The prices they offer are unreasonable.

Linda: If they could reduce the prices, our profit next year may reach the set goal.

Kathy: What will we do if the negotiation fails?

Linda: We may change to another company. In fact, I know 3 competing companies, who can also provide us with the raw materials.

Kathy: You did a really good job.

Linda: Thank you.

★全文中畫 ⬤ 色塊的地方，可以依自己的狀況套入不同的名字、公司名、職稱、學校名等等。

net profit 淨利

營業收入減掉成本與營業所花費用，就是「淨利」了。

中文翻譯1

凱西：這是我們今年的淨利潤，這些是其他銷售資料。

琳達：數字不是很樂觀。

凱西：是的，因為原料價格上漲和金融危機，我們的利潤沒有達到之前期望的水準。

琳達：妳有什麼建議嗎？

凱西：有，我想我們應該和原料供應商安排一次談判。他們的報價不太合理。

琳達：如果他們能降價的話，我們明年的利潤可能就達得到既定目標。

凱西：如果談判失敗，我們該怎麼辦？

琳達：我們可以換一家公司合作。事實上，我知道三家同類型的公司，他們也可以賣給我們原料。

凱西：妳做得很好。

琳達：謝謝。

Dialogue ❷ 談判沒有結果 (1) ◀ *Track 093*

像對話中凱西這樣直接把可以接受的底線（**bottom line**）說清楚，是在談判時幫助達成共識的一個好方法。

Kathy: I received your price list and think your price is a little too high.

Anna: These are our latest products with added features and improved performance.

Kathy: We want a 20% discount off the original price.

Anna: I'm afraid we cannot accept this.

Kathy: Actually your competitors have offered a reasonable price.

Anna: Our product is famous for its good quality.

Kathy: I know. What about 10% off? This is the bottom line for us.

Anna: How much will you order?

Kathy: It depends on the final price you offer.

Anna: Okay, I need some time to think it over.

★全文中畫 ⬤ 色塊的地方，可以依自己的狀況套入不同的名字、公司名、職稱、學校名等等。

中文翻譯2 ▸▸▸

- 凱西：我收到妳們的報價單了，但是我認為妳們的價格偏高。
- 安娜：這是我們的最新產品，增加了一些功能，性能也提高了。
- 凱西：我們希望以原價打八折。
- 安娜：我們恐怕不能接受。
- 凱西：事實上，你們的競爭對手已經提供了一個合理的價格。
- 安娜：我們的產品以品質優異著稱。
- 凱西：我知道。九折怎麼樣？這是我們可以接受的底線了。
- 安娜：你們想訂購多少呢？
- 凱西：這要看你們最後的價格。
- 安娜：好吧，我需要一些時間考慮一下。

Dialogue ❸ 談判沒有結果 (2) 🔊 *Track 094*

💬 像此段對話中，凱西直接說「如果價格合適，我們馬上就可以下單唷」，是個讓對方動心的好方法，因為大家都希望你下訂單。

Kathy: We can't accept the price for your product. It is too high.

Mr. Zhang: The price is based on the relative profits . It's reasonable.

Kathy: If we buy at this price, it will be hard to sell.

Mr. Zhang: These items are popular on the international market.

Kathy: I still can't accept your price. Can you reduce a little?

Mr. Zhang: You know the price for this commodity has gone up a lot in the last few months.

Kathy: If the price is favorable, we can book an order right away.

Mr. Zhang: How much will you need?

Kathy: It depends on your price.

Mr. Zhang: Okay, let me think about it.

★全文中畫 ⬤ 色塊的地方，可以依自己的狀況套入不同的名字、公司名、職稱、學校名等等。

凱　西：我們不能接受你們產品的定價。價格太高了。
張先生：這個價格是根據相關的利潤而定的,很合理。
凱　西：如果我們以這個價格買入的話,是很難出售的。
張先生：這些產品在國際市場很受歡迎。
凱　西：我還是不能接受你們的價格,能低一點嗎?
張先生：妳知道,這幾個月來,這種商品的價格上漲了很多。
凱　西：如果價格合理的話,我們可以馬上下訂單。
張先生：妳需要多少呢?
凱　西：這取決於你們的價格。
張先生：好吧,讓我考慮一下。

Dialogue 4 談判成功 (1) ◀Track 095

這段對話最後,凱西說:「**We are waiting for your reply**」(我們在等你回覆),雖然並沒有直接說出催促的話,但意思很明顯,就是「快點回答喔,我們可是在等唷」。

Kathy: This is our latest product price list. Have a look.

Mr. Liu: Do you have any samples of the new product?

Kathy: Yes. Compared with the original model, it can save 15% more energy.

Mr. Liu: I'm afraid your price is still a little high.

Kathy: But our price is realistic and based on reasonable profit margins.

Mr. Liu: We have done business with you for about 10 years . Could you reduce your price?

Kathy: As you know, our products are famous for their good quality, but if you could place a substantial order, we can reduce our price by 5% .

Mr. Liu: Let me think it over.

Kathy: This is the lowest price we can offer. We are waiting for your reply.

Mr. Liu: Okay, I will call you as soon as possible.

★全文中畫 ⬤ 色塊的地方,可以依自己的狀況套入不同的名字、公司名、職稱、學校名等等。

現在是不是回想起來了呢？

realistic 實際的

realistic指的是「實際的、辦得到的」的意思，而如果是「不切實際的」、「絕對辦不到的」事情，就會以unrealistic來形容。

中文翻譯4

凱　西：這是我們最新的產品報價單。您參考一下。

劉先生：妳有新產品的樣品嗎？

凱　西：有。和原有的型號相比，新產品可以多節省15% 的能源。

劉先生：我覺得你們的價格仍然有點高。

凱　西：但是這個價格很實在，而且是以合理的利潤為基礎的。

劉先生：我們已經合作差不多10年了，你們能算便宜一點嗎？

凱　西：就你所知，我們的產品以高品質著稱。但是如果您的訂貨量大的話，我們可以打九五折。

劉先生：讓我考慮一下。

凱　西：這是我們所能報的最低價了，我們等您回覆。

劉先生：好的，我會儘快回電話給妳的。

Dialogue ❺ 談判成功 (2) ◀€*Track 096*

人家踢爆你說你們公司賣得比人家貴，你該怎麼辦？像此對話中凱西的作法，說「因為我們品質比較好」，就很聰明。

Kathy: This is our price list. Here you are.

Linda: Your price has gone up a lot this year. Could you lower it?

Kathy: Actually our price is reasonable, compared with that on the international market.

Linda: I'm afraid I don't agree with you. Your competitor's quotation is lower.

Kathy: You should take quality into consideration. Our merit is high quality .

Linda: But if we buy at this price, it will be hard to make any sales.

Kathy: The price of raw material rose last year, so we have to raise the price, but we can offer you 20% off. This is the bottom line.

Linda: I think this price is reasonable. I can make an order right away.

Kathy: Okay. We will dispatch the goods as soon as possible.

Linda: Thank you.

★全文中畫 ⬤ 色塊的地方，可以依自己的狀況套入不同的名字、公司名、職稱、學校名等等。

中文翻譯5

凱西：這是我們的報價單。請看。

琳達：妳們的價格今年上漲了很多，能便宜一點嗎？

凱西：事實上，我們的價格與國際市場的價格相比，還是很合理的。

琳達：我不認同妳的看法。妳們的對手的報價比妳們還低。

凱西：妳們應該考慮到產品品質。良好的品質是我們的優勢。

琳達：但是如果我們以這個價格買入的話，很難進行銷售。

凱西：去年原物料漲價了，所以我們不得不提高價格，但是我們可以打八折給妳。這是最低價了。

琳達：我覺得這個價格還算合理。我馬上就可以下訂單。

凱西：好的。我們會儘快送貨給您。

琳達：謝謝。

Dialogue ❻ 談判成功 (3) 🔊 *Track 097*

💬 「跟國際上相比，我們的價格並不算高」也是個很好的說法，因為大家聽到「國際」就會覺得聽起來好像很有道理。

Kathy: Can you reduce your price?

Mary: I'm afraid we can't. Our price is reasonable as compared with that on the international market.

Kathy: It is difficult for us to sell the goods, as your price is so high.

Mary: The price for this commodity is $25 per pound on the international market, so our price is not too high. Besides, this article is our best seller.

Kathy: If your price is favorable, we can book an order right away.

Mary: How much do you want to order?

Kathy: At least 1 ton.

Mary: We can give you a (10%) discount. What do you think?

Kathy: Okay, that sounds good.

Mary: Let's sign the contract now.

★全文中畫 ⬤ 色塊的地方，可以依自己的狀況套入不同的名字、公司名、職稱、學校名等等。

現在是不是回想起來了呢？

best seller 最暢銷的商品

也可省略中間的空格，說bestseller。像在美國的小說封面上，我們就常會看到有人寫「這本書是哪家哪家報紙的bestseller」。

中文翻譯6

凱西：你們的價格可以低一點嗎？

瑪麗：恐怕不行。我們的價格和國際市場的價格相比，還是很合理的。

凱西：你們的價格太高了，這樣我們很難銷售。

瑪麗：這種商品在國際市場的售價是每磅25美元，所以我們的價格並不算太高。況且，這也是我們最暢銷的商品。

凱西：如果你們價格合理的話，我們可以馬上下訂單。

瑪麗：妳要訂多少？

凱西：至少一噸。

瑪麗：我們可以給妳打九折。妳看怎麼樣？

凱西：好的，聽起來還不錯。

瑪麗：我們現在簽合約吧。

Dialogue ❼ 談判成功 (4)　🔊 *Track 098*

💬 … 和對方達成成功的談判後，可以如本篇對話中的凱特一樣，多貼心地問一句：「你們有沒有什麼特別擔心的事？」

Kathy: The price you quoted us is a little too high. I want a (20%) discount.

Cate: I'm afraid we can't give you that kind of reduction. Our price is reasonable.

Kathy: If your price is favorable, we can make an order right now.

Cate: How much will you order?

Kathy: About　1 ton . Can you reduce the price for us?

Cate: We could offer you　10%　off, but we will not pay the shipping fees.

Kathy: Okay, we could pay after the goods arrive.

Cate: Do you have any concerns?

Kathy: Actually we are quite in need of the goods, so if the shipment is too late, we'll withdraw the contract.

Cate: Don't worry. We will deliver the goods as soon as possible.

★全文中畫 ● 色塊的地方，可以依自己的狀況套入不同的名字、公司名、職稱、學校名等等。

中文翻譯7

凱西：你們的報價有點太高了。我希望能打八折。

凱特：我們恐怕不能給妳那個折扣。我們的價格很合理了。

凱西：如果你們能給優惠價格的話，我們馬上就可以下訂單。

凱特：你們會訂多少？

凱西：大約1噸吧。你們可以便宜一點嗎？

凱特：我們可以打九折給妳，但是我們不會負擔運費。

凱西：好的，貨到之後我們會支付運費的。

凱特：有什麼特別擔心的事嗎？

凱西：事實上我們很需要這批貨物，所以如果貨送得太晚的話，我們將會終止合約。

凱特：別擔心，我們會儘快送貨的。

商務小常識

　　雖然說談價格是比較困難的一件事，但是經過努力而成功的例子也相當多。當然，在談判中必須要遵循一些技巧，才能讓談判更順利的進行。

　　(1) 列明客戶公司資料，越詳細越好。

　　(2) 掌握國內主要競爭對手名單以及老闆名字。

　　(3) 對方關注的是什麼，也就是他為什麼要購買該產品，是自用還是轉賣，要考慮相應的對策。

　　(4) 對自己的產品、技術特色一定要非常熟悉。

　　(5) 不要和客戶糾纏於自己的產品和同類產品的價格比較。避免這種比較，要岔開話題，或者直接說「沒有可比性」。

SOS Unit 18 品牌

Dialogue ① 品牌名稱的作用 🔊 *Track 099*

💬 明明就是天經地義的事，同事卻跟你說「我不太懂耶」……這時，可以像凱西一樣，用「Let's say it this way」（我這樣說好了）當開頭，來把事情解釋得更詳細。

● ●

Kathy: We've discussed a lot about the new brand but haven't found a good name for it.

Linda: To tell you the truth, I don't know why we've spent so much time on it.

Kathy: Competition between similar products on today's market is much more fierce than we expected.

Linda: I know that, but can the brand name be of any advantage to our business?

Kathy: Sure. A good brand name is very important for the product.

Linda: I don't quite understand.

Kathy: Let's say it this way. A good brand name is easy to pronounce, recognize and remember, for example Nike and Shell. Almost everyone knows them.

Linda: I never thought of that before. It's really interesting.

Kathy: More than that, an effective brand name can even be regarded as the best advertisement for the product itself.

Linda: You're right. Let's keep working on it.

★全文中畫 ⬤ 色塊的地方，可以依自己的狀況套入不同的名字、公司名、職稱、學校名等等。

be of advantage 有幫助

這是個代表「對某人有幫助、帶來優勢」的片語。用在這個對話中，就表示「品牌名稱對我們的銷售有幫助」的意思。

中文翻譯1

凱西：新品牌的問題我們已經討論很久了，但是還沒找到一個合適的品牌名稱。

琳達：說實話，我不知道為什麼我們在這個問題上花了這麼多時間。

凱西：現在市場上同類商品的競爭，比我們預計的還要激烈得多。

琳達：這個我知道。但是品牌名稱對我們的業務能有什麼幫助嗎？

凱西：當然。一個好的品牌名稱對產品很重要。

琳達：我不是很明白。

凱西：我這樣說好了，一個好的品牌名稱會很好念，也容易辨別和記憶，比如耐吉和殼牌，幾乎所有人都知道。

琳達：這點我以前從來沒想過。真有趣。

凱西：不止這些。一個好的商標名稱甚至可以看成是產品本身最好的廣告。

琳達：說得對。那我們繼續努力吧。

Dialogue ❷ 品牌標誌設計 🔊 *Track 100*

💬 這段對話中，王先生是凱西的老闆，所以他可以說「我好累喔」，但要是你是下屬，可別跟老闆說你思考得很累啊！

Kathy: What about the design of the brand logo? Do you have a suitable one?

Mr. Wang: Not yet. I have spent lots of time looking for a proper one but haven't found it yet.

Kathy: What's the problem? Can't we use the domestic logo?

Mr. Wang: I'm afraid not. This is the first time we have entered the European market and our market report says that our brand isn't accepted well by the local people because of cultural difference.

Kathy: I know. Lenovo Group had to change their brand name when they entered the American market.

Mr. Wang: Yes, so we have to choose a new brand name and logo for the European market.

Kathy: It's worth our while to find a good logo.

Mr. Wang: Yes, but it is not easy. I have been thinking about this all the week. Actually I'm really tired.

Kathy: Let's take a rest. Sleep on it and we'll start fresh in the morning.

Mr. Wang: Okay.

★全文中畫 ● 色塊的地方，可以依自己的狀況套入不同的名字、公司名、職稱、學校名等等。

現在是不是回想起來了呢？

sleep on it 再想想

這個片語不是叫你「睡在上面」，而是說「再考慮一下，至少再想個一個晚上再決定」。

中文翻譯2

凱　西：品牌標誌設計得怎麼樣了？有合適的了嗎？
王先生：還沒有。我已經花了很多時間找合適的標誌，但是還沒找到。
凱　西：有什麼問題嗎？我們不能用國內的標誌嗎？
王先生：恐怕不能。這是我們第一次進入歐洲市場，而且市場報告顯示，由於文化差異，我們的品牌在當地的接受情況不是很好。
凱　西：我知道了。就像聯想集團進入美國市場要改換品牌名稱一樣。
王先生：是的。因此我們不得不為歐洲市場選用新品牌名稱和標誌。
凱　西：花時間選一個好標誌很值得。
王先生：是呀，但不是很容易。這個禮拜以來我一直在思考這事。事實上我真的很累。
凱　西：休息一會兒吧。明天早上再來想這件事。
王先生：好吧。

Dialogue ❸ 品牌推廣 (1) ◀ Track 101

想請對方把事情說得更仔細，你可以像對話中的琳達一樣，說：「Could you go into detail please?」（可以說得詳細些嗎？）

Kathy: What do you think of our new brand?

Linda: I'm satisfied with the design of the logo, but I'm worried about its acceptance in a new market.

Kathy: I'm worried about this, too.

Linda: So do you have any suggestions? What could we do to create brand awareness?

Kathy: I think the company should launch an advertising campaign.

Linda: Could you go into detail please?

Kathy: That is to say we could put ads on television or other media, to acquaint people with our goods.

Linda: What about free samples? We could also consider that too.

Kathy: It is okay. We could combine the two together.

Linda: So I will prepare a plan about the publicity of our new brand, and hand it in in (two) days.

★全文中畫 ⬤ 色塊的地方，可以依自己的狀況套入不同的名字、公司名、職稱、學校名等等。

中文翻譯3

凱西：妳覺得我們的新品牌怎麼樣？
琳達：我很滿意品牌標誌的設計，但是我擔心它在新市場上的接受問題。
凱西：我也在擔心這件事。
琳達：那妳有什麼建議嗎？為了建立品牌知名度，我們應該做些什麼？
凱西：我認為公司應該進行一次廣告宣傳。
琳達：能說清楚一點嗎？
凱西：就是說我們可以在電視或其他媒體上登廣告，讓大眾瞭解我們的產品。
琳達：免費的試用樣品呢？我們也可以考慮這種方法。
凱西：可以的。我們可以把兩者結合起來。
琳達：那麼我會準備一份我們新品牌的宣傳策劃方案，兩天後會把企劃案給妳。

Dialogue ❹ 品牌推廣 (2) 🔊 *Track 102*

當對方說了一句有點籠統的話時，你可以用「**Could you elaborate?**」（可以說得具體一點嗎？）請他跟你講清楚。看看對話中怎麼用的吧！

Kathy: Our new brand didn't go over very well.

David: I can understand it. Well-known brands influence consumers a lot.

Kathy: Exactly. When I choose expensive goods, I will not consider unknown brands, either.

David: So what should we do?

Kathy: This is our second brand and I believe it will be popular.

David: Could you elaborate?

Kathy: Our first brand takes the largest market share in the high-end customers and has a good reputation for its quality, but it's much more expensive for the lower range customers. So we launched our second brand to cater to this segment of customers. What we should do now is inform more customers about it.

David: You mean we could use ads to let people know our second brand?

Kathy: That's it. It will be successful.

David: I think so, too.

★全文中畫 ⬤ 色塊的地方，可以依自己的狀況套入不同的名字、公司名、職稱、學校名等等。

現在是不是回想起來了呢？

ad 廣告

ad是advertisement的縮寫，是「廣告」的意思。現在ad是個你會經常看到的字，因為網路上常有一堆pop-up ads（會跳出來的廣告），所以你也需要ad blockers（擋廣告的程式）幫忙。

中文翻譯4

凱西：我們新品牌的接受度不是很高。

大衛：我可以理解。知名品牌對消費者的影響太大了。

凱西：確實如此，當我買貴重物品的時候，我也不會去考慮不知道的品牌。

大衛：那我們該怎麼做呢？

凱西：這是我們的第二品牌，我相信它會受歡迎的。

大衛：妳能說得明白一點嗎？

凱西：我們的第一品牌在高端客戶群體中佔據了最大的市場份額，並且因為品質優良，而享有很好的聲譽。但是我們的第一品牌對於較低端的消費者來說相對較貴。因此我們創立了第二品牌來滿足這部分消費者的需求。我們現在要做的就是讓更多的顧客知道這個品牌。

大衛：妳的意思是說，我們可以用廣告讓人們瞭解我們的第二品牌？
凱西：是的。這會成功的。
大衛：我也這麼認為。

Dialogue ⑤ 品牌形象 🔊 *Track 103*

💬 注意看看對話中，王先生問：「**What's your problem with the new brand?**」（你對這個新品牌遇到什麼困難？）這聽起來是很正常的一個句子，不過要注意，不能只問「**What's your problem?**」，意思是「你是怎樣？」喔！

Kathy: It is really difficult to create a proper brand name.

Mr. Wang: Yes, I kept on thinking about the right one but failed.

Kathy: I can understand. When consumers are buying something they need, brand is an important factor.

Mr. Wang: Yes, a well-known brand offers good quality and reliable after-sale service.

Kathy: Our brand is well-known domestically. Why do you want to choose another one?

Mr. Wang: This one is for the foreign market. We have to consider different cultural backgrounds.

Kathy: That's right. A good brand name can help push sales.

Mr. Wang: What's your problem with the new brand?

Kathy: I'm trying to combine our company values with the brand but I still can't find a solution.

Mr. Wang: Maybe we should have a meeting with the design department and brainstorm some new ideas.

★全文中畫 ⬤ 色塊的地方，可以依自己的狀況套入不同的名字、公司名、職稱、學校名等等。

中文翻譯5

- 凱　西：確立一個合適的品牌名稱確實很難。
- 王先生：是的。我一直想找一個合適的名稱，但是沒有成功。
- 凱　西：可以理解。當消費者購買產品的時候，品牌是一個很重要的因素。
- 王先生：是的。知名品牌有優良的品質和值得信賴的售後服務。
- 凱　西：我們的品牌在國內市場很有名氣，為什麼你要換呢？
- 王先生：這個是針對國外市場的，我們得考慮不同的文化背景。
- 凱　西：對。好的品牌名稱可以促進銷售量。
- 王先生：妳對這個新品牌有什麼問題？
- 凱　西：我想把我們公司的價值觀和品牌結合在一起，但是還是沒有找到解決方案。
- 王先生：也許我們應該和設計部門一起開個會，大家交流一下想法，想一點新的主意。

商務小常識

　　消費者在購買商品的時候通常會選擇比較熟悉的品牌。因此選擇一個合適的品牌名稱，對任何一家公司來說都是一件很重要的事情。產品銷往多個國家的公司必須決定是使用同一品牌還是不同品牌。因為在一個國家受到歡迎的品牌在其他國家不見得有好的表現，這是由於文化差異所致。有的跨國公司會為了適應地區市場，而採用不同的品牌名稱。有些公司甚至在還沒有生產出產品時就註冊了品牌名稱，為的是防止競爭者使用同樣的名稱。

包裝

Dialogue ❶ 貨物包裝談判 (1) 🔊 *Track 104*

💬 packing也可說packaging，看看這個對話裡面如何使用這個單字吧！出現了很多次。

● ●

Kathy: Now that we have agreed on the price, shall we discuss the packing now?

Harvey: Okay, go ahead.

Kathy: What kind of packing do you plan to use?

Harvey: Actually we haven't decided yet. What's your opinion?

Kathy: I think proper packing is most important.

Harvey: We think so, too. As you know, packing is extremely important for frozen food delivery.

Kathy: What will you do?

Harvey: We plan to use double packing .

Kathy: That sounds good. Do you have a sample?

Harvey: Yes, here you are.

★全文中畫 ⬤ 色塊的地方，可以依自己的狀況套入不同的名字、公司名、職稱、學校名等等。

中文翻譯1

凱西：既然我們已經談妥價格了，現在能談談包裝的事項嗎？

哈威：好的，請說。

凱西：你們想用哪種包裝？

哈威：實際上我們還沒決定。你們有什麼意見？

凱西：我認為妥善包裝非常重要。
哈威：我們也這麼認為。如你們所知，對冷凍食品的運輸來說，包裝是非常重要的。
凱西：你們會怎麼做？
哈威：我們計畫用雙層包裝。
凱西：這聽起來不錯。你們有樣品嗎？
哈威：有，請看。

Dialogue ❷ 貨物包裝談判 (2) ◀️*Track 105*

對話中E.T.A的完整說法是Estimated Time of Arrival（預計到達時間），在和客戶談論時也可以適時穿插這種聽起來很專業的詞語，讓對方印象深刻。

Kathy: Shall we talk about the packing now?

Betty: Okay, go ahead.

Kathy: How will you pack our goods? We pay great attention to the safety of the goods.

Betty: We plan to use double packing : both inner and outer packing to protect your goods.

Kathy: Could you elaborate?

Betty: Shirts are easily wrinkled so we will lay them flat, and use fancy plastic bags as inner packing. We put every 100 pieces into a case and use waterproof paper to keep them intact.

Kathy: That sounds good. By the way, could you deliver the goods as soon as possible?

Betty: Okay, after we pack all the goods, we will deliver them.

Kathy: What is the E.T.A of the goods?

Betty: You should receive the goods by next Friday .

★全文中畫 ⬤ 色塊的地方，可以依自己的狀況套入不同的名字、公司名、職稱、學校名等等。

waterproof 防水的

「-proof」這個字尾表示「防……」的意思，例如「soundproof」是「隔音的」、「bulletproof」是「防彈的」。

中文翻譯2

凱西：我們現在能談一下包裝的事宜嗎？

貝蒂：可以，請說。

凱西：妳們會怎樣包裝我們的貨物呢？我們很關心貨物的安全性。

貝蒂：我們打算用內外兩層包裝，以保證貨物的安全。

凱西：能說得具體一些嗎？

貝蒂：襯衫很容易產生褶皺，我們會把它們平放，用精美的塑膠袋作為內包裝。每100件裝進一個箱子裡，然後再用防水紙保護襯衫。

凱西：聽起來不錯。順便問一下，你們能儘早出貨嗎？

貝蒂：可以，等所有商品都包裝完，我們就出貨。

凱西：貨物預計什麼時候可以到？

貝蒂：下禮拜五之前你們就能收到貨了。

Dialogue ❸ 貨物包裝談判 (3) ◀ *Track 106*

這段對話中，凱西再三強調「如果貨物遲交，我們『有權』取消合約」，使用「有權」（**have the right to**）帶有一點威嚇、警惕的作用，讓對方更清楚知道絕不能遲交。

Kathy: What about your packing?

John: It is very safe. During delivery, goods are at risk of damage. We will try our best to protect the goods.

Kathy: Could you elaborate?

John: Yes, we use outside and inside packing in case of damage.

Kathy: That's good.

John: Within every box, we also use waterproof paper . I'm sure that you will be satisfied with the packing.

Kathy: I saw the sample just now and I am satisfied. By the way, when will you deliver the goods?

John: We plan to ship them this (Friday) and you will receive the goods before next weekend.

Kathy: Okay. We are in need of them soon, so if they can't arrive by the deadline, we have the right to cancel the contract.

John: Don't worry. We will deliver them on time.

★全文中畫 ⬤ 色塊的地方，可以依自己的狀況套入不同的名字、公司名、職稱、學校名等等。

中文翻譯3

凱西：你們的包裝怎麼樣？

約翰：很安全。因為運輸過程中，貨物容易受損，我們會盡最大努力保護貨物的。

凱西：你能說得更具體一些嗎？

約翰：好的，為了防止損壞，我們使用內外雙層包裝。

凱西：那很好。

約翰：在每個盒子裡，我們還使用了防水紙。我確信你們會滿意這種包裝的。

凱西：我剛才看了樣品，確實很滿意。順便問一下，你們什麼時候出貨？

約翰：我們計畫這個禮拜五出貨。最晚下週末你們就可以收到貨。

凱西：好的。因為我們急著需要這批貨，所以如果貨物不能在截止時間之前到達的話，我們有權利取消合約。

約翰：別擔心。我們會按時出貨的。

Dialogue ❹ 產品包裝設計 (1) 🔊 *Track 107*

💬 從這段對話中，我們可以看出李先生一開始不同意凱西的話，卻逐漸被說服。她是如何做到的？仔細看看兩人對話的過程！

Kathy: I don't think our packaging design is very attractive.

Mr. Lee: Why do you say so?

Kathy: Our cosmetics aim for the (office ladies from 30 to 40), who have good taste.

Mr. Lee: I know that, but our goods are famous for their quality.

Kathy: That's right, but the packaging is out of date. I prefer more delicate packaging.

Mr. Lee: That will increase our cost and we will have to increase our price.

Kathy: I know that, but don't forget our customers are people who can afford a relatively high price.

Mr. Lee: You mean our customers are not price-sensitive?

Kathy: That's it. I think a delicate packaging makes us more competitive.

Mr. Lee: I agree with you.

★全文中畫 ⬤ 色塊的地方，可以依自己的狀況套入不同的名字、公司名、職稱、學校名等等。

現在是不是回想起來了呢？

delicate 精美的

除了「精美的」以外，delicate也帶有「脆弱的」的意思，所以如果有人說自己很delicate，別以為他在稱讚自己精美，他可能只是想表達他很容易生病受傷而已。

中文翻譯4

凱　　西：我認為我們的包裝設計不具有吸引力。
李先生：為什麼這樣說呢？
凱　　西：我們的化妝品是針對30到40歲的職業女性，她們很有品味。
李先生：我知道。不過我們的產品向來以品質著稱。
凱　　西：沒錯。但是我們的包裝過時了。我比較想要使用更精緻的包裝。
李先生：那樣會增加我們的成本，這樣一來，我們不得不提高價格。
凱　　西：我知道，但是別忘了我們的顧客有能力支付相對較高的價格。
李先生：妳是說我們的顧客對價格不敏感？
凱　　西：是的。我認為一個精美的包裝會讓我們更具有競爭力。
李先生：我同意妳的說法。

Dialogue ❺ 產品包裝設計 (2) 🔊 *Track 108*

💬 在說服同事時，可以適時使用一些家喻戶曉的實例來讓對方容易瞭解你的觀點。琳達在此對話中說「Think of...」（想想……）就是要對方考慮她即將舉出的例子。

Amy: What do you think of the packaging design?

Linda: To tell you the truth, I don't think it is an appropriate one.

Amy: Nor do I. I hope we could have a more attractive design.

Linda: Think of Coca Cola and its classic bottle design.

Amy: Yes, I am seeking a design like that, but haven't found a powerful one yet.

Linda: Our new eye shadow emphasizes traditional Chinese culture . Why not use china to contain it?

Amy: That sounds like a good idea.

Linda: As for the delivery, we can use double packing to protect our goods. What do you think?

Amy: I think the packaging will attract more customers.

Linda: I hope so.

★全文中畫 ⬤ 色塊的地方，可以依自己的狀況套入不同的名字、公司名、職稱、學校名等等。

現在是不是回想起來了呢？

china 瓷
我們都知道China是中國的意思，但它也可以當作「瓷、瓷器」，第一個字不必大寫。

中文翻譯5
艾咪：妳覺得這個包裝設計怎麼樣？
琳達：說實話，我覺得這種設計不是很合適。
艾咪：我也覺得不合適。我希望我們會有一個更有吸引力的包裝。
琳達：想想可口可樂和它經典的瓶裝設計。

艾咪：是的，我一直在找一個那樣的設計，但是還沒找到很棒的。
琳達：我們新的眼影強調中國傳統文化，為什麼不用瓷器來做容器呢？
艾咪：這個主意真不錯。
琳達：至於運送問題，我們可以使用雙層包裝來保護產品。妳覺得呢？
艾咪：我想這種包裝會吸引更多顧客的。
琳達：希望如此。

Dialogue ❻ 產品包裝設計 (3) ◀ *Track 109*

樂觀地想和同事說「我們沒什麼好擔心的，狀況良好」，可以用下列對話中的「**we are in good shape**」這句話。

Ann: Do you have a marketing plan for our new ice cream sandwich?

Linda: Yes, after the market research, I think we are in good shape. One of our main strengths is the quality of our ice cream, and our market share has been increasing all through last year.

Ann: What do you think of the sales for this summer?

Linda: I think we don't need to worry about the new flavor.

Ann: Why do you think so?

Linda: The statistics show our 5 flavors put into the market as samples are very popular among young people.

Ann: That's good. What about the packaging?

Linda: I'd suggest we improve the packaging. We could package it in gold foil with dark brown lettering to simulate chocolate, and price it 20% higher than our chocolate-covered ice cream bar.

Ann: Sounds good. What about advertisements?

Linda: We haven't decided yet. I will inform you when it's ready.

★全文中畫 ⬤ 色塊的地方，可以依自己的狀況套入不同的名字、公司名、職稱、學校名等等。

現在是不是回想起來了呢？

simulate 模擬

如果有在玩遊戲的人，可能會發現有種類型的遊戲叫做「simulation games」。
這些就是模擬遊戲，像是模擬開飛機啦、模擬城市啦、模擬經營餐廳等等都
是。

中文翻譯6

安：妳對我們新的冰淇淋三明治有什麼行銷計畫嗎？

琳達：有，在做過市場調查以後，我認為我們的經營良好。我們的一個主要優勢是冰
淇淋的品質，同時我們的市場份額去年全年一直在增加。

安：妳覺得這個夏天的銷量會如何呢？

琳達：我想我們不必擔心新口味的問題。

安：為什麼妳會這麼認為？

琳達：資料顯示，我們作為樣品上市的5種口味很受年輕人歡迎。

安：這很好。包裝方面怎麼樣？

琳達：我建議我們應該改進包裝方式。我們要用金箔紙來包裝，上面有深褐色字
母，像是巧克力的顏色，但是定價要比我們的巧克力脆皮冰淇淋貴20%。

安：聽起來不錯。那廣告呢？

琳達：我們還沒決定。等準備好了我會通知你的。

商務小常識

商品的包裝被稱為「無言的推銷員」，是品牌視覺形象設計的一個重
要部分。一項市場調查表明，家庭主婦到超級市場購物時，由於精美包裝
的吸引而購買的商品通常超過預算的45%左右，可見包裝的魅力之大。包
裝設計已成為現代商品生產和行銷最重要的環節之一。

交貨

Dialogue ❶ 交貨談判 (1) 🔊 *Track 110*

💬 要讓步配合客戶，答應一些事務時，也別忘了像文中的露西一樣，加一句「we can't guarantee...」（我們不能擔保……），到時候如果出差錯，還可以說「我們都說過不能擔保了」。

Kathy: Is it possible to ship the products in September ?

Lucy: I don't think we can.

Kathy: Then when can we expect the earliest shipment?

Lucy: By the middle of October , I think.

Kathy: That's too late. You see, November is the peak season for this commodity in our market.

Lucy: We know, but we can't guarantee your goods will arrive in time.

Kathy: We want to point out that if you fail to execute shipment within the time specified, we shall not be able to fulfill the contract with our clients.

Lucy: Don't worry. We will try our best to deliver the goods as soon as possible.

Kathy: Thank you.

Lucy: Not at all. I will inform you when we deliver the goods.

★全文中畫 色塊的地方，可以依自己的狀況套入不同的名字、公司名、職稱、學校名等等。

凱西：可否能在9月份出貨？

露西：我覺得不行。

凱西：那最早什麼時候可以出貨呢？

露西：我覺得要到10月中旬。

凱西：那太晚了。妳知道，在我們這裡，11月是這個商品的銷售旺季。

露西：我們知道，但是我們不能保證你們的貨能及時到達。

凱西：我們必須指出，如果你們不能在規定的時間內出貨，我們將無法與我方客戶履行合約。

露西：別擔心。我們會盡最大的努力儘早出貨的。

凱西：謝謝。

露西：不用謝。出貨後我會通知妳。

Dialogue ❷ 交貨談判 (2) 🔊 *Track 111*

想請合作的公司多為你們出一點力時，可以用對話中的「**Could you do something to...**」（可不可以做點什麼來……），以表達出迫切希望對方幫忙的意思。

Kathy: When can you ship the items?

Lucy: Next Monday at the earliest.

Kathy: Could you do something to speed up the shipment?

Lucy: I'm afraid we can't. Our manufacturers are swamped at the moment.

Kathy: Can they speed up their production? We need the goods urgently.

Lucy: We rearrange their schedule according to our orders almost every day, but there are many more than we could have expected.

Kathy: I understand. The busy season is coming.

Lucy: Yes, this is the busiest time of the year.

Kathy: Well, in that case, there is nothing more to say. When you deliver the goods, please inform me.

Lucy: Okay, I will.

★全文中畫 ⬤ 色塊的地方，可以依自己的狀況套入不同的名字、公司名、職稱、學校名等等。

speed up 加速

加速又稱accelerate。相反地，減速則叫做reduce speed或decelerate。

中文翻譯2 •

凱西：你們什麼時候能出貨？

露西：最早下個禮拜一。

凱西：你們能不能想辦法讓出貨提前？

露西：恐怕沒辦法。現在我們工廠的訂單多得都應付不過來。

凱西：他們能加快生產速度嗎？我們急著需要這批貨。

露西：我們基本上每天都根據訂單調整他們的進度，但是訂單比我們預期的要多出很
　　　多。

凱西：我理解。旺季馬上就到了。

露西：是的，這是全年最忙的時候。

凱西：既然這樣，我就不多說什麼了。你們出貨的時候，請通知我。

露西：好的，我會的。

Dialogue ❸ 催運貨物 (1) ◀ *Track 112*

對話中，凱西表示「若貨物太晚到，就要取消訂單」，但畢竟是天氣因素，
對方也很無辜，所以我們可以看到凱西刻意用了「**I'm sorry to say**」（很抱
歉）、「**will be forced to**」（不得不）等詞語以表達對對方公司的同情。

• •

Linda: Hello, ABB Company, this is Linda. How may I help you?

Kathy: Hello. This is Kathy. It is over two months since we sent the order for
the TV sets, yet we are still waiting for delivery. Is there a problem?

Linda: I see. Let me check... We sent them two weeks ago, they should have
arrived by now.

Kathy: After your delivery, your service staff called me, but I don't know why
they haven't arrived yet.

Linda: I think perhaps the heavy snow storm delayed the delivery. Don't worry.

Kathy: I'm sorry to say that if the goods don't arrive in time, we will be forced to
withdraw the order.

Linda: We can track the trucks with GPS and report their location to you by (fax).

Kathy: Thank you. I will call you if we receive the goods.

Linda: Thank you.

★全文中畫 ⬤ 色塊的地方，可以依自己的狀況套入不同的名字、公司名、職稱、學校名等等。

中文翻譯3

琳達：妳好，這裡是ABB公司，我是琳達。您有什麼需要？

凱西：妳好，我是凱西。兩個月前我們下了電視機的訂單，但是我們還在等待交貨，出什麼問題了嗎？

琳達：我瞭解了，讓我查一下訂單……我們兩個禮拜前就出貨了，它們現在應該到了呀。

凱西：出貨後，你們的客服打電話給我過，但是我不知道為什麼它們還沒到。

琳達：我想可能是暴風雪導致送貨延誤。別擔心。

凱西：很抱歉，但我還是要說，如果貨物不能及時送到，我們會被迫中止訂單。

琳達：我們可以用全球定位系統追蹤訂單，並且將追蹤結果傳真給妳。

凱西：謝謝，如果收到貨我會打電話跟妳說。

琳達：謝謝。

Dialogue ❹ 催運貨物 (2)　🔊 *Track 113*

💬 打電話催運貨物時，對方卻跟你講一堆有的沒的包裝的事，該怎麼把話題拉回正題？可參考這個對話中，凱西一邊稱讚對方的主意很好，一邊卻又馬上說「but are you aware...」（但是你知道嗎……），把話題導入重點。

Kathy: We haven't received your notice of the shipment yet. Is there anything wrong?

Mr. Wang: I'm sorry. The delay is because we changed the packing.

Kathy: What's wrong with it?

Mr. Wang: The original packing allowed more breakage of the (machines) during the shipment, so we decided to take measures to reduce the breakage.

Kathy: What did you do?

Mr. Wang: We finally packed each of the machines in wooden cases supported with soft materials to ensure that the machines would not shift inside the cases.

Kathy: That's a good idea, but are you aware if the machines cannot arrive on time, we have the right to cancel the order according to our contract?

Mr. Wang: We are aware of this. We will deliver them as soon as possible.

Kathy: Thank you so much. We really need the goods urgently!

Mr. Wang: Don't worry. We will inform you the moment we send the items.

★全文中畫 ⬤ 色塊的地方，可以依自己的狀況套入不同的名字、公司名、職稱、學校名等等。

現在是不是回想起來了呢？

shift 移動

大家對shift的印象，很可能是電腦鍵盤上的那個shift鍵對吧！其實在以前還是用打字機的時代，按這個shift鍵會把整排的字「移動」，從小寫變成大寫。也難怪它會叫做shift了！

中文翻譯4

凱　　西：我們還沒有收到你們的出貨通知。出了什麼事嗎？

王先生：很抱歉。出貨延遲是因為我們更換了包裝。

凱　　西：出什麼問題了？

王先生：原本的包裝讓機器在運輸中出現很多破損，因此我們決定採取措施，來降低損壞風險。

凱　　西：你們是怎麼做的？

王先生：我們最後決定用填充了軟材料的木箱包裝，來保證機器不會在箱子內移位。

凱　　西：這個辦法很好。但是你們知道嗎，如果機器不能按時到達，根據合約，我們有權利取消訂單。

王先生：我們明白這一點。我們會儘快出貨的。

凱　　西：十分感謝。我們真的急著需要這批貨！

王先生：不用擔心，一出貨我們就會通知你們。

Dialogue ❺ 貨運要求 ◀ *Track 114*

當客戶要求你做某些事，你卻無法一口答應時，你可以像這段對話中的王先生一樣，說：「我們很不想讓你們這樣的老顧客失望」，以表示自己就算沒辦法馬上達到對方的要求，但還是有把他們放在心上。

Kathy: When can we expect shipment?

Mr. Wang: I think the middle of October.

Kathy: That's too late. Could you possibly make your delivery date no later than the end of September? October is the prime season for the goods, and we can't afford to miss it.

Mr. Wang: I see your point, but our factory is fully committed for the third quarter. In fact, many of our clients are placing orders for delivery in the fourth quarter.

Kathy: Time of delivery is a matter of great importance to us. I sincerely hope you will give our request your special consideration.

Mr. Wang: The last thing we want to do is to disappoint a customer, especially a loyal customer like you.

Kathy: We've also enjoyed our long partnership.

Mr. Wang: But the fact is our factories all have quite a load of orders.

Kathy: Can you find some way to get round your producers for an earlier delivery?

Mr. Wang: OK, I will try.

★全文中畫 ⬤ 色塊的地方，可以依自己的狀況套入不同的名字、公司名、職稱、學校名等等。

現在是不是回想起來了呢？

a load of 很多的
除此之外，還有a lot of、a heap of、a bunch of、a ton of等，都是指「一堆的、很多的」的意思。

凱　西：你們什麼時候能交貨？

王先生：我想要到10月中旬。

凱　西：這樣太晚了。你們交貨日期能趕在9月底前嗎？10月是這批貨的銷售旺季，我們不能錯過。

王先生：我明白妳的意思。但是我們工廠第三季度的訂單都滿了。事實上，很多客戶正在下第四季度的訂單。

凱　西：交貨時間對我們來說很重要。我希望你能對我們的要求特別考慮一下。

王先生：我們最不想做的事就是讓顧客失望，尤其是像妳這樣的老顧客。

凱　西：我們也對雙方長期的合作感到很愉快。

王先生：但事實就是我們的工廠都有很多訂單。

凱　西：你能想辦法讓廠商提前交貨嗎？

王先生：好吧，我會試試看。

商務小常識

　　交貨期是指賣方將貨物裝上運往目的地的運輸工具或交付承運人的日期，習慣上稱為「裝運期」。海運提單的出單日期是指貨物裝上船的日期，而鐵路運單、航空運單、郵包收據和國際多式聯運單據的出單日期，是指貨物裝上運輸工具或承運人收到並接管貨物的日期。很多國外進口商，他們跟客戶的付款方式是出貨後30天甚至60天才收款，是一種常見的賒銷方式，這在交涉的時候需要相當注意。

SOS Unit 21 合約

Dialogue ❶ 交貨合約 ◀ *Track 115*

想與人討論一件事時，可以一開頭就開門見山地說：「**Let's discuss...**」
（我們來討論一下……），這會給人一種你很幹練的感覺。

• •

Kathy: Let's discuss the delivery date. When will you deliver the finished goods?

Susan: Usually we offer to deliver within six months after the contract signing.

Kathy: The interval is too long. We are in urgent need of the goods now. Could you advance the shipment?

Susan: There is very little we can do, but we'd like to continue to hear your feedback on the matter. We shall see what can be done.

Kathy: We thought you would deliver within three months after the contract signing.

Susan: Impossible! As you know, we have to order the raw materials from the European market.

Kathy: I see. We still hope you can advance our shipment.

Susan: I think if we step up production, we can deliver the goods a month early. What do you think of that?

Kathy: That's really kind of you, but you must know, if there is any delay, we will reject the goods.

Susan: Don't worry. We will do our best to make the shipment early.

★全文中畫 ⬤ 色塊的地方，可以依自己的狀況套入不同的名字、公司名、職稱、學校名等等。

step up 加快

除了這個對話中當作「加快」的意思外，step up 還可以當作「增加、增強」的意思，例如叫人家認真點，不要表現得那麼爛，就可以說：「Step it up!」

中文翻譯1

凱西：我們商量一下交貨日期吧。你們什麼時候能交貨？

蘇珊：通常在合約簽署後6個月內交貨。

凱西：時間間隔太長了。我們現在急著需要這批貨。你們能提前出貨嗎？

蘇珊：我們無能為力，但是我們願意持續聽聽你們在這方面的感想，看看我們可以做些什麼。

凱西：我們以為你們會在合約簽署後3個月內交貨。

蘇珊：不可能！妳知道，我們必須從歐洲市場訂購原料。

凱西：我明白了。我們還是希望你們能提前出貨。

蘇珊：我想如果我們加快生產的話，我們可以提前一個月出貨。你們看怎麼樣？

凱西：太好了。但是得說明一下，如果有任何延誤，我們將拒收這批貨。

蘇珊：別擔心，我們會儘量提前出貨的。

Dialogue ❷ 合約草稿 ◀ *Track 116*

想讓同事或客戶感覺到你很認真，可以像本文中的凱西一樣，在講正題的同時，若無其事地提到「我昨晚認真看了……」，讓人覺得你晚上還在工作，表示你非常重視他們。

Kathy: I made a very close study of the draft contract last night.

Linda: Any questions?

Kathy: Yes, there are several points I'd like to bring up. First is the packing. I think your packing could allow breakage. Please fill the boxes with cushioning material.

Linda: Okay, no problem.

Kathy: Another is the terms of the payment. We prefer to have the payment made by letter of credit.

Linda: I will discuss this with my manager and then get back to you.

Kathy: OK, I can wait.

Linda: Is there anything else?

Kathy: As far as the contract stipulations are concerned, there is nothing more. After you confirm the payment terms, we can arrange a time to sign the contract.

Linda: OK, I will inform you the moment we have made a decision.

★全文中畫 ⬤ 色塊的地方，可以依自己的狀況套入不同的名字、公司名、職稱、學校名等等。

中文翻譯2

凱西：昨晚我仔細審閱了合約草案。

琳達：有什麼問題嗎？

凱西：是的，有幾點我想說明一下。首先是包裝問題。我認為你們的包裝可能會造成產品損壞。請在箱子裡填充緩衝材料。

琳達：好的，沒問題。

凱西：另一個問題是支付條款。我們希望使用信用證支付。

琳達：這個問題我要和經理討論一下，然後再給妳答覆。

凱西：好的，我可以等。

琳達：還有別的問題嗎？

凱西：以合約條款來說，沒有問題了。在你們確認支付條款後，我們可以安排時間簽署合約了。

琳達：好的，我們一決定，我就立刻通知妳。

Dialogue ❸ 仲裁條款 ◀ Track 117

想和客戶表示親切，以下對話中的「personally」（個人地）是一個很好用的字。聽到你說「我個人建議你怎樣怎樣」時，客戶會覺得你不是考量你公司的利益，而是以你本人的立場提供意見，感覺就會和你親近很多。

Miranda: I don't understand the arbitration clause. In all our past contracts signed with you, it was stipulated that arbitration took place in a third country.

Mr. Wang: That's right.

Miranda: Can we use the original arbitration clause?

Mr. Wang: Personally I hope you'll accept this clause. The Arbitration Commission of CCPIT enjoys a good reputation in settling disputes.

Miranda: I have to discuss this point with my manager later.

Mr. Wang: That's okay. But as you know, the disputes that have arisen from our business transactions were all settled through friendly consultations. Very rarely was arbitration necessary.

Miranda: I'm afraid I still cannot answer you right away.

Mr. Wang: Okay, I will wait for your reply.

★全文中畫 ⬤ 色塊的地方，可以依自己的狀況套入不同的名字、公司名、職稱、學校名等等。

中文翻譯3

米蘭達：我不太明白你們的仲裁條款。在之前我們和你們簽訂的所有合約中都規定仲裁在第三國進行。

王先生：是這樣沒錯。

米蘭達：我們能用以前的仲裁條款嗎？

王先生：個人來說，我希望你們可以接受這項條款。中國貿易促進委員會的仲裁委員會在解決爭端上擁有很好的聲譽。

米蘭達：我之後得和我的經理討論一下這個問題。

王先生：好的。但如妳所知，我們生意中出現的爭端都是透過友好協商解決了，很少進行仲裁。

米蘭達：我恐怕還是不能馬上給你答覆。

王先生：好的，我等妳的答覆。

Dialogue ❹ 時間條款 🔊 *Track 118*

💬 簽合約前，再次確認交貨時間是一個很聰明的作法。看看此段對話中，凱西一開始就說了「another discussion」，「another」（另一次）這個字用得很好，暗示了「關於這個題材我們之前已經討論過幾次了，現在再來討論一次，你看這個話題有多重要」的意思。

Kathy: We would like to have another discussion about delivery time before it is finally included in the contract.

Linda: Okay, go ahead.

Kathy: We need you to execute the shipment on time.

Linda: Can we deliver (a month) later? There are more orders than we expected.

Kathy: I'm afraid not. We need the goods urgently.

Linda: Okay, we will monitor our factory's progress regularly.

Kathy: Thank you, but if the shipment cannot be made within (three) months as stipulated, the contract will become void.

Linda: That's acceptable. No one wants to miss the peak period of sales.

Kathy: Okay, we don't have any other issues with the contract.

Linda: I will revise the contract and we will sign it officially as arranged.

★全文中畫 ⬤ 色塊的地方，可以依自己的狀況套入不同的名字、公司名、職稱、學校名等等。

現在是不是回想起來了呢？

peak 高峰

peak指山的頂峰，也可以引申為某事物抵達「巔峰」。這裡的「peak period」就是「銷售旺季」的意思，也就是銷售達到高峰的這段時間。

中文翻譯4

凱西：在最後列入合約之前，我想再商量一下交貨時間。

琳達：好的，請說。

凱西：我們需要你們按時出貨。

琳達：我們可以晚一個月交貨嗎？訂單比我們預期的還要多。

凱西：恐怕不能。我們急著需要這批貨。

琳達：那好，我們會定期檢查工廠進度的。

凱西：謝謝。但是如果不能按原規定在3個月內交貨，合約就會作廢。

琳達：可以。沒有人想錯過銷售旺季。

凱西：好吧，對於合約我們沒有任何問題了。

琳達：我會修改合約，然後我們按計劃的時間正式簽約。

SOS Unit 22
產品代理

Dialogue ❶ 申明優勢 ◀≲ *Track 119*

在此段對話中，凱西用了「I have confidence...」（我有信心……）這句當開頭。在做生意時相當適合用這一句，因為就算對方知道你說說而已，但就是會不知不覺被影響，真的開始有信心起來。

Kathy: I want you to know that our clients are very satisfied with your garments. They find the styles and colors meet the customer's tastes perfectly.

Raymond: We've received similar comments from other firms as well.

Kathy: This is just what I want to discuss with you. We want to be your sole agent in China.

Raymond: What's your advantage?

Kathy: We've been in this field for 15 years and enjoy a good business relationship with all the leading wholesalers and retailers in this industry.

Raymond: I see. We appreciate your efforts in promoting our garments, but as far as I know, your total amount of order last year was moderate, which was not satisfactory enough.

Kathy: In fact we want to expand our business in the years to come. I have confidence we will have a larger market share in the near future.

Raymond: But I still want to see the related market statistics.

Kathy: This is the market research report. Here you are.

Raymond: Okay, I will discuss it with my manager and then give you our response.

★全文中畫 ●●● 色塊的地方，可以依自己的狀況套入不同的名字、公司名、職稱、學校名等等。

現在是不是回想起來了呢？

response 答覆

response是名詞，而如果要用動詞說「答覆」，可以用respond。

中文翻譯1

凱　西：我想告訴你，我們的客戶對你們的服裝非常滿意。他們認為服裝的樣式和顏色都符合消費者的要求。

雷蒙德：我們從其他公司也得到類似的評價。

凱　西：這正好是我想和你們討論的問題。我們想做你們在中國的獨家代理。

雷蒙德：你們的優勢是什麼？

凱　西：我們在這一行業已經有15年的經驗，而且與這一行所有大批發商和零售商都有很好的業務聯繫。

雷蒙德：知道了。我很感謝你們為推銷我們的服裝所做的努力。但據我所知，你們去年訂的貨總額不大，還不太讓人滿意。

凱　西：事實上我們想在以後的幾年擴大業務。我有信心我們在不久的將來會有更大的市場份額。

雷蒙德：但是我還是想看一下相關的市場統計資料。

凱　西：這是市場調查報告。請你過目。

雷蒙德：好的，我會和我的經理討論一下，然後再給妳答覆。

Dialogue ❷ 申請代理權　🔊 *Track 120*

可以在這段對話中，看到琳達使用了「**You've really thought this through**」稱讚對方「考慮得很周到、很深入」，這是稱讚工作上合作夥伴時，非常適合使用的一句。

Kathy: As we have learned from our customer Mr. Harry, you are anxious to expand your activity in our market and are not represented at present. We would like to act as your sole agent.

Linda: We appreciate your interest in our company. As you know, the demand for this item in your market is substantial. However, your turnover last year didn't reach our requirement.

Kathy: We will expand our business this year, so I believe the turnover shouldn't be a problem.

Linda: If possible, I'd like to know your plan to improve the sale of our products.

Kathy: We will combine traditional advertising with the Internet.

Linda: It sounds like a good idea, but would you please let us know the sales prospects for our products in your market and your programme in detail?

Kathy: We've prepared everything already. Here is the related information.

Linda: You've really thought this through.

Kathy: Thank you. We want to fully illustrate the advantages of picking us as your sole agent.

Linda: Okay, I will inform you after we have made a decision.

★全文中畫 ⬤ 色塊的地方，可以依自己的狀況套入不同的名字、公司名、職稱、學校名等等。

中文翻譯2

凱西：從我們的顧客哈利先生那裡得知，貴公司想拓展在我們市場上的業務，且目前還沒有代理商。我們想擔任貴公司的獨家代理商。

琳達：我們很感謝貴公司對我們公司有興趣。如您所知，你們市場對這一商品的需求量很大。但是你們去年的銷售額沒有達到我們的要求。

凱西：今年我們將拓展業務，所以我想銷售額不會是個問題。

琳達：如果可能的話，我想知道你們將怎麼計劃推廣我們的產品。

凱西：我們會把傳統廣告和網際網路結合起來。

琳達：聽起來不錯。但是妳能談談看我們的產品在你們市場上的銷售前景和你們的詳細計畫嗎？

凱西：我們已經都準備好了。這是相關的資訊。

琳達：你們確實考慮得很全面。

凱西：謝謝。我們想充分展示我們做你們獨家代理商的優勢。

琳達：好吧，我們決定後我會通知您。

Dialogue ❸ 公司運營 🔊 *Track 121*

林先生在此段對話中說了「**go ahead**」（請說），這是用於下屬、同事的一句話，注意別和你的老闆說「**go ahead**」了，會顯得你很忙、對方的事不重要似的。

Kathy: I want to go over the details with you in person, so you can fully understand the operation of our company.

Mr. Lin: Okay, go ahead.

Kathy: We specialize in this line of business and have six sales representatives. They are on the road all the time, covering the whole Chinese market.

Mr. Lin: Do you sell directly to shops?

Kathy: Yes, we have well-established channels of distribution.

Mr. Lin: What about your annual turnover?

Kathy: It is high this year and more than meets your requirements.

Mr. Lin: It seems you are our best choice but I have to discuss it with the board first.

Kathy: Okay, I will wait for your answer.

★全文中畫 ⬤ 色塊的地方，可以依自己的狀況套入不同的名字、公司名、職稱、學校名等等。

現在是不是回想起來了呢？

on the road 在外面

「on the road」可不是「在馬路上面」的意思，而是指在外頭搭乘交通工具到處移動旅行、到處忙著辦事。

中文翻譯3

凱　西：我想親自同您談談細節問題，這樣可以讓您充分瞭解我們公司的運營情況。

林先生：好，請說。

凱　西：我們公司專營這項業務，有6名推銷員長年在外，涵蓋整個中國市場。

林先生：你們是否直接賣給商店？

凱　西：是的，我們有穩定可靠的銷售管道。

林先生：你們的年營業額呢？

凱　西：今年營業額很高，比你們所要求的還要高。

林先生：看來你們是我們的最佳人選，但是我還是得和董事會討論一下。

凱　西：好的，等你的回覆。

Dialogue ➍ 產品推廣 🔊Track 122

💬 踏入還不熟悉的市場，想請當地的專家替你分析局勢時，可以像這段對話中的琳達一樣，問：「我們在中國市場有競爭對手嗎？」

Linda: If we choose you as our sole agent, what is your advertising plan?

Kathy: We will use the (Internet) as the main mode of advertising.

Linda: This will cost you a lot.

Kathy: Yes. Because the (Chinese) market is not familiar with your products, this investment is necessary.

Linda: Do we have rivals in the (Chinese) market?

Kathy: You have keen competitors from (Japan) and (European) countries.

Linda: It is a difficult environment for us to sell our products.

Kathy: Yes. We will use various advertising methods to publicize and promote your products.

Linda: It sounds good. We'd like to select you as our agent. What about negotiating the contract this (Friday)?

Kathy: Okay, I'll be there.

★全文中畫 ⬤ 色塊的地方，可以依自己的狀況套入不同的名字、公司名、職稱、學校名等等。

中文翻譯4

琳達：如果我們選你們做我們的獨家代理商，你們有什麼廣告計畫？
凱西：我們主要會利用網際網路進行廣告宣傳。
琳達：這樣你們的費用會很高。
凱西：是的。因為中國市場對你們的產品還不熟悉，這樣的投資是必不可少的。
琳達：我們在中國市場有競爭對手嗎？
凱西：你們主要的對手來自日本和歐洲。
琳達：這種環境對銷售我們的產品很不利。
凱西：是的。我們會利用各種廣告形式來宣傳促銷你們的產品。
琳達：聽起來不錯。我們願意選擇你們做我們的代理商。這個禮拜五討論一下合約事宜行嗎？
琳達：好的，我會去的。

Dialogue ❺ 拒絕授予代理權 ◀ *Track 123*

如果談合作被拒絕了，像這段對話中的凱西一樣，直接問清楚「要怎麼樣做你們才會接受」，聽起來好像有點太直截了當，但也會讓對方覺得你很有誠意，是真的非常想要和他們合作。

Kathy: Our company wants to sign a sole agency agreement with you for a period of 3 years. As it is in our mutual interest, I am sure you'll have no objection.

Tom: Thank you for your interest, but we think it's premature for us to discuss the question of sole agency at this present stage.

Kathy: Why do you say so? Our company specializes in handling shoes of all sorts.

Tom: We know that, but we think your volume of business is not big enough. Thus we can't grant you the agency appointment.

Kathy: If we want to gain the agency appointment, what should we do?

Tom: You must increase your turnover and extend your business.

Kathy: What's your requirement of the turnover for an agency?

Tom: At least $200,000 per year should be your turnover. If you can improve sales greatly for the next year, we may appoint you as our agent.

Kathy: Okay, we will try our best to improve the sales.

★全文中畫 ⬤ 色塊的地方，可以依自己的狀況套入不同的名字、公司名、職稱、學校名等等。

> **現在是不是回想起來了呢？**
>
> **premature 過早的**
> mature是「成熟的」的意思，加上了pre-這個字首，表示「還沒成熟的」，也就是「太早了」。

凱西：我們公司想和你們簽一項為期3年的獨家代理協定。因為這符合雙方利益，我想你們是不會反對的。

湯姆：謝謝你們的垂青，但是我們認為現在討論代理問題還不夠成熟。

凱西：為什麼這樣說？我們公司專營各種類型的鞋子。

湯姆：我們知道，但是我們認為你們的業務量不夠大。因此我們不能授予你們代理權。

凱西：如果我們想取得代理權，我們該做些什麼？

湯姆：你們必須提高你們的銷售額並且擴大業務。

凱西：你們對代理商銷售量的要求是多少？

湯姆：一年至少20萬美金。如果你們能在明年大大改善銷售狀況的話，我們會指定你們為代理商的。

凱西：好的，我們會盡最大努力提高銷量的。

Dialogue ❻ 市場調查研究 🔊 *Track 124*

💬 有人跑來找你們談合作的事，而且一開口就說得好像已成定局一樣，嚇你一跳！這時可以參考對話中王先生的作法，說一句：「Before we go any further...」（在我們深入談這個問題以前……），要對方先別想太遠，你還沒答應要合作呢。

Kathy: We are confident in our local knowledge and widespread connections.

Mr. Wang: Your report says you specialize in the production and sale of cosmetic products.

Kathy: Yes. So we want to be your sole agent in the Asian market.

Mr. Wang: Before we go any further, I'd like to ask several questions about the market prospects. How much turnover will you reach if you are our sole agent?

Kathy: It is really hard to say. Because the Asian market isn't familiar with your products till now, the sales at the beginning might be sluggish.

Mr. Wang: According to your estimate, what is the maximum annual turnover you could fulfill? In round figures, of course.

Kathy: We will always do our utmost to enlarge the business, but we cannot guarantee anything, at least not to begin with.

Mr. Wang: You'd better do some market research and then give us a detailed market forecast report.

Kathy: You mean we can't be your agent?

Mr. Wang: No, we can't give you exclusive agency of the whole (Asian) market without having the slightest idea of your possible annual marketing turnover.

★全文中畫 ⬤ 色塊的地方，可以依自己的狀況套入不同的名字、公司名、職稱、學校名等等。

現在是不是回想起來了呢？

round figures 大概的數字

會說到「round figures」，就是要對方不用給你很精確的數字，說個大概就好。順帶一提，四捨五入的英文說法也和round相關，例如把六round up，就會變成十。畢竟四捨五入也是「算個大概的數字」嘛！

中文翻譯6

凱　西：我們瞭解本地市場，而且通路廣泛，我們對此很有自信。

王先生：你們的報告說你們專門從事化妝品的生產與銷售。

凱　西：是的。因此我們想做你們在亞洲的獨家代理商。

王先生：在我們深入談這個問題之前，我想問幾個有關市場前景的問題。如果成為我們的獨家代理商，妳們能完成多少銷售額？

凱　西：這很難說。因為到目前為止亞洲市場並不熟悉你們的產品，因此開始的銷售情況可能會有點緩慢。

王先生：妳估計能完成的最大年銷售量是多少？當然，概數就可以。

凱　西：我們會盡最大努力來擴大業務，但是我們不能保證什麼，至少一開始我們不能保證什麼。

王先生：你們最好做個市場調查，然後給我們一份詳細的市場預測報告。

凱　西：你是說我們不能做你們的代理商？

王先生：是的。在一點都不瞭解你們年銷售額可能會有多大的情況下，我們無法給你們整個亞洲市場的獨家代理權。

Dialogue ❶ 轉讓形式 ◀€ *Track 125*

不願意答應合作的廠商某些事，難免會讓你覺得對方有些抱歉。此段對話中傑夫的作法就很好，他雖然沒有答應對方的要求，但卻說「we're quite willing...」（我們很願意……）以表示「雖然我們不能答應這件事，但要是其他的事，我們倒挺樂意幫忙的」。

● ●

Kathy: We'd like you to provide us with the equipment.

Jeff: I'm afraid that we can't.

Kathy: Why not?

Jeff: Because the production costs have risen a great deal and we are now losing money.

Kathy: Are there any other channels?

Jeff: No. However we're quite willing to transfer the patent.

Kathy: In what form will you transfer the patent?

Jeff: We'd like to transfer the right to use the patent in the form of a licence .

Kathy: That sounds good. Would you like to talk about it this afternoon ?

Susan: Okay.

★全文中畫 色塊的地方，可以依自己的狀況套入不同的名字、公司名、職稱、學校名等等。

中文翻譯1

凱西：我們希望貴公司能提供設備給我們。
傑夫：我們恐怕無法。
凱西：為什麼呢？
傑夫：因為生產成本已經上漲了很多，我們現在在虧損。
凱西：沒有其他管道了嗎？
傑夫：沒有。不過，我們非常願意轉讓專利。
凱西：貴公司將以什麼形式轉讓專利？
傑夫：我們想以許可證的形式轉讓專利使用權。
凱西：這主意聽起來不錯。我們下午討論好嗎？
傑夫：好的。

Dialogue ❷ 轉讓需求　◀ *Track 126*

戴安娜在此段對話中，要求對方提供一些管理技術，但卻說是「為了幫助兩方的合作」，是個有技巧性的說法。

Diana: Good morning. Shall we discuss the technology transfer briefly now?

Susan: Okay, go ahead.

Diana: We want to import your medicine technology in order to compete successfully in the domestic market. The technology we acquire should be truly appropriate to our needs.

Susan: No problem. We have taken it into account.

Diana: To help our joint venture, we hope that you will keep supplying us with advanced medicine production management techniques.

Susan: That's no problem. We shall help you update the present and future technology.

Diana: We sincerely hope that we can build a long-term business relationship with you.

Susan: I am sure that this will be a successful venture.

★全文中畫 色塊的地方，可以依自己的狀況套入不同的名字、公司名、職稱、學校名等等。

take into account 考慮到

這個片語通常是理性地「考慮到某件事」，而非「考慮到某個人的心情」這種比較感性的「考慮」。例如若我們說「take Jenny into account」，意思會是「考慮到該怎麼處置珍妮這傢伙」，而不是「考慮到珍妮的心情」。

中文翻譯2

戴安娜：早安！我們現在來簡要地討論一下技術轉讓問題，好嗎？

蘇　珊：好的，請說。

戴安娜：為了能在國內市場成功地競爭，我們想向你們進口醫學技術。我們購買的技術要能夠真正滿足我們的需求。

蘇　珊：沒問題。我們已經考慮到這點了。

戴安娜：為了幫助我們的合資企業，希望你們能不斷向我們提供先進的製藥管理技術。

蘇　珊：沒問題。我們會幫助你們更新現有的以及將來的技術。

戴安娜：我們真誠地期待與你們建立長期的合作關係。

蘇　珊：我相信我們的合資企業會很成功。

Dialogue ❸ 專有技術和專利使用權轉讓 Track 127

如果遇到像王先生這樣，一開口就不明不白地說「我們想轉讓專利」之類的話，可以像對話中的戴安娜一樣，問一句「**What do you mean?**」（您的意思是？）請對方說清楚。

Mr. Wang: We'd like to transfer the patent.

Diana: What do you mean?

Mr. Wang: We'd like to transfer the right to use the patent.

Diana: In what form?

Mr. Wang: In the form of a licence.

Diana: That's good. What rights will the licence grant us?

Mr. Wang: It will grant rights to both manufacture and transport our products.

Diana: But the licence only supplies the right to produce the equipment. What about the technology not included in the patent?

Mr. Wang: We'll provide you with all the information, including another two technicians that can help you manufacture the equipment.

Diana: Does the licence include the patent?

Mr. Wang: Yes. It does.

Diana: How long will you allow us to use the patent?

Mr. Wang: Four years.

Diana: Well, sounds good.

★全文中畫 ⬤ 色塊的地方，可以依自己的狀況套入不同的名字、公司名、職稱、學校名等等。

中文翻譯3

王先生：我們想轉讓專利。

戴安娜：您的意思是……？

王先生：我們想轉讓專利使用權。

戴安娜：以什麼形式？

王先生：以許可證的形式。

戴安娜：好。這項許可證會給予我們什麼權利？

王先生：會給予生產和運輸我們產品的許可。

戴安娜：但是許可證只給予生產設備的權利，那麼不包括在專利中的技術，該如何處理呢？

王先生：我們會向貴公司提供所有資訊，還會再提供兩名技術人員，幫助您生產設備。

戴安娜：這項許可包括專利嗎？

王先生：是的，包括。

戴安娜：那麼貴公司將允許我們使用多久時間的專利？

王先生：四年。

戴安娜：好的，聽起來不錯。

Dialogue ❹ 轉讓洽談　🔊 *Track 128*

💬 洽談成功後，可以像此段對話一樣，以「很高興這次洽談圓滿成功」收尾。也隱含有「那就說定囉，不能反悔囉」的弦外之音。

Anne: We'd like to know if you'd be willing to transfer the pharmaceutical technology to our company.

Lily: We are quite willing to help you.

Anne: The know-how we need to import should help our products achieve significant economic results as well as make us competitive in the export market.

Lily: Definitely. Our technology meets international standards and is competitive in the domestic market.

Anne: Could you please explain it in detail?

Lily: We will send you a report on the feasibility of the entire plan as soon as possible.

Anne: Since the current know-how from your company will soon become obsolete, we hope that you will continue offering us improved technological expertise.

Lily: If our transfer documents are not applicable to your actual production condition, we will assist you in modifying the technical documents.

Anne: I'm glad our negotiation has reached such a successful conclusion.

★全文中畫 色塊的地方，可以依自己的狀況套入不同的名字、公司名、職稱、學校名等等。

現在是不是回想起來了呢？

know-how 專業技術
其實「know-how」的意思光看字面上大概就可以猜到：know是「知道」，how是「如何」，而「知道如何做某件事」不就等於是在某方面有專業知識、專業技術了嗎？

中文翻譯4

安妮：我們想知道妳們可否轉讓製藥技術給我們。
莉莉：我們非常願意幫助妳們。
安妮：我們引進的專業技術，應該要能讓我們的產品取得可觀的經濟效益，並能使我們在出口市場上具有競爭力。
莉莉：當然了。我們的技術符合國際標準，在國內市場上很有競爭力。
安妮：您能詳細說明一下嗎？
莉莉：我們會儘快向貴公司寄一份整個計畫可行性的調查報告。

安妮：由於你們轉讓給我們的現有專業技術很快就會過時，希望你們能持續不斷地向我們提供改進的專門技術。

莉莉：我們提供的轉讓資料如果不適合貴公司的實際生產條件，我們會幫助貴公司修改技術資料。

安妮：我很高興這次洽談圓滿成功。

商務小常識

技術轉讓的內容包括：

(1) 有工業產權的技術，如專利、商標等。

(2) 無工業產權的技術，主要是指技術訣竅，一般包括藍圖、配方、設計方案、技術記錄、技術示範、操作方法說明、具體指導等。

(3) 轉讓單機、成套設備、整套工廠等。

招標投標

Dialogue ❶ 邀請投標 ◀Track 129

邀請公司投標時，順便稱讚對方贏面很大，讓對方開心之外，也更容易激起對方參加投標的興趣。

Kathy: Tom, we are inviting tenders for the power station construction project in Southeast China . I wonder if you would like to join them.

Tom: Yes, that's our area of expertise and I am very interested in it. Could you tell me what we should do when we send our bid?

Kathy: As a rule, you have to submit a report on the cost, the construction time, etc. of the project. The bidding paper should be as well appended.

Tom: What about the photocopies of the business licence and qualification certificates?

Kathy: Sure. Needless to say, these are essential.

Tom: Right, we will try to complete it as soon as possible, but we would also like to know the other regulations of the tender committee.

Kathy: Sure, we will give you the complete set of the relevant documents, so you can calculate the cost and study the details of the construction.

Tom: All right. What are our chances, in your opinion?

Kathy: Your company is experienced and well-regarded in this area, so I think you have a good chance.

Tom: Thank you. We will take action right away.

★全文中畫 ⬤ 色塊的地方，可以依自己的狀況套入不同的名字、公司名、職稱、學校名等等。

現在是不是回想起來了呢？

tender 投標

此外，tender還有「軟、嫩」的意思，像在餐廳經常可以點到chicken tender，也就是嫩雞條。

中文翻譯1

凱西：湯姆，我們正在為中國東南部的發電站建立專案進行招標。您是否參加投標？

湯姆：當然，那是我們擅長的領域，我對這項工作很感興趣。您能否告訴我，如果我們投標，應該做些什麼嗎？

凱西：作為規定，你們必須繳交一份有關費用、建設週期等內容的報告。投標書也應該一併附上。

湯姆：營業執照和資格證書的影本呢？

凱西：當然要。不用說，這些是必不可少的。

湯姆：好的，我們會儘早完成這件事情。不過我們也想知道投標委員會的其他規定。

凱西：當然，我們會給你們一套完整的相關檔，這樣你們就可以計算費用、研究工程建設的細節了。

湯姆：好的。您認為我們有多大的機會？

凱西：你們是資深公司，在這個領域很有聲望，所以我認為你們贏的機會是很大的。

湯姆：謝謝。我們會馬上行動。

Dialogue ❷ 闡明投標意見 🔊*Track 130*

明明是自己的公司的事，卻被別的公司的人知道了！這時可以像這個對話中的史蒂夫一樣說一句「**You are quite informed!**」（你的消息真靈通！），其實背後的含意是：你怎麼會知道啊？

Mary: I've heard that your company is planning to invite bids for a commercial residential building contract in Dalian. Is that true?

Steve: Yes. We must make arrangements now because the invitation must be sent out. You are quite informed!

Mary: When do you intend to start the tender?

Steve: We expect that next month.

Mary: What kind of material would you like to buy?

Steve: We'd like to buy rolled steel .

Mary: I was wondering whether we should make a cash deposit.

Steve: Yes, certainly. According to international practice, bidders need to hand in a cash deposit or a letter of guarantee from a commercial bank.

Mary: When do the bidders have to submit their bids?

Steve: The time is tentatively set from the 10th of October to the end of October .

Mary: Shall I get the address?

Steve: You may send it to: International Tendering Department, China National Real Estate Agency, Dalian, China 116044 .

★全文中畫 ⬤ 色塊的地方，可以依自己的狀況套入不同的名字、公司名、職稱、學校名等等。

中文翻譯2

瑪　麗：聽說貴公司計畫為大連的一個住商大樓專案進行招標，這個消息是真的嗎？

史蒂夫：是的。我們現在必須做準備，因為招標通知得寄出去了。妳的消息真靈通！

瑪　麗：你們打算什麼時候開始招標呢？

史蒂夫：我們預計在下個月開始招標。

瑪　麗：貴公司想購入什麼材料？

史蒂夫：我們想購入鋼材。

瑪　麗：我想知道我們是否需要繳納保證金？

史蒂夫：那當然，根據國際慣例，投標人要繳納保證金或提供商業銀行出具的保證函。

瑪　麗：投標期限定在什麼時候？

史蒂夫：我們暫定從10月10日到10月底。

瑪　麗：可以告訴我地址嗎？

史蒂夫：妳可以寄到中國大連房地產公司國際招標部。郵遞區號是116044。

Dialogue ❸ 詢問具體事宜 (1)　🔊 *Track 131*

對話中的王先生問了很多的問題，所以最後有禮貌地說了一句「很抱歉耽誤你這麼多時間」，是很禮貌的作法，因為他實在問超多的。

Mr. Wang: When do you expect to open the tender? And where?

Kathy: 1st of November , in Beijing .

Mr. Wang: Will the tender-opening be done publicly?

Kathy: Yes, tender-opening must be done publicly this time. All the bidders shall be invited to join us to supervise the opening.

Mr. Wang: Would you please let me know more about your conditions for a tender?

Kathy: Invitations will be sent next month, you can read about the details then.

Mr. Wang: Our corporation is very much interested in this tender. We will try our best to win the contract.

Kathy: I understand fully how you feel. If the conditions of your tender prove to be most suitable, of course we'll accept it.

Mr. Wang: I'm sorry to have taken so much of your time today.

Kathy: That's all right. You may contact Lily , our staff member, for further details, or ask me directly if you'd like.

★全文中畫 ● 色塊的地方，可以依自己的狀況套入不同的名字、公司名、職稱、學校名等等。

中文翻譯3

王先生：貴公司準備什麼時候開標？在哪裡開標？

凱　西：11月1日在北京開標。

王先生：打算進行公開招標嗎？

凱　西：是的。此次必須進行公開招標，到時候會請所有投標人來監督投標。

王先生：能否請您把招標條件詳細地向我介紹一下？

凱　西：下個月我們就發出招標通知，到時你可以看到詳細的介紹。

王先生：我們公司對這次招標非常感興趣。我們一定會盡力爭取標下它。

凱　西：您的心情我完全理解。如果貴公司的投標條件是最合適的，我們當然會接受。

王先生：很抱歉今天耽誤您這麼多的時間。

凱　西：沒關係，今後您還有什麼細節需要瞭解，可以找我們的業務員莉莉聯繫，也可以直接找我。

Dialogue ④ 詢問具體事宜 (2) ◀Track 132

💬 詢問招標事宜時，有些人也會先問一句：「我們的贏面有多大？」，用英文說就是「**What are our chances of success?**」

••

Tom: Can you elaborate more on your conditions for the bid?

Kathy: You're required to come to our office for the bid documents, and we hope you read all the provisions set forth in them carefully, including the technical specifications.

Tom: Do we have to guarantee our participation in the tender?

Kathy: As this is a large project involving a large amount of capital, we require a letter of guarantee from an approved bank.

Tom: That sounds reasonable.

Kathy: Anything else you want to ask me?

Tom: I'd also like to know the requirements of the tender committee.

Kathy: Certainly. We shall get a complete set of tender documents for you and you will be able to study the requirements. The expenses involved will be charged to your account, though.

Tom: Well, no problem. What are our chances of success?

Kathy: We know that you are rich in experience in this field and that you offer technical assistance on favorable terms. I think you may win the tender.

Tom: We hope so.

現在是不是回想起來了呢？

committee 委員會
委員會叫committee，那委員呢？可以說committee member。

中文翻譯4

湯姆：妳能否再詳細介紹一下招標的條件？
凱西：您需要到我們辦公室來領取標書。希望你們仔細閱讀標書中包括技術指標在內的所有條款。
湯姆：我們參加投標需要擔保嗎？
凱西：因為這是一項大工程，需要巨額資金，我們公司要求由一家經認可的銀行出具擔保書。
湯姆：聽起來很合理。
凱西：還有想瞭解的問題嗎？
湯姆：我還想瞭解一下投標委員會的要求。
凱西：好的，我們會給貴公司提供一整套招標資料，你們可以研究相關要求。但所涉及費用需由你們承擔。
湯姆：好的，沒問題。我們中標可能性有多大？
凱西：我們知道在這個領域你們有豐富的經驗，而且提供的技術支援條件很優惠。我認為你們可能會中標。
湯姆：希望如此。

Dialogue ❺ 招標競爭　Track 133

這段對話的最後，琳達說了一句「I want...」（我要……），從這句可看出琳達在公司的地位比班還要高，因為是不會對上司說「我要……」的。

Jack: Have you seen the report for the tender? Who do you think is our biggest competitor?

Linda: It seems Tom is our biggest competitor; Mr. Wang is also a major contender in the market.

Jack: I don't know how they do it, our competitors have undercut us by ten percent on the price. There is no way we will be able to compete against that.

Linda: The bottom line figure is disastrous for us. If they are ten percent less than we are, we've got to find a way to lower our price while maintaining a profit.

Jack: Profits are non-existent now.

Linda: We can try to lower our production cost then; we need a competitive price.

Ben: But the competition is cut-throat. And here is the information about our competitors' recent market activities.

Linda: Thanks! This would be a big help.

Ben: We're in a very competitive environment.

Linda: We've got to find a way to outsmart the other guys. I want a strategic marketing plan on my desk by next Tuesday . The competition never sleeps, and neither should we.

★全文中畫 ⬤ 色塊的地方，可以依自己的狀況套入不同的名字、公司名、職稱、學校名等等。

現在是不是回想起來了呢？

cut-throat 激烈的

cut-throat直翻就是「割喉」的意思，常用來形容「競賽」、「競爭」。一場「割喉般」的競爭，想必很激烈，兩邊的人都不顧一切地想贏，到就算把對方的喉嚨給割了也沒關係的程度。

中文翻譯5

傑克：妳看過招標報告了嗎？妳認為誰是我們最大的競爭對手？

琳達：湯姆似乎是最大的競爭對手，王先生也是市場上的一個主要對手。

傑克：我真不知道他們是怎樣做到的，價格比我們低了10%。這樣我們以現在的價格根本無法跟他們競爭。

琳達：這個底價對我們來說很糟糕。如果他們的價格比我們低10%，我們必須在保證利潤的前提下降低我們的價格。

傑克：現在根本就沒利潤了。

琳達：那我們可以盡力降低生產成本；我們需要一個有競爭力的價格。

班：但競爭太激烈了。這是我們對手最近的市場活動資訊。

琳達：謝謝！這對我們有很大的幫助！

班：我們現在的環境競爭很激烈。

琳達：我們得找到擊敗對手的方法。下週二前，我要你們交一個市場戰略計畫。市場競爭一刻不停，我們也一刻不能怠慢。

Dialogue ❻ 遞交標書 🔊 *Track 134*

💬 決定遞交投標書時，負責收投標書的人可能會很親切地表示：「很高興聽到你們決定要參加投標了」，因為要是沒人來投標，他們也會很傷腦筋的。

• •

Mr. Wang: Good morning, Kathy . We have carefully studied the tender documents and decided to take part in the tender.

Kathy: I'm glad to hear that. Have you prepared your tender?

Mr. Wang: Yes, we have prepared a competitive tender.

Kathy: How did you assess the amount of work involved in the project?

Mr. Wang: We assessed the amount of work according to the data acquired.

Kathy: All right, thank you. Have you brought the tender?

Mr. Wang: Yes, here it is, together with the information on the cost, construction time and amount of work.

Kathy: Are the prices stated in Chinese RMB ?

Mr. Wang: Yes.

Kathy: What kind of guarantee will you provide us with?

Mr. Wang: A standby letter of credit established by Bank of China .

Kathy: All right.

★全文中畫 ⬤ 色塊的地方，可以依自己的狀況套入不同的名字、公司名、職稱、學校名等等。

中文翻譯6 •

王先生：早安，凱西。我們認真地研究了投標資料，決定參加這次投標。

凱　西：很高興你們來投標。你們準備好投標書了嗎？

王先生：是的，我們已經準備好了很有競爭力的投標書。

凱　西：你們是如何確定工程量的？

王先生：我們是根據獲取的資料計算工程量的。

凱　西：好的，謝謝你。標書帶來了嗎？

王先生：帶來了，在這裡，還附有該項目的費用、施工時間和工程量。

凱　西：價格是按人民幣計算的嗎？

王先生：是的。

凱　西：貴公司向我們提供什麼形式的擔保？

王先生：由中國銀行開立的備用信用證。

凱　西：好的。

公司併購

Dialogue ❶ 併購分類 🔊 *Track 135*

💬 在服務業工作，常會有需要解答人家問題的時候。參考這段對話中馬婭的說法：**We are pleased to offer you help. What do you want to know?**（我們很高興幫助您。您想知道些什麼呢？）是非常好的一句會話。

● ●

Maya: What can I do for you, sir?

Ben: Well, we are planning to take over other firms as part of our expansion strategy.

Maya: We are pleased to offer you help. What do you want to know?

Ben: We are not clear enough about the type of M&A so far. Could you introduce this to us first?

Maya: Yes, no problem. M&A can be divided into horizontal integration, vertical integration, lateral integration and diversified integration.

Ben: What do they mean respectively?

Maya: Horizontal integration occurs when two companies in exactly the same line of business and the same stage of production merge.

Ben: What about vertical integration and lateral integration?

Maya: Vertical integration means that one firm, for example a manufacturer, joins together with another firm in an earlier stage of production such as a raw material supplier or in the next stage of production such as a retailer. Lateral integration involves the merging of two firms with related goods which don't compete directly with each other.

Ben: Then, how can we understand "diversified integration"?

Maya: "Diversified integration" refers to two firms in completely different lines of business who join together to explore new and different market opportunities and reduce risks of operation.

Ben: Thank you very much for your help.

Maya: You are welcome.

現在是不是回想起來了呢？

take over 收購

在這段對話中「take over」是「收購」另一間公司的意思，如果規模再小一點，你可以說「take over別人的工作」（即「接手」之意）；如果規模再大一點，你可以說「take over別的星球」（即「佔領」之意）。總之，take over 指的就是把本來不是自己的東西變成自己的。

中文翻譯1

馬婭：先生，需要什麼服務嗎？

　班：嗯，我們計畫收購其他公司作為我們擴張戰略的一部分。

馬婭：我們很樂意向您提供幫助。您想瞭解什麼情況？

　班：我們目前對併購的類型還不夠清楚。您能先向我們介紹一下嗎？

馬婭：好的，沒問題。併購可以分為水平整合、垂直整合、橫向整合和多元整合。

　班：它們各自是什麼意思？

馬婭：處於完全同一行業和生產階段的兩家公司合併就是水平整合。

　班：垂直整合和橫向整合呢？

馬婭：垂直整合是指一家公司，比如製造商，和另一家位於上一個生產階段的公司，比如原料供應商，或一家位於下一個生產階段的公司，比如零售商，聯合在一起的情況。橫向整合涉及兩個相關商品企業的聯合，這兩家公司並不直接相互競爭。

　班：那「多元化整合」又是什麼呢？

馬婭：多元化整合指兩個處在完全不同行業的企業合併在一起，以挖掘新的、不同的市場機會並降低經營風險。

　班：非常感謝您的幫助。

馬婭：不客氣。

Dialogue ❷ 合併的利弊 ◀ Track 136

💬 當其他人有疑慮的時候，說「我完全知道你在顧慮什麼，但是請放心」，是個非常不錯的說法，對方會覺得你考慮得很周到，連他在想什麼都先替他考慮好了。參考這一段對話中傑夫怎麼說的吧！

••

Jeff: Now, I'd like to get things under way. I'm thinking of merging with another company.

Kathy: That's great. Conditions are certainly in our favor. Do you have any particular company in mind?

Jeff: Yes, in fact, I'd prefer a foreign company .

Kathy: That's a very wise choice. However, I'm concerned about the results of this merger.

Jeff: I know what's on your mind, but please rest assured. There are so many potential benefits in mergers and acquisitions.

Kathy: Could you go into more detail on that?

Jeff: In the long run, it will be advantageous for us to keep costs low by transportation cost reduction . As a result, we'll have an enhanced ability to create long-term growth and increase value for our shareholders.

Kathy: I see. Are there any risks in this merger?

Jeff: Sure. The biggest challenge lies in integration.

Kathy: What do you mean by that?

Jeff: The way I see it, a merger happens when two firms agree to go forward as a single new company rather than remain separately owned and operated. The new company should perfectly integrate the previous two companies in all aspects of culture, strategy and operation, etc.

Kathy: So, it's important to integrate successfully.

★全文中畫 ⬤ 色塊的地方，可以依自己的狀況套入不同的名字、公司名、職稱、學校名等等。

現在是不是回想起來了呢？

in our favor 對我們有利

「in 某人的 favor」指的就是「（情勢）對某人有利」。前陣子受到歡迎的《飢餓遊戲》（*The Hunger Games*）中就有一句經典台詞：「May the odds be ever in your favor.」（願情勢一直對你有利）。

中文翻譯2

傑夫：現在，我們來處理一下業務。我正在考慮與另一家公司合併。

凱西：太好了。形勢確實對我們有利。您有特別想選的公司嗎？

傑夫：是的，實際上，我希望是一家外國公司。

凱西：真是非常明智的選擇。但是，我有點擔心這次合併的結果。

傑夫：我瞭解你的顧慮。但是請放心，併購有很多潛在的益處。

凱西：你能說得具體一點嗎？

傑夫：從長遠角度來看，這有利於公司透過減少運輸開銷來降低成本。這樣一來，我們就更有能力來實現長期的增長，為我們的股東增加價值。

凱西：我明白了。這次合併有風險嗎？

傑夫：當然有。最大的挑戰在於整合。

凱西：什麼意思？

傑夫：在我看來，當兩家公司同意作為一家單獨的新公司一同前進，而並非獨立掌控、獨立運營時，合併就發生了。新公司應該在文化、戰略及運營等方面完美整合兩家公司。

凱西：那麼說，成功整合非常重要啦。

Dialogue ❸ 聯合發展的評估事宜 🔈*Track 137*

在職場稱讚人時，此段對話最後的「**insightful**」是非常好用的一個單字。它的意思是「有洞察力的」、「有見地的」，可稱讚別人想得非常深入，或想法非常特別，將別人從來不會考慮到的事情都想到了。

Kathy: Good morning, Mr. Wang . What can I do for you?

Mr. Wang: As you know, the company we intend to merge with has offered us the price and settlement method for the merger programme. How is our evaluation going?

Kathy: Pretty smooth. We have referred to comparable companies in our industry in the same situation.

Mr. Wang: What was the result?

Kathy: Their bidding price is comparable to the sum of all our equipment and staffing costs and proves to be reasonable compared with similar cases.

Mr. Wang: How about the settlement method? Is there any disagreement?

Kathy: Yes. As for that matter, we have sought advice from our shareholders. Most of them prefer cash, because transferring between different accounts seems risky to them.

Mr. Wang: Okay, we can negotiate that with that company.

Kathy: What's more, payment in shares, in my opinion, should also be suggested so that we can gain more say in the future business operation.

Mr. Wang: That's very insightful.

★全文中畫 ⬤ 色塊的地方，可以依自己的狀況套入不同的名字、公司名、職稱、學校名等等。

中文翻譯3

凱　西：早安，王先生。有什麼事嗎？

王先生：妳知道，我們準備與它合併的那家公司已經給我們提供了要合併項目的價格及結算方式。我們的評估進行得怎麼樣了？

凱　西：很順利。我們參考了具有相同情況的同業類似公司。

王先生：那麼結果如何？

凱　西：他們的競標價格與我們的設備總額及員工成本是相當的，與類似的案例相比也是很合理的。

王先生：那麼結算方式呢？有什麼不同意見嗎？

凱　西：是的。在這個問題上，我們徵求了股東的意見。他們中的大多數人希望能得到現金，因為轉帳對他們來說似乎風險較大。

王先生：好吧，我們可以跟那家公司就此協商一下。

凱　西：而且，我認為應該提議以股票的方式付款，這樣我們在將來的商業運營中可以更有發言權。

王先生：很有見地。

Dialogue ❹ 兼併價格與結算 🔊*Track 138*

💬 可以看看這段對話中，凱西將「我方」稱為「our party」，對方稱為「your party」。這裡的party可不是開趴的那種party，而是表示「我們團隊」、「我們這一群人」。像在玩RPG時，用一群角色組一隊一起去打怪時，這也是一個party。

· ·

Kathy: Good morning, sir.

Mr. Green: Morning. Nice to see you again!

Kathy: Now, let's discuss the issue of price and settlement method for the merger programme!

Mr. Green: All right. Our bidding price is $1 billion. Is that acceptable?

Kathy: Yes, it is. Our board of directors has voted and accepted the bidding price. But, concerning the means of settlement, there are still conflicting ideas.

Mr. Green: Like what?

Kathy: Some shareholders think that settlement by cash payment is their best choice because they can immediately get their money back. Others prefer to settle it by means of shares so that they will continue to be the owners of the new firm and can still have some influence over the company.

Mr. Green: I see. What is your current plan for the settlement method?

Kathy: Our party would like to solve the problem by means of payment with half in cash and half in shares. Is that acceptable to your party?

Mr. Green: Yes, it is.

★全文中畫 ⬤ 色塊的地方，可以依自己的狀況套入不同的名字、公司名、職稱、學校名等等。

凱　　西：早安，先生。

格林先生：早安！很高興又見面了！

凱　　西：現在，我們討論一下這次合併專案的價格和結算方式吧！

格林先生：好的。我們投標的價格是10億美元。您接受嗎？

凱　　西：是的，我們接受。我們董事會已經表決通過了該價格。不過，關於結算方式問題還是有一些不同的意見。

格林先生：有什麼不同意見呢？

凱　　西：有些股東認為現金付款結算是他們的最佳選擇，這是因為他們可以馬上獲得資金。其他股東更希望以股票方式結算，這樣一來他們可以繼續成為新公司的所有權人，仍然能夠對公司施加一些影響力。

格林先生：我明白了。您現在希望用怎樣的結算方式呢？

凱　　西：我們想通過一半使用現金，一半使用股票的付款方式來解決問題。你們接受嗎？

格林先生：好的，接受。

Dialogue ❺ 聯合發展的動機 🔊 *Track 139*

若對於某些重大決定還有疑慮時，可參考亨利在此段對話中的作法，說：「I'm still not convinced...」（我對……還是心存疑慮），既沒有無禮地否定對方的想法，也清楚地表達了自己的立場。

Henry: Good morning.

Kathy: Good morning. Pleased to see you again.

Henry: I've reviewed your proposal for the merger between our two firms, but I am still not convinced we need to merge.

Kathy: Both our firms will benefit a lot from this merger. It's a clear win-win situation.

Henry: For example?

Kathy: Both of us are now facing fierce competition in the global market. Our merger would enhance our competitiveness.

Henry: How can we become a stronger competitor if we join together?

Kathy: Your company has efficient distribution channels in the local market, and we have state-of-the-art technology. Thus, merging will mean the integration of our advantages.

Henry: I see. Such a strategic alliance between us has obvious advantages, that is, your fast expansion into the marketplace and our faster upgrading of technology. Am I correct?

Kathy: You are absolutely right.

★全文中畫 ⬤ 色塊的地方，可以依自己的狀況套入不同的名字、公司名、職稱、學校名等等。

現在是不是回想起來了呢？

state-of-the-art 最先進的
這是一個看起來蠻有趣的片語，雖然有「art」這個字，但和「藝術」不見得相關，指的是某事物（尤指科技）走在時代的尖端，是目前這個時代發展出最優秀也最進步的一種。

中文翻譯5

亨利：早安。

凱西：早安。很高興再次見到您。

亨利：我已經審閱了你們關於我們兩家公司合併經營的建議書。不過，我對是否需要合併還是心存疑慮。

凱西：我們兩家公司都可以從這次合併中獲得諸多好處，這顯然是一個雙贏的局面。

亨利：舉例來說呢？

凱西：我們雙方目前都面臨全球市場的激烈競爭壓力，我們的合併經營會增強我們的競爭力。

亨利：如果合併，我們怎麼能成為更加強大的競爭者呢？

凱西：貴公司在本地市場有高效率的銷售管道，而我們擁有最先進的技術。因此，合併經營將意味著我們雙方優勢的整合。

亨利：我明白了。我們之間的這種戰略聯盟擁有明顯的優勢，即你們可以更快擴展市場，而我們可以加快技術升級。我說得對嗎？

凱西：你說得完全正確。

Dialogue ❻ 聯合發展的策略 ◀ Track 140

💬 凱西在這段對話裡說了「Thank you for putting my mind at ease.」，意思是「謝謝你讓我安心」。在職場上也可以用這一句，言外之意就是：「你這樣說我就安心了，但接下來要是你們做出什麼讓我不太安心的事的話，我會覺得好像被騙一樣喔」，會讓對方更謹慎地達到你的要求。

• •

Kathy: The merger is complete. What will be your next step?

Mr. Wang: The clear and tight management control of all new interfaces as well as the full integration of the new company.

Kathy: Tight management control? I'm afraid that will be difficult for our staff.

Mr. Wang: Let me assure you that with the implementation of this control, we will ensure that the staff will work together more systematically, easily and efficiently within the company.

Kathy: Thank you for putting my mind at ease. So is this management control a prelude to upcoming fuller integration?

Mr. Wang: Definitely. We will focus on a few major issues which improve efficiency and save money.

Kathy: But some merging companies focus too intently on cost-cutting and neglect day-to-day business, thereby prompting nervous customers to flee.

Mr. Wang: We will always have our stellar customer service, the best practices and approaches to create a profitable new company, and a deep respect for different cultures.

Kathy: It's important to take people's different cultural backgrounds into consideration.

Mr. Wang: We can minimize cultural clashes across geographic boundaries by bearing in mind that we are dealing with people, who need to be treated with respect and sensitivity.

Kathy: Indeed, they are the resource which will make the merger a success.

現在是不是回想起來了呢？

prelude 序曲

prelude在音樂中是「序曲」的意思，在這段對話中表示「為……揭開序幕」的事物。

中文翻譯6

凱　西：合併已經完成了。您下一步的打算是什麼呢？

王先生：對所有新的交接點進行明確而嚴格的管理監控，以及新公司的全面整合。

凱　西：嚴格管理監控？這恐怕對我們的員工來說有難度。

王先生：我向妳保證，實行這種管理監控會確保員工們在公司內更加系統、輕鬆、有效地工作。

凱　西：謝謝您讓我安心。那麼此次的管理監控是在為即將到來的全面整合拉開序幕嗎？

王先生：是的。我們將專注於能夠提升效率和節約成本的幾個主要問題。

凱　西：但是一些公司在合併後，由於過分關注節約成本而忽略了日常運營，因而導致焦慮的客戶流失。

王先生：我們會始終保持一流的客戶服務，用最好的做法創造一個新的可盈利的公司，並深切尊重不同的文化。

凱　西：考慮人們不同的文化背景這點很重要。

王先生：我們應該記住我們一直是在跟人打交道，我們應該尊重並且謹慎地對待他們，這樣我們可以把地理界限上的文化衝突最小化。

凱　西：的確，員工就是使合併取得成功的資源。

Dialogue ❼ 聯合發展的成敗 ◀ Track 141

在職場上說服人時，有時會用到一些聽起來很厲害（但其實還好）的字，像在這段對話的「synergy」就是。它的中文翻譯是「協同作用」，但聽起來還是不明不白的對吧？簡單地說，就是「一加一大於二，兩方合作後激起了不得了的火花，默契十足，創造出很好的效益，超級神奇」這樣的感覺。聽起來果然是個好像很厲害的字吧！

Kathy: It is said that the success rate of acquiring and merging companies is between 40% and 50%. Fortunately, we have been able to make it as part of that 40% to 50%. What do you think is the key to our success?

Mr. Wang: All mergers and acquisitions have one common goal, that is, to achieve synergy by all means. The success of the merger or acquisition depends on it.

Kathy: What is synergy?

Mr. Wang: Synergy is the magic force that allows for enhanced cost efficiencies of the new companies, making the value of the combined companies greater than the sum of the two parts.

Kathy: So it takes the form of revenue enhancement and cost savings.

Mr. Wang: Right. Mergers are extremely hard to get right, so we looked for a company with a healthy grasp of reality.

Kathy: Yes. But sadly, companies sometimes have a bad habit of biting off more than they can chew in mergers.

Mr. Wang: That's true. They miss the whole point of the mergers and acquisitions; because in a merger and acquisition, we are not trying to beat the other company but to win the whole market.

Kathy: Success in the market needs to be our priority, right?

Mr. Wang: Yes, and to this end, some sacrifices from both parties are imperative.

★全文中畫 ⬤ 色塊的地方，可以依自己的狀況套入不同的名字、公司名、職稱、學校名等等。

現在是不是回想起來了呢？

bite more than one can chew 貪多
這個片語直翻就是「咬的比能嚼的還多」。人的嘴巴也就那麼大，要是咬太大一口，根本沒辦法嚼，結果你反而會嗆到或吐出來，得不償失。這個片語的意思也就是「想要的比能承受的還多，反而招致反效果」。

中文翻譯7

凱　西：據說合併公司的成功率只有40%到50%。幸運的是，我們能夠躋身於這40%到50%之中。您認為我們成功的關鍵是什麼呢？
王先生：所有的合併都有一個共同的目標，也就是透過各種手段達到協同作用。合併的成功取決於它。
凱　西：什麼是協同作用？
王先生：協同作用是提高新公司成本效益的神奇力量，能夠使合併後公司的價值比兩部分的總和要高。

凱　西：那麼它的形式就是收益增長與成本節約了。
王先生：是的。合併後的公司是很難步入正軌的，所以我們尋找了一個能夠好好把握
　　　　實際情況的公司。
凱　西：是的。但遺憾的是，有時公司習慣於貪多。
王先生：是的。他們沒有抓住合併的整個重點，因為在合併中，我們不是要打敗另一
　　　　家公司，而是要贏取整個市場。
凱　西：取得市場成功應是我們的首要任務，對嗎？
王先生：是的，為了這個目的，雙方做一些犧牲也是必要的。

Dialogue ⑧ 談論公司收購 ◀ Track 142

對於連自己都還不確定是否會成功的事，要如何說服別人接受？可以參考這
段對話中王先生的說法：「現在還很難說，但我覺得長期下來會是值得的」。

Mr. Wang: I'm pleased to tell you that M&G Company has agreed to negotiate with us on acquiring their company.

Kathy: Purchasing their company? I thought we were planning to establish a subsidiary company.

Mr. Wang: That was the original plan, but as you know, we are only in need of a raw material processing factory, which is a totally new field for us.

Kathy: Yes, that can be risky. So, what are the costs like?

Mr. Wang: In fact, the cost of both moves would be equal according to the assessment.

Kathy: Is this acquisition worth it?

Mr. Wang: It's hard to say right now. However, I believe it will be in the long run. This acquisition will assemble good management, obtain valuable property andget the right equipment for us.

Kathy: Absolutely. This acquisition means we can have everything prepared for us.

Mr. Wang: So I need you to draft the negotiation plan before next Friday. Is that okay?

Kathy: No problem. Is there anything I should be cautious about?

Mr. Wang: So far they intend to keep this secret. You can understand how news like this negatively influences the company.

★全文中畫 ● 色塊的地方，可以依自己的狀況套入不同的名字、公司名、職稱、學校名等等。

中文翻譯8 ●●●●●●●●●●●●●●●●●●●●●●●●●●●

王先生：有件高興事告訴妳，M&G公司已經同意與我們公司就收購他們公司進行談判。
凱　西：收購他們公司？我以為我們在計畫創辦子公司呢。
王先生：那是原來的計畫。但是，如你所知，我們只是需要一個原材料加工廠，這對我們來說是全新的領域。
凱　西：是的，這很有風險。那麼成本怎麼樣呢？
王先生：事實上，根據評估，兩種方式的成本是不相上下的。
凱　西：那麼這次收購划算嗎？
王先生：現在還很難說。但是，我覺得從長期來看是值得的。此次收購會為我們集合優秀的管理、帶來有價值的資產和合適的設備。
凱　西：是的。這次收購意味著我們需要的一切都為我們準備好了。
王先生：所以我需要妳在下個禮拜五之前起草好談判方案，可以嗎？
凱　西：沒問題。我有什麼需要注意的嗎？
王先生：目前為止，他們希望能夠保密。妳明白這樣的消息會給公司帶來多麼負面的影響。

商務小常識

　　無論是與國內或國外企業，在談併購時，都特別要注意幾種涉及法律的應付責任：

(1) 產品責任（product liability）

(2) 環保責任（environment liability）

(3) 租稅責任（tax liability）

(4) 退休金責任（pension liability）

(5) 契約責任（contractual liablity）

(6) 訴訟責任（litigation liability）

(7) 行政責任（administrative liablity）

(8) 保證責任（guarantor liablity）

(9) 資產負債表以外的交易責任（off-blance sheet transctions liablity）

Dialogue ❶ 商談出資比例 🔊 *Track 143*

> 在職場上，有時稱讚別人經常是為了打聽更多東西，對方也心知肚明，但還是會回答你。像這段對話第一句處，我們可以看到凱西說：「你們動作很快啊」，其實意思就是要問：「你們怎麼會這麼快決定的？背後有什麼原因嗎？」

Kathy: I'm glad you've decided to join hands with us in the venture. You move quickly.

Ben: To tell you the truth, we have been considering a joint venture for some time to cope with new developments in China.

Kathy: Our market analysis has predicted an active market for this product, so I think we stand a fair chance to do well.

Ben: I fully agree.

Kathy: Ben, how many production lines are needed in the joint venture?

Ben: At the initial stage, there will be only one production line.

Kathy: How much are you prepared to invest?

Ben: We'll supply the machinery and equipment estimated at about 40% of the total investment.

Kathy: To take a long-term view, assuming this sells well in this market, we may consider the possibility of producing it here.

Ben: If such a condition materializes, our company will be your ideal partner.

★全文中畫 ⬤ 色塊的地方，可以依自己的狀況套入不同的名字、公司名、職稱、學校名等等。

中文翻譯1

凱西：很高興你們決定與我們合作建立一家合資企業。你們行動很快啊。

班：不瞞您說，為了跟上中國發展的腳步，對建立合資企業的事，我們已經考慮一段時間了。

凱西：我們的市場分析預測到這種產品的市場將會很活躍，所以，我認為我們成功的機率很大。

班：我完全同意。

凱西：班，這次合資企業需要幾條生產線？

班：一開始只需要一條。

凱西：你們願意投資多少？

班：我們將提供機器和設備，大約占總投資額的40%。

凱西：從長遠角度考慮，如果這個產品在當地市場銷量不錯的話，我們會考慮在當地直接生產。

班：如果這種情況真的實現的話，我們公司將會是你們的理想夥伴。

Dialogue ❷ 投資地點 ◀ *Track 144*

從凱西在此段對話中說「I've no idea.」（我不知道），我們可以判斷她和布朗先生的關係應該是蠻熟的，因為對於上司或不熟的客戶，都不該直截了當地說「I've no idea」喔！

Kathy: Would you be willing to set up a joint venture with us?

Mr. Brown: Yes, we may be interested. Could you elaborate?

Kathy: I'm planning to build a production base in your economic zone. What do you think about that?

Mr. Brown: What a great idea! Where are you going to set up your production base?

Kathy: I've no idea. I'm here to ask you for help.

Mr. Brown: In my opinion, Pudong is the most ideal place.

Kathy: All right, I'll think it over.

Mr. Brown: May I ask how much we'd invest?

Kathy: How about investing 50% of the total amount respectively?

Mr. Brown: Then we can share the profit evenly, am I right?

Kathy: Yes, quite right.

★全文中畫 色塊的地方，可以依自己的狀況套入不同的名字、公司名、職稱、學校名等等。

中文翻譯2

凱　　西：你們願意與我們一起創辦合資企業嗎？
布朗先生：是的，我們或許會有興趣。妳能詳細說明一下嗎？
凱　　西：我計畫在你們的經濟區建立一個生產基地。你認為如何？
布朗先生：好主意！你們打算在什麼地方建立生產基地？
凱　　西：我還不知道。所以來向你請教。
布朗先生：我看浦東是最理想的地方。
凱　　西：好的，我考慮一下。
布朗先生：我能否問一下，我們應該出多少資金？
凱　　西：雙方各自投入50%的資金怎麼樣？
布朗先生：那麼我們可以均分利潤，是嗎？
凱　　西：是的，沒有錯。

Dialogue ③ 投資風險 ◀ *Track 145*

當有別的公司的人問你一些你也無法決定的事情時，你可以把事情推給上面的人：像是這段對話中的公司總裁和董事們。凱西還加一句「It depends」（這得看情況），就是要讓對方明白決定權並不在她的手中。

Mr. Zhang: Is it possible for us to introduce capital from your company?

Kathy: What would be the purpose?

Mr. Zhang: We need money to extend our factory.

Kathy: It depends. If our president and the directors think your conditions are favorable and the investment is safe, they may agree.

Mr. Zhang: It is obvious that the extension of the factory is necessary and will be beneficial in the long run. Don't you think so?

Kathy: Yes, I'm confident in your company and your products.

Mr. Zhang: Could you help us persuade the directors of your company board to make the investment?

Kathy: I'll give them a call and see what they say.

Mr. Zhang: Thank you very much.

Kathy: It's my pleasure.

★全文中畫 ⬤ 色塊的地方，可以依自己的狀況套入不同的名字、公司名、職稱、學校名等等。

現在是不是回想起來了呢？

in the long run 長期來說

這是個代表「長期來說」的片語，相反地也可以說「in the short run」來代表「短期來說」。

中文翻譯3

張先生：我們有可能從你們公司挹注資金嗎？

凱　西：目的是什麼？

張先生：我們需要資金擴建工廠。

凱　西：這得看情況。如果我們公司總裁和董事們認為你們條件優惠而且投資安全，他們或許會同意。

張先生：很顯然，工廠的擴建是必要的，而且從長遠來看也是大有益處的，您不這樣認為嗎？

凱　西：是的，我對你們的公司和產品都很有信心。

張先生：您能幫我們說服你們的董事會投資嗎？

凱　西：我打電話給他看看他們怎麼說。

張先生：好的，非常感謝。

凱　西：不客氣。

Dialogue ❹ 投資雙方的責任與義務 ◀ *Track 146*

討論完一個議題，該怎麼「無縫接軌」地進入下一個議題呢？可以參考這個對話的第一句：「**Shall I move on to the next item on the agenda?**」（我現在可以進入程序中的下一個議題嗎？）

● ●

Kathy: Shall I move on to the next item on the agenda—the issue of the responsibilities of each side?

Jim: Sure. Firstly, we should have a look at each party's responsibility.

Kathy: If the joint venture is to be equally owned, we'll have equal rights. Accordingly, we have to be prepared for a situation where two of us have some serious disagreement, which cannot be solved.

Jim: I'm confident that some compromise can be reached.

Kathy: I hate to be persistent, but what if we cannot find a solution even then? Shouldn't some mechanism be established beforehand?

Jim: I agree with you. Do you have any ideas?

Kathy: Let me propose a plan, which has been very successful in other joint ventures. If the matter is still unsolved after a discussion at the board meeting, the matter is referred to a meeting of the presidents of the parent company for a final decision.

Jim: But what if even the presidents cannot agree?

Kathy: Either the matter goes to arbitration or the JV is dissolved.

Jim: I see.

中文翻譯4 ●

凱西：現在可以進入議程的下一個議題——雙方的責任嗎？

吉姆：我同意。我們首先應該看一下雙方各自的責任。

凱西：如果合資公司我們各占一半，則享有同等權利。因此，我們必須事先考慮到雙方存在嚴重分歧、無法調和的情況。

吉姆：我相信我們能達成某種折衷的方案。

凱西：我不想爭個沒完，但如果我們到那時找不到解決辦法呢？是不是應該事先建立某種機制呢？

吉姆：我同意。妳有什麼想法嗎？
凱西：我提議一個方案，這個方案在其他合資企業非常成功。如果經過董事會討論後事情還是無法解決，那麼就由母公司的總裁會議作出最終決定。
吉姆：但如果總裁們也達不成一致意見呢？
凱西：那麼不是提交仲裁，就是合作關係解除。
吉姆：我明白了。

Dialogue ❺ 施工建設 ◀Track 147

這段對話中，湯尼所說的「**That can be arranged.**」（這些可以安排），是一句非常好用的商用會話，不但表達了一種「你對對方有求必應」的周到感覺，同時也表達你們這一方很有能力，對方一有要求，你馬上「可以安排」。

Kathy: To ensure proper work on the construction site and the installation and operation of the equipment you supply, it's necessary that some specialists be sent here to supervise work.

Tony: That can be arranged.

Kathy: Can you give me an indication of the number of specialists required and their roles?

Tony: For this project, I think it's necessary to send a civil engineer as the chief engineer and three mechanical engineers .

Kathy: And what will be their period of stay here?

Tony: The chief engineer will stay until after the completion of the construction, and the three mechanical engineers after the trial operation of the equipment.

Kathy: Okay.

Tony: I hope the living quarters for the experts are well furnished.

Kathy: Everything will be provided according to the terms stipulated in the contract and the living quarters will be well furnished.

Tony: Good. I will call you tonight about other details.

★全文中畫 ● 色塊的地方，可以依自己的狀況套入不同的名字、公司名、職稱、學校名等等。

role 角色

在戲劇中，role常指「角色」，也指遊戲中的「角色」。在這段對話中，role是指這些專家「扮演的角色」，也就是他們的「分工」。

中文翻譯5

凱西：為確保建築工地以及你們所供應的設備在安裝、運轉方面順利進行，你們派遣幾位專家監督工程是必要的。

湯尼：這些可以安排。

凱西：你能大概說一下要派遣的專家人數以及他們如何分工嗎？

湯尼：我想，這個案子有必要派一名土木工程師擔任總工程師，還需要三名機械工程師。

凱西：他們在這裡需要待多久時間？

湯尼：總工程師需要待到工程完工，三個機械工程師在設備初試成功以後才可以離開。

凱西：好的。

湯尼：我希望專家們的宿舍設備能夠齊全。

凱西：一切都會按合約條款提供，宿舍會配備有良好的設施。

湯尼：好。晚上我再打電話跟妳商量其他細節。

Dialogue ❻ 董事會組成 (1) ◀ *Track 148*

這段對話中，出現了「請問這些想法是建議還是要求？」這樣的會話，這是個雖然沒有直接拒絕對方的意見，但也非常直接堅定地表達自己立場的優秀說法，說出來會嚇人一跳的那種。

Kathy: We'd like to have a few other promises.

Danny: What do you have in mind?

Kathy: We'd like to have the head of the management board be rotated every three months. We'd also like the board to have an odd number in our favor.

Danny: Can I ask if these are proposals or demands?

Kathy: It's not that we don't trust you, Danny . We just must be sure we cover all contingencies.

Danny: I understand. But we would like the top person on the board to be rotated every (six) months.

Kathy: We can agree to that. Why is that a sticking point for you?

Danny: (Three) months isn't enough time to establish one's authority, but (six) months will allow for the proposal of new ideas.

Kathy: I have no problems with that.

Danny: Okay. Deal.

★全文中畫 ⬤ 色塊的地方，可以依自己的狀況套入不同的名字、公司名、職稱、學校名等等。

現在是不是回想起來了呢？

sticking point 癥結
「stick」有「黏住」的意思，要是整個話題都黏在某個點動彈不得，就表示是那個「點」害你們的談判卡住啦！在這段對話中，凱西就是要問：「為什麼你們會執著在這一點？」

中文翻譯6

凱西：我們希望得到其他一些承諾。

丹尼：您有什麼想法嗎？

凱西：我們希望管理委員會主席每三個月輪換一次。同時委員會的人數為奇數，而且我們的人占多數。

丹尼：請問這些想法是建議還是要求？

凱西：丹尼，不是我們不相信你。我們只是得確保預防所有可能發生的意外情況。

丹尼：我理解。但我們希望委員會主席6個月換一次。

凱西：我們可以同意這一點。為什麼這點會讓你們擔心呢？

丹尼：短短的3個月不可能建立權威，但待了6個月的人才能夠提出新的想法。

凱西：這個我不反對。

丹尼：好的，就這麼決定了。

Dialogue ❼ 董事會組成 (2) ◀️ *Track 149*

不確定在某些人面前是否可以談論某個話題時，可以如對話中的傑克一樣先問：「Is it appropriate to go into this subject now?」（現在談論這個話題合適嗎？）

Jack: We have some issues with the structure of the Board of Directors in the joint venture. Is it appropriate to go into this subject now?

Kathy: I'm interested to hear what you have to say. Please go ahead.

Jack: We believe the number of directors from each partner should reflect the ratio of ownership. If the ownership is 50/50 and the number of Board members is six, it should be three each. Any objections?

Kathy: I don't think that's reasonable. I suggest that four should come from our company and two from yours.

Jack: The shares of our investment basically determine that, I don't have any authority to reconsider that.

Kathy: This will be a tough issue.

Jack: Okay. We will talk about it later. Now I have a question for you: how long do you think the term of the directors, chairman and vice chairman should last? Would a two-year period be reasonable?

Kathy: From the perspective of the continuity and stability of a company's policy, I think four years are better.

Jack: I think that's reasonable. It's decided then. I will include these new details in the contract.

Kathy: Okay. We will discuss the issue of the number of directors later.

★全文中畫 ● 色塊的地方，可以依自己的狀況套入不同的名字、公司名、職稱、學校名等等。

中文翻譯7

傑克：我們對合資企業的董事會結構有幾個問題。現在合適提出討論嗎？

凱西：我很想聽聽你們的意見，請說。

傑克：我們認為各方在董事會的人數應該依據股權的比例而定。如果股權是50/50，而董事會的席位為6人，則雙方應該各占3席，你們同意嗎？

凱西：我認為這並不合理。應有4位來自我們公司，2位出自貴公司。

傑克：這基本上是由投資額決定，我沒有重新考慮的權力。

凱西：這個問題會很棘手。

傑克：好吧，我們等一下再談這個問題。現在，我有一個問題：您認為董事、主席和副主席的任期為多久比較合適？兩年合適嗎？

凱西：從公司政策的連貫性和穩定性角度來看，我認為4年會更好。

傑克：我覺得這樣很合理。就這麼決定了，我會把這些新細節寫入合約內。

凱西：好的。我們一會兒再討論董事會人數的問題。

Dialogue ❽ 催促資金匯入 🔊 *Track 150*

> 這段對話中的董先生打電話催促一些相關設備，然而我們可以看到他非常有技巧性地沒有說他擔心對方會動作很慢，而是說「以往運送時間需要幾個星期」，把責任怪到運送公司上。這樣既達到催促的效果，也不需要說對方動作慢。

● ●

Kathy: Kathy speaking.

Mr. Dong: Hi! Kathy. This is Dong Ming.

Kathy: Hi! Mr. Dong. How is everything?

Mr. Dong: I'm calling to tell you that we have received the first sum of your credit of $200,000 for the building of the power station's housing, which has now begun, and everything is getting on well.

Kathy: Well, I'm pleased to hear of the start of the housing construction. I'm sure you must have been working very hard and efficiently.

Mr. Dong: Thank you, Kathy. According to schedule it should be finished by the end of next May. I want to know if the relevant machines will be sent from your place in time as we planned. You know, it usually takes weeks to arrive here, and we hope it won't fail to meet the assembling time. We have no time to lose!

Kathy: Well, don't worry. We'll get it sent to you as soon as possible, but allow us some time. We need more time.

Mr. Dong: I know, but our time is also limited.

Kathy: You are right. We shall do everything necessary.

Mr. Dong: Thank you, Kathy.

★全文中畫 ⬤ 色塊的地方，可以依自己的狀況套入不同的名字、公司名、職稱、學校名等等。

現在是不是回想起來了呢？

have no time to lose 時間寶貴

這句直翻就是「沒有時間可以浪費」，也就是說時間非常珍貴，一點點也不能「lose」（失去）。

中文翻譯8

凱　西：我是凱西。

董先生：妳好，凱西。我是董明。

凱　西：你好，董先生。一切都好嗎？

董先生：我這就要告訴妳呢。我們已經收到你們所給的用於建造電廠廠房的第一筆信貸款 20 萬美元，現在發電廠廠房的建設已經開始，一切都進展得很順利。

凱　西：聽到發電廠廠房開始動工，我很高興！我敢肯定你們工作一定非常賣力，很有效率。

董先生：謝謝凱西！按照行程，發電廠廠房的建設將在明年5月末完成，我想問一下，你們是否能把有關的機器設備按照計劃發配下來？妳知道的，從你們那裡運貨到這裡常常需要幾個禮拜的時間，我們不希望耽誤我們的裝機。我們浪費不起時間。

凱　西：哦，別擔心。我們會儘快出貨給你們，但給我們一點寬限。我們還需要一些時間。

董先生：我知道。但我們的時間也很緊迫。

凱　西：你說得對，我們會盡力的。

董先生：謝謝妳，凱西。

商務小常識

　　不同的合資形式決定著雙方責任和義務的分擔，所以要成立合資公司，一定要從多方面衡量，確定最為合適的合作形式。一般來說，合資企業雙方應以各自所占的出資額對合資公司的債務承擔責任。雙方可以以現金、實物、工業產權等形式進行投資。

SOS Unit 27
產品糾紛

Dialogue ❶ 出錯貨物 ◀Track 151

仔細看看這段對話，會發現凱西先將錯誤怪在工廠上（「也許是工廠送錯了」），結果對方不高興了，叫她不要找藉口，她立刻說會負全權責任，對方便沒有再追究。看來面對某些客戶時，還是誠實地攬下責任比較有效。

● ●

Kathy: Good morning, Kevin, how have you been?

Kevin: Not so well, I'm afraid.

Kathy: What's the problem? How can I be of help?

Kevin: I'm here regarding our order No. TJ 205 placed three months ago. We've received the consignment, only to find that two cases of your products were not up to the standard of your samples.

Kathy: I don't know why that happened. Nothing like this has happened before. Maybe the factory sent you the wrong cases.

Kevin: There is no excuse. If we can't get the products we've ordered by the end of this month, I'm afraid that we have to lodge a claim against you.

Kathy: I've contacted our factory and we will be responsible for our mistake. I deeply apologize for that. We'll exchange all the goods that fall short of our samples.

Kevin: Just make sure it's delivered before the end of this month.

Kathy: I assure you that the order will reach you in time and I promise there won't be such mistakes again.

Kevin: We will not pursue it since this is the first time such a mistake has been made.

★全文中畫 ⬤ 色塊的地方，可以依自己的狀況套入不同的名字、公司名、職稱、學校名等等。

中文翻譯1

凱西：凱文，早安，最近過得怎麼樣？

凱文：恐怕不是很好。

凱西：怎麼了？我能幫什麼忙嗎？

凱文：我來這裡，是為了3個月前下的TJ 205號訂單。我們已經收到了這批貨，但是卻發現有兩箱貨物與樣品標準不符。

凱西：我不知道是什麼原因，之前從來沒有發生過這樣的事情。也許是工廠發錯了貨物。

凱文：不要找藉口。如果我們在月底之前不能收到預訂的貨物，恐怕只好向你們提出索賠了。

凱西：我已經和工廠聯繫過了，我們會對我們的錯誤負責。我為此深感抱歉。我們會把沒有達到樣品標準的貨物全部予以調換。

凱文：確保在月底前交貨。

凱西：我向您保證這批貨物會按時運達你們那裡的，並且我保證以後不會有類似的事情發生了。

凱文：這是第一次出現這樣的問題，所以我們就不再深究了。

Dialogue ❷ 產品包裝糾紛 ◀ *Track 152*

凱西在這段對話中，特別強調「之前從來沒有發生過這個問題」、「我們公司一向很看重包裝」，目的是要一而再再而三地告訴對方：「這件事就只有這一次，以後絕對不會再發生」，以獲取信任。

Chris: Well, if you don't mind, I'll get straight down to business.

Kathy: Not at all. Please go ahead.

Chris: I must say your deliveries have so far been satisfactory; however, your last lot was found damaged on delivery.

Kathy: I'm sad to hear that. What is the cause of the damage determined by your people at the port?

Chris: According to the checker's report, nearly 25% of the cases had been broken and, therefore, the contents had been badly damaged, obviously attributed to improper packaging.

Kathy: Our company has always attached great importance to proper packaging and never before has such a thing happened. There is absolutely nothing wrong with the packaging.

Chris: As I said, your deliveries have so far been satisfactory; but the damage was unbearable for us. If this can't be settled amongst us, then we have to file a claim.

Kathy: That's totally understandable. As you know, before the shipment, international authorities had also inspected the products. We can present you the certification for the intact packaging, if necessary.

Chris: All right. It seems that we have more investigations to make.

Kathy: We'll be in touch.

★全文中畫 ● 色塊的地方，可以依自己的狀況套入不同的名字、公司名、職稱、學校名等等。

現在是不是回想起來了呢？

get straight down to business 開門見山
這句直翻就是「直接開始幹正事」，也就是「馬上切入正題，不拐彎抹角地做一些有的沒的其他的事」的意思。

中文翻譯2

克里斯：嗯，如果妳不介意，我就開門見山了。

凱　西：不介意，請說。

克里斯：我必須要說，你們的貨物一直都很令人滿意；但是，你們的上批貨物卻在抵達時有破損。

凱　西：聽到這個消息，我感到很遺憾。你們在碼頭時，有確定貨物破損的原因是什麼嗎？

克里斯：根據檢驗員的報告，近25%的包裝箱已經破損，所以裡面的貨物已經嚴重損壞，很明顯是因為包裝不當造成的。

凱　西：我們公司一直高度重視包裝，並且之前從未有過類似事情發生。貨物的包裝絕對沒有問題。

克里斯：就像我說的，你們的貨物一直都很令人滿意；但是這一次的損失我們無法承受。如果這件事不能妥善解決，我們不得不提出索賠。

凱　西：完全可以理解。如您所知，在運輸之前，國際權威機構也檢驗了我們的產
　　　　品。如果必要的話，我們可以出示包裝完好證明。
克里斯：好吧，看來我們要做更進一步的調查了。
凱　西：保持聯繫。

Dialogue ❸ 產品品質糾紛 🔊 *Track 153*

想對別的公司提出產品方面的抗議，但對方一直堅持說自己的產品沒問題，
到底要怎麼講才會讓對方聽得進去？凱文在這段對話中的作法就很好，他說：
「我很懷疑你方合作的誠意」，絕對會讓對方開始緊張。

Kevin: Good morning, Kathy !

Kathy: Good morning, Kevin ! Did you receive our last delivery?

Kevin: Yes. It was just in time; however, I'm afraid that I've got a bone to pick with you about the quality.

Kathy: I hope it's not serious.

Kevin: I hate to say this but the products you exchanged for us last time were in a bad state. Half of them are deteriorated.

Kathy: A complaint of this sort is very rare indeed. You know our exports have to pass rigid inspection prior to shipment.

Kevin: With all due respect, I found your recent lot very disappointing. I seriously doubt your sincerity in cooperation.

Kathy: Kevin , I can't tell you how much effort we've made to remedy our mistakes and I can promise you things like this have never once occurred. We're at a loss to understand the current situation.

Kevin: Because of the defective products, we'll miss the sale on Women's Day . How much clearer can I make it?

Kathy: We'll make a thorough investigation and we won't dodge our responsibility.

★全文中畫 ● 色塊的地方，可以依自己的狀況套入不同的名字、公司名、職稱、學校名等等。

have got a bone to pick with you 有點事情要抱怨

看到「bone」（骨頭）和「pick」（挑選），是不是很自然地就會以為這個片語是「雞蛋裡挑骨頭」的意思呢？其實意思不完全一樣，這個片語表示「有點事要抗議、找碴」的意思。

中文翻譯3

凱文：早安，凱西！

凱西：早安，凱文！你收到我們最近的那批貨了嗎？

凱文：是的。它剛好按時抵達；但是，我恐怕得批評品質了。

凱西：希望不嚴重。

凱文：我不想這樣說，但是很嚴重。你們上次為我們調換的貨物情況糟透了。一半的貨物都已經變質了。

凱西：這類的抱怨的確很少見。你知道我們的出口貨物在運輸前都必須經過嚴格的檢驗。

凱文：請恕我直言，我覺得你們最近的貨物很令人失望。我很懷疑你們合作的誠意。

凱西：凱文，我無法告訴你我們為彌補錯誤做了多少努力。我可以向你保證這類事件之前從未發生過。對於現在的狀況，我們同樣一頭霧水。

凱文：因為這次的缺陷產品，我們將要錯過婦女節特賣了。還用我解釋得更清楚嗎？

凱西：我們將進行徹底調查，並且不會推卸責任的。

Dialogue 4 產品運輸糾紛 🔊 *Track 154*

這段對話中，我們發現凱西提出證據證明貨物糾紛的問題並不出在她這一方後，對方本來還兇巴巴地問她有沒有證據，結果態度立刻改變，還說「我很感謝貴方在這次調查中所付出的努力」。在這段對話中注意看看他語氣的轉變也是很有趣的事！

Kathy: Glad to meet you, Chris !

Chris: Glad to meet you, too! How is your investigation?

Kathy: According to our survey, the damage of the packaging as well as the products was caused during transit.

Chris: What is your conclusion, then?

Kathy: We found compensations unacceptable for the damage happening during transit, according to our contract terms. What's more, another survey of ours showed that the products were actually still in good condition upon the arrival in Canada .

Chris: That means the products were damaged when discharged at our port?

Kathy: I'm afraid so. Your claim should be referred to the carrier.

Chris: Do you have any proof?

Kathy: Here you are. This is the survey conducted by a prestigious lab in Canada , whose testimony is absolutely trustworthy.

Chris: I really appreciate your diligence in this investigation.

★全文中畫 ⬤ 色塊的地方，可以依自己的狀況套入不同的名字、公司名、職稱、學校名等等。

中文翻譯4

凱　西：很高興見到你，克里斯！
克里斯：我也很高興見到妳！你們的調查進展得如何？
凱　西：根據我們的調查，包裝及產品的破損是運輸途中發生的。
克里斯：那你們的結論是什麼？
凱　西：我們認為，根據合約條款，對運輸途中導致的破損進行賠償是我們難以接受的。而且，我們的另一份調查顯示此批貨物在抵達加拿大時還是完好的。
克里斯：那就表示貨物是在我們碼頭卸貨時破損的？
凱　西：恐怕是這樣的。你們應該向承運人提出索賠。
克里斯：你們有證據嗎？
凱　西：給你。這是加拿大一所知名的實驗室進行的調查，他們的證言絕對可靠。
克里斯：我真的很感謝你們在此次調查中所付出的努力。

Dialogue ❺ 投訴出錯貨物 🔊 *Track 155*

同樣是有貨物的問題要抗議，凱西走比較溫和客氣的路線，我們可以看到在這段對話中她先稱讚對方值得信賴的品質，再提到這次貨物的問題，這也是一個溫和的抗議法。

Mr. Jackson: Hello, Kathy !

Kathy: Hello, Mr. Jackson ! I must say, as our raw material supplier , your quality has been reliable; however, to our disappointment, there was something wrong with your recent lot.

Mr. Jackson: Hold on. Before you go any further, may I have the contract number, please?

Kathy: COB0812/11 .

Mr. Jackson: OK, I'll write it down. What is the problem?

Kathy: You have delivered the wrong products to us.

Mr. Jackson: But if memory serves me right, we delivered that order almost three months ago!

Kathy: Yes, that's right. That is what makes the current situation complicated and our loss huge. We never found that out until we received a complaint from our client and carried out detailed investigation.

Mr. Jackson: That does not look so good. I will check with the party concerned regarding that order.

Kathy: I look forward to hearing back from you.

★全文中畫 ⬤ 色塊的地方，可以依自己的狀況套入不同的名字、公司名、職稱、學校名等等。

現在是不是回想起來了呢？

if memory serves me right 如果我沒記錯的話
長得很像的片語還有「serves me right」，但它的意思是「我應得的、我自找的」，兩者的意思完全不同，別搞混了。

中文翻譯5

傑克遜先生：妳好，凱西！

凱　西：你好，傑克遜先生！我得說，作為我們的原料供應商，你們的品質一直值得信賴。然而，令我們失望的是，你們近期的貨物出了問題。

傑克遜先生：等一下，您能告訴我合約號碼再繼續嗎？

凱　西：COB0812/11。

傑克遜先生：好的，我把它記下來。有什麼問題？

凱　西：你們為我們出錯貨了。

傑克遜先生：但是，如果我沒有記錯的話，我們出貨給你們是快三個月前的事！

凱　　西：是的，就是這樣。就是因為這個原因，現在的情況才變得很複雜，使我們的
　　　　　損失慘重。我們在收到客戶的投訴並進行了詳細的調查之後，才發現這件
　　　　　事。
傑克遜先生：看起來不太妙啊。我會與相關方面就那批訂單進行核實。
凱　　西：我等您的消息。

Dialogue ❻ 協商糾紛未果 ◀︎ *Track 156*

這段對話中，凱西一開口居然就要求對方全額賠償。如果你也遇到這樣的狀
況，而認為這好像不太合理，可以像傑克遜先生一樣說「**I beg your pardon?**」
（您能再說一遍嗎？）其實並不是要叫對方再說一遍，而是要表達「欸，我沒聽
錯吧……」這樣的情緒。

Mr. Jackson: I've already consulted the party concerned and as you said, we made the wrong delivery due to negligence. I'm sorry to have caused you so much inconvenience.

Kathy: I'm glad to hear that. I have little doubt that the problem will be solved through friendly consultation.

Mr. Jackson: Exactly. What is your proposed compensation?

Kathy: We think you are completely responsible for our huge losses.

Mr. Jackson: I beg your pardon? Full responsibility? You should have realized our mistake on delivery. I'm afraid you also have to share part of the responsibility.

Kathy: The difference between these kinds of herbs is extremely difficult to tell. Don't you think we would have informed you about this and wouldn't have produced those products if we had known that earlier?

Mr. Jackson: But that should have been revealed if proper measures had been taken to ensure the finished products met quality checks.

Kathy: Please don't question the quality of our products. The fact is that these two kinds of ingredients showed little disparity during the analysis.

Mr. Jackson: Anyway, full responsibility is out of the question on our side.

Kathy: I find your attitude in this case quite unreasonable. If this is what you insist on, we will end this discussion right now and directly appeal to arbitration.

Mr. Jackson: Fine.

★全文中畫 ⬤ 色塊的地方，可以依自己的狀況套入不同的名字、公司名、職稱、學校名等等。

現在是不是回想起來了呢？

out of the question 絕不可能

這個片語的意思是「完全不可能，說都不用說」的意思。例如：

A: Can I buy this house? 我可以買這棟房子嗎？

B: That's out of the question. We have no money.
　不用說，不行。我們又沒錢。

中文翻譯6

傑克遜先生：我們已諮詢了當事人，如您所說，我們由於疏忽出錯了貨物。很抱歉給你們造成如此大的不便。

凱　西：很高興能聽到您這樣說。我深信此次問題會透過友好協商的方式予以解決。

傑克遜先生：沒錯。你們就賠償問題有什麼建議？

凱　西：我們認為你們對我們的損失負有全責。

傑克遜先生：您能再說一遍嗎？全部責任？你們應該在收貨時就意識到我們的錯誤。你們恐怕需要分擔部分責任。

凱　西：這些草藥很難區分。您難道不認為，如果我們早就發現了，就會及時通知你們，也不會生產那些產品了嗎？

傑克遜先生：但如果你們採取了適當措施來保證貨品品質檢合格，就會發現這個問題。

凱　西：請不要懷疑我們產品的品質問題。事實是，這兩種成分在分析過程中，差異很小。

傑克遜先生：不管怎樣，我們無法接受全責。

凱　西：我覺得您對此事的態度非常不合理。如果您堅持己見，我們將立即結束討論而直接訴諸仲裁了。

傑克遜先生：好吧。

Dialogue ❼ 產權糾紛 ◀ *Track 157*

要請對方放心，這段對話中的「**please rest assured**」（請放心）是很棒的
一個說法，可以參考凱西怎麼說的。

● ●

Tina: Hello, Kathy !

Kathy: Hello, Tina ! How is our product selling?

Tina: Pretty well, in fact, even better than we expected. It flew off the shelves like hot cakes.

Kathy: I'm so happy to hear this. It's really encouraging.

Tina: But I also got some bad news. We've been informed that this brand belongs to another company, which means we are not authorized to sell the products.

Kathy: That is completely impossible. We've bought the trading rights from an entrepreneur in 2009 to promote our men's skin care range.

Tina: This is an entirely different story from theirs. I'm afraid if we get sued, we have to hold your company responsible for our cost.

Kathy: This brand has already generated annual sales of $215 million for us. We will do battle over ownership of the brand with any party.

Tina: I suggest you negotiate with the other party concerning the ownership of the brand.

Kathy: Please rest assured, we'll straighten things out.

★全文中畫 ⬤ 色塊的地方，可以依自己的狀況套入不同的名字、公司名、職稱、學校名等等。

現在是不是回想起來了呢？

sell like hot cakes 銷售極好
熱騰騰的蛋糕剛出爐，誰都想買吧！賣得像熱蛋糕一樣好，就表示賣得非常
好，很快就搶購一空。

蒂娜：妳好，凱西！

凱西：妳好，蒂娜！我們的產品銷售得怎麼樣了？

蒂娜：非常好，甚至比我們預想的還要好。像剛出爐的蛋糕一樣，一上市馬上就銷售一空了。

凱西：聽到這個真讓人高興。真是振奮人心啊。

蒂娜：但是我也有壞消息。我們被告知這個品牌屬於另一家公司，也就意味著我們無權銷售這項產品。

凱西：那是絕對不可能的。我們在2009年從一位企業家手裡購買了交易權，來擴展我們的男士皮膚護理領域。

蒂娜：這與他們的說法完全不同。如果我們被起訴的話，我們只能要求貴公司承擔我們的費用。

凱西：這個品牌已為我公司帶來了2.15億美元的年銷售額。我們會為此品牌的所有權與任何一方奮戰的。

蒂娜：我建議妳們與相關的另一方品牌，就所有權問題進行協商。

凱西：請放心。我們會把事情解決好的。

Dialogue ❽ 產品召回 🔊 *Track 158*

在這段對話中，凱西被老闆訓後，還順便捅自己一刀，說自己「short-sighted」（眼光短淺、短視近利），以表示自己知錯，也是個不錯的作法。

Kathy: Things have been a little bit messy recently. We've had so many disputes over the products.

Mr. Lee: Indeed, tough days. How is everything now?

Kathy: Concerning the dispute with our supplier, they have sent another person this time instead of Mr. Jackson to negotiate with us to express their earnest wish to be our supplier as usual, and we've reached an agreement of 85% compensation.

Mr. Lee: Good. How is our brand dispute?

Kathy: The dispute is now about to hit the Supreme Court. We have a good chance of winning the lawsuit.

Mr. Lee: Keep me posted of the latest news. How have we dealt with our defective products?

Kathy: We have stopped producing them and replaced the raw materials in a timely manner.

Mr. Lee: How about those that have been delivered to our clients?

Kathy: We have transferred new cargo to (Kevin) so that he can still sell it for (Women's Day) and guaranteed to cover his total losses. He seems to be pleased. So far we haven't heard any other complaints from clients.

Mr. Lee: This is not the right strategy. A stitch in time saves nine. We have to recall all the leftover defective products before they go to market in spite of the losses. This will maintain our brand power and save our long-term interest.

Kathy: I'm sorry for being short-sighted. I will release product recall announcements and notify the clients right away.

★全文中畫 色塊的地方，可以依自己的狀況套入不同的名字、公司名、職稱、學校名等等。

中文翻譯8

凱　西：最近事情有些亂。我們產品出現了很多糾紛。

李先生：的確如此，日子不好過啊。現在一切怎麼樣了？

凱　西：關於與我們供應商的糾紛，他們這次派另一個人替代傑克遜先生來與我們談判，以此表達其希望繼續做我們供應商的誠意。我們達成賠償85%金額的協議。

李先生：很好。我們的品牌糾紛怎麼樣了？

凱　西：這個糾紛很快就要送達最高法院了。我想我們勝算很大。

李先生：即時通知我最新的進展。對於有缺陷的產品，我們是怎麼處理的？

凱　西：我們已經及時停止生產，也替換了原料。

李先生：那些已經送達我們客戶的產品呢？

凱　西：我們已經為凱文調送了一批新的貨物，這樣他還可以趕上婦女節的特賣，並且保證彌補他的全部損失。他似乎很高興。到目前為止，我們還沒有從客戶那裡收到新的投訴。

李先生：這不是正確的決策。及時一針頂九針。儘管會有損失，我們還是要在剩餘缺陷產品投放市場之前，召回所有產品。這樣可以維護我們的品牌力量並且挽回我們的長期利益。

凱　西：很抱歉，我沒考慮那麼多。我會馬上發出產品召回通知，並告知我們的客戶。

交貨糾紛

Dialogue ❶ 貨物損壞 🔊 *Track 159*

💬 「進入重點」用英文可以說「get to the point」。在這段對話中,我們可以看看凱西如何用這個片語,將話題迅速從旅館很舒服轉移到貨物損壞的問題。

● ●

Kathy: Hello, Mr. Brown , how are you? It is nice to see you again.

Mr. Brown: How are you, Kathy ? It certainly is a pleasure to see you here again. I hope you had an enjoyable trip from Shanghai .

Kathy: The flight was really long, but it was comfortable so I didn't feel too tired.

Mr. Brown: I am glad that you had a pleasant trip. I hope you are comfortably settled and find things at the hotel satisfactory.

Kathy: Everything is perfect. Thank you. Well, now, Mr. Brown , if you don't mind, I'll get to the point.

Mr. Brown: Okay. You want to discuss the quality of the products, don't you?

Kathy: That's right. You see, Mr. Brown , you have probably been advised of the serious damage done to the last consignment of 60 cases of products. Upon its arrival in Shanghai it was found, much to our regret, that about 50% of the cases were leaking.

Mr. Brown: Just a minute, if you please, Kathy . Have your people in Shanghai discovered what the exact cause of the leakage was? It was rather a singular case, for thousands of tons of this product have been exported and this seems to be the only case of a shipment being damaged en route.

Kathy: I am sorry I have to say it was not en route. It was definitely damaged prior to loading onto the ship. You may think it a singular case, yet the fact remains that this has made it necessary for us to file a claim against you.

Mr. Brown: As I have said before, the whole business is most unfortunate. We have never come across such a case of damage during loading. Don't worry, we will find the problem and give you a satisfactory answer at once.

★全文中畫 ⬤ 色塊的地方，可以依自己的狀況套入不同的名字、公司名、職稱、學校名等等。

現在是不是回想起來了呢？

en route 在途中

這是個代表「在路上、在途中」的片語。沒見過「en」吧！它真的是一個英文單字嗎？原來，它的確不是一個英文單字，這是從法文借過來的。

中文翻譯1

凱西： 布朗先生，你好。很高興再次見到你。

布朗： 凱西，妳好。很高興在這裡又見到妳。希望妳從上海來的時候旅途愉快。

凱西： 飛行時間雖然很長，但客機很舒適，所以也不覺得很累。

布朗： 很高興妳旅途愉快。希望妳住得舒適，對旅館設備滿意。

凱西： 謝謝你，一切都很好。噢，布朗先生，要是你不介意的話，現在我們就開始談業務吧。

布朗： 好，妳想談談產品品質的事，對不對？

凱西： 對。布朗先生，也許你已經知道最後一批60箱的產品嚴重損壞的情況。貨物一到上海，我們就遺憾地發現其中有一半左右的箱子滲漏。

布朗： 凱西，請等一下。請問你們上海的人有沒有發現滲漏的確切原因？這件事還是第一次發生，我們已經出口好幾千噸了，中途損壞還是第一次。

凱西： 很抱歉，我得說清楚，損壞不是在運輸途中發生的。很明顯，損壞是在裝上船之前發生的。你可能認為這種事很少發生，可是事實不得不讓我們向你們提出索賠。

布朗： 我剛才說過，整個事件實在是很遺憾。我們從未遇到過在裝船時發生這樣的損壞。別擔心，我們會找出問題並且及時給妳一個滿意的答覆。

Dialogue ❷ 貨物短缺 🔊 *Track 160*

💬 麥克在此段對話中先是採取全盤否認自己一方有錯的態度，最後卻有一百八十度的轉變，答應盡快調查此事。到底是什麼讓他有這個轉變呢？就是凱西從頭到尾都屹立不搖的態度。只要一直堅持重複一樣的事情，對方很可能就會受不了然後投降了。

• •

Mike: Good morning, ABC Company.

Kathy: Hello, Mike. This is Kathy, from Shanghai, China.

Mike: Hi, Kathy. How are you?

Kathy: Fine, thank you. I'm calling about the 80 cartons of Lion soap shipped by your company.

Mike: Yes? Haven't you received them?

Kathy: Yes. They arrived here on the 20th of August, but unfortunately, we found that there were only 70 cartons instead of the 80 you said you'd ship.

Mike: Really? Have you checked the order?

Kathy: Yes, certainly. We were told by the shipping company that only 70 cartons had been loaded on board.

Mike: Well, that's impossible.

Kathy: But it is true, and our customers are waiting for delivery of the goods, and we can't because of the shortage in quantity.

Mike: Don't worry. I will check it out as soon as possible.

★全文中畫 ⬤ 色塊的地方，可以依自己的狀況套入不同的名字、公司名、職稱、學校名等等。

中文翻譯2 •
麥克：早安！這裡是ABC公司。
凱西：你好，麥克，我是中國上海的凱西。
麥克：嗨，凱西。妳好嗎？
凱西：很好。謝謝。我打這通電話是為了你們公司送來的那80箱獅牌肥皂的事。
麥克：怎麼了？你們沒收到嗎？

凱西：收到了。是8月20號到的。但遺憾的是，你們只運送了70箱而不是所說的80箱。

麥克：真的嗎？你們核對訂單了嗎？

凱西：是的，當然核對了。船運公司告訴我們裝船的時候就是70箱。

麥克：啊，那不可能。

凱西：但這是事實。現在我們的客戶正在等著我們供貨，而因為數量短缺我們無法供貨。

麥克：別著急。我會儘快調查此事。

Dialogue ❸ 提前交貨 🔊 *Track 161*

在和其他的公司溝通時，最好的作法就是白紙黑字，以書信的方式確認，這樣到時候如果對方出爾反爾，你就有證據可以咬死對方。在這段對話中就是這麼做的。

Kathy: Mr. Black , when is the earliest you can make a shipment?

Mr. Black: In April or early May .

Kathy: I am afraid shipment by early May would be too late for us. Our customs formalities are quite complicated, and it takes time to distribute the goods to our customers. The cosmetics must be delivered before April , or else we can't make it in time for the spring sale .

Mr. Black: In that case, we will have to move shipment up a month earlier. It's now January . The cosmetics should be shipped before the end of March , only 2 months are left. Time is too limited.

Kathy: You understand a timely delivery is very important to us.

Mr. Black: All right. You can rest assured that we will do everything possible to speed up shipment. The cosmetics will be delivered before April .

Kathy: I am so glad to that. Shall we send you a letter confirming this?

Mr. Black: As soon as you send us a letter confirming this conversation, we'll send you a reply immediately.

Kathy: Thanks ever so much for your cooperation, Mr. Black . Good bye.

Mr. Black: Good bye.

★全文中畫 ⬤ 色塊的地方，可以依自己的狀況套入不同的名字、公司名、職稱、學校名等等。

rest assured 安心

rest有「休息」的意思，而assured有「安心、放心」的意思。安心到可以跑去休息，可見這個片語有多「安心」了。

中文翻譯3

凱　西：布萊克先生，你們最早能什麼時候出貨？

布萊克先生：四月或者是五月初。

凱　西：五月初出貨的話，對我們來說恐怕太晚了，我們的海關手續比較複雜，而且還需要一定的時間才能把貨物發到我們顧客手中。化妝品必須在四月之前交貨，否則我們趕不上春季特賣了。

布萊克先生：這樣的話我們必須再提前一個月出貨。現在是一月，化妝品應該在三月底前出貨，只剩下兩個月了，時間太緊了。

凱　西：你知道及時交貨對我們來說很重要。

布萊克先生：好吧，妳放心，我們會盡我們所能提前出貨，化妝品會在四月前交貨的。

凱　西：聽你這樣說，我很高興。我們寄信給你們確認一下這個安排好嗎？

布萊克先生：我們一旦收到你們針對此次談話內容的確認信，就會立即回覆。

凱　西：十分感謝您的合作。布萊克先生，再見。

布萊克先生：再見。

Dialogue ❹ 分批交貨 ◀ Track 162

轉換話題時，可用「let's turn to...」（我們來改談談……）的說法，可以看看這段對話中是怎麼用的。

Danny: Now let's turn to the delivery. When is the soonest you can deliver?

Kathy: You can have the first five thousand pieces before the end of this month.

Danny: I want ten thousand by the end of this month.

Kathy: Well, Danny, that will be difficult, but since you have compromised on the question of price, I think we can arrange that.

Danny: What about the balance of the order?

Kathy: We can deliver that in three consignments over the following three months.

Danny: I'd rather have everything delivered by (the end of May).

Kathy: I can't promise that, but I shall do my best.

Danny: Thanks for your cooperation, (Kathy). Good bye.

Kathy: Good bye.

★全文中畫 ⬤ 色塊的地方，可以依自己的狀況套入不同的名字、公司名、職稱、學校名等等。

中文翻譯4

丹尼：現在我們來談談交貨的事情。你們最快什麼時候可以交貨？
凱西：這個月底前你可以收到首批5,000件。
丹尼：月底前我想要1萬件。
凱西：嗯，丹尼，這太難了，不過有鑒於你在價格上的讓步，我認為我們可以安排。
丹尼：訂單餘下的部分呢？
凱西：我們將在隨後的3個月內分3批交貨。
丹尼：我傾向要你們在5月底前交清所有貨物。
凱西：我不能保證做到，不過我會盡力。
丹尼：謝謝妳的合作，凱西。再見。
凱西：再見。

Dialogue ❺ 交貨日期 🔊 *Track 163*

💬 這段對話中的湯姆在答應幫對方協商事情時，還不忘加一句「考慮到我們之間長期的友好業務關係……」，來鞏固雙方的交情，是個行走商場江湖好用的說法。

Kathy: Can you execute shipment during (September)?

Tom: I don't think we can.

Kathy: Then when is the earliest we can expect the shipment?

Tom: By (the middle of October).

Kathy: It's too late. You see, in our market, (October) is the peak season for this kind of commodity, so the goods must be shipped before (October), or we won't be ready for the peak season.

Tom: Well, considering our long-standing good business relationship, we'll try hard to negotiate with our manufacturers for an earlier delivery.

Kathy: Thanks. Then may I suggest that you put down in the contract "shipment on September 15th or earlier"?

Tom: Let me see. Now the workers will have to work on three shifts for it. Well, we can manage it on the 20th of September. That is the best we can do.

Kathy: Oh, that's very considerate of you. I'll take your word for it.

Tom: It's my pleasure.

★全文中畫 色塊的地方，可以依自己的狀況套入不同的名字、公司名、職稱、學校名等等。

現在是不是回想起來了呢？

long-standing 長期的
這個字字面上的意思是「站得很久的」，引申為「長久以來屹立不搖的」的意思。

中文翻譯5

凱西： 你們能在9月裝運嗎？

湯姆： 我看不行。

凱西： 那麼最早什麼時候能裝運？

湯姆： 到10月中旬。

凱西： 那太晚了。你知道，在我們這邊，10月份是這類商品的銷售旺季。因此，貨物必須在10月之前裝運，否則就無法趕上銷售旺季了。

湯姆： 嗯，考量到我們之間長期的友好業務關係，我們將儘量跟廠方磋商，想辦法早一點交貨。

凱西： 非常感謝。那麼，可否請你在合約上寫清楚「9月15日或之前出貨」？

湯姆： 讓我看看，這樣，工人就得輪三班了。嗯，我們可以在9月20日之前出貨，這是我們最快的出貨時間了。

凱西： 噢，你太周到了，那就這樣決定了。

湯姆： 不必客氣。

Dialogue ❻ 協商賠償 🔊 *Track 164*

💬 請對方賠償時，也要察言觀色。這段對話中，凱西發現對方講話非常客氣又抱歉，就可以使用非常堅定的口氣要求對方賠償，甚至用了「**have to**」（一定要）。如果對方比較兇或感覺不能惹，則不會用這麼直接而強制的語氣。

• •

Kathy: Hello, Kathy speaking.

Lily: Hello, Kathy, this is Lily, UK.

Kathy: Oh, yes. Lily, may I help you?

Lily: We received your fax, and found the problem. We sincerely regret the mistakewe made, and apologize for the inconvenience caused by it.

Kathy: I'm sorry, too, because some of our customers raised a claim against us for not being able to get the delivery in time.

Lily: Oh, I'm sorry for that.

Kathy: Unfortunately there's nothing we can do to change the past. Now, we have to give our customers some compensation, and in turn we will also lodge our claim against your company. You have to make up for the loss.

Lily: Well, it's our fault. We are very sorry about that.

Kathy: I'm faxing you the claim documents.

Lily: Well, all right. We'll discuss it.

★全文中畫 ⬤ 色塊的地方，可以依自己的狀況套入不同的名字、公司名、職稱、學校名等等。

中文翻譯6 •

凱西：你好，我是凱西。

莉莉：你好，是凱西嗎？我是英國的莉莉。

凱西：哦，莉莉，妳有什麼事嗎？

莉莉：我們收到了妳的傳真，找到了問題所在。我們為所發生的失誤深感遺憾，並對給你們帶來的不便表示歉意。

凱西：我也為此感到遺憾，因為我們的一些客戶因我們沒有按時供貨，對我們提出索賠了。

莉莉：噢，很抱歉。

凱西：很遺憾，對發生的事我們無法改變。我們必須給我們的客戶一些補償，而我們
　　　也要向妳們公司提出索賠。妳們必須補償我們的損失。

莉莉：嗯，是我們的過失。我們對此非常抱歉。

凱西：我現在將索賠資料傳真給你們。

莉莉：好的，傳過來吧。我們會對這件事進行討論的。

商務小常識

　　在業務中常見的是買方向賣方提出索賠，如賣方拒不交貨、逾期裝
運、數量短缺、貨物的品質規格與合約不符、錯發錯運、包裝不妥、隨船
單證不全或漏填錯發等致使買方遭受損失時，買方可向賣方提出索賠。但
是在某些情況下，如買方拒開或遲開信用證、不按時接收貨物、無理毀約
等致使賣方遭受損失時，賣方也會向買方提出索賠。

Dialogue ❶ 要求合理解釋未加薪 ◀ *Track 165*

在這段對話中,莉莉用了「**you can be totally honest with me**」(你可以跟我開誠布公沒關係)這一句。這在職場上是很好用的一個句子,能用來博得他人的信任,讓對方不知不覺就跟你吐實。

• •

Mr. Wang: Good morning, Lily ! How is your project going?

Lily: Good. Is it a convenient time to talk?

Mr. Wang: No problem. What's the matter?

Lily: It's just a minor problem but it's been bothering me. Everyone in my department got a pay raise except me.

Mr. Wang: You see, we are limited by budget constraints and cannot afford a raise for all our employees in spite of our desire to do so.

Lily: Mr. Wang, you can be totally honest with me. Despite the budget constraints, there are still employees receiving the raise.

Mr. Wang: Okay. To be frank, our performance management system aligns performance with pay raise, unfortunately, you were disqualified.

Lily: Will you explain, please?

Mr. Wang: You just don't seem to have enthusiasm for your job; like just now, I asked you about your recent project, but you didn't seem to be interested. If you don't love your job, you can hardly stand out in it.

Lily: I see your point now. Thank you for your advice. I will try harder.

★全文中畫 ⬤ 色塊的地方,可以依自己的狀況套入不同的名字、公司名、職稱、學校名等等。

to be frank 老實說

「to be frank」並不是要你成為法蘭克，而是表示「老實說」的意思。類似的用法還有「frankly」，可以互相替換著使用。

中文翻譯1

王先生：早安，莉莉！妳們的專案進行得怎麼樣了？

莉　莉：很好。您現在方便嗎？

王先生：沒問題。有什麼事嗎？

莉　莉：只是一個很小的問題，但是卻一直困擾我。我們部門除了我以外的每一個人都加薪了。

王先生：妳知道，我們受預算限制，儘管我們很希望，但是卻承擔不起給公司的每一個人都加薪。

莉　莉：王先生，您可以跟我開誠佈公。儘管有預算限制，但還是有員工加薪了。

王先生：好吧，坦白說，在我們的績效管理體系，員工的表現與加薪有關，可惜妳沒有通過。

莉　莉：你能說具體一點嗎？

王先生：妳看起來對工作沒有熱情；像剛才，我詢問了妳關於妳們最近專案的情況，但是妳卻似乎不是很感興趣。如果妳不喜歡妳的工作，妳就很難表現出色。

莉　莉：我現在明白了。謝謝您的建議。我會更加努力的。

Dialogue ❷ 正式提出加薪要求 ◀ *Track 166*

在這段最後，王先生說了「take it or leave it」，意思就是「不要拉倒」。但聽起來沒有我們中文的「不要拉倒」這麼任性，反而表示了自己的意志堅決與強勢，是可以在職場上使用的會話。

Kathy: Good morning, Mr. Wang !

Mr. Wang: Good morning, Kathy ! Take a seat, please!

Kathy: I think it's fair to say everyone knows the quality of work I've been doing here.

Mr. Wang: Right. That's why I promoted you several months ago.

Kathy: I suppose no pay raise also played a role. Perhaps now it's time for me to get what I missed out on since recent performance appraisals that document my job are everywhere.

Mr. Wang: Despite your best efforts, there may simply not be enough money in the budget to increase your salary. The company may also not want to create inequities by paying one person more than others in a similar position.

Kathy: (Mr. Wang), please don't press conference me.

Mr. Wang: All right. I'll discuss it with (Human Resources).

Kathy: (Mr. Wang), both of us know well that it's within your power. Please just give me an answer. This won't be the first time you have disappointed me. I did what you said last time but you gave me a promotion instead of a raise.

Mr. Wang: I can only grant you an extra couple of weeks paid vacation rather than a raise. Take it or leave it. It's up to you.

Kathy: It seems that I don't have any other alternative. Okay, I'll take it.

★全文中畫 ⬤ 色塊的地方，可以依自己的狀況套入不同的名字、公司名、職稱、學校名等等。

> **現在是不是回想起來了呢？**
>
> **don't press conference me 不要跟我說外交辭令**
> 「press conference」是「記者會」的意思，是當作名詞片語用，但在這裡則把它「轉品」變成了動詞，整句的意思是「別跟我講一堆像開記者會一樣假掰的話」。

中文翻譯2

凱　西：早安，王先生！
王先生：早安，凱西！請坐！
凱　西：我想公平地說，大家對我在這裡工作的品質有目共睹。
王先生：是的。所以我幾個月前讓妳升職了。
凱　西：我想沒有加薪也產生了一定的作用吧。也許現在是我加薪的機會了，因為最近對我工作表現的讚譽隨處可見。
王先生：儘管妳表現得很出色，但是預算裡還沒有足夠的錢替妳加薪，公司也不希望在同職位的員工中，造成薪酬不均的現象。

凱　西：王先生，請不要跟我說外交辭令。

王先生：好吧，我會與人力資源部談談這件事。

凱　西：王先生，我們都很清楚，這是在您的職權範圍內的。請給我一個答覆吧。這不是您第一次令我失望。我上一次已經按您說的做了，但是您卻給我升職而不是加薪。

王先生：我只能給妳額外兩週的有薪假，而不能加薪。同不同意，全在於妳。

凱　西：看來，我似乎沒有別的選擇。好吧，我接受。

Dialogue ❸ 要求提高加薪幅度 🔊 *Track 167*

張先生在這段對話中稱讚了蘇珊「是成熟的員工」，試圖以稱讚的方式讓對方接受加薪加很少的事實。也可以參考他的說法試試看！不過，這個作法對蘇珊管用，對一些其他的員工就不一定了。

Mr. Zhang: Hello, Susan !

Susan: Hello, Mr. Zhang ! I'm here to talk about the recent pay raise.

Mr. Zhang: If memory serves me correctly, I did give you a 3.59% salary increase this time.

Susan: Yes, but this is just the problem—even our receptionists received a 5.2% increase, and I have been with the company for 8 years , while they have worked here for only 2 years .

Mr. Zhang: That's true, but that's not the criteria we used. Besides, the receptionists have taken on some additional responsibilities.

Susan: But my levels of responsibilites are far greater. I have to deal with relationships of various kinds. I have a much heavier load on my shoulders.

Mr. Zhang: I need to shorten the "gap" among your salary ranges.

Susan: But actually the salaries of the five of us in our department have basically stayed in the same range over the years, while there has always been a "gap" between our salary and that of our receptionists.

Mr. Zhang: This is exactly what I am trying to change currently. They need to catch up. It's just the way it is. You're all mature staff; I think you all can understand.

Susan: I see now. I'll do my best to work with them.

★全文中畫 ⬤ 色塊的地方，可以依自己的狀況套入不同的名字、公司名、職稱、學校名等等。

criteria 標準

這個單字是「複數形式」喔！它通常都是以這個複數形式出現，它的單數形式是criterion，反而比較少看到。

中文翻譯3

張先生：妳好，蘇珊！

蘇　珊：你好，張先生！我是來跟您談最近加薪的問題的。

張先生：如果我沒有記錯的話，我確實替妳加薪了，漲了3.59%。

蘇　珊：是的，但是這正是問題所在——我們的接待人員薪水甚至漲了5.2%。我已經在公司工作八年了，可是她們在這裡卻只有兩年。

張先生：沒錯。但是，那不是我們的標準，況且接待人員又承擔了一些額外的任務。

蘇　珊：但是我的責任更重大。我要處理各種關係，肩負的擔子更重。

張先生：我需要縮小你們之間的薪酬差距。

蘇　珊：但是，這幾年下來，我們部門的五個人的工資基本上就在同一個範圍，而在我們和接待人員之間總是有「差距」的。

張先生：這正是我目前想改變的。她們要趕上來。就是這麼回事。你們都是成熟的員工了；我想你們能明白。

蘇　珊：我現在明白了。我會盡力與她們合作的。

Dialogue ❹ 見機要求加薪 🔊 *Track 168*

💬 這段對話正是見機行事的最好範例，南西一聽自己要被派去處理人家加薪的事，就藉機也來要求可加薪，難怪張先生會說她「**really didn't miss the boat**」（真不錯過機會啊）。

Mr. Wang: Nancy , since you are the executive of the Public Relation Department and you are proficient at communicating with people, I will assign you a very important task.

Nancy: I can feel the pressure now. I hope I can handle it.

Mr. Wang: Our company is facing an internal dispute currently. As you may have heard of the news, the workers in the production line have been on strike, demanding salary increases, so our company needs you to negotiate with them.

Nancy: I wish I had the expertise for this, but I'm afraid I don't.

Mr. Wang: Why not? I'm sure you can work it out.

Nancy: I do love my job of repairing relationships among people but I'm not so sure about my love for this company, since my demand for salary increases have also been denied several times.

Mr. Wang: You really didn't miss the boat. All right, how about this? If you can manage this case, I will give you a 6% increase.

Nancy: That's great. Mr. Wang , but to speak from a completely objective third party, I really believe they should get salary increases. They've been complaining about this for a long time.

Mr. Wang: That will be our last resort in this dispute.

Nancy: OK, I will do my best.

★全文中畫 ⬤ 色塊的地方，可以依自己的狀況套入不同的名字、公司名、職稱、學校名等等。

【 現在是不是回想起來了呢？ 】

last resort 最後手段

「last resort」指的是「實在沒有別的辦法了，只好用這個辦法了」。舉例來說，如果你在哪都找不到廁所，只好跑進路邊人家借，這個方法就是你的「last resort」。或如果你沒有錢，但全部的人也都沒錢，只有你的仇人有錢，你只好去跟仇人借錢，這也是你的「last resort」。

中文翻譯4

王先生：南西，既然妳是公共關係部的主管，又精於溝通，我要分配一項非常重要的任務給妳。

南　西：我現在就感覺到壓力了。希望我能處理好。

王先生：我們公司現在面臨一場內部糾紛。妳可能已經聽到這個消息了，生產線上的工人舉行了罷工，要求調漲薪資。所以，公司需要妳去跟他們談判。

南　西：我希望我能處理這件事，但是我恐怕不行。

王先生：為什麼不行？我相信妳會解決好的。

南　西：我確實是熱愛可以修復人們之間關係的這份工作，但是我不敢肯定自己也熱愛公司，因為我調漲薪資的要求也已經被公司拒絕好多次了。

王先生：妳真是不錯過機會呢！好吧，妳看這樣好不好？如果妳能處理好這件事，我就替妳漲6%的薪資。

南　西：很好。王先生，但從完全客觀的第三者角度來看，我確實覺得他們應該調漲工資。他們為此已經抱怨很長時間了。

王先生：先解決這次糾紛吧，如果沒有別的辦法，再漲薪資。

南　西：好吧。我會努力的。

Dialogue ❺ 協商薪資問題 ◀ *Track 169*

在這段對話中，最後南西使用了「that's beyond my reach」（這超出我能做的範圍了），這是很好用的一句會話，面對顧客，遇到不知道怎麼解決的事時，可以拿來用。

Joe: Good morning, my name is Joe. I am the workers' representative.

Nancy: Good morning, I'm Nancy. I'm here to resolve the dispute with you on behalf of our company. I can understand your stance of complaining about wages.

Joe: No, you can't. It is extremely difficult to obtain a pay raise in our company.

Nancy: But we have raised the pay twice just recently.

Joe: In fact, we have seen a pay raise only twice and it was done in order to comply with our national policies. However, the best rate we have is 5.6%. That is still below the national average of 6.5% and not everyone got the raise, especially not our production workers.

Nancy: I can see your point, but don't forget that we also have pension plans, medical insurance and paid vacations and other benefits.

Joe: That is what other companies also have. As for the paid vacation, we don't have time to enjoy it at all because of the extra work. What's worse, we work overtime without extra pay.

Nancy: That's because our budget is too tight.

Joe: The budget in every company is tight, but you can still find the money if you want. We insist on a 20% increase for us.

Nancy: That's beyond my reach. I have to call the manager.

Joe: Okay, we can take a break.

★全文中畫 色塊的地方，可以依自己的狀況套入不同的名字、公司名、職稱、學校名等等。

中文翻譯5

喬：早安，我叫喬，我是工人代表。

南西：早安，我是南西。我是代表公司來跟你們解決糾紛的，我能夠理解你們抱怨工資的立場。

喬：不，妳不能理解。在我們公司是很難得到加薪的。

南西：但是，僅僅是在最近，我們就有兩次加薪。

喬：事實上，我們只有兩次加薪，並且還都是為了迎合國家政策的需要。然而，我們最高的漲薪幅度是5.6%，還是低於6.5%的國家平均標準，而且並不是所有人都加薪了，尤其是我們生產工人沒有加薪。

南西：我能理解你的想法，但是不要忘了我們公司還有退休金、醫療保險、有薪休假等其他福利。

喬：這在其他公司也有。至於有薪休假，由於加班，我們根本沒有時間去享受休假。更糟糕的是，我們加班卻沒有加班費。

南西：因為公司的預算太緊了。

喬：每家公司的預算都很緊，但是，只要願意的話，總可以弄到錢。我們堅持要求加薪20%。

南西：這就超出我能做的範圍了，我得打個電話給經理。

喬：好，我們休息一下。

Dialogue ❻ 就加薪問題達成共識 🔊Track 170

💬 南西在這段對話的最後用了一個非常好的招數，表示自己會為了員工們說服經理加薪，馬上讓自己從員工們的敵人變成夥伴，是個在協商時很棒的作法。

● ●

Nancy: I just called the manager. 20% is too much.

Joe: No, it isn't. The average increase in other companies has already totaled 35%, but we've only had a 10% increase. This figure was put forward even without considering the compensations for working overtime.

Nancy: But work is not just about money, it is what we enjoy and strive for, and how we improve ourselves, isn't it?

Joe: No, it isn't. Work is about the money. We need money to support our families. Only with sufficient money can work be about other motivations. If we can't have what we deserve, we will take legal actions.

Nancy: It appears that we don't feel the same way about our jobs. Maybe that's why I've tolerated no increase in pay for such a long time. What about this? 15% pay raise and the other 5% will be transformed into the extra weeks of paid vacation.

Joe: But you just said the manager didn't agree.

Nancy: No, he didn't; but I'll persuade him into it. When I accepted this task, the party I intended to persuade was him not you.

Joe: Please accept my appreciation from the bottom of my heart! Thank you for your attempts regardless of the results!

★全文中畫 ⬤ 色塊的地方，可以依自己的狀況套入不同的名字、公司名、職稱、學校名等等。

現在是不是回想起來了呢？

take legal actions 採取法律手段

「take legal actions」是個文雅而不直接的說法，直接說的話就是we will sue you（我們告你喔）。類似的說法還有「we will take this to court」（咱們法庭上見）。

南西：我剛剛打電話給經理了。20%太多了。

喬：這不多。其他公司的平均漲幅已經達到了35%，但是我們卻只有10%的增長。我們提出這個數字，甚至還沒有算加班費。

南西：但是，工作不僅僅是為了錢，它是我們所喜歡、追求的，是提升自我的方式，對嗎？

喬：不對，工作就是為了錢。我們需要錢養家。只有有了足夠的錢，工作才有其他的動機。如果我們不能得到我們應得的，我們就要採取法律行動。

南西：看來我們對工作抱著不同的態度。也許這是我能長期忍受不加薪的原因吧。你看這樣好嗎？15%的加薪，另外的5%轉成帶薪休假的形式。

喬：但是，妳剛才說經理沒有同意。

南西：是的，他沒同意。但是，我會說服他的。當我接受這項任務時，我想說服的一方就不是你們，而是他。

喬：請接受我發自內心的感謝！無論結果如何，都感謝您的努力！

商務小常識

合理加薪三步走：

(1) 判斷崗位價值：包括該崗位的基班條件、基班職責、基班職位晉升途徑。

(2) 瞭解市場行情：可以對收集來的應聘資料進行分析或在人才仲介機構中尋找數據。

(3) 薪資談判方式：採取合理有力的薪資談判方式，談判之前組織好語言，以期達到最佳效果。

SOS Unit 30
人事糾紛

Dialogue ❶ 性別歧視 ◀ *Track 171*

在這段對話中，我們可以看到許多和女性問題有關的會話常用字句，如「孕吐」、「性別歧視」，大家可以看看兩人是怎麼說的。

• •

Coco: Good morning, Kathy ! Are you all right? You appear a little pale.

Kathy: I'm okay. It's just this morning sickness that is torturing me.

Coco: Morning sickness? Wow, you're pregnant?

Kathy: For three months. I'll give a notice to our manager later today. Coco , you seem worried. What's wrong?

Coco: Everyone except my sister in her department got promoted one after the other, even the one that entered after her.

Kathy: How come your sister never got a promotion?

Coco: Because she is a woman, they don't believe she can be a competent worker.

Kathy: This is gender discrimination. It's so unreasonable. Women can do as good a job as men or even better.

Coco: I know. She knows that she will never climb up the ladder, so she is considering getting out of this dead-end job.

Kathy: She cannot let them get away with it so easily. She has to demand for equal opportunities. Listen, I have a friend who is a lawyer. Here is her contact number. Your sister can consult her about this.

★全文中畫 ⬤ 色塊的地方，可以依自己的狀況套入不同的名字、公司名、職稱、學校名等等。

dead-end job 沒有前途的工作

dead-end指的是死路、死巷，如果你的工作是一條死路，那就表示它沒有前途啦！。

中文翻譯1

可可：早安，凱西！妳沒事吧？看起來臉色不太好。

凱西：我還好。就是孕吐一直在折磨著我。

可可：孕吐？哇，妳懷孕了嗎？

凱西：三個月了。今天晚一點我會告訴經理的。可可，妳看起來很困擾。怎麼了？

可可：我姐姐的部門裡除了她以外，每一個人都接二連三地升職了，甚至比她還晚進入公司的人也升了。

凱西：你姐姐為什麼一直沒有升職呢？

可可：因為她是女生。他們不相信她會是名稱職的員工。

凱西：這是性別歧視。太不合理了。女人可以和男人一樣有好表現，甚至會做得更好。

可可：我知道。她知道她永遠也不可能升職了，所以她在考慮擺脫這份永無出頭之日的工作。

凱西：她不能這麼輕易就放過他們。她得要求同等的機會。聽著，我有一個朋友，她是一名律師。這是她的電話，妳姐姐可以向她諮詢這件事。

Dialogue ❷ 不合理規定 🔊 *Track 172*

一般聽到自己的公司被告了可能會覺得有點恐怖，但凱西一開口就說「哇，真是令人刮目相看」，可見她對公司的遲到規定也不滿很久了。看看這段對話怎麼說的吧！

Coco: Have you heard the news?

Kathy: What news?

Coco: We don't have to worry about being late any more. The rule stating that employees that are late twice will be fired has been proved to be ineffective.

Kathy: How come?

Coco: Jimmy , the guy from the Sales Department , sued our company for being fired and he won the case with full compensation.

Kathy: Wow, that's so impressive!

Coco: It is said that this company rule isn't in line with our national laws, so they cannot expel us for being late anymore.

Kathy: And we never doubted this rule?

Coco: We are just used to obeying everything the company says and have become dumb. Obviously, we are not rebels.

Kathy: No, we are not. But who knows? Maybe one day we will also learn to stand up for our own rights.

★全文中畫 ⬤ 色塊的地方，可以依自己的狀況套入不同的名字、公司名、職稱、學校名等等。

中文翻譯2

可可：妳聽到消息了嗎？

凱西：什麼消息啊？

可可：我們不用再擔心遲到的事了，因為員工遲到兩次就要被開除這條規定已經被證實，是無效的。

凱西：為什麼呢？

可可：銷售部的那個吉米，因為被開除起訴了我們公司，他贏了，並得到了全額的賠償。

凱西：哇，真是讓人刮目相看啊！

可可：據說公司這條規定與國家法律不符，所以他們再也不能因為這個原因開除我們了。

凱西：我們怎麼就從來沒有質疑過這項規定呢？

可可：我們只是習慣了服從公司的決定，變得沒頭腦了。很顯然，我們不是反叛者。

凱西：是啊，我們確實不是。但是誰知道呢？也許有一天我們也會站起來維護自己的權利。

Dialogue ❸ 不合理安排 🔈 *Track 173*

💬 遇到不合理的安排時，最有效的對付方式就是搬出法律。因此我們可以在對話中看到凱西不但提到「這是受法律保護的」，最後並說會「尋求仲裁」，肯定會讓她的上司皮皮剉。

Mr. Wang: Hello, (Kathy)! So nice to see you back! How is everything with you and your baby?

Kathy: Pretty good. Thank you! (Mr. Wang), now that I'm back, I want to have my job back.

Mr. Wang: You know, during your leave, there was a job vacancy for your position, so we hired someone else.

Kathy: But it's a maternity leave. It is protected under the law.

Mr. Wang: I know, but it'll be really difficult for us to transfer him to some other position. Besides, you know how fast the business is changing every day. After this leave…

Kathy: I can familiarize myself with the work very quickly.

Mr. Wang: I don't believe so. Due to the distraction of your child, you cannot totally focus on the job. You know how important this position is to our company.

Kathy: I know its importance and that's why I must do it. I assure you I will be one hundred percent devoted to the job.

Mr. Wang: I'll take your word for it, but I'm sorry; it's just not how we do things here. I can fit you in at the (Sales Promotion Department) and…

Kathy: I will fight this and seek arbitration.

★全文中畫 ● 色塊的地方，可以依自己的狀況套入不同的名字、公司名、職稱、學校名等等。

現在是不是回想起來了呢？

I'll take your word for it 我相信你的話
這句話的意思是「我相信你的話」，但背後帶有「我可是很相信你喔！所以我們也不白紙黑字寫下來喔！接下來出什麼問題的話，你就背叛了我的信任喔！」，會讓聽的人有點壓力。

中文翻譯3 •

王先生： 妳好，凱西！很高興見到妳回來！妳和寶寶一切都好嗎？

凱　西： 很好。謝謝！王先生，既然我已經回來了，我想回到我原來的職務。

王先生： 妳知道，在妳請假期間，妳的職位出現了空缺，所以我們聘用了另外一個人。

凱　西：但是，我請的是產假。這是受法律保護的。
王先生：我知道。但是，要我們把他調到其他崗位確實有困難。而且，妳知道業務每天的變化有多快。在這次休假之後⋯⋯
凱　西：我能很快就讓自己熟悉起業務來的。
王先生：我不相信。來自孩子的干擾，會讓妳無法完全專注於工作的。而且妳也知道這個職務對我們公司有多重要。
凱　西：我知道它的重要性，這也是我必須要做這份工作的原因。我可以向您保證我一定百分之百地投入工作。
王先生：我相信妳的話。但是，我很抱歉，我們不是這樣做事的。我可以讓妳進入促銷部，並且⋯⋯
凱　西：我會據理力爭尋求仲裁的。

Dialogue ❹ 解雇費 🔊 *Track 174*

凱西在這段對話中依舊受到不合理的待遇，所以我們可以看到她再次強調「legal maternity leave」（合法的產假），硬是插入「legal」這個字，來顯示整件事情的不合理性。

Kathy: Hello, (Kathy) speaking. May I ask who's calling?

Mr. Lei: Hello, (Kathy). I'm (Mr. Lei), a representative from the company. I'm here to discuss your dispute with the company. The company offered you severance pay.

Kathy: What's that?

Mr. Lei: Severance pay is money that an employer will provide for an employee who is leaving their position.

Kathy: How much will that be?

Mr. Lei: For executives, the severance pay may constitute up to (a month's) pay for each year of service and might also include outplacement assistance.

Kathy: What do they ask for in return?

Mr. Lei: (Kathy), you are very smart! You must sign a release that frees the company from all potential law suits in the future.

Kathy: That means I lose my job and am not allowed to make a charge, but in return I get a few extra months' pay just because I had a legal maternity leave?

Mr. Lei: Technically, yes.

Kathy: This is ridiculous! I believe I will live a much better life working at my position.

★全文中畫 ⬤ 色塊的地方，可以依自己的狀況套入不同的名字、公司名、職稱、學校名等等。

中文翻譯4

凱　西：你好，我是凱西，請問你是……？
雷先生：妳好，凱西。我是小雷，公司的代表。我是來跟妳談妳跟公司之間的糾紛的。公司提供了解雇費。
凱　西：那是什麼？
雷先生：這是老闆為將被解雇的員工提供的一筆錢。
凱　西：那是多少錢？
雷先生：對於主管來說，每工作一年，將會獲得最多一個月的工資作為解雇費，可能還包括再就業援助。
凱　西：他們要求什麼作為回報呢？
雷先生：凱西，妳真是聰明！妳要簽訂一份聲明書，承諾以後絕對不會起訴公司。
凱　西：那就意味著我失去了工作，並且不允許起訴，但是作為回報，我得到了額外幾個月的工資，僅僅是因為我請了一個合法的產假？
雷先生：嚴格講，是這樣的。
凱　西：這太可笑了！我相信繼續在我的職務上工作的話，我會過得好得多。

Dialogue ❺ 法律諮詢 ◀ *Track 175*

在這段諮詢中，我們可以學到一個有用的說法：「in cases like yours」（像你這種情況）。在諮詢意見時，這是句常會出現的會話。

Melinda: Hello, Kathy! I heard you had a baby. How is everything?

Kathy: Not so good, actually. I was replaced by someone else in the company during my leave.

Melinda: This is illegal. What are you going to do?

Kathy: I just didn't take what they offered me. So here I am asking for your help.

Melinda: What did they offer you?

Kathy: They offered me severance pay, declaring it is for my own good.

Melinda: In cases like yours, they would most probably do that, because they know they'd lose in a court of law.

Kathy: What should I do now?

Melinda: You should try in good faith to resolve the problem yourself before seeking mediation assistance or taking legal action. Even if you do have to pursue the problem further, discussing and clarifying it first will save time later.

Kathy: Okay, I'll follow your advice.

★全文中畫 ⬤ 色塊的地方，可以依自己的狀況套入不同的名字、公司名、職稱、學校名等等。

【現在是不是回想起來了呢？】

for sb.'s own good 為了某人好

通常用這句會話時，說話者都不是真心地覺得是為了對方好，而是有別的目的。例如：

A: Dear, you should listen to your daddy, even though he beats you. It's for your own good. 親愛的，你應該聽你爸的話，雖然他會打你。這是為了你好。

B: Duh, I'm calling the police. 屁咧，我要去報警了。

【中文翻譯5】

梅琳達：妳好，凱西！我聽說妳生寶寶了。一切可好？

凱　西：實際上，不是很好。在產假期間，我被公司裡的其他人取代了。

梅琳達：這是不合法的。妳打算怎麼做？

凱　西：我沒有接受他們給我的條件。所以我來向妳求助了。

梅琳達：他們向妳提出什麼條件了？

凱　西：他們給我提供了解僱費，還說是為我好。

梅琳達：像妳這種情況，他們很可能這樣做。因為他們知道在法庭上他們是贏不了的。

凱　西：我現在應該怎麼辦呢？

梅琳達：尋求調停或者採取法律行動之前，妳應該好好努力自己解決這個問題。即使妳確實需要進一步追究這個問題，事先探討、澄清問題也會為以後節省時間。

凱　西：好的，我會接受妳的建議的。

Dialogue ❻ 提出和解 ◀Track 176

在這段對話中，我們可以學到一些與和解相關的說法，如「for peace」。看看在對話中怎麼用的吧！

Kathy: Melinda, the representative from the company came to see me again.

Melinda: What for?

Kathy: They asked me to go back to work, or else they will deem it as leaving the position on my own.

Melinda: How did you reply to them?

Kathy: I said I needed time to take care of a few things. Therefore, I came to you.

Melinda: You should turn them down immediately. Can't you see? They know their situation now, so they are here for peace. You shouldn't surrender.

Kathy: But they promised to give me my position back. I thought that's it. Otherwise, shouldn't I take legal responsibility for leaving the position automatically?

Melinda: But you've already sought for arbitration. We will win and the case is in the bag! That is exactly what they are trying to change now just like what they did when you first came to me.

Kathy: Yes, I see. You're really something! Thank you so much!

Melinda: Not at all. Just remember to take a firm stand, or I cannot help you, either.

★全文中畫 ● 色塊的地方，可以依自己的狀況套入不同的名字、公司名、職稱、學校名等等。

現在是不是回想起來了呢？

be in the bag 十拿九穩的

東西已經「在袋子裡」了，等於是幾乎已經得手了，不太可能還會從袋子裡掉出來。所以就是十拿九穩的意思啦！

中文翻譯6

凱　　西：梅琳達，公司的代表又來找我了。

梅琳達：為了什麼啊？

凱　　西：他們要我回去工作，否則將視為自動離職。

梅琳達：妳怎麼答覆他們的？

凱　　西：我說我需要時間處理幾件事情。所以，我來找妳了。

梅琳達：妳應該立刻拒絕他們。妳不明白嗎？他們現在已經知道他們的處境了。所以，他們來要求和解。妳不應該投降的。

凱　　西：但是他們保證會讓我回到原來的崗位。我以為就是這樣了。否則，我不會為自動離職負法律責任嗎？

梅琳達：但是妳已經要求仲裁了。我們幾乎要在這個案子裡勝利了。這就是他們現在想極力改變的，就像妳剛來找我時，他們做的一樣。

凱　　西：是啊，我明白了。妳真了不起！太感謝妳了！

梅琳達：不用客氣。要記住，要立場堅定，不然我也幫不了妳。

商務小常識

　　亞洲及歐美各國，職場上的性別歧視案例層出不窮，所幸現今的立法潮流，都是以職場必需兩性平等這個方向來修正。 在國外，尤其是美國，這類訴訟是比較普遍的，簡單講一般只要在聽証中，多數證詞證實存在著歧視情況，雇主又不能合理解釋其行為的合法性，即可認定性別歧視，依法便可向雇主開罰。

Dialogue ❶ 發生職業傷害 🔊 *Track 177*

💬 在這段對話中，我們可以看到喬說：「**just now you said...**」（你剛剛說……），這是個實用的會話句型，當你想請對方把剛剛講的話再講一次的時候可以用。

● ●

Joe: Oh, what happened to your finger, Kathy?

Kathy: I was injured by one of the machines in our workshop when I was handing out the newly released Safety Manual yesterday, and got a fracture in my middle finger.

Joe: How did it happen?

Kathy: I was walking down the aisle in the workshop with a large handful of the manuals, and I did not notice the box lying in front of me. Suddenly, I tripped and fell down.

Joe: And then?

Kathy: While falling down, my middle finger hit the running machine and got injured. It really hurt a lot.

Joe: Oh my god, what a pity!

Kathy: I was taken to the hospital by my colleagues. At the hospital, after a series of exams, the doctor told me that I have a fracture in my middle finger and need a plaster cast.

Joe: Wait, just now you said you were injured in your workshop?

Kathy: Yes, that's right. What is the matter?

Joe: That means your injury qualifies as an industrial injury, for which you should be given some compensation.

Kathy: Oh, I didn't realize that. Thanks for your suggestion. When I am out of the hospital, I will advocate for my rights and get what I deserve.

★全文中畫 ⬤ 色塊的地方，可以依自己的狀況套入不同的名字、公司名、職稱、學校名等等。

中文翻譯1 •

喬：天啊，凱西，妳的手指怎麼了？

凱西：昨天我在工廠發放新出版的《安全手冊》時，被一台機器傷到了，中指骨折。

喬：怎麼傷到的？

凱西：我捧著一大堆手冊，走在工廠的走道上，沒有注意到前面有個盒子。突然，我被絆了一下，就摔倒了。

喬：然後呢？

凱西：摔倒的時候，我的中指碰到了正在運轉的機器，受傷了，非常痛。

喬：哦，天哪，真可憐！

凱西：我被同事送到了醫院。在醫院，經過一系列檢查，醫生說我的中指骨折了，需要打石膏。

喬：等等，妳剛才說妳是在工廠受傷的？

凱西：是的，是這樣的，怎麼了？

喬：這也就是說妳受的傷屬於職災，應該得到賠償。

凱西：哦，我都沒意識這一點。謝謝你的建議，當我出院的時候，我會盡力爭取我的權利，得到我應得的。

Dialogue ❷ 拒付職災賠償 🔊 *Track 178*

💬 拒付賠償的時候，總會使用異常的親切態度，想矇混過去。我們可以看看這段對話中史密斯先生究竟用了多少裝親切與裝熟的說法呢？

• •

Mr. Smith: Good morning, Kathy !

Kathy: Good morning, Mr. Smith .

Mr. Smith: I was sorry to hear that your finger was injured the other day, but I think at the moment, you should be in the hospital. Why are you here?

Kathy: Thanks for your concern. I was discharged from the hospital yesterday.

Mr. Smith: How about your injury?

Kathy: The doctor got rid of my plaster cast the day before yesterday and said my finger recovered a lot but it needed some rehabilitation.

Mr. Smith: Oh, that's a great pity. I can give you more days to rest and rehabilitate.

Kathy: Thanks for being considerate, but today I came here to talk about something else with you. I think I should be given some compensation for my industrial injury, since my injury occurred while I was working.

Mr. Smith: Kathy, I'm sorry for your injury, but during your time in the hospital, our company still gave you sick pay and also offered you more days for rehabilitation. We have already offered you so much. Aren't you satisfied?

Kathy: Well, Mr. Smith, what you mentioned is what I deserve. However, besides that, I also should get my compensation.

Mr. Smith: Anyway, what I mentioned before is what we can offer you. That's all.

Kathy: I will do everything to make sure my rights are met.

★全文中畫 ⬤ 色塊的地方，可以依自己的狀況套入不同的名字、公司名、職稱、學校名等等。

現在是不是回想起來了呢？

discharge 退院

discharge這個字的意思很多，有「退出」、「流出」、「卸下」的意思，很常見的一個用法就是指從身體排出的體液。既然從醫院「排出來」，也就是離開醫院、退院的意思啦。

中文翻譯2 •

史密斯先生： 早安，凱西。

凱　　西： 早安，史密斯先生。

史密斯先生： 聽說妳前幾天手指受傷了，對此我深表遺憾。但是我想現在妳應該在醫院裡呀，為什麼來這裡呢？

凱　　西： 謝謝您的關心，我昨天出院了。

史密斯先生：妳的傷勢怎麼樣了？

凱　西：醫生前天為我拆了石膏，而且說我的手指好多了，但是需要進行一些復健。

史密斯先生：哦，太可憐了。我可以多給妳一些假期來休息恢復。

凱　西：謝謝您為我考慮。但是，今天我來是和您談一些別的事情的。我認為我應該得到一些職災賠償，因為我是在工作期間受傷的。

史密斯先生：凱西，我對妳受傷感到很遺憾，但是我認為在妳住院期間，我們公司還是付給妳病假工資，並且提供妳更多假期來進行復健。我們已經給了妳很多了，妳還感到不滿意嗎？

凱　西：那麼，史密斯先生，您所說的都是我應該得到的。但是，除此之外，我還應該得到賠償。

史密斯先生：無論如何，之前我提到的，就是我們能給妳的。就這些。

凱　西：我會盡各種可能來維護我的權利。

Dialogue ❸ 請求律師幫助 🔊 *Track 179*

請求律師幫助時，常會先提到是經由誰介紹、推薦的。在這段對話中，我們可以學到此會話的說法：「某人recommended you to me.」（某人推薦你給我）。

Kathy: Good morning, Mr. Yang .

Mr. Yang: Good morning, can I help you?

Kathy: I'm Kathy Li . My friend Joe recommended you to me.

Mr. Yang: Nice to meet you, Kathy . What seems to be the problem?

Kathy: I stumbled over a box and injured my finger on one of the machines in our workshop while I was handing out the newly released Safety Manual the other day, and got a fracture in my middle finger.

Mr. Yang: That qualifies as an industrial injury.

Kathy: I think so, but when I went to my manager, he told me that all I could get was my sick leave and my sick pay.

Mr. Yang: You mean you will not be given compensation for your industrial injury?

Kathy: That's right! I feel extremely angry at this decision, so I've come here to ask for your advice and help.

Mr. Yang: That violates the Law of the People's Republic of China on Work Safety . I'll help you to claim your rights.

Kathy: Thanks a lot, Mr. Yang . It's really kind of you to help me.

Mr. Yang: You are welcome.

★全文中畫 ⬤ 色塊的地方，可以依自己的狀況套入不同的名字、公司名、職稱、學校名等等。

中文翻譯3 ▶

凱　西：早安，楊先生。
楊先生：早安，我能為您做些什麼嗎？
凱　西：我是凱西‧李。我朋友喬向我推薦您。
楊先生：很高興認識妳，凱西。妳遇到什麼難題了？
凱　西：前幾天我在工廠發放新出版的《安全手冊》時，被一個盒子絆倒，然後被一台機器傷到了手指，中指骨折。
楊先生：這屬於職災。
凱　西：我也是這樣認為的，但是當我去找我的經理時，他告訴我我能得到的只有病假和病假工資。
楊先生：妳是說妳得不到職災賠償了？
凱　西：是的！我對這個決定氣憤極了，所以，我來這裡尋求您的建議和幫助。
楊先生：這個決定違反了《中華人民共和國安全生產法》。我會幫助妳維護妳的權利的。
凱　西：太感謝了，楊先生，您能幫助我，真是太好了。
楊先生：不用客氣。

Dialogue ❹ 協商解決 🔊 *Track 180*

💬 凱西在此段對話中使用了「令對方感到抱歉」的手段，說：「雖然我受傷了，我還是很有誠意地來這裡跟你協商，但你似乎不是很在意」。說對方「just don't seem to care」（似乎不是很在意）是個特別能讓對方感到抱歉的好用會話句。

Kathy: Hello, Mr. Wang !

Mr. Wang: Hello, Kathy ! I'm surprised to see you back so early! Have you fully recovered?

Kathy: Actually, I'm here to talk about my compensation again. I couldn't come to a satisfactory solution with (Mr. Smith) last time.

Mr. Wang: So you are still insisting on your compensation. I'm afraid things of this kind have never happened before. We can't give you compensation.

Kathy: We don't need any precedent at all, because there are laws for us to abide by. It was suggested by my lawyer that I come here to negotiate with you, but if you insist, I'm afraid we must start arbitration.

Mr. Wang: Okay. What figure do you suggest?

Kathy: Besides the sick pay and the medical care fees, I believe (5,000 yuan) is reasonable.

Mr. Wang: What? There is no way we can give you that much money!

Kathy: With all due respect, I've been so devoted to the company. Even though I'm injured, I still came here in good faith to negotiate a solution; but you just don't seem to care.

Mr. Wang: I do care—including that sum of money. I reckon the arbitration will work this out for both of us fairly and squarely.

★全文中畫 ⬤ 色塊的地方,可以依自己的狀況套入不同的名字、公司名、職稱、學校名等等。

中文翻譯4

凱　西:你好,王先生!

王先生:妳好,凱西!看到妳這麼早回來,我很驚訝!妳完全康復了嗎?

凱　西:實際上,我還是來談我的補償的。我上一次沒能與史密斯先生達成滿意的解決方案。

王先生:那妳還是堅持要妳的賠償嗎?這類事情在我們公司從來沒有發生過,我們不能給妳賠償金。

凱　西:我們不需要有先例,因為我們要遵守法律。律師建議我來跟你們協商一下。但是,如果您還是一味這樣,恐怕我們只能尋求仲裁了。

王先生:好吧,妳要多少?

凱　西:我認為不包括病假工資及醫療費用,5,000元是很合理的。

王先生:什麼?我們絕不可能給妳那麼多錢!

凱　西:恕我直言,我一直都為公司盡心盡力,即使是受傷了,我還是帶著誠意來到這裡跟您協商,但是您似乎不是很在意。

王先生:我確實是很在意——包括那筆錢。我想仲裁機構會秉公地為我們解決這件事的。

Dialogue ❺ 仲裁結果 ◀€ *Track 181*

仲裁結果常要簽合約，但合約裡卻又常常會有陷阱，很恐怖！在這段對話中看看兩人如何討論合約中的陷阱吧。

● ●

Kathy: Thank you so much, Mr. Yang ! I wouldn't have received justice without you.

Mr. Yang: I just did what I should. Just for your information, when you sign the contract again, be aware of the traps.

Kathy: I've learned my lesson. I didn't know they would set a cap on compensation in the contract.

Mr. Yang: No matter what they do, they have to obey the law; otherwise, the contract is invalid.

Kathy: I really learned something. When I return to my office, I will tell my colleagues about this lesson.

Mr. Yang: Speaking of your colleagues, I do think you should warn them of the potential hazards at your workplace.

Kathy: Or maybe I should just go to the manager to solve it once and for all.

Mr. Yang: Whatever works for you!

Kathy: Mr. Yang , I don't know how I can ever thank you enough for your help and constructive advice.

Mr. Yang: No sweat! I'm glad to be of any help.

★全文中畫 ⬤ 色塊的地方，可以依自己的狀況套入不同的名字、公司名、職稱、學校名等等。

現在是不是回想起來了呢？

no sweat 這沒什麼
sweat是「汗」的意思，既然連汗都不用流，可見是一件非常輕鬆的事，所以這只是舉手之勞，「沒什麼」。用於別人感謝你的時候。

凱　西：非常感謝您，楊先生！要不是您，我就無法獲得公道了。
楊先生：我只是做了份內之事。跟妳說一下，下次，在簽訂合約的時候，一定要當心裡面的陷阱。
凱　西：我已經得到教訓了。我不知道他們會在合約裡為賠償設定上限。
楊先生：不管他們做什麼，都必須遵守法律；否則，合約就是無效的。
凱　西：我真的學到了很多。等我回到辦公室，我一定把這個教訓告訴同事。
楊先生：說到妳的同事，我認為妳應該把工作場所內的潛在危險告訴他們。
凱　西：或許我該去找經理談談，徹底把這個問題解決掉。
楊先生：只要對你們能行得通就可以！
凱　西：楊先生，我真不知道該如何感謝您對我的幫助，以及提供這麼有建設性的建議。
楊先生：舉手之勞。很高興有幫助到妳。

Dialogue ❻ 和同事談論職災事故　◀ Track 182

此段對話中，凱西並沒有一見到同事就大肆抱怨，而是等到被問才平靜地解釋自己遭遇到的不公平待遇。這個作法更能讓她廣獲同事的支持喔！

Tina: Good morning, Kathy.

Kathy: Good morning, Tina.

Tina: How is your injury?

Kathy: It's getting better, but it needs some rehabilitation.

Tina: I hope you will recover from your injury soon. What kinds of compensations did our company give you?

Kathy: The manager told me that I could only get my sick leave and my sick pay.

Tina: Really unfair! Did you go to the lawyer?

Kathy: Sure, my lawyer said such a decision violated national laws and I should be given what I deserve.

Tina: The similar cases that I have heard of were also dealt with in this way.

Kathy: But the manager did not follow the law.

Tina: Now, he is doing something unfair to you and it is possible for him to do the same thing to us in the future. I will call our other colleagues to support you.

Kathy: Thanks for your support.

★全文中畫 ⬤ 色塊的地方，可以依自己的狀況套入不同的名字、公司名、職稱、學校名等等。

中文翻譯6

蒂娜：早安，凱西。
凱西：早安，蒂娜。
蒂娜：妳的傷怎麼樣了？
凱西：好多了，但是需要進行復健。
蒂娜：希望妳能早日康復。公司給妳什麼賠償了？
凱西：經理說他只能給我病假和病假工資。
蒂娜：太不公平了。妳找律師了嗎？
凱西：找了，律師說這樣的決定違反國家法律，我應該得到相應的賠償。
蒂娜：我聽說的類似案例都是這樣處理的。
凱西：但是經理不遵守法律。
蒂娜：現在他對妳不公正，將來對我們也會如此。我會聯合其他同事支持妳的。
凱西：感謝你的支持。

Dialogue ❼ 生產安全 🔊 *Track 183*

王先生聽了凱西的建議後，就說「**I'll take it under advisement**」（我會聽從你的建議，周密考慮）。這是一個表達自己有把對方的話聽進去，而且會思考處置方式的實用會話。

Kathy: They told me to come to your office. Anything I can help you with?

Mr. Wang: How is your injury?

Kathy: I'm feeling much better with the compensation now. Thank you for your concern!

Mr. Wang: Here is the thing. Other staff have been injured during office hours, so we decided to improve our safety measures.

Kathy: That is so nice!

Mr. Wang: You are one of the "victims" in our company, so you have the right to say something about our working conditions.

Kathy: To tell you the truth, our working conditions are good in general except for some minor details.

Mr. Wang: Like what?

Kathy: Like the machine directly exposed to the exterior, and the improper positioning of some tools . I think maybe some lectures on safety and first aid would work better than the manuals.

Mr. Wang: That is very insightful. Thank you! I'll take it under advisement.

★全文中畫 色塊的地方，可以依自己的狀況套入不同的名字、公司名、職稱、學校名等等。

現在是不是回想起來了呢？

first aid 急救

first aid指的是急救措施，如急救箱則是叫做「first aid kit」。

中文翻譯7 ● ● ● ● ● ● ● ● ● ● ● ● ●

凱　西：有人叫我來您的辦公室。需要我做什麼嗎？

王先生：妳的傷怎麼樣了？

凱　西：有了賠償，我現在感覺好多了。謝謝您的關心！

王先生：事情是這樣的。有別的員工在上班時受傷了，所以我們決定改善我們的安全措施。

凱　西：太好了！

王先生：妳是我們公司的「受害者」之一，因此妳有權利對我們公司的工作環境發表意見。

凱　西：說實話，我們的工作環境總體來說很好，只是有些微小的細節做得還不到位。

王先生：比方說？

凱　西：比如直接暴露在外面的機器，還有一些工具擺放的位置不適當。我想，關於安全與急救方面的講座也許會比手冊更加有效。

王先生：很有見地。謝謝！我會好好考慮的。

商務小常識

下列為職業傷害的標準：

(1) 在工作時間和工作場所內，因工作原因受到事故傷害。

(2) 在工作時間前後在工作場所內，從事與工作有關的預備性或收尾性工作受到事故傷害。

(3) 在工作時間和工作場所內，因履行工作職責受到暴力等意外傷害。

(4) 患職業病。

(5) 因工外出期間，由於工作原因受到傷害或者發生事故下落不明。

(6) 在上下班途中，受到機動車事故傷害。

(7) 法律、行政法規規定應當認定職災的其他情形。

勞資糾紛

Dialogue **1** 未按合約行事 ◀ *Track 184*

💬 想問對方在想什麼、打算接下來怎麼辦時，可以用此段對話中的「**What's on your mind?**」。在一些社群網站上，自己的頁面上也會有這樣的一個空格，要你填入「**what's on your mind**」，也就是你正在想的事情。

• •

Kelly: I was kicked out.

Kathy: But how come? I thought you would go abroad for the training.

Kelly: It seems that a relative of our manager is more important than me.

Kathy: It's so unfair, but still, why are you being dismissed?

Kelly: It was stated clearly in my employment contract that I would receive this training abroad three months after I got the job, but they failed to honor their promise and dismissed me to cover it up.

Kathy: Then, what's on your mind?

Kelly: I'll just find a job somewhere else. It is not like I can't find a job.

Kathy: Come on! Why don't you fight for your rights? How can you just give in like this?

Kelly: I don't want to make a fuss. It's not a big deal.

Kathy: Oh, yes, it is. I can't bear standing idly by. You just wait here, and I'll talk to our manager.

Kelly: Kathy, you don't have to.

★全文中畫 ⬤ 色塊的地方，可以依自己的狀況套入不同的名字、公司名、職稱、學校名等等。

凱莉：我被解雇了。

凱西：怎麼會這樣呢？我以為妳要去國外培訓呢。

凱莉：看起來，經理的某位親戚比我更重要。

凱西：這太不公平了。但是，妳怎麼會被解雇呢？

凱莉：在我的勞動合約裡明確規定了在得到這份工作三個月後，我會出國接受培訓。但是他們沒有信守承諾，還解雇我來掩蓋事實。

凱西：那妳有什麼計畫呢？

凱莉：我去找份別的工作就是了。我又不是找不到工作。

凱西：拜託！妳為什麼不爭取自己的權利呢？妳怎麼能這麼輕易就屈服了呢？

凱莉：我不想小題大做。沒有什麼大不了的。

凱西：噢，這是很嚴重的。我不能坐視不理。妳在這裡等著，我去和經理談。

凱莉：凱西，妳沒有必要這樣做。

Dialogue ❷ 聘用糾紛發生的原因 ◀ *Track 185*

王先生在說員工「壞話」（洩漏公司機密）時，使用了「**I really don't want to bring this up...**」（我本來很不想提起這件事的……），以表示自己本來不想張揚，是不得已才說出來的（其實說不定他心裡想說出來想得要命），是個可以參考的說法。

Kathy: Excuse me, may I come in?

Mr. Wang: Yes, please. What's the matter?

Kathy: I'm here to talk about Kelly. You can't just fire her like that. It's not fair to her. She will resort to employment arbitration.

Mr. Wang: It is fair and square. She can do whatever she pleases.

Kathy: In today's environment, an employment dispute like this can ruin a company's reputation.

Mr. Wang: I know. But it's not my fault.

Kathy: If you just fire her like this, it is your fault and it can really distract and unnerve an otherwise strong and efficient management team.

Mr. Wang: Okay, Kathy. I really don't want to bring this up, but Kelly let out our company's confidential files.

Kathy: It is not that she did it on purpose, right?

Mr. Wang: No, she didn't, but still I can sue her for all the losses. I am tolerant enough to just let her go.

Kathy: Please just give her another shot.

Mr. Wang: That's beyond my reach. Based on the contract, employment termination can be executed in case of a major misconduct.

★全文中畫 ⬤ 色塊的地方，可以依自己的狀況套入不同的名字、公司名、職稱、學校名等等。

現在是不是回想起來了呢？

unnerve 使不安、手足無措

相關的形容詞是「unnerving」，形容一件事令人有點不安、不舒服。例如若你同學很愛亂摸人，你就會覺得他的動作有點unnerving。

中文翻譯2

凱　西：打擾一下，我能進來嗎？

王先生：可以，請進。有什麼事嗎？

凱　西：我是來談關於凱莉的事的。您不能這樣解雇她。這對她太不公平了。她會尋求勞動仲裁的。

王先生：這是公平公正的。她想做什麼就去做什麼吧。

凱　西：在現今的環境中，像這樣的勞資糾紛會損害公司聲譽的。

王先生：我知道。但這不是我的過錯。

凱　西：如果您這樣解雇她，這就是您的過錯。這樣會導致我們強大有效的管理團隊人心渙散、士氣消沉。

王先生：好吧，凱西。我不想提起這件事，但是凱莉洩露了我們公司的機密檔案。

凱　西：她不是故意的吧？

王先生：是的，她不是故意的，但是我還是可以起訴她賠償所有損失。我這樣解雇她，已經對她很寬容了。

凱　西：請再給她一次機會吧。

王先生：那就超出我的能力範圍了。根據合約，由於重大行為過失，公司有權終止雇傭關係。

Dialogue ❸ 糾紛的解決辦法 🔊 *Track 186*

💬 凱莉在這段對話中說了「**give me a break**」（饒了我吧），是句很好用的會話，因為在生活中實在太容易發生讓你想嚷嚷「饒了我吧」的事了。

● ●

Kathy: You never told me you released our confidential file.

Kelly: I intended to, but you had already gone.

Kathy: You know that will affect the company's sales figures. You've been lucky enough not to be sued.

Kelly: I know. ⬤Kathy⬤, just give me a break. I've had a hard time already. I'm overcome by repentance.

Kathy: I thought maybe you could resort to employment dispute mediation or even arbitration if it's not your fault.

Kelly: I really appreciate your help in this incident. I'm sure I've learnt something from it.

Kathy: Live and learn. Remember better safe than sorry.

Kelly: This unfortunate incident is indeed a good lesson for me.

Kathy: What are you going to do?

Kelly: I will find a job in another company. It's not that hard for me, and if I have any problem in employment, I will come to you. You are an expert now.

Kathy: Glad to help!

★全文中畫 ⬤⬤⬤ 色塊的地方，可以依自己的狀況套入不同的名字、公司名、職稱、學校名等等。

> 現在是不是回想起來了呢？

better safe than sorry 小心總比難過好
這句話特別常用在當有人埋怨或笑你「想太多了」、「準備那麼充分幹嘛」時。這時你就可以用這句話回答對方：「現在先小心，總比之後難過好」。

中文翻譯3

凱西：妳沒有跟我說妳洩露了我們公司的機密檔案。

凱莉：我正打算跟你說，但是妳已經走了。

凱西：妳知道那會影響公司的銷售額的。妳沒有受到起訴已經很幸運了。

凱莉：我知道。凱西，饒了我吧。我已經很難受了，怎麼後悔都來不及。

凱西：我還以為如果不是妳的錯，也許妳可以求助於勞資糾紛協調甚至是仲裁。

凱莉：我真的很感激妳在這件事上對我的幫助。我確實已經從中吸取教訓了。

凱西：活到老，學到老。記得：小心總比難過好。

凱莉：這件倒楣的事確實給了我一個難忘的教訓。

凱西：那妳有什麼打算？

凱莉：我會在另一家公司再找一份工作。這對我來說不是什麼困難的事。如果我在就業方面有任何問題，我會來找妳的。妳現在是個專家了。

凱西：沒問題！

Dialogue ❹ 公司內部維權機制 🔊 *Track 187*

這段對話中，我們可以看到這位新同事很聰明，一開口就稱讚公司對員工權益的保障，其實她更是要順便套話，瞭解更多和權益相關的問題。

Coco: Hello, I'm Coco! I'm new here.

Kathy: I'm Kathy. Nice to meet you!

Coco: I heard that our company attaches great importance to employees' rights and there are a lot of measures to ensure our rights.

Kathy: Yes. We have implemented employment dispute resolution programmes requiring fair and reasonable investigation of complaints, and a dispute resolution mechanism involving mediation.

Coco: We can make a complaint?

Kathy: Certainly. In fact, we are seeing sophisticated employment policies that include an elaborate dispute resolution mechanism which may start with an internal complaint and investigation, peer review, non-binding mediation and then arbitration.

Coco: Wow, that's marvellous!

Kathy: We also have several rounds of meetings with the presence of both the employee and the employer, seeking to facilitate and improve communication before the dispute is resolved.

Coco: I'm sure in this way the dispute can be settled more efficiently and more peacefully.

Kathy: At least, in this way our side of the story can be heard.

★全文中畫 ⬤ 色塊的地方，可以依自己的狀況套入不同的名字、公司名、職稱、學校名等等。

中文翻譯4

可可：妳好，我是可可，新來的。

凱西：我是凱西。很高興見到妳！

可可：我聽說我們公司很重視員工的權利，並且這裡有很多措施來保護我們的權利。

凱西：是的。我們已經實行了勞資糾紛解決計畫，這個計畫要求公平合理地調查投訴，我們還有包含調停的糾紛解決機制。

可可：我們還可以投訴嗎？

凱西：當然。實際上，我們有很完善的聘用政策，包括詳盡的糾紛解決機制，該機制最先會進行內部投訴及調查、同事評審、非約束性調停，然後是仲裁。

可可：哦，真是不錯！

凱西：在糾紛解決前，我們還會有幾次由雇主及雇員都出席的會議，尋求改善交流、促進溝通。

可可：我相信按照這種方式，能夠更加有效平和地解決糾紛。

凱西：至少，按照這種方式，我們的心聲可以得到聆聽。

Dialogue ❺ 未按合約支付工資 🔊 *Track 188*

同事看起來不太開心的時候，可以像這段對話中的凱西一樣，問一句：「Anything I can do?」其實就是「Is there anything I can do?」的簡單說法，是「我可以幫你什麼忙嗎？」

Kathy: What's wrong, Coco? You seem to be worried. Anything I can do?

Coco: It's my cousin. She is thinking about switching to another job now.

Kathy: Why? I thought that she likes this job.

Coco: Yes, she does. The problem is that she has worked for this company for three months, but they always deduct her salary in one way or another.

Kathy: Is the deduction reasonable?

Coco: Of course not. That's why she is bothered.

Kathy: If the company doesn't pay her according to the employment contract, she has the right to take legal action.

Coco: She doesn't want to go through all that trouble.

Kathy: Maybe she can go to the Labor Union and get their assistance.

Coco: That's a great idea! I will tell her about it.

★全文中畫 ⬤ 色塊的地方，可以依自己的狀況套入不同的名字、公司名、職稱、學校名等等。

中文翻譯5

凱西：怎麼了，可可？妳看起來憂心忡忡的。我能幫忙嗎？

可可：是關於我表姐。她現在正在考慮換工作呢。

凱西：為什麼呢？我以為她很喜歡這份工作呢。

可可：是的，她很喜歡。問題是，她已經在這家公司工作了三個月，但是他們總是以各種方式扣減她的工資。

凱西：這樣扣工資合理嗎？

可可：當然不合理。所以她才很苦惱。

凱西：如果公司不按照合約付她工資，她就有權採取法律行動。

可可：她不想那麼麻煩。

凱西：或許她可以去找工會，尋求他們的幫助。

可可：真是好主意！我會告訴她的。

Dialogue ❻ 未按合約給予休假 ◀️ Track 189

這段對話的最後，主管用了一句「**suit yourself**」做結。suit是「適合」的意思，因此這句話直翻就是「適合你自己」，延伸來說就是「做自己覺得合適的事」。

Betty: Good morning, Allen! I'm here to ask for leave. A friend of mine was injured so I want to go and see her. You know, I haven't used my leave this year.

Allen: I know, but I'm afraid that is not permissible now.

Betty: Not permissible? It is specified in the contract in black and white that I can have three weeks' annual leave excluding public holidays.

Allen: That is not possible now, at least not for this month. You see, it is a busy season.

Betty: But that is not written in the contract. Besides, I thought that was my right.

Allen: You should be subjected to the interests of the company.

Betty: I insist on having my leave now.

Allen: If that's the case, you can have it forever and don't bother to come back again.

Betty: You can't fire me!

Allen: I can fire anyone I want. I'm the executive. Please pack your stuff and leave now.

Betty: There is no good cause for my termination. I'll sue you! By no means shall I give in.

Allen: Fine. Suit yourself.

★全文中畫 ⬤ 色塊的地方，可以依自己的狀況套入不同的名字、公司名、職稱、學校名等等。

現在是不是回想起來了呢？

give in 屈服

類似的片語還有give up（放棄），兩者看起來非常相似，但用法還是稍有不同。give in通常是「對某人、某事屈服」，而give up則不一定是「對特定的對象」屈服，有可能是自己在做某件事，做著做著就放棄了。

中文翻譯6

貝蒂：早安，艾倫！我是來請假的。我的一個朋友受傷了，我想去探望她。你知道，我一直都沒有用今年的年假。

艾倫：我知道，但是恐怕現在不行。

貝蒂：不行？但是合約中，白紙黑字明確規定：除公共假日之外，我可以有三週的年假。

艾倫：現在不行，至少這個月是不行的。妳知道，現在是旺季。

貝蒂：但合約中並沒有那樣規定。而且，我覺得這是我的權利。
艾倫：妳應該服從公司的利益。
貝蒂：我堅持現在就要休假。
艾倫：如果是那樣的話，妳就可以一直休假，不用再麻煩回來了。
貝蒂：你不能解雇我！
艾倫：我可以解雇任何人。我是主管。收拾妳的東西，現在就走吧。
貝蒂：沒有正當理由終止我的合約。我要起訴你！我絕不會屈服的。
艾倫：好，隨便妳。

Dialogue ⑦ 未按合約保保險 ◀ Track 190

💬 大家平常聊天時應該也常會說「比起這件事，另一件事又更糟」。這用英文如何表達？在這個對話中傑夫說到了：「**What's worse...**」（更糟的是……）

Kelly: How are you feeling now? I heard you broke your leg in the workplace.

Jeff: I'm feeling much better now. Thank you for coming to see me.

Kelly: How can you be so careless?

Jeff: There were wires all over the ground. I tripped and as a result my leg is broken.

Kelly: This is not right. Your company should maintain safe working conditions for their employees.

Jeff: What's worse, I just found out that they didn't cover my insurance.

Kelly: You definitely should take them to court.

Jeff: It's not that serious.

Kelly: Yes, it is. You shouldn't allow your rights to be abused like this. I'll go to the Employment Dispute Mediation tomorrow, because my company has also breached the contract. You should go with me.

Jeff: Okay, let's see what they can do.

★全文中畫 ⬤ 色塊的地方，可以依自己的狀況套入不同的名字、公司名、職稱、學校名等等。

中文翻譯7

凱莉：你現在感覺怎麼樣了？我聽說你在公司把腿摔斷了。

傑夫：我現在感覺好多了。謝謝妳來看我。

凱莉：你怎麼那麼不小心呢？

傑夫：地上都是電線。我被絆倒了，結果腿就骨折了。

凱莉：這是不對的。你們公司應該為雇員提供一個安全的工作環境啊！

傑夫：更糟糕的是，我剛剛發現他們沒有為我保險。

凱莉：你一定要告他們。

傑夫：沒有那麼嚴重。

凱莉：很嚴重。你不應該這樣放任自己的權利受到侵害。我明天去工作糾紛調停部門，因為我們公司也違反了合約。你應該跟我一起去。

傑夫：好吧。看看他們能怎麼辦吧。

Dialogue **8** 糾紛談判 🔊 *Track 191*

宋先生在這段對話中使用了哀兵政策，告訴貝蒂她如果告了公司，會對公司的名譽有很大的損傷。這個方法好像不怎樣，但對心軟的貝蒂就是有用，她後來還真的答應下來了。看看這段對話中兩人是怎麼說的吧！

Mr. Song: I heard that you have taken legal action against our company.

Betty: I can't just sit here and do nothing when my own rights are being infringed.

Mr. Song: You know our company has always tried very hard to maintain employee's rights and have implemented many programmes to guarantee it.

Betty: The law sets out certain minimum conditions that apply to all employees. You failed to carry them out. I did my bit, but I was sent away.

Mr. Song: It is Allen's decision, not mine, and I'm here on behalf of our company, saying he made the wrong decision. I assume you know the stake since you've told me how damaging a dispute with an employee can be to a business.

Betty: I believe so.

Mr. Song: So how about this? I grant you the leave and have you back, and you drop the charge.

Betty: I can't face (Allen) if I go back.

Mr. Song: (Allen) will apologize to you in public. As the saying goes, a gentleman rarely harbors grievance for past wrongs. What would you say to it?

Betty: Okay, let bygones be bygones.

★全文中畫 ⬭ 色塊的地方，可以依自己的狀況套入不同的名字、公司名、職稱、學校名等等。

現在是不是回想起來了呢？

let bygones be bygones 過去的就讓它過去

「bygones」（過去的事）是一個有點文謅謅、現在不常見到的字。這個字一般只會出現在這句格言中，不太會在一般的會話中見到它。

中文翻譯8

宋先生：我聽說妳對我們公司已經採取了法律行動。

貝　蒂：我不能放任自己的權利受到侵害。

宋先生：妳知道我們公司一直在極力維護員工的權利，並實行了很多計畫來保證這一點。

貝　蒂：法律規定了適用於所有員工的某些最低條件。您未能按此執行。我盡職盡責，卻被解雇了。

宋先生：那是艾倫的決定，不是我的決定。我來這裡是代表公司告訴妳他做了錯誤的決定。我想既然妳跟我說過，跟雇員的糾紛對一家公司是很大的傷害，妳應該明白其中的利害關係。

貝　蒂：我想是吧。

宋先生：那這樣可以嗎？我批准妳的假期，並且讓妳回來，而妳撤訴。

貝　蒂：如果我回去的話，我沒有辦法面對艾倫。

宋先生：艾倫會公開向妳道歉。俗語說得好，君子不念舊惡。妳覺得怎麼樣？

貝　蒂：好吧。過去的事情就讓它過去吧。

會前準備

Dialogue ❶ 通知客戶 🔊 *Track 192*

💬 在這段對話中，我們可以看到凱西不過是提了一個旅館選擇的建議，貝絲就若無其事地稱讚了她一句。在職場上多相互稱讚，是個增進感情與增加職場和諧氣氛的方法。

Kathy: Hello, Beth , please invite all our clients to the conference next week.

Beth: No problem. How should I get their contact info and addresses?

Kathy: I'll send you an email.

Beth: Which hotel would be better to put them up in?

Kathy: How about the Shangri-La ?

Beth: What a great choice! What else should I do, Kathy ?

Kathy: Please print out the conference agenda for me to look over.

Beth: Certainly.

★全文中畫 色塊的地方，可以依自己的狀況套入不同的名字、公司名、職稱、學校名等等。

中文翻譯1

凱西： 妳好，貝絲，請妳邀請我們所有的客戶參加下個星期的會議。

貝絲： 沒問題。我怎樣才能知道他們的聯繫方式和位址呢？

凱西： 我會寄郵件給妳的。

貝絲： 讓客戶在哪裡住宿呢？

凱西： 香格里拉大酒店怎麼樣？

貝絲： 好選擇！凱西，還需要我做什麼？

凱西： 請把大會議程表列印給我看看。

貝絲： 好的。

Dialogue ❷ 初步會見　◀ *Track 193*

這段對話中，莉莉替布朗先生擬了一個行程表，但沒有經過布朗先生的確認，她就沒有擅自說這是最終確定的行程表，而是說它是個「tentative」（暫時的）的行程表。

● ●

Lily: Good morning, ⬭Mr. Brown⬭. I hope you slept well last night. Have you recovered from the journey?

Mr. Brown: Oh, yes. I had a sound sleep last night and I enjoyed it a great deal. The hotel is fitted with modern comforts and conveniences and the food here is very much to my taste.

Lily: I'm very glad to hear that.

Mr. Brown: Ah, sit down, please. ⬭Lily⬭, would you like a cup of tea or coffee?

Lily: A cup of tea, thank you. Well, ⬭Mr. Brown⬭, I'm here to ask your opinion about the time schedule of the next ⬭six⬭ days. Is this a good time?

Mr. Brown: Perfectly all right.

Lily: Well, we've drawn up a tentative schedule for the following ⬭six⬭ days, which lasts from tomorrow till the day you board the plane to ⬭Shanghai⬭. And I was wondering whether it's acceptable or not.

Mr. Brown: Let me have a look.

Lily: What do you think of this arrangement?

Mr. Brown: It looks good to me.

★全文中畫 ⬭ 色塊的地方，可以依自己的狀況套入不同的名字、公司名、職稱、學校名等等。

現在是不是回想起來了呢？

to sb.'s taste 合某人胃口

不只是食物，無論是衣服、裝潢等，只要是合口味的東西都可以用這個說法。例如若你想說現在播放的音樂很合你的口味，就可以說：This music is to my taste.

莉　　莉：早安，布朗先生，但願您昨晚睡得還好。您休息過了嗎？
布朗先生：嗯，昨晚睡得很香，非常舒服。這家酒店配備有現代化設施，舒適方便，飲食也非常合我的胃口。
莉　　莉：聽您這樣說我很高興。
布朗先生：啊，請坐，莉莉，妳喝茶，還是來杯咖啡？
莉　　莉：來杯茶，謝謝。布朗先生，我來問問您的意見，看看接下來六天的行程怎麼安排，不知道現在談這個問題方便嗎？
布朗先生：好。很合適。
莉　　莉：從明天起到你們搭上去上海的飛機那天為止，一共六天的行程，我們做了個初步的安排，不知這個安排是否合適？
布朗先生：讓我看看。
莉　　莉：對這個安排您有什麼看法？
布朗先生：我覺得不錯。

Dialogue ❸ 準備演講稿 🔊 *Track 194*

💬 彼得在這段對話中詢問凱西意見時，用了「What do you think of...」，這個句型後面一般是接名詞的，但如要接動詞，則要改成「動名詞」（動詞＋-ing），例：**What do you think of going to the beach?**（你覺得去海邊怎樣？）

Kathy: What do you think of the invitation to give a speech at the conference in October?

Peter: Well, it's a great opportunity.

Kathy: I agree. It will help increase our influence in the marketplace.

Peter: And people are always interested to hear how new companies are getting on.

Kathy: We've certainly got nothing to be nervous about.

Peter: You are right. Who do you think should give the speech? You or I?

Kathy: Well, it's an important conference. I think it would look odd if I didn't speak myself. By the way, please hand me the budget. I should review the numbers and familiarize myself with them.

Peter: No problem.

★全文中畫 ⬤ 色塊的地方，可以依自己的狀況套入不同的名字、公司名、職稱、學校名等等。

現在是不是回想起來了呢？

get on 發展

get on在這段對話中是新公司「發展」的意思，此外，也可以拿來說兩人的相處情形「發展」得如何，例如：How are your kids getting on with each other?（你們的孩子們相處得如何？）

中文翻譯3

凱西：對於受邀在10月份的會議上發言，您的看法是？
彼得：我想這是個極好的機會。
凱西：我也這麼認為。這有助於提升我們在市場上的影響力。
彼得：而且人們總是對新公司的發展情況抱有很大興趣。
凱西：我們當然也沒有什麼要緊張的。
彼得：當然。妳去演講還是我去呢？
凱西：呃，這次是非常重要的大會。我想要是不親自演講，會看起來怪怪的。對了，把預算表交給我，我再回顧一遍資料，熟悉一下。
彼得：沒問題。

Dialogue ❹ 機場接待 ◀ Track 195

到客戶的國家參觀，不著痕跡地稱讚一下對方的城市是個很好的作法。這段對話中布朗先生就特別提到了上海的環境改變，以顯示自己對上海的印象有多深刻。

Kathy: Hello, Mr. Brown .

Mr. Brown: Hello, Kathy .

Kathy: It's nice to see you again in Shanghai .

Mr. Brown: Well, I'm so glad to be able to attend this meeting.

Kathy: How was your flight?

Mr. Brown: Just wonderful! Good food and perfect service!

Kathy: Now, Mr. Brown , if all is ready, we'd better head for the hotel.

Mr. Brown: I'd like to. After you.

Kathy: This way, please. The driver is waiting for us.

Mr. Brown: Okay. By the way, the airport and the surroundings look different from what I saw them last.

Kathy: The last time you were here was (two) years ago, is that right?

Mr. Brown: Yes, that is right.

Kathy: In the past (two) years, (Shanghai) has been given a facelift. You'll see more changes elsewhere.

Mr. Brown: That's why I like (Shanghai) so much.

★全文中畫 ⬤ 色塊的地方，可以依自己的狀況套入不同的名字、公司名、職稱、學校名等等。

現在是不是回想起來了呢？

give a facelift 整容

「lift」是「提起來」的意思。把臉「提起來」，就等於是把皺皺垮垮的臉皮拉得緊緻有彈性，也就是「整容」啦！在這段對話中，說上海被「整容」了，也就表示上海被翻新、整修過，難過看起來完全不一樣。

中文翻譯4

凱　　西：您好，布朗先生。
布朗先生：您好，凱西。
凱　　西：很高興再次在上海見到您。
布朗先生：是呀，能來參加這次會議我很高興。
凱　　西：您旅途怎麼樣？
布朗先生：好極了！食物很好，服務也很周到。
凱　　西：好的，布朗先生，沒有什麼事情的話，我們儘快出發去飯店吧。
布朗先生：好的。妳先請。
凱　　西：這邊請。司機在等我們。
布朗先生：好的。說起來，機場和周邊環境和我上次看到的有些不一樣呀。
凱　　西：您上次來是在兩年前，對吧？
布朗先生：是的。
凱　　西：在過去的兩年裡，上海市容進行了整修。您在別的地方會看到更多的變化。
布朗先生：這就是我非常喜歡上海的原因。

Dialogue ❺ 排定時程 ◀ *Track 196*

💬 凱西在這段對話中說了「it's all settled」，意思就是「那就都安排好囉」的意思，是句下結論時可以用的會話，給對方安心的感覺，同時也表示「如果你還有意見、還想改變安排，那現在就得說出來喔」。

• •

Jones: Kathy , would it be possible for a free afternoon to be arranged? You see, I have a friend here, and I want to take this opportunity to pay him a visit.

Kathy: I think that could be easily arranged. Anything else?

Jones: Nothing more.

Mr. Brown: You see, we are total strangers here, and I suppose the safest way is to put ourselves at your disposal.

Kathy: Thank you for saying so, and I'll make sure that your stay here is a pleasant one.

Mr. Brown: Thank you very much indeed.

Kathy: Then it's all settled. Finally, before the meeting this afternoon, the vice mayor of the city who is in charge of foreign trade would like to meet you at his office at 3 o'clock .

Mr. Brown: How nice of him. We will all be most delighted to meet him.

Kathy: Then I'll come for you at 2:30 this afternoon .

Mr. Brown: Okay. We'll wait for you.

★全文中畫 ⬤ 色塊的地方，可以依自己的狀況套入不同的名字、公司名、職稱、學校名等等。

中文翻譯❺ •

瓊　　斯：凱西，可以留一個下午不安排活動嗎？妳知道，我在這裡有個朋友，我想利用這次出差機會拜訪他。

凱　　西：我想這很容易安排，還有其他事嗎？

瓊　　斯：沒有了。

布朗先生：你知道我們在這裡人生地不熟，因此，我想對我們來說，在這裡，最保險的做法就是一切聽您的安排。

凱　　　西：謝謝您這樣說，我會保證你們在這裡過得愉快。
布朗先生：太謝謝您了。
凱　　　西：那麼行程的事就解決了。最後，今天下午在會前，負責外貿的副市長想要在3點鐘在他的辦公室接見你們。
布朗先生：他人真好，我們非常樂意去拜訪他。
凱　　　西：那麼我今天下午兩點半來接你們。
布朗先生：好的，我們等妳。

Dialogue ⑥ 準備材料 ◀Track 197

凱西在此段對話中講了反話，明明忘了重要的東西，還說了「wonderful」（太好了），很明顯是在反諷自己。所以這時她的好同事聽出了她的弦外之音，便趕快安慰她：「Don't worry」（別擔心）。

Kathy: Sally , have you looked over the budgets that I gave you?

Sally: Sure, Kathy . They looked okay, but I thought there should be more details.

Kathy: Okay. Such as?

Sally: Well, you should have included details on your market research spending and the interest you will have to pay back on the bank loan.

Kathy: Wonderful, I forgot those important items.

Sally: Don't worry. There is so much to remember when you write a business proposal.

Kathy: Do you think the budgets are ready for me to take to the investors for them to see at the meeting next week?

Sally: As your accountant, I think that they are ready and the investors will be excited when they see them.

Kathy: I couldn't have imagined that it would be such hard work! Thanks for all your assistance, Sally .

★全文中畫 ⬤ 色塊的地方，可以依自己的狀況套入不同的名字、公司名、職稱、學校名等等。

中文翻譯6

凱西：莎莉，妳看過我給妳的預算了嗎？

莎莉：看過了，凱西。看起來不錯，不過我覺得還需要更詳細一點。

凱西：沒問題，哪裡需要詳細一些？

莎莉：妳應該在市場調查費用，和銀行貸款利息方面描述得更仔細一點。

凱西：好建議，我忘了那些重要的項目了。

莎莉：別擔心。寫商務提案的時候要涉及的東西確實太多了。

凱西：妳覺得這份預算可以在下個禮拜的會議上拿給投資商看嗎？

莎莉：作為妳的會計，我認為可以了，投資商看到會很興奮。

凱西：我從沒想到會這麼難。謝謝妳給我的所有幫助，莎莉。

商務小常識

　　不論是正式還是非正式會議，在召開之前，都必須先考慮開會的原因和目的，以及是否有召開的必要，然後再開始著手進行規劃。確定與會人員是一項很重要的工作，也是一個變化較多的因素，而它的變化將影響到整個會議的規格與規模，進而影響會議的各個因素。比如，重要人物的出席和缺席都可能影響規格。有時為了方便起見，會議地點或會議的一部分內容改為在機場、貴賓室進行，有時還會調整會議時間。這些是總協調工作控制的重點，需要格外重視。

SOS Unit 34
主持會議

Dialogue ❶ 開場白 ◀ Track 198

你的公司或許也有這樣的人，在會議上總是不正經，而且愛講一些有的沒的。這段對話中的麥克就是一例，一開口就虧主持人「很有名」。也不必特別想辦法對付這樣的人，當與會人士都很安靜害羞不想講話，正好就可以叫這種人先來發表意見、開個頭。看看這段對話中凱西是怎麼做的呢？

Kathy: Good morning, everyone. First, I'd like to introduce myself.

Mike: There is no need, Kathy . You are famous.

Kathy: Well, thank you very much, but I thought I'd try and chair the meeting formally—at least for a while.

Mike: Okay, certainly!

Kathy: Now I will commence the meeting. The main topic on today's agenda is the exploration of the African market for our new product. I would like to hear all of your ideas. Mike , you seem in top form today. Could you start the ball rolling?

Mike: Uh, oh, sure, I'm always the first. Well, I think we should keep in mind that the key to good sales is definitely advertising.

Kathy: Well, that's kind of obvious.

Mike: Please don't interrupt me, Kathy .

Kathy: Uh, let's keep this going, shall we?

Mike: Okay.

★全文中畫 ⬤ 色塊的地方，可以依自己的狀況套入不同的名字、公司名、職稱、學校名等等。

284 |

in top form 狀態極好

「top」是「最上面的」、「最頂端的」，所以這個片語就是「狀態絕頂好」的意思。舉例來說，如果有個籃球選手一場就得了50分，你可以稱讚他：He's in top form today.（他狀態極好）。

中文翻譯1

凱西：早安，各位。我先向大家作一下自我介紹。

麥克：不用介紹了，凱西，妳很有名氣。

凱西：那真是謝謝你了。但是我想我應該儘量按照正規程式來主持這次會議，一下下也好。

麥克：好的，當然啦！

凱西：那麼，我現在就開始。今天主要的議題是有關我們的新產品在非洲的市場開拓。我想聽聽大家的意見。麥克，你今天看起來很有精神，你先開始發言怎麼樣？

麥克：呃，好的，我總是第一個。嗯，我想我們始終要認識到的一點是，產品銷路好壞的關鍵是把廣告做好。

凱西：這還用你說？

麥克：請不要打斷我，凱西。

凱西：嗯，請繼續，好嗎？

麥克：好的。

Dialogue ❷ 會議前提問　◀Track 199

會議開始前，主持的人可以先請大家提出可能有的問題。看看這段對話中，凱西是怎麼說的？

Kathy: Good morning, my fellow colleagues. I hope our meeting today will be productive.

Leo: We all hope so.

Kathy: First of all, look at the yellow sheet on your table. Let's review today's agenda. If you have any queries, please put them forth immediately. The meeting will be chaired by me as usual. Okay, back to the agenda, any questions?

Leo: Yes, I was just asked to attend this meeting this morning, because our team leader had an emergency business trip.

Kathy: That's all right. Don't be nervous. This is a big chance for you to learn new things. Just follow the others and report on your team projects. Let the other teams report first.

Leo: Thank you. I'll try my best.

Kathy: Any other questions?

David: Prior to the meeting, I wonder if we could get your personal support on the proposal for the exploration of (African) market I mentioned yesterday.

Kathy: I see. Let me go over the material today and let's talk about it tomorrow morning. Okay?

David: Certainly.

Kathy: Okay. Let's start our meeting.

★全文中畫 ⬤ 色塊的地方，可以依自己的狀況套入不同的名字、公司名、職稱、學校名等等。

> **中文翻譯2**
>
> 凱西：早安，各位同事。希望今天的會議有所成效。
> 里歐：我們也希望如此。
> 凱西：首先，讓我們看看今天的議程，就是放在你們桌上的那張黃紙。如果有什麼問題，請立刻提出。會議和往常一樣，由我主持。好吧，回到議程，有什麼問題嗎？
> 里歐：有。我今天早上才接到通知要出席這次會議，因為我們組的組長臨時出差。
> 凱西：沒關係，別緊張。對你來說這是一次很好的學習機會。只要照著其他人做，報告一下你們組的計畫進度就行了。那就讓其他組先報告好了。
> 里歐：謝謝，我會盡我所能。
> 凱西：還有其他問題嗎？
> 大衛：在開會前，我想知道您個人是否支持我昨天說的關於開拓非洲市場的事情。
> 凱西：我知道了，讓我今天看一下資料，明天早上我們再說，好嗎？
> 大衛：當然可以。
> 凱西：那好，我們開始開會吧。

Dialogue ❸ 安排討論 ◀ᛂ *Track 200*

在會議中擔任主持人，重要的是要能夠讓話題一直源源不斷地進行下去。看看這段對話中，「let me direct your attention to...」（讓我帶你們來看看……）、「the next issue is...」（下一個議題是……）、「another significant problem is...」（另一個明顯的問題是……），都是引導話題好用的句型。

• •

Kathy: Okay, let's call this meeting to order. As (Marketing Director), (Sam) will lay out the main points of the agenda today. (Sam), would you please?

Sam: Thanks, (Kathy). Well, let me direct your attention to the main issues. First, the laws in that area. Will they make it hard for us to do business there by controlling the tariff?

Kathy: As you know, we've asked a legal expert to come in today. He isn't here yet, so we'd better go on to the next topic.

Sam: Okay. The next issue is how to sell in that market. Should we get people there to sell for us? Or even build our factory there for the reduction of cost? Yes, (Kathy)?

Kathy: I think the construction of a factory nearby is more feasible. Could you make a detailed proposal for this idea?

Sam: Good idea. Does everyone agree? Good. Another significant problem is the poor hygiene conditions of that area.

Tom: Could you give us some details?

Sam: I'd like to invite (Dr. Vincent), our medical expert, to explain this. (Dr. Vincent)?

Vincent: Thank you, (Sam). The lack of precipitation has led to a lack of decent drinking water. Many people often become sick.

Kathy: That'll greatly increase our cost. I think we should reconsider the proposal to build a factory there.

Sam: I agree with you.

★全文中畫 ⬤ 色塊的地方，可以依自己的狀況套入不同的名字、公司名、職稱、學校名等等。

凱西：好，現在會議正式開始。作為行銷總監，山姆將詳細說明今天議程的重點。山
　　　姆，請。

山姆：謝謝凱西。請大家注意幾個重要問題：一是那個地區的法律，他們會不會透過
　　　控制關稅來影響我們的銷售？

凱西：你也知道，我們請了一位法律專家出席今天的會議，可是他現在還沒到場，所
　　　以我想直接進入下一話題。

山姆：好的，第二個主要問題是如何在當地市場銷售，我們是找當地人代售，還是節
　　　省成本在當地建工廠直銷？凱西？

凱西：我認為在附近建廠更有可行性。你可以擬一份詳細的提議嗎？

山姆：好主意。大家同意嗎？好。這個地區的另外一個主要問題，是衛生環境很差。

湯姆：能說得清楚一點嗎？

山姆：我想請我們的醫學專家文森博士解釋這個問題。文森博士，請！

文森：謝謝山姆。在那裡的乾旱導致人們缺乏乾淨的飲用水。許多人經常生病。

凱西：這會大大提高我們的成本。我想我們應該重新考慮一下建廠的提議。

山姆：我贊同。

Dialogue ❹ 轉移議題 ◀ *Track 201*

要轉移議題有許多說法，可以參考這段對話中的句型：「**let's turn to the next topic**」（我們來進行下一個議題）。

Kathy: Team 1 will carry out the plan we've discussed just now. Now let's turn to the next topic on the agenda. We will confirm who will go to the annual conference next month.

Anna: I think Marco's team is the most prepared.

Maria: I agree, I think Marco's team should go because this year they've made great progress in sales.

Kathy: I'd like to get your opinion on this matter, Marco.

Marco: Thanks, everyone. But there is just one more suggestion before you make the decision. Every member in our team has been working hard and if possible we should all attend the conference together.

Kathy: ◯Maria◯ and ◯Anna◯ have nominated ◯Marco's◯ team to attend the conference. I will consider your nomination and suggestion, and let you know tomorrow. Is there anything else to mention?

Maria: Nothing.

Kathy: Okay, and now I would like to invite our ◯General Manager◯ to conclude our meeting.

Jack: I am very delighted to have participated in today's meeting. I am encouraged by the number of good suggestions we've heard today. I believe we can achieve our goals and make greater progress within the next year. Let's continue to work hard! Thank you very much!

Kathy: Thank you, ◯Jack◯.

★全文中畫 ⬤ 色塊的地方，可以依自己的狀況套入不同的名字、公司名、職稱、學校名等等。

現在是不是回想起來了呢？

mention 提到

許多東方的英語學習者會犯一個錯誤，說「mention about某事」，但其實不需要這個about，說mention就夠了。例如：

I've mentioned this to him. 我跟他提過這個。✓

I've mentioned about this to him. 我跟他提過這個。✗

中文翻譯4 ●

凱　西：第一組將會按照我們剛剛討論過的計畫執行。現在讓我們進行下一個議題。我們需要確定出席下個月舉行的年會的人選。

安　娜：我認為馬可的團隊準備得最充分。

瑪麗亞：我同意，我認為馬可的團隊今年應該出席該會議，因為他們這一年來在銷售上有了很大的進步。

凱　西：馬可，我想知道你對這件事的看法。

馬　可：謝謝大家，但是我只有一點想要在你們做決定之前提出。我認為我們組的每一個人工作都非常努力，如果可能的話我們應該一起參加會議。

凱　西：瑪麗亞和安娜提名了馬可的團隊參加此次會議。我會考慮你們的提名和建議並在明天告訴你們結果。各位對此還有什麼意見嗎？

瑪麗亞：沒有了。

凱　西：如果沒有，有請總經理做會議總結。

傑　克：很高興參加了今天的會議。今天聽到各位提出這麼多好的建議，我備感鼓
　　　　舞。我相信明年我們一定能完成目標，取得更大的進步。讓我們繼續努力
　　　　吧！謝謝！
凱　西：傑克，謝謝你。

Dialogue ❺ 討論議題 ◀╴*Track 202*

在會議中打斷別人時，該怎麼說才不會顯得沒禮貌？參考一下這段對話中的
說法吧！插話的人都有說「sorry」或「excuse me」喔！

Kathy: Well, everyone is here. We'll start. The main reason for this meeting is to discuss the probability of expanding our business in South China, particularly whether we should open more agencies next year.

Mark: That's great! We all have something to say on this subject.

Kathy: Lily, as the manager of the Marketing Department, perhaps you can briefly introduce the situation.

Lily: Yes, I've kept an eye on sales figures over the past years, and the data shows that we should increase the number of agencies in new areas in which there is a great deal of demand for our services.

Mark: Sorry to interrupt, but I have a quite different understanding of the situation. Personally speaking, I'm in favor of expanding our present agencies rather than setting up new ones. Please take the cost of setting up new ventures into consideration.

Tom: Excuse me, Mark. I have to break in here. I agree with you that we have to increase the budget on facilities, staff training, advertising and so on, but Lily is right. There's a great demand! Maybe Peter can tell us some concrete information about Shanghai Company.

Peter: Yes. I was going to mention that. Yesterday, I heard that Shanghai Company is planning to add four more agencies in South China.

Lily: Well, if we don't jump at the opportunity, our competitors will take over our market. Don't you think so?

Tom: I agree with you.

Kathy: All right, I feel we've discussed this matter fully. I will present your ideas
to the board of directors. Are there any other questions? No? Okay, this
meeting is adjourned.

★全文中畫 ⬤ 色塊的地方，可以依自己的狀況套入不同的名字、公司名、職稱、學校名等等。

現在是不是回想起來了呢？

jump at the opportunity 抓住機會

光看字面上的意思，彷彿可以想像機會一出現，你就馬上跳上去抓著不放的畫
面，有點像貓抓老鼠一樣。這句話就是這樣，指的是一看到機會就毫不猶豫、
想都沒想就跳上去的意思。這句會話不見得是稱讚的意思，因為完全未經思考
就衝動地抓住機會，有時不見得是好事。

中文翻譯5

凱西：好，所有人都到了，我們開始吧。召集這次會議主要是為了討論擴大華南市場
　　　的可能性，尤其是明年是否應該增設代理商。

馬克：太好了，我們對這個問題都有話要說。

凱西：莉莉，妳是銷售部經理，或許妳可以簡單介紹一下情況。

莉莉：好的。我一直在關注過去幾年的銷售額，資料顯示我們應該在對我們服務需求
　　　較大的新地區增設代理商。

馬克：對不起，打斷一下，我對形勢有完全不同的分析。依我個人看來，應該擴大我
　　　們現有的代理業務，而不是增設代理點。請考慮建立新機構所需的成本。

湯姆：對不起，馬克，我得插一句。我同意我們需要在增添設備、培訓員工、廣告宣
　　　傳等方面增加預算。但是莉莉說得有道理，因為那裡的確有很大的的需求。也
　　　許彼得可以告訴大家一些關於上海公司的具體情況。

彼得：是的，我正要提這事。昨天我聽說上海公司計畫在華南增設4個代理商。

莉莉：嗯，如果我們錯過了機會，我們的對手就會搶佔我們的市場。你不覺得嗎？

湯姆：我同意妳的看法。

凱西：好吧，我覺得我們已經充分討論這個問題了。我會把你們的意見提交到董事
　　　會。還有別的問題嗎？沒有？好，那今天就到此為止。

Dialogue ❻ 主持表決 ◀ *Track 203*

在這段對話中，出現了 **propose a motion** 這個說法。它的意思是「提議」，但是個非常正式的說法，只會在工作場合用，你要提議午餐吃披薩的時候，不會用這一句。

● ●

Kathy: Excuse me, please address your remarks to the chair.

Tom: Certainly, Chairwoman. I can assure the members of the board that when this programme is finished, our production capacity will be doubled.

Kate: Excuse me, Chairwoman, on a point of order, I don't think that (Tom) should be talking about the capacity before the board has had the opportunity to vote on whether to approve the programme.

Kathy: Yes, indeed. (Kate), would you like to propose a motion?

Kate: Yes, Chairwoman. I move that the capital expenditure programme, as presented to the board, be adopted in its present form.

Kathy: Who will second the motion?

Lily: I will second the motion.

Kathy: Those in favor? Those against? Any abstentions? (Eight) in favor, (none) against. I declare the motion carried. The capital expenditure programme is now adopted. Shall we go on to the next item on the agenda?

Kate: Of course, Chairwoman.

★全文中畫 ● 色塊的地方，可以依自己的狀況套入不同的名字、公司名、職稱、學校名等等。

現在是不是回想起來了呢？

second the motion 附議

開會的時候，有人提議，接下來就要看有沒有人附議。附議就叫 second the motion，和 propose a motion 一樣，是在正式的場合用，日常生活中則不會這樣說。

中文翻譯6

凱西：對不起，請對主席發言。

湯姆：好的，主席。我向董事會成員保證，這個項目完成後，我們的產能將提高一倍。

凱特：對不起，主席，按照程序，我認為董事會應該先投票表決是否批准這個專案，然後湯姆才能談論項目的產能。

凱西：的確如此。凱特，妳來提議好嗎？

凱特：好的，主席。我提議遞交給董事會的資金開支計畫，以現有的形式通過。

凱西：誰附議？

莉莉：我附議。

凱西：同意的舉手……反對的舉手……有棄權的嗎？8人同意，無人反對。我宣佈通過提議。資金開支計畫現已被採納。我們繼續行程中的下一個議題好嗎？

凱特：好的，主席。

Dialogue ❼ 反對提議　Track 204

當你要表達同意某人說法，卻又不想表現得一副完全被說服的樣子時，可以像此段對話中一樣，說：「You can't argue against that」（這實在很難反對），表示「雖然我本來沒有特別想支持你，但，欸，你說得真好」的意思。

Kathy: Sorry, Vincent, but I have to object to your opinion on the sale of technology.

Vincent: That's all right. I would prefer you gave me some different suggestions.

Kathy: First of all, most workers there can't read English, so an English explanation won't help them at all.

Vincent: Oh, that will be a problem.

Kathy: Second, even if their government agrees to the import of our technology, other groups won't. They may call out the media hounds, and many people will be very, very dissatisfied with us. Expansion will fail.

Vincent: Hm... Kathy. Is there another reason you want to add?

Kathy: Yes, there is. Last but not least, our customers would be hurt because of it.

Vincent: Hm... You can't argue against that. How could we live with ourselves if we let that happen? Just because we wanted more money?

Kathy: It is about the reputation of our company.

★全文中畫 ⬤ 色塊的地方，可以依自己的狀況套入不同的名字、公司名、職稱、學校名等等。

中文翻譯7

凱西：抱歉，文森，我對你在出售技術方面的看法持反對態度。

文森：沒關係。我想聽聽你的不同意見。

凱西：首先，在那裡大部分的人都不懂英文，所以英文說明對他們根本沒有作用。

文森：哦，那確實是個問題。

凱西：第二，就算他們的政府同意引進我們的技術，但是其他團體不會同意的。他們或許會引起輿論的注意，許多人會對我們非常非常不滿，擴張計畫會失敗。

文森：嗯，凱西，還有其他要補充的嗎？

凱西：有。最後但同樣重要的一點是，我們的消費者因此而受傷害。

文森：嗯。我真無法反駁。如果我們坐視這種情形發生而不管，我們怎麼能心安理得？難道僅僅是為了賺取更多的錢嗎？

凱西：這是有關我們公司聲譽的問題。

Dialogue ❽ 結束會議 ◀《*Track 205*

💬 在這段對話中，凱西一開始說「**We'll adjourn our discussion for today**」（我們就要結束今天的討論）、最後說「**We have reached a conclusion today**」（我們今天達成了結論）、「**That's all for today**」（今天到此為止），都是結束會議時可能會說的話。

Kathy: We'll adjourn our discussion for today, but there are still several points that need further discussion. When shall we have our next meeting?

Danny: How about Tuesday afternoon?

Mike: I'm afraid I cannot make it on Tuesday. I have to go to Hong Kong.

Lily: Neither do I. On Tuesday, our team will have a trip to Shanghai for the conference there.

Kathy: Yes, that's a very important meeting. You should bring back useful information. If you have the chance, you'd better sign the contract.

Lily: Yes, we'll try our best.

Danny: How about ⬤Friday afternoon⬤?

Mike: That'll be good for me, but can everybody make it on ⬤Friday afternoon⬤?

Lily: I don't think it'll be a problem.

Kathy: Fine. I hope everyone will give some thought to the points we have discussed today. We have reached a conclusion today for the projects, and I hope we'll see some results on ⬤Friday afternoon at 2 o'clock⬤. That's all for today. Thank you, everyone.

★全文中畫 ⬤ 色塊的地方，可以依自己的狀況套入不同的名字、公司名、職稱、學校名等等。

中文翻譯8 ● ● ● ● ● ● ● ● ●

凱西：我們就要結束今天的討論，但還有幾點需要進一步討論一下。下一次會議定在什麼時候？

丹尼：星期二下午怎麼樣？

麥克：星期二我恐怕沒空。我要去香港。

莉莉：我也沒空。星期二我們小組要去上海參加一個會議。

凱西：是的，那是個非常重要的會議。妳們要帶回有用的資訊。如果有機會，最好能簽合約。

莉莉：是的，我們會盡最大努力。

丹尼：那麼星期五下午呢？

麥克：我可以，但其他人行嗎？

莉莉：沒問題。

凱西：好。我希望每個人都想想今天討論的重點。我們今天就專案已經得出了結論，我希望到週五下午兩點時，能看到一些成果。今天到此為止。謝謝大家。

商務小常識

　　開會時除非座位已事先安排好，否則宜選擇鄰近老闆或有實權者的座位。此舉並不是趨炎附勢的表現，而是若故意保持距離，在他人看來，是有欠團隊精神的表現。這種不願參與（成為一分子）的姿態，尤令高層主管不悅。

Dialogue ❶ 時間安排 ◀ *Track 206*

💬 在這段對話中，可以學到「在我的經驗中……」的說法（**In my experience...**），是個在商討事宜安排時實用的句子。

• •

Kathy: Please let me see the draft that you put together for Monday's meeting.

Flora: I'm still working on the agenda. There will be a lot to go over on Monday. Here's what I've got so far.

Kathy: Do you think we will spend more than twenty minutes on introductions? I think it should be pretty simple.

Flora: It shouldn't take too long, but there will be several dignitaries at the meeting. In the opening, we'll spend a little time introducing them, and I reckon it should take at least half an hour before we can even get to the minutes.

Kathy: Really? Well, at least the minutes shouldn't take too long to review. There shouldn't be a lot of unfinished business left over from the last meeting.

Flora: True, after review and acceptance of the minutes, we have several committee reports. Old business won't take up too much time, but sometimes the committee delegates can be a little verbose. Is there any way we can limit their speaking time?

Kathy: We can set a five-minute report time with a three-minute question and answer afterwards.

Flora: In my experience, question and answer periods always take forever because people usually get stuck on some irrelevant point. We'll lose control of the meeting if we open it up to questions too early.

Kathy: True, well, impose an (eight-minute) limit on the committee reports. Then, we'll save the question and answer period until the end.

Flora: Sounds good. We can probably finish the meeting within (two hours).

Kathy: Let's hope so.

★全文中畫 ⬤ 色塊的地方，可以依自己的狀況套入不同的名字、公司名、職稱、學校名等等。

現在是不是回想起來了呢？

dignitary 顯要人物、權貴人士

dignitary指的就是不能得罪的重要人物，尤其常指從其他國家來的重要人物。

中文翻譯1

凱　西：請讓我看一下妳整理的週一會議用的草案。

芙羅拉：我還在研究會議行程。週一會有很多事情。這是我目前為止所整理的。

凱　西：妳認為我們要花超過20分鐘作介紹嗎？我覺得作介紹應該很簡單。

芙羅拉：確實不需要那麼長時間，但是會有幾位高官與會。在開場白中我們會花一些時間來介紹他們。我估算在回顧會議紀錄前，至少需要花去半個小時。

凱　西：真的嗎？好吧，至少回顧會議紀錄的時間不應該太長。上次會議應該沒有留下太多沒解決的事情。

芙羅拉：是的，在回顧和通過會議記錄之後，我們還有幾份委員會報告。舊業務不會佔用太多時間，但有時委員會代表的報告會有點冗長。我們有什麼辦法來限制他們的講話時間嗎？

凱　西：我們可以限定5分鐘報告時間，之後是3分鐘問答時間。

芙羅拉：以我的經驗，問答環節總是沒完沒了，因為人們老是卡在一些不重要的小癥結上面。如果我們太早開始問答部分，我們將無法控制整個會議。

凱　西：確實是，嗯，那麼就把委員報告時間限制在8分鐘內。然後在會議即將結束前開始問答。

芙羅拉：聽起來不錯。這樣我們或許可以把會議長度限制在兩小時之內。

凱　西：但願吧。

Dialogue ❷ 修改議程 🔊 *Track 207*

💬 主持會議時被其他人糾正，怎麼辦？也不用表現得一副不高興或難過的樣子，像此段對話中凱西隨口說「I somehow overlooked...」（我不知怎麼地忽略了……）輕鬆帶過，就是個不錯的方法，讓別人不會覺得你這個人說不得，而且會很快地忘記你有疏漏過事情。

● ●

Kathy: Who'll motion to approve the draft from last meeting?

Flora: I motion it, and he seconds it.

Kathy: All in favor? Good, now what's next on the agenda? We have some new business. Flora , would you introduce Item B on the agenda for us?

Flora: Yes, but we should probably follow the agenda in order, shouldn't we? Item A is still pending.

Kathy: Oh, yes, I somehow overlooked Item A . Well then, Mark , can you report back to us on your project?

Mark: The agenda is a little out of order today. I'd prefer Flora to introduce her project first, then what I have to say might make more sense, technically.

Kathy: Oh, is that right? Well, let's rearrange the agenda then. We can move Item A to the end of our new business section. It will follow reports on Items B through D . Any objections?

Flora: Can we have Item A directly following Item B ?

Kathy: Fine, any objections? If there are no objections, then the modification to the agenda has been approved unanimously. We will proceed according to the amendments we've just made.

★全文中畫 ⬤ 色塊的地方，可以依自己的狀況套入不同的名字、公司名、職稱、學校名等等。

> **現在是不是回想起來了呢？**
>
> **pending 未定的**
> pending就是「還沒決定的」的意思，例如若你申請一間學校，但學校還沒放榜，你去網站上查榜時可能就會看到「pending」，指的是他們還沒有決定要不要收你。

中文翻譯2

凱　西：誰要來提議通過上次會議提出的草案？

芙羅拉：我提議，他附議。

凱　西：所有人都贊成？好的，下一項議程是什麼呢？我們有一些新業務。芙羅拉，妳能為大家介紹一下議程表上的B項嗎？

芙羅拉：好的。但我們應該按照議程表的順序來，是不是？A項還沒有解決呢。

凱　西：哦，是的，我不知道怎麼忽略了A項。那麼，馬克，你能向我們彙報一下你們的項目嗎？

馬　克：今天的議程有些混亂，我倒覺得芙羅拉先介紹她的專案比較好，然後我報告的內容嚴格說來才會更有意義。

凱　西：哦，是這樣嗎？好吧，那我們重新安排議程。我們可以把A項放到新業務後面討論。先討論B至D項。有異議嗎？

芙羅拉：我們可以在B項後直接討論A項嗎？

凱　西：好，有反對的嗎？如果沒有的話，那麼今天會議議程的修改就全體通過。我們將按照新的議程繼續進行。

Dialogue ❸ 協商議程 ◀ *Track 208*

請對方安排會面，想不到對方已經安排好了，真是設想周到。看看這段對話中，史密斯先生是如何稱讚凱西的安排：「**that's very nice of you.**」（你真是太好了）。

Kathy: Welcome to our company. My name is Kathy . I'm in charge of the export department. Let me give you my business card.

Mr. Smith: I'll give you mine too.

Kathy: How was your flight?

Mr. Smith: Not bad, but I'm a little tired.

Kathy: Here's your schedule. After this meeting, we will visit the factory and have another meeting with the Production Manager , then you'll be having dinner with our director .

Mr. Smith: Thank you very much. Could you arrange a meeting with your boss?

Kathy: Of course, I've arranged for 10 o'clock tomorrow morning .

Mr. Smith: Oh, that's very nice of you. Well, shall we get down to business?

Kathy: Of course.

★全文中畫 ⬤ 色塊的地方，可以依自己的狀況套入不同的名字、公司名、職稱、學校名等等。

中文翻譯3

> 凱　　西：歡迎來到我們公司。我叫凱西，負責出口部門。這是我的名片。
> 史密斯先生：這是我的名片。
> 凱　　西：您的旅途如何？
> 史密斯先生：還可以，不過我有點累。
> 凱　　西：這是您的行程。開完會後，我們去參觀工廠，再跟生產部經理開個會。晚上您將和我們的主任共進晚餐。
> 史密斯先生：非常感謝！您能安排我跟你們老闆會面嗎？
> 凱　　西：當然可以，我已經安排在明天上午10點。
> 史密斯先生：哦，那真是太好了！那我們開始談正事吧。
> 凱　　西：當然可以。

Dialogue ④ 會前協商 ◀ *Track 209*

看看這段對話中的議價方式，先說無法降價，又說如果下大批訂單就降價，是個技巧性的作法。

Kathy: Did you receive the samples we sent last week?

Mr. Smith: Yes, we finished evaluation of it. If the price is acceptable we would like to order now.

Kathy: I'm very glad to hear that.

Mr. Smith: What's your best price for that item?

Kathy: The unit price is $12.50 .

Mr. Smith: I think the price is a little high. Can't you reduce it?

Kathy: I'm afraid we can't. $12.50 is our rock bottom price. If you purchase more than 10,000 units we can reduce it to $12.00 .

Mr. Smith: Well, I'll accept the price and place an initial order of 10,000 units.

Kathy: Very good. It's a pleasure doing business with you, Mr. Smith .

Mr. Smith: The pleasure is all mine. Can you deliver the goods by ⟨March 31⟩?
Kathy: Of course.

★全文中畫 ⬤⬤ 色塊的地方，可以依自己的狀況套入不同的名字、公司名、職稱、學校名等等。

現在是不是回想起來了呢？

rock bottom 最低處

除了說「價格最低」以外，只要是講「最低」的時候，也都可以使用這個說法。例如你的心情盪到谷底就可以說I'm at rock bottom.。

中文翻譯4

凱　　　西：您有沒有收到我們上個禮拜寄給您的樣品？
史密斯先生：收到了，我們已進行了評估。如果價格合適，我們現在就想訂貨。
凱　　　西：聽到這個我很高興。
史密斯先生：這種貨你們最低價是多少？
凱　　　西：單價是12.5美元。
史密斯先生：我覺得這個價錢有點貴，能不能再低一點？
凱　　　西：恐怕不行，12.5美元是我們的底價。如果你們訂貨超過10,000件，我們可以降到12美元。
史密斯先生：好，我接受這個價格，第一批訂10,000件。
凱　　　西：太好了。史密斯先生，跟您做生意真是我的榮幸。
史密斯先生：是我的榮幸才對。你們能在3月31號前出貨嗎？
凱　　　西：當然可以。

Dialogue ❺ 部門會議　🔊 *Track 210*

💬 請同事告訴你一些你不知道的事時，可以用「**fill me in**」這個片語。在這段對話中，也使用了「**fill us in**」，就是請同事告訴大家一些他們原本不知道，但必須要知道的事。

Kathy: I call this meeting to order. Thank you for attending. I know it's a busy day for you all. Did everyone get the minutes for the last meeting?
Flora: I need a copy of the minutes for the last meeting.

Kathy: Okay, we can now begin.

Flora: May I suggest something? I know we have many points to review today, but would it be possible to limit our meeting time to finish before four o'clock ? Many of us still have a great amount of work to do before the day's end.

Kathy: We should be able to finish everything up before then. Let's run through the major points first and see where we're at. The first matter of business is to approve the minutes of our last meeting.

Flora: I propose we accept the minutes.

Kathy: Good, does anyone second the motion? Good, motion carried. Now next on our agenda is our budget review. Margaret , could you please fill us in on where the budget review stands?

Margaret: We've had a review board going over everything, and we have come up with a final review. Here is a copy for everyone and if you have any questions, you can talk to me after the meeting. Basically, the budget review has been completed with maybe a few polishing details left.

Flora: What kind of action is required?

Kathy: If everyone could take a look at the final review handout, if there're any objections or corrections, let me know. Next week, we can cast the final approval.

★全文中畫 ⬤ 色塊的地方，可以依自己的狀況套入不同的名字、公司名、職稱、學校名等等。

中文翻譯5 •

凱　西：我宣佈會議開始。非常感謝大家的參加。我知道大家今天都非常忙。每個人都拿到上次的會議紀錄了嗎？

芙羅拉：我還需要一份上次的會議紀錄。

凱　西：好了，我們可以開會了。

芙羅拉：我可以提個建議嗎？我知道今天會議有很多事情要回顧，但能否把會議限制在4點前結束？我們很多人在今天下班前還有大量工作要做。

凱　西：我們在4點之前應該能完成所有事情。我們先快速流覽一下重點，然後看看我們目前所處的情況。第一件事就是要通過上次會議的紀要。

芙羅拉：我提議通過。

凱　西：好的，有人同意嗎？好的，提議通過。下一項是預算評議。瑪格麗特，你能告訴大家預算審議現在到哪一步了嗎？

瑪格麗特：我們有請評議委員會仔細審查了每項內容，並給出了最終的審議意見。現在給大家每人一份影本，如果大家有任何問題，可以會後找我談。除了一些要改善的細節，預算審議基本上完成了。

芙羅拉：我們需要做什麼呢？

凱　西：如果大家都能仔細閱讀最終的審查報告，有任何反對意見和修改建議，那麼就通知我一聲，下週我們就可以通過最後的決議。

Dialogue ❻ 會議間歇 🔊 *Track 211*

想問人家為什麼會到你們公司來拜訪，可以用這段對話中的「**what brings you to...?**」句型。直翻是「是什麼把你帶來的？」，確切意思則是「你是為什麼會來這裡？」，有一種「是什麼風把你吹來的」的感覺。

Kathy: Hi. I'm Kathy Li.

Gail: My pleasure. I'm Gail Mirabel.

Jody: My name's Jody Fowler. Nice to meet you all.

Kathy: So what brings you to this seminar?

Jody: I'm a manager in the Marketing Department at ABC Incorporated. We're interested in the potential advertising capabilities this new technology offers.

Gail: I'm the CMO for Asco International. My CEO is highly interested in this new technology. What about you, Kathy? Where do you work?

Kathy: I work for ABB Company. I'm a supervisor in Sales there. I think something like this would inject new life into our sales campaigns.

Jody: That seems to be a prevailing opinion here. Well, looks like the seminar's about to continue. It was a pleasure meeting you all. Maybe we can get together again over dinner.

★全文中畫 色塊的地方，可以依自己的狀況套入不同的名字、公司名、職稱、學校名等等。

inject 注入

inject通常是「注射」、「打針」的意思。在這段對話中，說的就是把新的活力像打針一樣「注入」銷售活動中。

中文翻譯6

凱西：你好。我是凱西・李。

蓋爾：幸會。我是蓋爾・米拉貝爾。

喬迪：我叫喬迪・福勒，很高興見到大家。

凱西：那麼，你們是為什麼來參加這次研討會？

喬迪：我是ABC公司行銷部的經理。我們對這個新技術蘊含的廣告潛力很感興趣。

蓋爾：我是阿斯科國際公司的首席行銷長。我們的首席執行長對這個新技術有極大的興趣。妳呢，凱西？妳在什麼地方工作？

凱西：我在ABB公司工作，我是那裡的銷售主管。我認為像這樣的技術可以給我們的銷售活動注入新的活力。

喬迪：大家的看法好像是一致的。哦，看來研討會又要繼續了。很高興見到你們，也許我們能夠在晚餐時再見面。

商務小常識

　　會議通常有一個或幾個相關的議題。若有多個議題，負責秘書應根據這些議題的內在聯系、主次編排議程，列印成文，將議程表在會前發給與會人員。會期超過一天的會議，還應制訂出日程表和作息時間表，讓與會人可以更清楚整體流程。

詢問意見

Dialogue ❶ 詢問客戶意見 ◀ *Track 212*

大家應該也有這樣的經驗：在餐廳填完問卷，如果填的都是「滿意」，服務生就不會多問你問題，而如果有「不滿意」，則會有人過來問你是怎麼回事。在這段對話中，我們可以學學看朱莉所問的：「**What went wrong exactly?**」（確切地講到底是哪裡出錯了？）

● ●

Julie: First of all, thank you for filling in our questionnaire.

Charley: No problem, how can I help you?

Julie: Well, you made a few interesting comments that I'd like to ask you about, if that's all right.

Charley: Sure, go ahead!

Julie: You said that the customer service you received was "shoddy". What went wrong exactly?

Charley: Well, the guy who served me didn't really seem to know what he was doing.

Julie: Do you mean he was rude?

Charley: No, not rude; he just didn't know where to find things in the store. Things like that.

Julie: I see, but you were happy with what you bought?

Charley: Yes. They're absolutely fine.

Julie: Good. And you thought they were reasonably priced?

Charley: Yes. They weren't cheap, but they're of high quality, so I didn't mind paying a bit extra.

★全文中畫 ⬤ 色塊的地方，可以依自己的狀況套入不同的名字、公司名、職稱、學校名等等。

現在是不是回想起來了呢？

shoddy 劣質的

shoddy常指「破破爛爛的」，尤其常拿來形容破車之類的物品。在這裡是說服務品質很爛，有如破車一樣爛。

中文翻譯1

- 朱莉：首先感謝您填寫我們的調查問卷。
- 查理：沒什麼。需要我做什麼？
- 朱莉：嗯，如果不介意的話，我想就你作的幾條有趣的評論問幾個問題。
- 查理：當然可以，問吧。
- 朱莉：您說您遇到的客戶服務很差，究竟是怎麼回事呢？
- 查理：嗯，那個為我服務的小夥子好像根本不知道他在做什麼。
- 朱莉：您的意思是他很粗魯？
- 查理：不，不是粗魯。他只是不知道商品的擺放位置這類的事情。
- 朱莉：我知道了。但是您對所購買的東西還是滿意的吧？
- 查理：是的。東西非常棒！
- 朱莉：好的。您認為這些東西價格合理嗎？
- 查理：合理。它們不便宜，但品質非常好，所以我不介意多花一些錢。

Dialogue ❷ 徵求下屬意見 🔊 *Track 213*

💬 想請人提供意見時，可以像此段對話中一樣，說：「I want your feedback」（我要聽你的意見）。feedback是個聽起來帶點專業感的字，在職場上非常適用。

Gregory: Kathy , before I officially announce the reorganization, I want your final feedback.

Kathy: I've gone through the entire plan again, and I'm sure the impact will be minimal since we're not planning large-scale lay-offs.

Gregory: That was a key objective from the start. Qualified staff holding positions that are being cut will be offered retraining for our new positions. If they accept, they have the job.

Kathy: That's the best policy. Nevertheless, some employees may not want to change career paths mid-stream, and will probably hand in their resignations.

Gregory: I know, and we have a very fair compensation package for those who decide to quit. In this case, this may be a good opportunity to fire under-performers. This reorganization and the new company policies will make us leaner and meaner. Are the new employee contracts ready?

Kathy: Yes, they are, and all other appropriate forms have been modified. We're ready to go.

Gregory: Great! I think we've covered all the bases. I'll set up a general meeting for (next Monday) to make the announcement.

★全文中畫 ⬤ 色塊的地方，可以依自己的狀況套入不同的名字、公司名、職稱、學校名等等。

現在是不是回想起來了呢？

cover all the bases 各方面都考慮周全

打棒球的時候，那些壘包都叫做base。既然你每一個壘包都顧到了，那就表示你準備萬全、什麼都考慮到了，也不用擔心有人盜壘之類的意外啦。所以 cover all the bases就是考慮周全的意思。

中文翻譯2

葛列格里：凱西，在我正式宣佈重組之前，我想聽一下妳最終的意見。

凱　　西：我把整個計畫又仔細研究了一下。我肯定這次重組帶來的影響會非常小，因為我們沒有大規模的裁員計畫。

葛列格里：這一開始就是我們的一個重要目標。而且，假如被裁的職員符合我們的用人要求，我們會向他們提供再培訓的機會，讓他們適應我們新職務的需要。如果他們接受這樣的安排，就仍有工作做。

凱　　西：這樣最好。但即便是這樣，可能會有些人不願意中途更換工作類別，他們
　　　　　仍有可能提出辭呈。
葛列格里：這點我也想到了。我們會給決定辭職的員工一筆相當公道的補償金。說不
　　　　　定這還是我們解雇不稱職員工的好機會呢。這次重組加上新的公司政策會
　　　　　使我們減輕負擔、提高效率。對了，新的雇傭合約準備好了嗎？
凱　　西：是的，已經準備好了。其他相關的表格也都經過改進了。一切都已就緒。
葛列格里：好極了！我想我們已把所以方面都考慮周全了。下週一我會召開全體大會
　　　　　宣佈進行重組。

Dialogue ❸ 徵求同事意見 (1) 🔊 *Track 214*

看看這段對話中，用了不少假設語氣，例如「**if I were you...**」（如果我是
你的話……）。我當然不可能會是你，所以要用「**were**」這個假設語氣的字。

Anna: I think I need to check this report again before I hand it in.

Kathy: Good idea!

Anna: What would you suggest I do for the cover page?

Kathy: I would use an old one so you don't have to spend a lot of time on it.

Anna: I might do that. By the way, have you read the presentation I gave you?

Kathy: It was good overall, but you need to make some small changes.

Anna: What do you suggest I do?

Kathy: If I were you, I would put the production information before the cost so
　　　　that it sounds justified.

Anna: Anything else?

Kathy: Just speak with more confidence.

Anna: Thank you very much.

★全文中畫 ⬤ 色塊的地方，可以依自己的狀況套入不同的名字、公司名、職稱、學校名等等。

中文翻譯3

安娜：我認為在呈交報告之前應該再檢查一下。
凱西：好主意！
安娜：妳對封面有什麼建議嗎？

凱西：我會用一個用過的封面，這樣就不用花費太多的時間在這上面了。

安娜：那我也這麼做。對了，妳看過我給你的報告了嗎？

凱西：總體看非常好。但妳還要做些細微的改進。

安娜：妳建議我怎麼做呢？

凱西：如果我是妳的話，我會把生產資訊放在成本前面，這樣更加合理。

安娜：還有別的嗎？

凱西：那就是發言時要更有自信一點。

安娜：非常感謝。

Dialogue ❹ 徵求同事意見 (2)　🔊 *Track 215*

💬 突然要倉促通知大家某件事，可以參考此段對話中的用法，說：「**sorry about the short notice**」（很抱歉這麼倉促通知）。

Kathy: Good morning, everyone. Sorry about the short notice, but the CEO just informed me that the board has approved the project for expansion to the East Coast as we proposed. They want it done in four months, which is one month shorter than the timeframe we proposed. I need to know who's available for the project team. Jenny, let's start with you. We need an experienced report analyst.

Jenny: Ken Green's our best bet for this type of project.

Kathy: When can he start?

Jenny: I'll reassign some of his current responsibilities, so he can start almost right away.

Kathy: Fine. How about you, Nigel? Who can look after the office space? According to the floor plan, we'll need 1,200 square metres in the center of downtown.

Nigel: Uh, let me see. Jake Williams could start in a few days. He has numerous contacts on the East Coast.

Kathy: Okay. Lily, we need a materials specialist to purchase office equipment and supplies, get rental cars, etc. Who can handle that for us?

Lily: (Sherry) is my choice. She's an expert at getting quality material and staying under budget.

Kathy: I'll go along with that. Last but not least, (Lyle), since we're under tighter time restraints, I'll need someone to assist me with workflow management. What's your recommendation?

Lyle: (Julie Stevens) can help you there, and the timing's just right. She's just finished another major assignment.

Kathy: Alright, everything's settled. I'll talk to HR about staffing tomorrow. I'm setting the project's start date for (Monday).

★全文中畫 ● 色塊的地方，可以依自己的狀況套入不同的名字、公司名、職稱、學校名等等。

workflow 工作流程

flow的意思是「流動」，像是河水的流動就可以用這個字。在它的前面加上「work」，就表示「工作的流動過程」，也就是「工作流程」。

中文翻譯4

凱　西：各位早安，首先對倉促通知各位表示抱歉，執行總裁剛剛告知我董事會已經通過了我們提議的那個往東海岸擴張的項目，不過他們希望在四個月之內完成，這就比我們所建議的進度提前了一個月。我需要知道誰能參加專案小組。珍妮，就從妳開始吧，我們需要一個資深的報告分析師。

珍　妮：對這種項目來說肯・格林是我們的最佳候選人。

凱　西：他什麼時候可以開始工作？

珍　妮：我會重新分配他現在的工作量，那麼他差不多可以立刻開始了。

凱　西：好的，那你呢，奈傑爾？誰能負責管理辦公地點？根據樓層平面圖，我們在市中心需要一個1,200平方公尺的地方。

奈傑爾：嗯，讓我想想。傑克・威廉斯可以在幾天內開始，他在東海岸人脈很廣。

凱　西：好的。莉莉，我們需要一個物資專家來採購辦公設備和用品以及租車等事宜。誰能負責這個部分？

莉　莉：我選雪莉。她擅長採購優質材料，同時又不會超出預算。

凱　西：就這麼辦。最後還有一件重要的事，萊爾，由於時間緊迫，我需要一個人協助我做工作流程管理，你認為誰合適？

萊　爾：朱莉・史蒂文斯可以。而且時機也剛剛好，她剛完成了一項重要工作。

凱　西：好的，一切都定下來了，我明天會跟人力資源部談有關的人員安排問題。我會把項目安排在星期一開始實施。

Dialogue ❺ 詢問合作方市場意見　◀ *Track 216*

和曾用e-mail和電話等方式聯絡過，卻從未見過面的人，第一次見面時，可以像這段對話中一樣說說看「it's very nice to finally meet you」（很高興終於見到您）。其中使用「finally」（終於）這個字，可以表示「在電話與郵件往返過程中，我一直很想見到您，現在終於讓我見到了，真開心！」的意思。

Ben: Mr. Sun , I'd like you to meet Ms. Kathy Li , Sales Manager for our company.

Mr. Sun: It's very nice to finally meet you, Ms. Li , especially after so many phone calls and faxes. I'd like you to have my business card.

Kathy: Thanks very much, Mr. Sun . Please accept mine, and please, call me Kathy . Can you tell me in a nutshell what the retail market is like at your place?

Mr. Sun: Well, as per capita income goes up, high-end products are increasingly popular.

Kathy: Retail is going upscale? Your place is certainly growing more quickly than I had imagined.

Mr. Sun: Yes. Things certainly have changed since I was a boy. We've developed very quickly.

Kathy: Do you think the trend will continue?

Mr. Sun: I don't see why not. We do have some problems, but we are still willing to work hard and wages aren't too high at this point.

Kathy: Everything I've seen so far is very impressive.

Mr. Sun: We'd be very pleased to welcome your investment here.

★全文中畫 ⬤ 色塊的地方，可以依自己的狀況套入不同的名字、公司名、職稱、學校名等等。

in a nutshell 總括來說

nutshell是「核桃殼」。核桃非常地小，要把一切想說的話都塞進核桃殼裡，當然也就得把要說的話「塞得很小」，也就是「精簡來說」、「總括來說」。

中文翻譯5

班：孫先生，我來替你介紹我們公司的銷售經理凱西·李女士。

孫先生：多次電話、傳真往返之後，非常高興終於見到您，李女士，請收下我的名片。

凱　西：謝謝您，孫先生。也請收下我的名片，叫我凱西就行了。可以簡單地跟我說一下你們這裡零售市場的現況嗎？

孫先生：好的，由於個人平均收入不斷增高，高階產品越來越受歡迎。

凱　西：零售向高階發展？你們這裡的發展比我想像的要快多了。

孫先生：沒錯，情況和我小時候完全不一樣了，這裡發展得非常快。

凱　西：你認為這種趨勢還會持續下去嗎？

孫先生：我想沒有理由不持續。雖然有一些問題存在，但我們仍願意勤奮工作，而且現階段薪水仍不算太高。

凱　西：到目前為止，我所看到的一切都令人讚歎。

孫先生：我們十分歡迎妳們能到這裡投資。

Dialogue ❻ 徵求參展商意見 ◀ *Track 217*

💬 和第一次參展的客戶聊天，可以問對方對此展覽的感想。那若對方已經來過很多次了呢？凱西在這段對話中問：「您有發現什麼不一樣的地方嗎？」就是個好問題。

Kathy: Good afternoon, Mr. Brown. My name is Kathy Li, the Sales Manager.

Mr. Brown: Nice to meet you, Kathy.

Kathy: Nice to meet you too, Mr. Brown. Is it your first trip to the Fair?

Mr. Brown: No, it's the fourth time.

Kathy: Good. Is there anything you've found different this year?

Mr. Brown: Yes, a great deal. The business scope has been broadened, and there are more visitors than ever before.

Kathy: Really? Did you find anything interesting?

Mr. Brown: Oh yes. Quite a bit, but we are especially interested in your products.

Kathy: We are glad to hear that. What items are you particularly interested in?

Mr. Brown: Women's dresses . They are fashionable and suit Australian women well, too. If they are of high quality and the prices are reasonable, we'll purchase large quantities of them.

★全文中畫 ● 色塊的地方，可以依自己的狀況套入不同的名字、公司名、職稱、學校名等等。

中文翻譯6

凱　　西：布朗先生，午安！我是凱西‧李，銷售部的經理。
布朗先生：見到妳很高興，凱西。
凱　　西：布朗先生，我也很高興見到您。這是您第一次參加展覽會嗎？
布朗先生：不，這是第四次了。
凱　　西：太好了。您有發現今年展覽會有什麼變化嗎？
布朗先生：有的，變化很大。經營範圍擴大了，而且客戶比以前也多了很多。
凱　　西：真的嗎？您有沒有發現感興趣的商品？
布朗先生：有，有很多。我們對妳們的產品尤其感興趣。
凱　　西：聽您這樣說我們真高興。您對什麼產品特別感興趣呢？
布朗先生：洋裝。這些洋裝的款式不僅時髦，而且很適合澳洲的女性穿著。如果這些衣服品質好而且價格合理的話，我們會大量訂購。

Dialogue ❼ 徵求合作意見 ◀Track 218

這段對話中的最後一句，不但說雙方都會得到很多利益，還說希望能夠長期成功合作，是段讓對方聽起來會很開心的好用會話。

Richard: How about 15% for the first six months, and 12% for the next, with a guarantee of 3,000 units?

Kathy: That's a lot to sell, with very low profit margins.

Richard: It's about the best we can do, Kathy . We need to hammer something out today. If I go back empty-handed, I may be coming back to you soon to ask for a job.

Kathy: Okay, (17%) for the first (six) months, (14%) for the second?

Richard: Good. Let's iron out the remaining details. When do you want to take delivery?

Kathy: We'd like you to execute the first order by the (31st).

Richard: I'd prefer the first shipment to be (1,000) units, the next (2,000). The (31st) is quite soon. I can't guarantee (1,500).

Kathy: I can agree to that. Well, if there's nothing else, I think we've settled everything.

Richard: (Kathy), this deal promises big returns for both sides. Let's hope it's the beginning of a long and prosperous relationship.

★全文中畫 ⬤ 色塊的地方，可以依自己的狀況套入不同的名字、公司名、職稱、學校名等等。

現在是不是回想起來了呢？

iron out 解決、消除（困難等）

iron是「熨斗」或「燙（衣服）」的意思。燙衣服的時候，衣服不是都會有皺褶或不平整嗎？燙衣服就是要把這些麻煩處去掉，而這個動作就叫做iron out。用在這段對話中，意思就是要把剩下一些麻煩的小細節「燙掉」，也就是解決、消除這些麻煩啦。

中文翻譯7

理查：前6個月8.5折，後6個月8.8折，保證訂貨3,000件，妳意下如何？

凱西：這樣我們要賣的貨太多，而毛利又太低了。

理查：凱西，我們沒辦法再讓步了。今天我們一定要把事情搞定。如果我空手回去，大概很快就會來找妳要份工作嘍。

凱西：好吧，前6個月8.3折，後6個月8.6折？

理查：好！那麼我們來解決剩下的細節問題。妳想要什麼時候收到貨？

凱西：我們希望貴公司能在31號前履行第一筆訂單。

理查：我希望第一批貨運1,000件，下一批2,000件。31號就快到了，我不能保證能做1,500件。

凱西：這我可以同意。那麼，如果沒有其他問題，我想事情都敲定了。

理查：凱西，這筆生意保證能讓雙方得到很大回報。希望這一次是我們長期成功合作的開始。

Dialogue **1** 詢問準備事項 🔊 *Track 219*

💬 在這段對話中，我們可以看到馬婭向上司稟報事情的方式非常地詳細，雖然上司並沒有要她一條一條列出來，她卻將所有會議相關的用具如何處置通通告訴他了。這能讓上司知道你準備得非常充足，是個不錯的作法。

• •

Mr. White: Maya , I was wondering if Room 503 is ready for the business conference this afternoon.

Maya: Yes, it's all set up. We've put a copy of the agenda, a pencil and some paper for each attendant on the conference table. Also, we've got the microphones and speakers ready.

Mr. White: Thank you. How about the slide projector?

Maya: I've checked it. It works fine.

Mr. White: Good. Could you tell Jenny to take the minutes this afternoon?

Maya: Mr. White , Jenny is in Shanghai on a business trip.

Mr. White: Oh, yes, I forgot. Can you take her place?

Maya: Okay, but I've never done that job before. Should I write down every word that everyone says?

Mr. White: No, that's not necessary. You just need to take short notes of the topics that are discussed and the results of the discussion.

Maya: I see.

Mr. White: And please type out the minutes after the conference.

Maya: Sure!

★全文中畫 ⬤ 色塊的地方，可以依自己的狀況套入不同的名字、公司名、職稱、學校名等等。

懷特先生：馬婭，我想知道503房間是否為今天下午的商務會議佈置好了。

馬　　婭：是的，都佈置好了。我們已經在會議桌上為每個與會者準備了議程表、鉛筆和紙。麥克風和喇叭也都準備就緒了。

懷特先生：謝謝。投影機怎麼樣？

馬　　婭：我已經檢查過了，沒有問題。

懷特先生：好。妳能通知珍妮今天下午做會議記錄嗎？

馬　　婭：懷特先生，珍妮在上海出差呢。

懷特先生：哦，是的，我忘了。妳能代替她嗎？

馬　　婭：好的，但是我以前沒做過這項工作。我是否需要把每個人說的每個字都記錄下來？

懷特先生：不，不必那樣。妳只要把討論的事項和結果簡短記下來就行了。

馬　　婭：明白了。

懷特先生：請在會議之後將會議記錄打出來。

馬　　婭：沒問題！

Dialogue ❷ 合作意向 🔊 *Track 220*

當有人跟你說「很高興認識你」，不是都會回答「我也很高興認識你」嗎？在英文中，就可以像此段對話中一樣，來一句：「**The pleasure is mine.**」（我才高興認識你呢）。

Mr. Black: Hello, Ms. Li, it's a pleasure to meet you.

Kathy: The pleasure is mine, Mr. Black.

Mr. Black: I came to get acquainted with your company.

Kathy: Great. It's also our policy to develop strong relationships with potential business partners.

Mr. Black: Our company specializes in the import of cosmetics, and we are very interested in the products made by your company.

Kathy: Our products have been exported to over 50 countries and regions around the world. We have enjoyed great popularity abroad.

Mr. Black: Yes, that's why I am here. I sincerely hope that we can establish a business relationship.

Kathy: I will tell my boss, and I can assure you, (Mr. Black), I'll give it top priority.

Mr. Black: Thanks, (Ms. Li). Here is the address of our bank. They will provide you with the information about our business and finances.

Kathy: Thank you, (Mr. Black). We will contact them in the near future.

★全文中畫 ⬭ 色塊的地方，可以依自己的狀況套入不同的名字、公司名、職稱、學校名等等。

現在是不是回想起來了呢？

get acquainted with 認識

這個片語可以用於人們認識、熟悉，例如：Go get acquainted with your new classmates! 就是「去跟你的新同事認識一下啊！」的意思。此外，也可以表示認識、瞭解新的事物，例如：I want to get acquainted with the tables. 就是「我要瞭解一下這些表格」。

中文翻譯2

布萊克先生：您好，李女士，很榮幸見到您。

凱　　西：這是我的榮幸，布萊克先生。

布萊克先生：我是來貴公司做進一步了解的。

凱　　西：太好了。與潛在的商業合作夥伴發展牢固的關係也是我們的原則。

布萊克先生：我們的公司專營化妝品進口業務，我們對貴公司生產的產品非常感興趣。

凱　　西：我們的產品已出口到世界50多個國家和地區，在國外深受歡迎。

布萊克先生：是的，這就是我來這裡的原因。我真誠地希望我們能建立業務關係。

凱　　西：我會向我的老闆彙報，我可以向您保證，布萊克先生，我會優先處理這件事。

布萊克先生：謝謝，李女士。這是我們銀行的地址。他們會向您提供我們的經營及財務狀況。

凱　　西：謝謝您，布萊克先生。我們會在近期與他們聯繫的。

Dialogue ❸ 建立業務關係 ◀ Track 221

💬 帶來好消息的時候，可以說：「I am very pleased to inform you...」（我非常高興可以告訴您……），是個實用的句型。

Kathy: Mr. Black , nice to see you again.

Mr. Black: Yes, nice to see you again too. I hope you have some good news for me.

Kathy: Yes, I am very pleased to inform you that we would be happy to work with you.

Mr. Black: Great. As I mentioned last time, our company specializes in importing cosmetics .

Kathy: Yes, here is the catalogue of our products. We are confident that we will be able to supply you with any kind of product you wish to order.

Mr. Black: Thank you. I have no doubt of that. Your products have a solid reputation for quality and price.

Kathy: Yes. Nearly all our customers say that our products are very attractive. If you place large orders regularly, we can give you a competitive offer.

Mr. Black: Yes, we are going to place substantial orders with you.

Kathy: Great. Then let's talk about the details at the conference this coming Friday .

★全文中畫 ● 色塊的地方，可以依自己的狀況套入不同的名字、公司名、職稱、學校名等等。

中文翻譯3

凱　西：布萊克先生，很高興再次見到您。

布萊克先生：能再次見到您我也很高興。我希望您為我帶來了好消息。

凱　西：是的。我非常高興地告訴您，我們將很樂意與您合作。

布萊克先生：太棒了。正如我上次所說，我們是一家專營化妝品進口業務的公司。

凱　西：是的，這是我們的產品目錄。我們有信心能夠為您供應任何一款您想訂購的產品。

布萊克先生：謝謝。我對此毫無疑問。你們的產品在品質與價格上擁有良好的聲譽。

凱　西：是的。幾乎所有的客戶都說我們的產品很具吸引力。如果您能定期大量訂購，我們可以給予有競爭力的報價。

布萊克先生：是的，我們準備在您這裡大量訂購。

凱　西：太好了。那麼在本週五的會議上我們來討論一下細節問題。

Dialogue ④ 商討廣告事宜 ◀Track 222

這段對話中，里歐說：「**We don't think that will be suitable for a company like you.**」（我們覺得這不太適合你們這樣的公司）。這會讓對方覺得你有認真思考他們公司的性質，且對他們非常瞭解，是個不錯的說法。

• •

Kathy: Leo, how's our project going?

Leo: It's going smoothly. We have done some tactical planning, and we think we've come up with a good plan.

Kathy: What media do you plan to use? You know, we need the right kind of media to achieve our market goals.

Leo: We've asked our copywriter to prepare a version for online magazines and search engines first.

Kathy: Sounds great. Will there be any direct mail?

Leo: No. We don't think that would be suitable for a company like you.

Kathy: You're right.

Leo: We'll also run billboard and newspaper ads to help create broad brand recognition.

Kathy: Great. Would you please prepare a more detailed proposal?

Leo: We'll get started right away and give it to you as soon as possible.

★全文中畫 ⬤ 色塊的地方，可以依自己的狀況套入不同的名字、公司名、職稱、學校名等等。

> **現在是不是回想起來了呢？**
>
> **copywriter 文案撰寫人**
> 光看字面上會覺得copy是「複製」的意思，所以copywriter就是複製、抄寫文字的人，但其實並不是這樣！他是在廣告公司與許多其他公司都會用到的「文案撰寫人」。

中文翻譯4 •

凱西：里歐，我們的項目進行得怎麼樣了？

里歐：進行得很順利。我們已經完成一些策略計畫，而且我們認為我們已經想出了一項不錯的計畫。

凱西：你準備用什麼媒體？你知道，我們需要合適的媒體來實現我們的市場目標。

里歐：我們已要求撰寫文案的同事首先準備好電子雜誌及搜尋引擎用稿。

凱西：聽起來不錯。會有直接郵件廣告嗎？

里歐：沒有。對像你們這樣的公司來說，我們並不認為那是恰當的做法。

凱西：你說得對。

里歐：我們還會同時使用戶外看板及報紙廣告來擴大品牌認知。

凱西：太好了。請你準備一份更詳細的提案好嗎？

里歐：我們馬上準備，會儘快給妳。

Dialogue ❺ 運營計畫 🔊 *Track 223*

和合作的公司談論計畫時，不時稱讚一下對方，可以增進兩方感情，像凱西在這段短短的對話中就一口氣稱讚了人家好幾次。同時也順便不著痕跡地稱讚了自己公司眼光很好，選擇了優秀的合夥人。

Kathy: Okay, the main purpose of our talks today is to discuss the joint venture in Germany. Our company considers it vitally important.

David: So does our company. We have established a (50/50) ownership structure for this joint venture operation.

Kathy: Good. As far as I know, your company operates in a number of countries in (Asia). I believe that your company has the skills to make this joint venture a profitable one.

David: Yes, we are very confident about that.

Kathy: So have you done any recruiting yet?

David: Yes, we have already arranged some suitable local employees to start operations.

Kathy: Great.

David: We have also drawn up some basic operation plans. Here, take a look.

Kathy: Thanks. We have certainly selected a good local partner.

David: Well, we are trying to make sure we have attended to every detail. We look forward to working with you.

★全文中畫 ⬤ 色塊的地方，可以依自己的狀況套入不同的名字、公司名、職稱、學校名等等。

中文翻譯5

凱西：好，我們今天談論的主要項目是關於在德國的合資企業。我們公司認為它極其重要。

大衛：我們也有同感。我們已經為這個合資企業的營運建立好了一個50/50所有權架構。

凱西：好。就我所知，貴公司在亞洲數個國家都有經營業務。我相信貴公司有能力讓這家合資企業有盈利。

大衛：是的，我們對此充滿信心。

凱西：那麼你們已經招募員工了嗎？

大衛：是的，我們已經為開始運營安排好合適的本地員工了。

凱西：太好了。

大衛：我們也擬定了一些基本的運營計畫。在這裡，請看。

凱西：謝謝。顯然我們選擇了一位優秀的本地合夥人。

大衛：嗯，我們一直努力確保把每一個細節都考慮到。我們期待與貴公司合作。

Dialogue ❻ 進一步商討提案 ◀ *Track 224*

💬 對方不願意同意合約時，可以參考對話中法蘭克的說法：「I'm sorry to hear that.」（聽到這個消息我很遺憾），非常有禮貌，但背後卻順便表達了「我方很願意合作、很好配合，你們卻不願意配合，真可惜呢」的感覺，讓對方不知不覺有點歉疚。

Frank: Have you discussed the proposals I made with your management team ?

Kathy: Yes, I have, but they are unwilling to agree to the terms of the contract.

Frank: Oh, I'm sorry to hear that.

Kathy: Yet they are willing to continue negotiations.

Frank: Oh good! Let's try to find a mutually beneficial outcome.

Kathy: Yes. But…

Frank: Is there another problem?

Kathy: Yes, they feel it's necessary to discuss your proposals in more detail, so they have asked to delay the next round of negotiations.

Frank: I see. So when can we recommence negotiations?

Kathy: Will next Thursday be good for you?

Frank: Sure.

★全文中畫 ⬤ 色塊的地方，可以依自己的狀況套入不同的名字、公司名、職稱、學校名等等。

中文翻譯6

法蘭克：您和您的管理團隊已經討論過我的提案了嗎?

凱　西：是的，但他們不同意合約條款。

法蘭克：哦，聽到這個消息我很遺憾。

凱　西：但他們願意繼續談判。

法蘭克：哦，好的。讓我們試著找到一種雙方互利的結果。

凱　西：是的。但是⋯⋯

法蘭克：還有別的問題嗎?

凱　西：是的，他們覺得有必要更詳細地討論妳的提議，所以他們已經要求推遲下一輪談判。

法蘭克：明白了。那我們什麼時候可以重新開始談判?

凱　西：下週四你方便嗎?

法蘭克：當然。

Dialogue ❼ 協商投資意見 ◀ *Track 225*

這段對話最後的地方，萊斯利說「We'll keep in touch」（我們要保持聯繫），不只是一般朋友說要「保持聯絡」的意思而已，更包含了「關於前面所說的『明確答覆』的事情，我會再跟你聯絡」的意思。

Leslie: Hello, Ms. Li, have you got some good news?

Kathy: Yes, we'd like to establish an equity joint venture as you have proposed.

Leslie: That's great!

Kathy: For the financial outlay, we need about 15 million dollars.

Leslie: How much would you like to invest in it?

Kathy: In general, we can lay out about 55% of the total investment, which will be allocated to help cover land, building, and labor costs.

Leslie: And what's the proportionate investment that the foreign participant should make?

Kathy: According to Chinese regulations, the foreign investment proportion shall be not less than 25% .

Leslie: Is there a top limit?

Kathy: No, there isn't.

Leslie: I see. Well, I'm afraid I can't give you a definite answer for the moment, but I'll let you know in a few days. We'll keep in touch.

★全文中畫 ⬤ 色塊的地方，可以依自己的狀況套入不同的名字、公司名、職稱、學校名等等。

現在是不是回想起來了呢？

proportionate 成比例的

proportionate這個字與它的相反詞disproportionate（不成比例的），不只用在數字方面的比例，也可以用來講「大小比例」等等其他的比例。例如說一個人的頭超大，跟身體不成比例，就可以說His head looks disproportionate to his body.（他的頭跟身體不成比例）。

中文翻譯7

萊斯利：妳好，李女士，您有好消息嗎？

凱　西：是的，我們願意建立您所提議的股權式合資企業。

萊斯利：太好了。

凱　西：關於資金開支，我們需要大約1,500萬美元。

萊斯利：妳們出資多少？

凱　西：一般來說，我方可以出資總投資額的55%左右，用來幫助支付土地、廠房和人工費。

萊斯利：那外資的投資比例應是多少？

凱　西：根據中國的規定，外資投資比例不應低於25%。

萊斯利：有上限嗎？

凱　西：沒有上限。

萊斯利：明白了。嗯，我恐怕不能馬上給您明確的答覆，但幾天後我會告知您的。保持聯繫。

工作計畫會議

Dialogue ❶ 市場計畫 🔊 *Track 226*

💬 這段對話中，凱西一開始就和上司說「我一直在找您呢」，展現出自己對這件事非常積極、想要趕快稟報給上司知道的態度。就算你其實沒有一直在找上司，有事要報告時也可以有技巧地說這一句，讓他對你印象加分。

● ●

Kathy: Hi, Mr. White , I've been looking for you.

Mr. White: Hello. So you've brought me your new marketing plan?

Kathy: Yes, here you are.

Mr. White: Thanks.

Kathy: How do you like it?

Mr. White: It's full of originality. Good job!

Kathy: Thank you, Mr. White .

Mr. White: Would you please fill me in on all the details?

Kathy: Sure. Our products haven't entered the African market yet, so it is almost a blank market. I think it's our opportunity to seize this market.

Mr. White: Yes, I agree with you. You may start work on it right away.

★全文中畫 ● 色塊的地方，可以依自己的狀況套入不同的名字、公司名、職稱、學校名等等。

現在是不是回想起來了呢？

originality 創造力、獨創性

original是「原本的」、「原始的」的意思，所以originality就是「能夠創造出獨一無二的新事物的能力」。這個字實際在句子中怎麼用呢？舉幾個例子：

· His work lacks originality. 他的作品缺乏獨創性。
· She expresses her originality through her songs.
她用她的歌曲表達她的創造力。

中文翻譯1

凱　　西：你好，懷特先生，我一直在找您。
懷特先生：妳好。那麼妳帶來了新的市場計畫？
凱　　西：是的，給您。
懷特先生：謝謝。
凱　　西：您覺得怎麼樣？
懷特先生：很有創意。做得好！
凱　　西：謝謝您，懷特先生。
懷特先生：可以跟我詳細講解一下嗎？
凱　　西：當然。我們的產品還沒有打入非洲市場，所以這幾乎是一個空白市場。我想這是我們搶佔這個市場的機會。
懷特先生：對，我同意。妳可以馬上著手去辦。

Dialogue ❷ 新財務計畫 ◀ *Track 227*

當上司和你說一些事情，但跟你原本想的不同時，也別急著糾正上司，而是應該像此對話中的凱西一樣，說：「but I thought...」（可是我以為……），不但能確實傳達出「這怎麼跟我想的不一樣」的意思，又不會讓對方覺得你在糾正他。

Mr. Green: Kathy, we need to start some urgent preparations for next year's financial planning.

Kathy: But I thought we didn't need to start that until next month.

Mr. Green: Well, due to some recent business changes, our senior management has requested us to start it earlier.

Kathy: I see.

Mr. Green: So could you please arrange a department meeting for this afternoon around 3?

Kathy: Sure. But what about the project we're working on now?

Mr. Green: How many people in the department are working on it?

Kathy: Probably about two thirds.

Mr. Green: Well, you may need to consider reassigning people from other departments to help.

Kathy: Okay, I will.

★全文中畫 ⬤ 色塊的地方，可以依自己的狀況套入不同的名字、公司名、職稱、學校名等等。

現在是不是回想起來了呢？

two thirds 三分之二

英文中的分數說法是把分子放在前面，分母放在後面，但分母的數字要以「序數加-s」（thirds、fourths、fifths...）來表達，例如五分之一就是one fifths，不過二分之一不會說one seconds，一般就直接說「一半」（half）即可。

中文翻譯2

格林先生：凱西，我們得為明年的財務計畫趕快開始做一些準備。

凱　　西：我還以為下個月才開始準備呢。

格林先生：嗯，由於近期的一些業務變化，我們的高級管理層要求我們提前動工。

凱　　西：明白了。

格林先生：那麼妳能在今天下午3點左右安排一個部門會議嗎？

凱　　西：當然。但我們手頭正在進行的項目怎麼辦？

格林先生：部門裡有多少人在做這個？

凱　　西：可能有三分之二的人員。

格林先生：嗯，你也許需要考慮從其他部門調人來協助。

凱　　西：好，我會的。

Dialogue ❸ 參加產品推銷計畫會 🔊 *Track 228*

💬 在會議上做報告時，雖然當然也不能說得太短，但比起來又更忌諱說得太長，尤其不能壓榨到其他人報告的時間，就算其他人嘴上不說，心裡肯定是不爽。此段對話中，王先生說「we're running short on time」（我們時間不多了），就是提醒對方沒有很多的時間可以慢慢報告。

● ●

Mr. Wang: Hi, everybody. I don't think you've met Oliver Li , the newest member of our sales team . He's quite an experienced sales representative .

Oliver: Thank you, Mr. Wang . I'm very glad to meet you all.

Mr. Wang: We're looking forward to your analysis of the new products.

Oliver: No problem. May I start my presentation now?

Mr. Wang: Yes, but we're running short on time here.

Oliver: My presentation should only take about 45 minutes.

Mr. Wang: Could you shorten it?

Oliver: Okay, I could omit a section or two.

Mr. Wang: All right. We can discuss the omitted sections at a later time if needed.

Oliver: Okay.

★全文中畫 ⬤ 色塊的地方，可以依自己的狀況套入不同的名字、公司名、職稱、學校名等等。

中文翻譯3 ●

王先生：大家好。我想你們還不認識奧利弗‧李，我們銷售團隊的新成員。他是一位很有經驗的銷售代表。

奧利弗：謝謝您，王先生。很高興認識大家。

王先生：我們很想聽聽你對新產品的分析。

奧利弗：沒問題。我可以現在開始我的報告了嗎？

王先生：是的，但我們現在時間不多了。

奧利弗：我的報告只需要45分鐘左右。

王先生：能縮短一些嗎？

奧利弗：好，我可以省略掉一兩個部分。

Dialogue ④ 行銷方案計畫 ◀ Track 229

💬 在這段對話中，我們可以看到海倫問：「**Do you really think...?**」（你真的覺得……嗎？），雖然和「**Do you think...?**」（你覺得……？）只差一個字，但意思差很多，前者帶有明顯的質疑意味，彷彿在問「媽媽樂，你怎麼會這樣想啊？」

Helen: Since we've decided to go global, we need to think of an effective plan to penetrate the Australian market in the shortest time possible.

Kathy: Absolutely!

Helen: So what is your suggestion then?

Kathy: Well, as I have written in my strategic plan, I think a joint venture would be the best choice.

Helen: Do you really think that we need a local partner?

Kathy: Yes, I believe that their local market knowledge will be valuable. A joint venture would be the easiest way to gain that local knowledge.

Helen: I agree. But it's also a very expensive way.

Kathy: So what's on your mind?

Helen: I think finding a distribution agent and a business consultant would be much less expensive.

Kathy: Great idea! We can establish a small office in Australia to organize marketing and sales campaigns through outside marketing agencies.

★全文中畫 ⬤ 色塊的地方，可以依自己的狀況套入不同的名字、公司名、職稱、學校名等等。

中文翻譯4

海倫：既然我們已經決定走全球化路線，我們應該想一個有效的計畫，以便在最短的時間內打入澳洲市場。

凱西：沒錯。

海倫：那麼你的建議是什麼？

凱西：嗯，正如我在策略計畫中所寫，我認為創辦合資企業將是最好的選擇。

海倫：你真的認為我們需要一位本地合夥人嗎？

凱西：是的，我相信他們關於本地市場的知識將是極其寶貴的。合資企業將是獲得本地知識最容易的方法。

海倫：我同意。但它也是一種很昂貴的方式。

凱西：那麼你的想法是什麼？

海倫：我認為找一位經銷代理人和一名業務顧問將會划算得多。

凱西：很棒的主意。我們可以在澳洲設立一個小型辦事處，透過外面的行銷代理公司來組織行銷和銷售活動。

Dialogue ⑤ 部門招聘計畫 ◀ *Track 230*

這段對話中凱西說「I'll say」，是一句同意對方所說的話時可以用的會話，頗有輕描淡寫帶過的意味。

Kathy: You know what? Bill handed in his resignation letter last Friday. We'd better find someone to fill his position.

Anna: Oh, no! Does that mean that my workload will double?

Kathy: I'm sorry, but yes, as he only gave two weeks' notice.

Anna: That doesn't give us enough time to hire and train a replacement. We need at least one month.

Kathy: I'll say. But let's face it head on. Please help me outline the requirements for the job ad.

Anna: All right.

Kathy: We'll require a Bachelor's degree, preferable in business or marketing, and three years of work experience. What else would you suggest?

Anna: The person needs to be outgoing and have the ability to work both with a team and independently.

Kathy: Good suggestion. Could you start typing up the job ad?

Anna: Yes, boss. Extra work already!

★全文中畫 ⬤ 色塊的地方，可以依自己的狀況套入不同的名字、公司名、職稱、學校名等等。

現在是不是回想起來了呢？

head on 直接

「head on」常用來說「直接」撞上某物，例如「the cars crashed into each other head on」（那兩台車直接相撞了）。在這段對話中則是「直接」面對問題的意思。

中文翻譯5

凱西：你知道嗎？比爾上週五提辭呈了。我們最好找人替補他的職位。

安娜：啊，不！那是不是意味著我的工作量會加倍？

凱西：我很抱歉，但是確實是，因為他只提前兩個禮拜通知我們他要辭職。

安娜：那沒有給我們足夠的時間去招聘和培訓新人。我們至少需要一個月的時間。

凱西：對啊。我們只能硬著頭皮向前走了。請幫我想想這個徵人廣告裡要寫哪些要求吧。

安娜：好的。

凱西：我們要求學士學位，最好是主修商務或市場行銷的，還要有三年工作經驗。妳還有什麼建議？

安娜：這個人必須外向，而且具備團隊合作和獨立工作的能力。

凱西：好建議。妳可以把徵人廣告打出來嗎？

安娜：好的，老闆。現在這就是額外的工作了！

Dialogue ❻ 銷售計畫 ◀Track 231

開始討論時，總要有個人當第一個發言的。這個人做的事就是「start the ball rolling」（擔任開場）。在這段對話中可以看到這個說法怎麼用。

Kathy: Hi, everyone, we are having this meeting to discuss how to improve our sales volume and market share in the coming year. Peter, could you start the ball rolling?

Peter: Sure. Well, in my opinion, the key to good sales is advertisement. So improving our advertising strategy is a must.

Kathy: I couldn't agree more.

Peter: And of course, quality is always the most important thing. In order to maintain our reputation as a supplier of superior products, we need to put more effort into product quality.

Kathy: And what do you think is the best way to improve on the current situation?

Peter: Well, we should definitely guarantee quick after-sales service, because I've heard complaints from some of the customers saying our customer service has been going downhill recently.

Kathy: I'll meet the service manager to find out what's going on. Anything else to add?

Peter: I also think that our prices are a little too high. Even though we have great products, I think we're losing customers to lower priced competitors.

Kathy: All right. Thanks for your contribution.

★全文中畫 ⬤ 色塊的地方，可以依自己的狀況套入不同的名字、公司名、職稱、學校名等等。

中文翻譯6

凱西：大家好，我們開這個會是為了討論在新的一年裡如何提高銷量和市場佔有率。彼得，你先開始發言好嗎？

彼得：當然可以。嗯，在我看來，好的銷量的關鍵是廣告，所以我們必須要改進廣告策略。

凱西：非常贊同。

彼得：當然，品質總是最重要的一環。為了保持我們作為優質產品供應商的聲譽，我們需要在產品品質管制方面投入更多的精力。

凱西：那你認為改善現有狀況的最佳方法是什麼？

彼得：嗯，我們一定要保證迅速的售後服務，因為我已聽到有客戶抱怨說我們的客戶服務最近每況愈下。

凱西：我會和客服部經理碰個頭，看看究竟出了什麼問題。還有什麼要補充的嗎？

彼得：我還覺得我們的定價有點高。儘管我們有很棒的產品，我想我們的客戶正向定價較低的競爭對手那裡流失。

凱西：好。感謝你的發言。

Dialogue ❼ 下一年工作計畫 🔊 *Track 232*

對於他人在會議中發表的建議，身為主持人的你可以像這段對話中一樣，在最後說：「我會把這些建議加到工作計畫中」，讓對方知道自己的建議被聽進去了。

● ●

Kathy: I believe that everyone has a copy of the draft of our work plan for next year. I would really appreciate it if you guys could offer some feedback. Mike, could you start?

Mike: I see that expanding the production line will be our top priority next year.

Kathy: Yes. What do you think of it?

Mike: Well, I think upgrading the distribution network is also very important.

Kathy: Yes, you are absolutely right. I've already asked the Marketing Department to follow up on that.

Mike: We should also have a brainstorming session with the Advertising Department to make sure we can achieve our market goals.

Kathy: Good point. I'll talk to the Assistant Director in the Advertising Department right after this meeting.

Mike: That'll be great!

Kathy: Thanks, Mike. I'll incorporate these suggestions into our work plan before I submit the final report and forward it to the other departments.

★全文中畫 ⬤ 色塊的地方，可以依自己的狀況套入不同的名字、公司名、職稱、學校名等等。

現在是不是回想起來了呢？

submit 提交
在網路上填訂單、填問卷、甚至在某些討論區PO文時，都可以看到submit這個按鍵。按下去就表示你的訂單（或問卷、或文章）已經送出去了，不能更改囉！

中文翻譯7

凱西：我想每個人都拿到了一份我們明年的工作計畫草案。非常歡迎大家給一些意見。麥克，你能先說說看嗎？

麥克：看起來擴大生產線將是我們明年的首要任務。

凱西：是的。你對此有什麼意見？

麥克：嗯，我認為改進我們的配售網路也是非常重要的。

凱西：是的，你說得非常對。我已經要求行銷部門對此跟進。

麥克：我們還應該和廣告部門集體腦力激盪一下，以確保我們能實現我們的市場目標。

凱西：好主意。會議之後我會馬上和廣告部副經理商量一下。

麥克：那太好了。

凱西：謝謝，麥克。在我呈交最後的報告並把它轉給其他部門之前，我會把這些建議加到我們的工作計畫中。

商務小常識

　　小型會議座次安排：小型會議可以依門設座。一般面對會議室正門的是會議主席的座位。其他與會者在其兩側自左而右依次就座。在國內，座位是左尊右卑，國際上是以右為上。小型會議也可以依景設座，即會議主席的具體位置不必面對會議室正門，而是應該要背對著會議室內的主要景致所在，如字畫、講臺等。

SOS Unit 39
工作總結會議

Dialogue ❶ 準備年度總結會 🔊 *Track 233*

得到同事的幫助時，別忘了要像這段對話中一樣，說一句「You are very helpful」（你幫了大忙）來感謝對方。

●●●

David: Hi, Kathy, I really need your help.

Kathy: Yes?

David: I'm preparing for an annual summary meeting. Could you please tell me what kind of preparations I should make?

Kathy: No problem. First of all, you need to get the agenda ready beforehand. Then you should make sure that everyone has been informed about the meeting.

David: I see. Should I print out the documents and the information relevant to the meeting?

Kathy: Yes, it'll be better that way.

David: And what should I do during the meeting?

Kathy: You should take the minutes. And don't forget to type the minutes up after the meeting, and keep proper records of the resolutions passed.

David: Thanks a lot. You are very helpful.

Kathy: You're welcome.

★全文中畫 ⬤ 色塊的地方，可以依自己的狀況套入不同的名字、公司名、職稱、學校名等等。

中文翻譯**1**

大衛：你好，凱西，我非常需要妳的幫忙。
凱西：什麼事？
大衛：我正在準備一個年度總結會。妳能告訴我應該做哪些準備工作嗎？
凱西：沒問題。首先，你要提前準備好議程，然後確保每個人都有被通知到。
大衛：明白了。我應該把有關會議的檔案和資料列印出來嗎？
凱西：是的，這樣比較好。
大衛：那麼在會議期間我要做什麼呢？
凱西：要做記錄。會後別忘了把會議紀錄列印出來，並把通過的決議妥善歸檔。
大衛：非常感謝。妳真幫了我大忙。
凱西：不客氣。

Dialogue ❷ 總結成功經驗 ◀ *Track 234*

對於同事的成就，在稱讚的同時，也可以像這段對話中的薩姆一樣，問一句「**How did you manage that?**」（你們怎麼辦到的？），不但表達佩服的心情，也可以順便從對方那裡學到一些。

Kathy: Our present negotiations are the most successful in this company's history.

Sam: Great! All your hard work has finally paid off!

Kathy: Yes, we were able to negotiate two new supply contracts.

Sam: I heard that they were highly profitable. How did you manage that?

Kathy: We made very good preparations, so we were able to answer every query, and resolve potential problems quickly.

Sam: Have you completed your report yet?

Kathy: No, not yet. I'm still working on it together with my team members.

Sam: I see.

Kathy: Hopefully we'll be able to give the management team a full report next Monday.

Sam: That would be great. Then you can make a presentation at the summary meeting next Tuesday .

★全文中畫 ⬤ 色塊的地方，可以依自己的狀況套入不同的名字、公司名、職稱、學校名等等。

pay off 得到回報

這個片語通常會和「hard work」（努力工作）之類的概念用在一起。例如：

· My hard work has finally paid off! I got an A+ on my report.

　我的努力終於得到回報了！我的報告拿了A＋的高分。

中文翻譯2

凱西：我們這次洽談是公司成立以來最成功的。

薩姆：太棒了！妳所有的辛勞終於有了回報！

凱西：是的，我們談成了兩份新的供貨合約。

薩姆：我聽說這兩份合約有很高的利潤。妳是怎樣做到的？

凱西：我們準備得很充分，所以我們可以回答每個問題，並能迅速解決一些潛在的問題。

薩姆：妳寫完報告了嗎？

凱西：還沒有。我還在和團隊成員一起寫呢。

薩姆：明白了。

凱西：希望下週一我們能給管理團隊一個完整的報告。

薩姆：那太好了。這樣你就可以在下週二的總結大會上作報告了。

Dialogue ❸ 財務部門階段總結 ◀ *Track 235*

上司問到你是否有加班時，可別對他說「有啊，加班加得要死要活的」。像這段對話中凱西一樣，輕描淡寫地說「我們是有多工作幾個小時」就行了。

Mr. White: Kathy , has the financial review been completed yet?

Kathy: Yes, it has. Our accountants managed to finish it last Friday .

Mr. White: Good. How did we perform in the last financial period?

Kathy: Pretty good, our profits increased by 15% .

Mr. White: So how did the market react to this?

Kathy: The last time I looked, our stock was up 4% .

Mr. White: Great! I was wondering how you guys managed to complete both the financial review and the new business plan. I mean, your department must have been working overtime lately.

Kathy: Ah, yes. We did have to put in quite a few extra hours.

Mr. White: I hear your department has recently hired some new members. Is that true?

Kathy: Yes, they're currently going through our training programme.

★全文中畫 ⬤ 色塊的地方，可以依自己的狀況套入不同的名字、公司名、職稱、學校名等等。

中文翻譯3 •

懷特先生：凱西，財務審查已經做完了嗎？
凱　　西：是的，做完了。我們的會計上週五做完的。
懷特先生：好。公司上個財經年度的表現怎麼樣？
凱　　西：滿好的。公司利潤增長了15%。
懷特先生：那麼市場對此有何反應？
凱　　西：我上次看，我們的股票上升了4%。
懷特先生：太好了。我在想妳們是怎麼同時完成財務審查和新業務計畫的。我的意思是，妳們部門最近肯定一直在加班。
凱　　西：啊，是的。我們的確不得不加了很多班。
懷特先生：我聽說妳們部門最近招募了一些新員工，真是這樣嗎？
凱　　西：是的，目前他們正在接受我們的培訓。

Dialogue ❹ 銷售團隊階段總結 🔊 Track 236

在會議上報告時，要顧到現場很可能有其他部門的人在，或許根本聽不懂你講的那一串數字是什麼。他們想要知道的是你所說的數字對公司、對他們有什麼「影響」、會造成什麼「改變」。參考一下這篇對話中的報告方式吧！

Kathy: Okay, everyone, let's start our summary meeting right now. (Harry), would you please start first with the progress report of our sales team?

Harry: Yes, I'd love to. I have to say that things couldn't have gone any better.

Kathy: Could you elaborate on the progress?

Harry: Sure, so far our actual sales figure is (130%) above our expected level. The team has been subdivided into smaller teams.

Kathy: And what effects has that had?

Harry: It has made them more focused and they are now able to concentrate on the most important details.

Kathy: But it says that smaller groups often result in more inefficiency.

Harry: You mean things like overlapping or breakdowns in communication?

Kathy: Yes.

Harry: Oh, you don't have to worry about that. Our sales team has been kept in communication through tightly controlled management.

Kathy: Great! This is a remarkable change.

★全文中畫 ⬤ 色塊的地方，可以依自己的狀況套入不同的名字、公司名、職稱、學校名等等。

現在是不是回想起來了呢？

overlap 重疊
overlap指的是兩個範圍或兩樣東西互相重疊，而用在工作上則表示「有不只一個人做了重複的工作」，其實明明只要一個人做的事情，卻因為溝通不良而造成好幾個人都在做。

中文翻譯4

凱西：好了，大家，現在開始我們的總結會議。亨利，可以請你先談談我們銷售團隊的進度報告嗎？

亨利：好，我很樂意。我得說，情況再好不過了。

凱西：你能詳細說明一下進展嗎？

亨利：當然可以。迄今我們的實際銷售額高出預期水準130％。銷售團隊已被進一步細分為小組。

凱西：這有什麼作用？

亨利：這使銷售小組工作能更有針對性，他們現在能夠把精力放到最重要的細節上。

凱西：但據說小團隊往往會導致低效率。

亨利：您是指工作重疊或溝通障礙之類的問題嗎？

凱西：是的。

亨利：噢，您不必擔心。透過嚴密的管理，我們的銷售團隊已經能很流暢的溝通。

凱西：不錯！這是個了不起的變化。

Dialogue ❺ 團隊內部小結會 🔊 *Track 237*

想建議大家幫忙解決一個問題，但又很清楚知道大家一定很不想幫忙的時候，可以參考這段對話中的「Shouldn't we do something about that?」（我們不應該做點什麼嗎？）。其中的「we」表達了「不是要求你們做而已，我也要做，我們一起做」的團結合作態度，而「do something about...」也暗示了這件事情非得找個方法解決不可。

Henry: Thank God, we got the final order!

Kathy: Yeah, we will be able to meet our target.

Henry: Great! Let's celebrate!

Kathy: Well, it's a little too early to do so.

Henry: Why? We've met our quarterly sales target, and we're sure to get nice bonuses, right?

Kathy: You're right. But look around at the building. It is full of our products. Shouldn't we do something about that?

Henry: But we are short of hands right now. It's almost impossible to get everything packed or shipped.

Kathy: True. So I'm afraid we have to work overtime tonight.

Henry: Oh no! No one is going to like that!

Kathy: I know. Well, let's get it done quickly so that we can all go home and rest.

Henry: Okay.

★全文中畫 ⬤ 色塊的地方，可以依自己的狀況套入不同的名字、公司名、職稱、學校名等等。

中文翻譯❺ ▶

亨利：感謝上帝，我們拿到了最後一筆訂單！
凱西：是啊，我們能實現我們的目標了。
亨利：太好了。讓我們慶祝一下吧。
凱西：嗯，要慶祝還太早了。

亨利：為什麼？我們已經完成了本季度的銷售目標，而且我們一定能獲得可觀的獎金了，對吧？

凱西：你說得沒錯。但看看這棟大樓周圍，到處堆滿了我們的產品。我們是不是應該做點什麼？

亨利：但是我們現在缺人手，要把東西都裝好或運走幾乎是不可能的。

凱西：是這樣沒錯。所以我們恐怕今晚得加班了。

亨利：哦，不！沒有人會喜歡加班！

凱西：我知道。嗯，我們快點把事做完，這樣就都能回家休息了。

亨利：好吧。

Dialogue ❻ 產品銷售總結會 🔊 *Track 238*

不想很直接地說不同意對方的主意，卻又不得不表達不同意的意見，就可以像這段對話中的凱西一樣，說一句非常實用的「I have some reservations.」（我還有點疑慮）。

Mr. White: We believe that this product will sell well, and we should put it on the market right away. (Kathy), what's your opinion on this?

Kathy: Well, to be honest, I have some reservations.

Mr. White: Could you tell me what they are? As you know, our department has done a lot of research on it.

Kathy: Would you mind telling us what kind of research you have done?

Mr. White: We've tested the product in the (Indian) market and (Japanese) market, and it sold very well.

Kathy: But are you sure that we will have a large enough budget for a big advertising campaign?

Mr. White: So you are saying that we'd better wait?

Kathy: I'm afraid so. I don't think we should put it on the market right away.

Mr. White: Okay, I'll think about it. Thanks.

Kathy: Thanks for hearing me out.

★全文中畫 ⬤ 色塊的地方，可以依自己的狀況套入不同的名字、公司名、職稱、學校名等等。

現在是不是回想起來了呢？

hear sb. out 聽聽某人說話

這個片語指的不只是「聽」而已，更是指「把某人的話聽完、聽進去」的意思。只有很認真地聽、並考慮對方的意見，這樣的情況才可以用hear sb. out。

中文翻譯6

懷特先生：我們相信這款產品會暢銷的，我們應該現在就上市。凱西，妳對此有什麼看法？

凱　　西：嗯，說實話，我對此有一些保留意見。

懷特先生：妳能告訴我是什麼意見嗎？妳知道，我們部門已經做了大量的調查研究。

凱　　西：你能告訴我們你們做了什麼調查嗎？

懷特先生：我們在印度和日本市場試銷了這款產品，賣得很好。

凱　　西：但你確定我們有足夠的預算來進行大規模廣告宣傳嗎？

懷特先生：所以妳的意思是我們最好等一等？

凱　　西：恐怕是這樣。我覺得我們不該立即上市。

懷特先生：好吧，我會考慮的。謝謝。

凱　　西：謝謝你聽我的意見。

Dialogue ❼ 項目小結會 🔊 *Track 239*

想說某件事「看來」是某個情形，就可以用此段對話中鮑勃所說的「apparently」（很明顯地、看來）。

Kathy: How's our project going, (Bob)?

Bob: Hmm, I'm afraid it's not going very well.

Kathy: What's the problem?

Bob: Well, we are having some trouble with the figures.

Kathy: What kind of problems are you having exactly?

Bob: Apparently some of the figures are not accurate.

Kathy: How do you know?

Bob: I checked last year's figures, and I found that they are not even close.

Kathy: Well, then we'd better find a solution as soon as possible.

Bob: Yes, we'll fix it as quickly as possible.

★全文中畫 ⬤ 色塊的地方，可以依自己的狀況套入不同的名字、公司名、職稱、學校名等等。

中文翻譯7

凱西：鮑勃，我們的專案進行得怎麼樣？

鮑勃：嗯，恐怕進展得並不順利。

凱西：有什麼問題呢？

鮑勃：嗯，我們在數據方面遇到了一些問題。

凱西：具體是什麼樣的問題呢？

鮑勃：很明顯有些數據並不準確。

凱西：你是怎麼知道的？

鮑勃：我核對了去年的資料，我發現它們相差很大。

凱西：嗯，那我們最好儘快找到解決的方法。

鮑勃：是，我們會儘快弄好的。

商務小常識

　　公司每年的年度工作總結會往往是最耗費精力的，在開總結會前的一兩個月，各部門就要開始準備五花八門的總結材料：銷售部要彙報年度銷售目標的完成情況，廣告部要彙報所做廣告宣傳的預算和效果，市場部要彙報對市場的調研和預測，財務部要彙報公司的利潤和債務情況……諸如此類，不一而足。

Note

為什麼?

為什麼有人的台語講得不輪轉,卻也能聽得懂台語?

小孩子不都是先學會聽跟說,才能更進一步學寫字?

英聽已是未來學習語言新趨勢,

聽得懂英語才能真正實際應用在生活上,

本書告訴你聽懂英文的關鍵絕竅,

讓英聽不再是恐懼!

聽力正是一切的開始、所有英語學習的起點!

讓你重拾信心的關鍵解析!

一網打盡所有情境的廣泛題型!

還有**連音教學**與**母語人士**常用會話!

附贈外師親錄英聽救星MP3+300句老外最愛說短句下載!
學英文無極限!隨時隨地隨你聽!

早就還給老師的英文文法
就由這本書從頭開始！

韓國百萬讀者擁護暢銷作者
姜守慶◎著　洪梅◎譯

救回已經忘掉的英文文法 SOS

挽救百萬韓國讀者對文法的學習熱忱，
史上絕無僅有的英文文法救世主！

學英文也能吃回頭草，這一次你肯定忘不了！

就是忘不掉！例句＋表格＋易疏漏小專欄，由淺入深，想起學校之前所教過的文法！
就是忘不掉！會話訓練與寫句子練習，文法不是紙上談兵！想看不懂說不出口都很難！
就是忘不掉！表格、專欄、情境圖片，最條列清楚的學習方式！想要混亂都很難！
就是忘不掉！學文法外還一起學發音規則，看字讀音、聽音拼字！想學不會都很難！

必備專業
外師親錄 MP3
英文文法念念不忘！

姜守慶/著　**洪梅**/譯

定價：台幣499元 / 港幣166元
1書＋1光碟＋1解答本 / 16開 / 雙色 / 頁數：400頁

捷徑 Book站

現在就上臉書（FACEBOOK）「捷徑BOOK站」並按讚加入
粉絲團，就可享每月不定期新書資訊和粉絲專享小禮物喔！

http://www.facebook.com/royalroadbooks
讀者來函：royalroadbooks@gmail.com

以為曾經學過卻記不得的文法，
像變了心的女友一樣回不來了嗎？
別放棄！
史上絕無僅有的英文救世主！
4步驟拯救你遺忘的文法記憶

① **例句＋表格＋易疏漏小專欄**，實在夠詳細、夠基礎，
以前就算再健忘，這次也絕對忘不了！

② **會話訓練＋句子練習**，一改過去被動地讀與聽，
要你以說、寫為出發點學文法，才能根深蒂固記牢牢！

③ 其實學過的你並沒忘，只是太久沒使用而混亂了！
讓這本的**情境圖片＋表格**，幫你理清思緒，回復文法記憶！

④ **自然發音**順便一起學，看字讀音、聽音拼字，
口說能力加倍佳，英語能力勢如破竹無人擋！

早就還給老師的**英文文法**，
讓百萬暢銷作者幫你找回來
想吃文法回頭草，就由這本書開始！

原來如此 系列 E149

史上最速衝刺！
2000句職場生存必備英文會話

39大情境 × 239段職場萬用對話

作　　　者	朱傳枝、夏洋
顧　　　問	曾文旭
總 編 輯	王毓芳
編 輯 統 籌	耿文國、黃璽宇
主　　　編	吳靜宜
執 行 編 輯	林冠妤
行 銷 企 劃	姜怡安
美 術 編 輯	王桂芳、王文璇
特 約 編 輯	盧惠珊
法 律 顧 問	北辰著作權事務所　蕭雄淋律師、嚴裕欽律師

印　　　製	世和印製企業有限公司
初　　　版	2016年09月
出　　　版	捷徑文化出版事業有限公司
電　　　話	（02）2752-5618
傳　　　真	（02）2752-5619
地　　　址	106 台北市大安區忠孝東路四段250號11樓之1

定　　　價	新台幣349元／港幣116元
產 品 內 容	1書+1光碟

總 經 銷	采舍國際有限公司
地　　　址	235 新北市中和區中山路二段366巷10號3樓
電　　　話	（02）8245-8786
傳　　　真	（02）8245-8718

港澳地區總經銷	和平圖書有限公司
地　　　址	香港柴灣嘉業街12號百樂門大廈17樓
電　　　話	（852）2804-6687
傳　　　真	（852）2804-6409

本書原由外語教學與研究出版社有限責任公司以書名《商務英語如此聽說─新手篇》首次出版。此中文繁體字版由外語教學與研究出版社有限責任公司授權捷徑文化出版事業有限公司在台灣、香港和澳門地區獨家出版發行。僅供上述地區銷售。

捷徑 Book站

書中圖片由Shutterstock網站提供。

現在就上臉書（FACEBOOK）「捷徑BOOK站」並按讚加入粉絲團，
就可享每月不定期新書資訊和粉絲專享小禮物喔！
http://www.facebook.com/royalroadbooks
讀者來函：royalroadbooks@gmail.com

國家圖書館出版品預行編目資料

史上最速衝刺!2000句職場生存必備英文會話 /
朱傳枝, 夏洋編著. -- 初版. -- 臺北市: 捷徑文化,
2016.09　面；　公分（原來如此：E149）
ISBN 978-986-93561-0-7（平裝）
1. 英語　2. 會話

805.188　　　　　　　　　　　105015445